THE RECKONING

SAGA OF A CIVIL WAR BLOCKADE RUNNER

Bob Larranaga

EAN-13: 978-1478177296
ISBN-10: 1478177292

www.the-reckoning.net
www.theuscivilwar.info

The Reckoning

ACKNOWLEDGMENTS

Writing this book about a blockade runner would not have been possible without a great crew of editors, starting with my first mate and wife of five decades, Mary. I was also lucky enough to receive the invaluable help of Roy and Karen Thorpe whose knowledge of the sea was a great help to this landlubber. Many thanks to them for their time, effort and insightful comments.

Inspired by actual events, the setting for this novel is Florida's Gulf Coast during the Civil War when swift and daring blockade runners challenged the Union navy's supremacy of the seas.

CHAPTER ONE

Crack-Crack-Crack!

The staccato sound of small arms fire shattered the stillness of the night. I gasped, threw myself out of bed, hit the floor rolling and groped around for the handgun that I kept under my bunk. Then nothing. Nothing but a sore rib and the scolding bark of a distant dog.

I raised my head warily; rubbed my eyes and squinted, searching for the source of the sound. Another gust of wind, another *Crack-Crack*—and the real source of the sound revealed itself—the wooden shutters of a drafty window. I cussed, sat up cross-legged on the floor and stared at the ragged shadows cast across my cabin walls by a guttering candle. The dim flame flickered futilely, unable to ward off the shape-shifting haunts.

I took a shallow breath, coughed, rubbed my eyes and squinted at the clock beside my bed: 3 a.m. I reached for the half-empty rum bottle lying beside me; uncorked it; raised it to my lips and swallowed. Hard. Then I put down the bottle and saw the letter from Charleston balled up on the cabin floor where I had thrown it.

The handwriting on the envelope had been a dead giveaway. I knew who'd sent it. But I'd opened it any way. I'd picked at the scab of an invisible wound of a long ago war.

After warring, most soldiers lay down their weapons, hang up their uniforms and go on about their lives as civilians. Not me. After I came home from the Mexican-American War, I burned my uniform. But nothing rid me of the nightmares that stuck with me like a burr on the hind end of a mangy dog. Night after night I fought an endless series of bloody skirmishes with demons that had no need of sleep. Always on edge and ready for a fight, I drifted from one dead-end job to the next like a man on the dodge. I didn't fit in.

But, I'm a Canfield—one of the Beaufort County Canfields—and there is no quit in us. I pushed on, struggling to find my way out of the fog of war.

Years passed, things slowly began to improve and I thought the worst was behind me. Then the saber rattling started up again. This time the big wigs talked about seceding from the Union. They spoke about slavery being divinely inspired. They said it was a boon to mankind. That letter balled up on the floor put it much plainer. In it, my ex-wife said the South was fixing to fight a Second American Revolution.

The firebrands thought a decorated war veteran like me—a "hero of the row with Mexico"—would take up arms in defense of the South. But that's not how I saw things.

To my way of thinking, slavery was wrong. War was wrong. And, as for being a hero, the real heroes of the Mexican-American fracas were the men who didn't live to see our flag waving over Chapultepec Castle. The restless ghosts of those brave soldiers still mustered in my dreams. In the dead of the night, I could hear the drummers beating the long roll, calling us to line of battle. I could hear the artillery exploding and the cries of the wounded and dying. I kept dreaming this would be the night that I would die. I thought I deserved to die. I'd thrash about in my bed, unable to sleep, shivering one minute, sweating the next, until suddenly, I'd sit bolt upright in bed, wide-eyed, gasping for air, a man at war with himself.

Getting that letter from Charleston pricked at my conscience. It reminded me of the men I had killed and the ones I had seen killed. It called to mind my first nightmare, when in a panic-attack I had scared the bejezzus out of my pregnant wife as she lay beside me in bed. She went into labor the next morning—only eight months after I had returned from Mexico. Eight months! I didn't believe the boy was my own flesh and blood. The day he came into this world I went off on another drunken bender. When I sobered up and came to my senses, it was too late. Like a fool, I had signed up for another tour of duty and was being posted to Fort Zachary Taylor, Key West, Florida.

There wasn't enough time to make things right between the wife and me, not that she didn't try. As best I recall, she wrote me five letters, but back then I couldn't read or write to save my life. So I didn't reply. The last letter came from a lawyer in Charleston. He said my wife had divorced me.

Next thing you know I got myself court-martialed and sent to Fort Jefferson in the Dry Tortugas. My cellmate, Rudy Povich, was the fair-haired, clean-shaven, pinch-faced son of a preacher and the fort's paymaster—until they discovered he had sticky fingers. When I asked him why preachers' boys always seemed to get in the most trouble, Rudy just laughed and said:

"There's good and evil in all of us, and both sides are constantly at war."

Rudy liked nothing better than to run his mouth. Every now and again, a big word would come out sideways and I'd stop him and ask what it meant. Before long, Rudy was teaching me to read the Good Book and put pen to paper. After that, I read everything I could get my hands on: newspapers, dime novels, anything to improve my mind.

Nothing much came of all my learning until I got that letter from Charleston stirring up bitter memories. That's when I realized I would never put the past behind me until I accepted what I'd done in answering duty's call. At first, I only spoke about it here and there in brief snatches. Then my new wife said the best way to rid myself of the war memories was to write them all down and burn the pages. I wasn't so sure that would help, but nothing else had put an end to the nightmares. So I decided to give it a try, writing a few pages at a time whenever I could summon the courage. Putting my thoughts in writing was painful. I would just as soon have forgotten the past. But, I kept at it.

When I finished my scrawling, my wife asked to read what I had written. I gave it to her hesitantly and studied her face for some reaction as she read. After a few minutes, she looked up with tear rimmed eyes and said:

"Ed, you can't burn this."

I stared at her in disbelief. "But burning it was your idea."

"Yes," she said, "I know. But now I realize you have to share your story."

"Share it?" I said. "I don't want to draw attention to what I did."

She fixed me with one of her school teacher's unblinking stares and said:

"You once told me that I had a duty to teach my students what war is really like. Well, as a veteran, you have a duty to tell your story. You owe that much to the fallen heroes who fought side by side with you. You have to be their voice. This is their story, too."

The intensity of her gaze disarmed me.

"But I'm no author."

"No, you're not," she smiled gently. "But I can help."

And so, kind reader that is how one old veteran came to tell more or less every soldier's story of what it's like to fight an endless war. In sharing these recollections, I hope to show there is hope for those who struggle—as I did—with what doctors called "soldier's heart."

~

After my stint in the army, I couldn't see the point in going home to Charleston so I took a job as a land surveyor in Florida. In those days, a surveyor had to be quick with a gun because squatters drew their property lines in blood. I was no stranger to danger, and I needed a job, so I put my misgivings aside and told myself it was just temporary, until something better came along. I strapped on my revolver quick-draw style, and went to work.

Then the Eberhard Faber pencil company hired me to survey a huge tract of cedar forest near Cedar Keys on Florida's west coast. A cluster of small islands, the Cedar Keys lie just below the mouth of the Suwannee River. The ready supply of lumber and access to shipping made the keys an ideal spot for a pencil manufacturer.

The fresh scent of those towering trees said to me that Cedar Keys was also good a place to get a fresh start in life. I moved there, saved enough to buy a parcel of slash pine timber on a land contract and built a turpentine still deep in the woods.

I was scratching out a living, minding my own business, when, from out of the blue, I got that letter from my ex-wife, triggering new wartime memories. I can't recall her exact words, as I'm relying on memory, but the gist of it went something along these lines:

Your son is now a teenager and itching to fight in a Second American Revolution. He's a chip off the old block, and ought to live with his father.

The last sentence really caught my attention:

He goes by the name Jesse Beecham, but he's a Canfield through and through. You'll see.

"Jesse." That was the first time in 16 years I had uttered the boy's name.

~

I can't say I welcomed Jesse with open arms. When he arrived by steamer at Cedar Keys, I met the ship more out of curiosity than anything else. I took one look at the way he dressed and shook my head in disbelief. The boy wore flannel pants, a frilled shirt with a turned out collar, buckled shoes and a wide-brimmed, low-crowned felt hat. That may have been the way they dressed in Charleston, but this was Florida's gulf coast. I wore a soiled cotton shirt, pants stained with fish blood and pine tar, a sweat-rimmed hat and tar-caked boots.

He looked me up and down, too, rolled his eyes, muttered something under his breath, took off his hat and wiped the sweat from his brow. As soon as he did that, I knew what a fool I'd been. Jesse was a Canfield all right. The same broad shoulders, fair skin, raven-colored hair tied in a pigtail and coal black eyes. He stood a good six feet tall in his fancy shoes and weighed 160 pounds or better. He was the spitting image of me at 16. I felt like I'd been hit by a brick on the end of a rope.

We didn't hug or shake hands or anything like that, and I don't remember what I said. But I do remember one of the first things out of his mouth. He turned completely around, pointed to his steamer trunk and said, as if dumb-founded:

"Don't you even own a horse and wagon?"

My throat swelled with the effort of holding my tongue. I spat to ease the pressure and said, "I reckoned it would do you good to stretch your legs after a long sea voyage."

"It's not my legs I'm worried about," he said. "It's this steamer trunk."

The trunk was huge—bigger than I had expected. He had come to stay.

"I'd keep a tight grip on that trunk," I said. "The mosquitoes down here are big enough to carry it off."

He didn't appreciate my sense of humor any more than his mother had, though he did follow in my wake as I headed out of town.

"Just how far is your cabin?" he asked.

"A fair piece," I answered. "Shake a leg."

But he kept dogging it, hauling that steamer trunk behind him, stirring up the dust and pine needles like a dragline dredging up murky memories of my past. With each step, I traveled further back in time to a place I didn't want to visit, to a day when my anger got the best of me and blinded me to the truth. There was no way to deny it now. I had messed up. Jesse was bone of my bone, flesh of my flesh. Finally, I stopped and gave him a hand with the trunk.

"What in hell do you have in here?" I asked. "Rocks?"

"Books," he said.

"Books? What kind of books?"

"History, biography—"

"How much learning do you have?"

"Eight years, more or less."

"Eight? Well, down here," I said, "you're going to learn things those books don't teach. You're going to learn what it means to be a gladesman."

By the time we reached my place deep in the pinewoods, sweat beaded Jesse's brow and stained the armpits of his frilly shirt. He dropped his side of the steamer trunk and sighed in exasperation on seeing my weather-beaten, one-room cabin. It sat two feet off the ground on dwarf cypress poles in the middle of the turpentine patch. The cabin had a pitched roof made of palmetto fronds and walls of rough-hewn yellow pine logs that I had notched, fitted up at the ends and chinked with mud, straw and moss. A chunk burner in the middle of the room kept the place comfortable on cold winter nights. The over-hanging branches of a laurel oak and a sycamore shaded the swayback roof on hot summer days.

In back of the cabin, I had built two open-air huts, the kind the Seminoles called chickees, one for cooking on a four-hole stove, and the other one a tool shed. Behind them, I had a small smokehouse and a garden plot where I grew maize, turnip greens, collard greens, potatoes and onions—until armyworms got at them. Beside the garden stood a stable and corral for my chestnut quarter horse.

"What's her name?" Jesse asked with the nearest thing to a smile I'd seen from him.

"Mosey," I said. "I use her when riding the timber and hauling our product to market."

Mosey lowered her muzzle to sniff Jesse and he asked, "You ever race her?"

I knew what the boy had in mind so I ignored the question.

"That there is the outhouse," I said. "And those shacks yonder are for the foreman and my eight-man crew. Come on. I'll show you the rest of the place."

My turpentine still sat among the slash pines in a ravine on the edge of a creek that provided the water for distilling. I had built the still with my own hands out of rough pine with a copper retort set into a brick furnace fired by pine logs. Beside it sat the cooper's shed where we made the barrels, which we used to stow our product.

The clearing was heavily scented with the aroma from the gum patch where the bark of the longleaf pines remained deeply notched and coated with congealed rosin. To my way of thinking, it was the smell of money.

"This is it?" Jesse sighed. "This is what you call home?"

His attitude galled me and I had to hold my temper in check. I let it pass this time, but I was counting.

"Built it myself," I said. "Proud of it, too."

That first afternoon, we scarcely knew what to say to each other. I found myself studying him when he wasn't looking, caught him doing the same to me. I told him to make himself at home. But it felt like we were opposing sides in a war, two wary foes separated by a no-man's land that was a minefield of unspoken words.

Toward the end of the workday, I introduced him to my good friend and foreman, Adam Broady, and his three-legged dog, "Beau." Adam was a big bear of a man with a full beard, a quirky sense of humor and the ability to kid me out of the dark moods that sometimes came over me. I asked him to introduce Jesse to the rest of my crew—the cooper, chippers, pullers and dippers—the freed blacks that did piecework for me.

As they walked off, I heard Jesse ask, "Where did your dog lose his leg?"

Without hesitation, Adam said, "Lose it? Hell, we breed them that way down here. It gives the varmints a running head start."

When Jesse didn't laugh, Adam added, "Where did you lose your grin?"

Adam was bound and determined to make Jesse smile. If anyone could get a rise out of my sourpuss son, it was Adam. While they met with the other men, I fed my horse and rustled up some grub. Adam and Jesse returned a half hour later and this time both of them wore sour expressions.

"I think we're in for some gloomy weather," Adam said out of the side of his mouth. "I'll see you in the morning."

He left us with Beau trailing behind, snout hung low to the ground as if he sensed trouble coming. Jesse and I ate in silence and soon called it a day.

The boy seemed to sleep like a log on the bunk bed I had built for him, but I wasn't so lucky. I tossed and turned, thinking about all I had lost out on in the past 16 years. The missed birthdays, the holidays that had come and gone. The hunting and fishing trips I could have taken with my son.

Had anyone taught Jesse how to read the stars and sail by dead reckoning? Could he tie a square knot or clove hitch? Track and field dress a deer? Did he know how to set a trap or start a fire with one match?

Those were things a father ought to teach his son—leastways, a good father.

I had no idea who my son was or what he was like. I knew less about Jesse than about the men who had served with me in the army.

My troubled thoughts circled back to my army days. They always did at times like this. Whenever I felt uneasy about something, the nightmares returned . . .

It was hot and muggy in the cabin, the way it had been on that Godforsaken day outside Mexico City. My pillow felt as hard as the boulders I had crouched behind while the greasers' artillery rained down on us. I was about to jump up and charge into a hail storm of lead when a voice from behind said, "Don't throw caution to the wind." I spun around to see Private Abner Winslow hunkered down behind me, his face ghostly white, his eyes blank as a washed blackboard. He held out his cartridge box and I took it. When I looked up again, he was gone. I opened the box and saw to my horror that it contained a beating heart . . .

I woke with a start, threw off the mosquito netting, reached under my bunk bed for a rum bottle and went outside for a swig and a smoke.

~

Early the next morning I rode into town and bought Jesse some work clothes, boots, a Bowie knife and a .58 caliber Springfield rifle-musket. When I returned to the shack, he was half-dressed and rummaging through his steamer trunk for something.

"See you finally woke up." I was on edge and didn't mean for it to sound as harsh as it did. He grunted something I couldn't hear and that I didn't care to have repeated.

"Brought you some things you're going to need," I said with a tight grin.

He raised his head, took one look at the Springfield, then at me. "What is this?" he said. "Am I supposed to think this makes everything right between us?"

My mouth cinched tighter than a wet knot.

"Look," I said through clenched teeth, "in case you forgot, this isn't my idea, you being here."

"It wasn't my idea, either," he said. "It was ma's."

"Well, like it or not, you are in my house now and, as long as you are living under my roof, you will show me some respect."

I threw the rifle and knife onto his bunk.

"House?" he said with a scornful laugh, a laugh that sounded just like his ma's. "You call this place a house? This is a pigsty. How can you live like this? It smells like an ashtray in a two-bit saloon. There are three empty rum bottles under your bunk."

"I see you're thrifty with your compliments," I shot back. "Just like your ma."

Tears welled up in his eyes and he said, "What did ma ever see in you, anyway?"

I would have laid him out right then and there, except for what he said next.

"And why in God's name did you walk out on us?"

Just like that, he spat it out. He wasn't wasting any time getting into it, but his tears got to me and doused the fire burning within me.

"The army sent me to Key West."

"And you never came back. You abandoned us."

"In case you haven't heard, it was your ma who filed for divorce."

"After you deserted us. What's the penalty for a soldier who deserts his post?"

"Shut your trap or I'll shut it for you." I threw the work clothes at him and said, "Put these on. You're going to earn your keep around here."

I stomped out of the cabin, slammed the door behind me, picked up my axe and strode over to the stump that I used for splitting wood and releasing demons. I put a cedar log on the stump and started wailing away at one log after another until I was drenched in sweat and covered with wood chips.

Jesse dragged his sorry ass out into the yard a half hour later. I put him to work making staves for the barrels that I used to haul turpentine, pine tar and rosin to the harbor. We worked together in silence, except for when he complained about it being "boring, stupid nigger work."

"It's Negro," I said, "Not nigger."

"Negro, nigger, it's all the same to me."

"Well, just so you know," I said. "This gum patch isn't part of the slavocracy. We do our own work around here."

"Well, if this isn't part of the slavocracy, how much are you aimin' to pay me?"

"Pay you?" I laughed. "So you can go gadding about?"

When he spoke, his voice had found a lower register. "I mean to send the money to ma."

"To your mother?"

"Yeah. Your ex-wife, Ellen. Remember her? She's on hard times; renting a small room in the back of another family's house; getting by as a seamstress. A good one, too."

I was stunned. "Your ma never remarried?"

He shook his head in disbelief at my ignorance.

"What about Beecham?"

"Ma did what she had to do. When you didn't come back, we moved in with the widower Beecham; lived in his manse for a couple of years; but he never actually married ma. Never legally gave me his name, either. I just took it. When he died, we had to fend for ourselves again."

Up until I laid eyes on Jesse, I had assumed my ex had married the man who got her pregnant. Then, I figured she had latched onto someone named Beecham. It never occurred to me that a good looker like her wasn't hitched.

I thought she lived high on the hog and a damn site better than I did. In all those years, I had never sent her a dime. Now, the full meaning of my mistake was staring me right in the face. I felt lower than a snake in a wagon wheel rut.

"How much were you bringing home in Charleston?" I asked.

"I made $8 a month," he said, "cleaning out stalls and such until the farmer's son made the mistake of taking a switch to me—like I was some field nigger. Then ma said I best high tail it down here."

"You didn't—"

"Kill him? No such luck. But don't change the subject. We were talking about me not being a slave."

"Right," I coughed. "Well, it is a helluva lot harder working down here in this heat and humidity. Tell you what, I'll pay you $11 a month. And, trust me, you will earn every penny."

That was damn good money in those days. But it was a debt way past due. Jesse didn't say a word; he just kept on working; probably figured he had won the first skirmish in what would become a long-running battle.

After I put in my chops, I went back to the cabin. That's when I saw why Jesse had been rummaging through his steamer trunk. A framed daguerreotype of his mother sat on the shelf next to his bed. Ellen was still a looker. I'll give her that.

~

The tension between Jesse and me never let up. In fact, it got a whole lot worse as the presidential election of 1860 approached. Abe Lincoln ran for president with solid support from the Northern abolitionists, which set Southern rabble-rousers to ranting and raving. They called Abe an ape and a black Republican and nine Southern states refused to put his name on the ballot. Yet, Lincoln out-polled all the other candidates and (near as I recall) won the election with something like 39 percent of the popular vote.

Talk of secession kept the "sparkie" at the telegraph office working over time. I thought secession was the stupidest thing I had ever heard. I mean Florida had only entered the Union 16 years earlier. Now the fire-eating radicals demanded that we fight our way out. In the entire South we had only a handful of iron works capable of producing cannons. There was no way we could beat the North.

Of course, Jesse saw things differently. My hotheaded son said:

"Secession would be the best thing to happen to the South since the invention of the cotton gin."

"Really," I said. "How many bullets can a cotton gin fire?"

"Whose side are you on anyway?"

"I'm on the side of peace."

"Well, you're on the wrong side of history," he shot back.

It just so happens heaps of people sided with Jesse.

They believed it when the politicians claimed we had a constitutional right to withdraw from the Union. They trusted the blowhards who said we could throw off the shackles of import taxes. They "Amen-ed" when the preachers claimed that slavery was part of the Almighty's plan.

My drinking buddies at the Salty Dog Saloon and Gambling Hall thought that secession would lead to a new golden age for the South. Of course, they said, there might be a little dust up with the North; but, they wagered, it would be over in time for spring planting.

None of those high-minded fellows had anything to say about the possibility of losing. Most of them had never fired a shot in anger. They'd never felt what it's like to see your friends bleed out in front of you. They'd never heard men crying out, begging to be put out of their misery. They'd never smelt the stench of a battlefield littered with the bloated bodies of men and horses. They'd never heard the deafening roar of cannons or the ping of a bullet that has narrowly missed your head.

I knew a hundred ways a man could die and I saw them all play out, night after night, in my dreams. I knew war was insane, especially a civil war.

CHAPTER TWO

On January 8, 1861, the first shots of the war rang out in Pensacola, Florida. A jittery federal sentry pulled down on some rebel scouts skulking around Fort McRee in the dead of night. But the sentry drew no blood, and he was only a lowly private, so the big wigs were not about to bestow on him the "honor" of starting the whole shebang. You might not read about it in your history books, but truth be told, the ruckus commenced in Florida. We were itching for a fight. Two days later, we became the third state to secede from the Union. Our forces quickly seized the Pensacola naval yard and arsenals throughout the state. An uneasy truce followed while the political windbags tried to outshout one another.

In her next letter, Jesse's mother couldn't contain herself. She wrote that on January 9th cadets from the Citadel had fired on a federal ship delivering supplies to Fort Sumter in Charleston's harbor. No one was injured in that first attack on the fort, but the news of that melee created quite a hullabaloo in Washington. "War is in the stars," Jesse's mother claimed. She and her lady friends were sewing ribbons into cockades for the soldiers' hats. I caught Jesse reading her letter and chortling about how the South was on the rise.

As if to prove better days were ahead, seven weeks later the Florida Railroad drove the final spike linking Cedar Keys to the state's east coast. The know-it-alls said it was a sure sign of the prosperity heading our way. The entire town turned out to cheer and a brass band played when the Abner McGehee, an eight-wheel locomotive, chugged into our new depot pulling a coal tender and two passenger cars. It was an older, second-hand locomotive gussied up for the big event with colorful bunting and flags; but its appearance was enough to briefly banish all thoughts of a looming war.

When the train crawled to a stop, three quick blasts from its whistle set the eager onlookers to cheering. The heads of young boys bobbed up and down among the crowd, each one trying to get a better look at the fire-breathing, mechanical marvel. Several men threw their hats in the air. Steam from the engine's boilers enveloped the entire scene, wreathing the heads of the arriving passengers.

The last person to exit a passenger car was a tall, comely woman holding an embroidered lace parasol. She stood there, as if on a cloud, her chin tilted slightly up to see over the throng, her trim figure backlit by the sun. She wore a simple straw hat and riding jacket. A breeze whisked away the last of the steam engine's smoke to reveal the rest of her outfit: a short, straight dress and just the hint of bloomers underneath. An audible gasp went up from a nearby clutch of women whose fashion sense bound their thinking tighter than a whalebone corset.

Jesse saw the look on my face and laughed. "She's our new school teacher, the daughter of Peter Foster."

"The owner of the salt works?"

"Right, Miss Maureen, the stepsister of my friend, Caleb Foster."

I couldn't take my eyes off her. Her face was free of all pretence—no make-up, no jewelry, no curls in her auburn hair that fanned out in the breeze like spun gold. Her eyes were blue, her nose slim and her lips seemed moist, as if expecting to be kissed. I found myself wondering how old she might be.

Twenty? Twenty-five?

"Isn't Caleb Foster," I asked Jesse, "the boy who wanted a job in the gum patch?"

"One and the same. You should have hired him."

At that moment, Peter and Caleb Foster drew up to the depot in a one-horse phaeton. The boy jumped down, ran over and hugged his sister and chatted with her as he carried her luggage to the waiting carriage. Peter Foster gave his daughter a peck on the cheek and they took off.

The next day, as I rode the timber, checking on my crew, I saw a rider in the distance racing across an open field. It was Maureen Foster mounted on one of her father's horses. She rode western style, not sidesaddle like the other ladies. I began to see why no man had been able to win her heart.

~

Three days later, on March 4, 1861, Abe Lincoln took office and the war mongering and caterwauling about the Confederacy's future reached a fevered pitch. With the threat of war at hand, shipbuilding boomed. Overnight, the shipwrights couldn't get enough of the pitch and tar I sold to make their vessels watertight. I'd already bought a small sloop to ship my product down the coast; and, when Caleb Foster got wind of it, he started pestering me for a job, again.

"Your dad wouldn't want you working the pines," I said. "It's tough, dangerous work."

Turpentine can blister your skin and burn your lungs. And, a gum patch crawls with timber rattlers coiled up in the pine needles beneath the trees, ready to strike. The crew has to cut the bark of the trees throughout the growing season to keep the sap flowing. When a sap bucket fills up, they scoop the gum out, empty it into barrels and haul them to the still. Then we cook it in huge kettles to separate the turpentine from the tar. In the winter, when the sap stops flowing, we rake around the trees to prevent forest fires; then hunt out the poisonous snakes.

When I finally relented and hired Caleb, I told him, "Stay the hell out of the pinewoods. Your job is to help the cooper build barrels."

He gave me a look I couldn't read but shook my hand. The next thing I heard, he was shooting snakes, skinning them and selling the white meat in town for 10 cents apiece. (In case you've never had rattlesnake steak, it's some kind of good.)

Then Jesse started bragging on Caleb and how he had killed a gator with one shot; could read sign and hunt down wild boar; knew where the best fishing was. It was Caleb this and Caleb that. The boy was a few months younger than Jesse but my son surely looked up to him. I can't say Jesse felt the same way about me.

~

Shortly after I hired Caleb, I saw his sister walking past the Salty Dog Saloon with a hymnal under her arm, heading straight for the church that rented space in the back of one of our stores. Up close she looked a lot like my first wife, Ellen. Right then and there, I decided to join that congregation.

That Sunday I began singing in the choir next to Miss Maureen Foster. When I left the prayer service, Jesse approached me with a puzzled look on his face.

"I thought you couldn't read." He pointed to the hymnal in my hand.

"A man can learn a lot in 16 years," I answered, "provided he has an open mind."

He shook his head. "Well, let me know if you need help with any of the big words—words like temperance, fatherhood and character."

"Keep your voice down," I snapped back. "It just so happens, I've read the Bible three times, cover to cover, including the big words." (No sense mentioning that I had read it in prison.) "That's probably three times more than you've read it."

"All that studying doesn't seem to have stuck," he said.

"How would you know?"

"Because," he hissed, "you never wrote one solitary letter to Charleston."

"How come you never wrote to me?" I shot back.

"Easy. I thought you were too dumb to read."

My blood was up. "If you're so smart," I said, "how come you never learned to respect your elders?"

"Respect isn't given," he said as he walked off. "It's earned. By the way, you can't sing."

He knew damn well that I wouldn't cuff him in front of all those church ladies. When I turned around, I saw Miss Maureen walking off with the other members of the choir. I had missed my chance to get to know her better. Just as well, I thought. I needed a drink.

~

In the days leading up to the next choir practice, I went over in my mind how I might approach Miss Maureen. I thought of a dozen things to say to her before hitting on the idea of leaving my hymnal at home so she'd have to share her copy with me. It worked, too, but to my surprise, she was the first to speak up after choir practice.

"Mister Canfield, may I have word with you in private?"

"I hope it isn't about my singing," I said.

She smiled at my quip then replied in kind. "No," she said, "it would take more than a word or two to address that subject."

We both smiled but I held my grin while hers faded.

"Shall we talk as we walk?" I asked hesitantly.

She took my arm and we began walking side-by-side. "It's about my brother Caleb," she said.

"He's a fine boy and a hard worker," I told her. "He does your family proud."

"He likes working at the turpentine still," she said. "This is Caleb's first job and he wants to prove himself to our father. So I hope what I'm about to say will be taken in the right spirit."

"Speak freely, Ma'am."

"Caleb says one of his jobs is shooting poisonous snakes. Is that true?"

"Actually, his job is to help the cooper build barrels."

"But he is shooting snakes and I've seen how big they can be," she said.

I felt her tense. This was not going the way I wanted.

"Most are under six feet," I said apologetically.

"My father has no idea what Caleb is up to and if anything should happen to him, it would devastate our entire family."

I nodded. "I'll see to it that nothing happens to him."

"Then you'll put a stop to it?"

She smiled and I crumbled. "Sure," I stammered, "I'll talk to him as soon as I get back to the still."

"Thank you," she said. "There's just one other thing."

"Anything. Anything at all."

"Please don't let Caleb know that I spoke to you."

After that, I walked Miss Maureen home after every choir practice. She had a graceful bearing, a profile that would do a bowsprit proud and a keen mind. Beneath the lace mantilla she wore to church services, I found a free spirit open to new ideas, a woman of strong views and one willing to speak freely about the folly of war. She wasn't concerned about what others thought, or what they might whisper about the way she spoke, dressed or mounted a horse. She did as she pleased. She was strong, independent and placed a high value on her liberty. Above all, I liked her wry sense of humor. She could make me laugh, something I hadn't done in quite a spell.

~

Before I could make much headway with Miss Maureen, General P.T. Beauregard—the "Little Napoleon"—attacked Fort Sumter in Charleston, South Carolina. Three days later, on April 15, 1861, Lincoln called for 75,000 volunteers to suppress the rebellion and Jefferson Davis countered by authorizing private ships to attack and capture enemy ships. The following week Lincoln declared a blockade of southern ports. The war was on. With the onset of fighting, the beacon of the Cedar Keys' lighthouse went dark and, to my way of thinking, the South's hopes for a brighter future dimmed.

The next Sunday, Brother Storter, our circuit preacher, took to his pulpit like an Old Testament prophet—like Elijah himself. I can still see him standing there: a tall, imposing figure robed in black with gray hair, mutton chops and a porcelain complexion that glistened with sweat as he warmed to his subject.

His sermon that day sounded to me like a political harangue. He began in the most strident tones that he could muster, building to a climax in words that the *Florida Sentinel* saw fit to re-print, word for word in Letters to the Editor. A yellowed copy of that rag lies before me as I write.

"As you know," Storter said, "I have studiously avoided using the pulpit to comment on the headlines of the day.

But the gravity of the current crisis compels me, as a devout Christian, to speak out when God's divine order is challenged by the forces of evil."

He grasped the lapels of his coat, jutted out his lower lip and surveyed the congregation before continuing.

"As God's chosen people, we are duty bound to uphold the Lord's plan of salvation. There is no denying the fact that we are the guardians of the institutions he has entrusted to us. As such, we must be prepared to make whatever sacrifice might be necessary to pass on to future generations the blessings of the Southern way of life.

"Our self-preservation depends on the current social order and on the peculiar institution of servitude, which has been a boon to the South and to other nations of the world.

"Those who would usurp God's authority and challenge the role of slavery in man's relations ignore at their peril the lessons of history and the example of Ham and Canaan."

Then he told us to open our Bibles to Genesis 9: 25-27 where he proceeded to use Holy Scripture to justify slavery. I glanced over at Miss Maureen and thought I saw a troubled look on her face.

"Brothers and sisters," Storter rumbled on in his booming voice, "it's as plain as the printed word. Slavery is part of God's plan and we will be held accountable on the Day of Reckoning, if we do not preserve it. We answer only to God in shouldering the white man's burden. We know our place in the social order and the niggers know theirs. They are far too indolent and ignorant to fend for themselves. They cannot be entrusted with liberty. Freedom would spell their doom. They need our guardianship."

Heads started nodding and Storter's braying grew louder.

"In the march of history," he shouted, "the destiny of a nation is revealed in the character of its people and in their response to calamity. Brothers and sisters, I say to you this day that we must rise up and confront the Northern devils."

He slapped the palm of his hand down on the pulpit with such force that it sounded like a gunshot. Several young men jumped to their feet. Maureen glanced nervously at her brother, Caleb, whose head bobbed up and down.

Brother Storter thundered on, his eyes focused directly on me as if by force of will alone he could compel me to rise.

"We must rise up with all the strength we can muster."

Another thwack of his hand reverberated throughout the church. Two more men jumped up, ramrod straight, to murmurs of approval. I didn't budge.

"We must drive them out of the South and back into their squalid, soulless, barren cities of the North."

A third whop of his hand ricocheted off the walls. With his Bible held high above his head, Storter ended with a flourish that lacked for nothing but thunderbolts:

"Surely God is on our side and the forces of evil will know the bitter taste of defeat at our hands."

He swept across the front of the makeshift altar to within two feet of where I sat in the choir.

"All the Lord asks of us," he said, "is the courage to answer the clarion call of history. Who else among us is brave enough, faithful enough and patriotic enough to echo the words of Isaiah 6: 'Here I am Lord! Send me?'"

By the time Storter finished, seven young men stood ready to receive their baptism by fire. Most of the congregation clapped and raised their arms in jubilation, claiming that a prophet had been revealed to us this day. But to my way of thinking, Brother Storter was a prophet of doom. I knew some of those boys would be coming home in coffins. My blood was boiling. When I looked over at Miss Maureen, she was grim-faced and pale.

~

In a dream that night, I saw myself standing over a fire pit in the backyard of my old home in Charleston, watching the flames consume my army uniform. The thick black smoke swirled about my head, choking me, blinding me to what was happening. I coughed, blinked, opened my eyes and saw that the soot from the fire had draped itself over me as if it were a black funeral shroud. Still dreaming, I gasped, tore at my blanket and threw myself out of bed.

"You O.K.?" Jesse asked.

"Yeah," I said. "Go back to sleep."

He grunted, shook his head and did as he was told. But I couldn't sleep. I couldn't help but wonder what my firebrand son thought about Storter's sermon.

~

For a brief spell everyone's spirits rose with news that Confederate forces had captured the federal arsenal at Harpers Ferry and the naval yard at Norfolk Virginia—without firing a single shot. In Norfolk, the Yanks' attempts at destroying the yard had failed and huge stores of war materiel remained behind when they abandoned the yard.

As I recall, the seized weaponry totaled close to 1,200 heavy cannons, including 300 Dahlgren guns, and vast quantities of ammunition. With the amount of armaments more closely balanced on both sides of the conflict, there was talk of a 90-day war followed by a truce. Folks started gathering daily at the telegraph office hoping for more good news from the war front. And they weren't disappointed.

Word soon reached us of a southern victory at the Battle of Big Bethel, Virginia. The attacking Union regiment actually mistook another Union regiment dressed in gray for Confederates and fired on them. Of course, the southern papers mocked the hapless Union commanders, and my know-it-all son had to joke about it.

"Those blue bellies," Jessie chuckled, "can't even shoot straight."

But I wasn't laughing. I knew how easy it is to kill one of your own men in the heat of battle.

On July 21, 1861, our southern boys won another big victory, one I wager you've heard about. The clash took place at Manassas Junction, Virginia where, in the first major land battle of the war, we routed the northerners. The Yankee newspapers called it the Battle of Bull Run. The southern papers called it the Great Skedaddle. They said it was proof that God was on our side. But, if memory serves me right, we lost close to 400 men on that battlefield with another 1,500 or so wounded, and Lord only knows how many boys deserted. That didn't sound like much of a rout to me, nor to Miss Maureen.

With tears in her eyes, and a lump in her throat, she said, “It’s a sad day when we count our losses as victories.”

Then she told me the husband of one of her good friends was missing in action. Dabbing at her tears with a hankie, she added, “And no one knows what has become of him.”

I tried to comfort her by saying, “If he’s been taken prisoner, there is still hope.”

“How do you mean?”

“He could become part of a prisoner exchange,” I said. “There is talk of exchanging one general for 46 privates; one colonel for 15 privates and so on.”

“That is like bargaining with the Devil.”

“Well,” I said, “war is hell on earth.”

“My daily prayer,” she said, “is that both sides will come to their senses and lay down their arms before any more blood is shed.”

~

But Maureen’s prayers went unanswered. By and by, the tide of war turned against the South as the federal army swelled in size, quickly outnumbering the Confederate army by more than two-to-one.

At the same time, the growing federal navy began seizing one rebel ship after another. The Yanks meant to cut off trade with northern Europe and strangle our economy.

“Just you wait and see,” Jesse said. “The embargo will bring England and France into the conflict on our side.”

But it never happened. Europe turned to Egypt and India for its cotton and southern farmers started turning their cotton fields into cornfields. King Cotton was dethroned.

We began to feel the effects of the war on the home front. Store shelves emptied quickly and we learned to do without.

Brother Storter saw this turn of events as a sign that God was testing us, purifying His people, chastising the sinners among us. (“You know who you are.”) He said that we were being tried in the fire, like tempered steel, being prepared to smite the Lord’s enemies with “His terrible swift sword.” The preacher pounded the pulpit and called down fire and brimstone on the heads of our foes. To hear him talk, the Yanks were going to burst into flames and go straight to hell on the Day of Reckoning.

The faithful "Amen-ed" and beat their breasts every time the preacher paused to catch his breath. The good folks just couldn't get enough of that divine retribution. I couldn't understand praying for vengeance out loud, and in the middle of a prayer meeting no less. In my mind, it didn't square with what the Good Book said. It sounded as if Brother Storter changed the rules as he went along. But no one seemed to mind.

In fact, so many folks congratulated the preacher on his "mighty fine, edifying and inspiring" sermon that he started delivering the same one, more or less, at every prayer meeting. The man was a regular player piano. Just tap on the bellows and off he'd go. And, after every sermon, more and more of our young men would heed his windbaggery and enlist in the rag tag Confederate army.

On the way home from one prayer meeting, Caleb Foster took to mimicking the preacher's rant. I thought the boy was hysterical, but Maureen told him to hush up, and Caleb tramped off to join some of his friends in a game of mumbly peg.

"Caleb's big for his age," she said, "but he's still a boy and some days he doesn't have the sense of a June bug."

"He's just trying to lighten things up a bit," I said.

"War is no laughing matter." She shook her head and added, "Thanks be to God, Caleb isn't old enough to volunteer."

I knew better. Boys like Caleb were lying about their age; marching off to what they thought would be certain victory. It struck me that Caleb had mocked the way Brother Storter spoke but not what he had actually preached. I couldn't help wondering if the boy was talking himself into joining the fight. But I did not trouble Miss Maureen with such thoughts.

~

As prices rose, the rich grumbled but paid up; the poor tightened their belts a notch or two. Some began hoarding, stockpiling and speculating on anything the rest of us couldn't grow, net, hunt or trap. Seafood was readily available. And we had plenty in the meat line—deer, turkey, birds, and such. But we saw a steep run-up in the price of just about everything else. As best I recall, I soon paid $3.30 for a bushel of corn; $2.00 for a pound of butter; and $28 for a barrel of weevily flour. (By war's end, that same barrel of flour would cost $100.) If this was a hiding, we were the ones feeling the switch.

I could be off a bit on my prices (as I'm relying on memory), but one thing I know for certain: the Confederate treasury couldn't print money fast enough to paper over all our troubles. Bartering for what you needed often took the place of cash. In some cases, salt became the medium of exchange, a practice, Maureen said, that dated back to the Roman Empire when soldiers were paid in salt.

Her father saw in the Yankee embargo a business opportunity and borrowed money to expand his salt works. Before the war a 33-pound bag of salt from England or the West Indies sold for 50¢. But, once those sources of supply dried up, that same bag sold for $1.00 and, by war's end, went for $13. Of course, that was $13 in Confederate graybacks.

At first, Peter Foster's decision to expand his business seemed like a very shrewd business move. His salt works soon challenged the area's largest salt works on James Island near Depot Key. But the temptation of easy money became too great for some thieves. They broke into Foster's warehouse; made off with all his salt; and left him was a mountain of debt. He immediately filed a claim with Lloyd's of London.

~

The harder things got the more Brother Storter stepped up his fulminating rhetoric, enflaming the passions of our patriotic young men. He never missed an opportunity to recount in detail stories of Yankee atrocities, which he gleaned on his circuit riding.

"I heard tell," he'd say, "that them blue bellies treat civilians in the most vile and ungodly manner. Why those demons steal horses, rob hen roosts and slaughter livestock. They rip the laundry off the clotheslines and fill the sheets with everything they can haul away. Then they pour out the molasses, scatter the flour and salt on the ground, and trample the preserves underfoot."

He said the Yanks had stripped one house of everything but a pile of straw for a bed; said those "poor souls might as well have been sleeping in slave quarters." And, any one who dared to speak back to the Yanks, had their home put to the torch, or so he claimed.

"Brothers and sisters," he sighed, "let us bow our heads and pray that our soldiers will have the strength to drive these heathen hordes to the very gates of hell."

I took about as much of Brother's bombast as I could stomach before pulling him aside.

"Brother Storter," I said, "I must be missing something because I don't see how all this rabble rousing relates to the gospel message."

He looked at me as if I had two heads and said, "I'll pray that you see the light."

The truth was he only had three basic sermons in his arsenal: one for prayer services, one for weddings and one for funerals. His wedding sermons were in high demand as a growing number of young couples were rushing to get hitched before the grooms went off to become cannon fodder. Demand for the funeral sermons would come later.

After the choir sang at one of the weddings, I walked Miss Maureen home as usual.

"It's a comfort to know," she said, "that your naval stores are considered vital to the war effort and that you will be remaining here in Cedar Keys, Mister Canfield."

I was too surprised by her show of concern to reply; luckily, I didn't have to. We had just reached the Foster home where their Negro, Minny, came out on the verandah with a silver tray balancing a pitcher of lemonade and two glasses.

"Ma'am," Minny asked, "would your gentleman caller care for a glass of lemonade fore Marse Caleb drinks dah whole pitcher hisself?"

Minny was a short, round-shouldered woman with a face as wrinkled as a raisin and a toothless gap in her smile, but on that day that old black woman won my heart.

There was an awkward pause before Miss Maureen said, "Where are my manners? Why, of course; by all means, do sit down, sir."

Minny placed the tray on a table on the verandah, and Maureen and I sat there making small talk for close to fifteen minutes about how beautiful the wedding had been. But all the while I could sense something troubled her. Finally, she took a sip of her lemonade, cleared her throat and said what was on her mind.

"That boy who works for you," she said hesitantly, as if afraid of what my answer might be. "He looks a lot like you. Caleb tells me Jesse Beecham is your son; yet he goes by another name."

My hand shook and the lemonade spilled over the side of my glass. I didn't want to visit this subject, not just yet.

"Are you a widower, Mister Canfield?" Her lower lip trembled; her voice reached just above a whisper.

I put down my glass, swallowed hard and chose my words sparingly. "Yes, Jesse is my son. The boy's mother is still alive. We're divorced; have been for a long time."

She hesitated, but her curiosity got the best of her. "I'm sorry," she said, "I didn't mean to bring up a painful past, it's just that his last name—"

"No. It's fine," I said. "I was getting around to telling you."

I could see her searching my face for some explanation as I ran an index finger around the rim of my glass and gathered in my thoughts. I said I'd gotten married as a teen-ager just before going off to war and that I had returned a changed man. Always angry. Always primed and ready to go off. I didn't mention my drinking, but I did say the breakup was my fault, not my wife's. I said she was a good woman and deserved better.

"If I had known then what I know now," I added, "things might have worked out differently."

That answer seemed to satisfy her for the moment. "I apologize," she said, "for bringing up such hurtful memories."

"No apology is called for," I replied.

We spoke for a few more minutes. Then I drained the last of my lemonade and stood, eager to leave before she could delve deeper into my past.

"I best be going," I said. "Would you excuse me?"

"Most assuredly and do say hello to young Jesse for me."

"May I walk you home again next Sunday?"

"I will look forward to that," she said.

I bowed, tipped my hat and turned to leave. At that moment, a sudden movement caught my attention. I turned and saw Minny holding back a lace curtain in the drawing room window, the hint of a grin on her face.

When I returned to the cabin, I found Jesse practicing in earnest with his Springfield. I gave him a few pointers and thought to myself that I just might make a gladesman out of him yet.

~

But Jesse had something else in mind as he practiced target shooting. At first, he could only hit a target at 50 yards, but by and by, he got the hang of it and started hitting it at 300 yards or more. I made the mistake of telling him he was becoming a fair hand with a firearm. That's when he spoke up about joining the rebel army.

"Over my dead body," I said.

"Your body?" he said. "This is my life we're talking about, not yours. It's my life and, in case you've forgotten, I'm old enough to decide for myself."

"Old enough?" I said. "Hell, boy, you're still wet behind the ears."

That's when the sparks flew between us like embers from a roaring fire. I told him there was no way he could join up because naval stores were considered critical to the war effort. The pitch and pine tar from turpentine stills like ours kept the ships watertight and afloat. I said I needed him in the gum patch and that was that. He didn't say peep, but I knew damn well that he still itched to go off to war like the other local boys.

Wouldn't you know it? Just when I thought I'd had the last word on the subject, his mother wrote him a letter saying his two cousins on her side of the family had just signed up and that she hoped Jesse would do her proud.

"She'll change her tune," I told him, "when your cousins come home in pine boxes."

"It ain't fair," he said. "You had your chance to fight the Mexicans."

"What did you say?" I growled.

"I know about your Certificate of Merit for distinguished service," he said. "You had a chance to cover yourself in glory."

"Glory?" I bellowed. "I covered myself in blood and gore."

"Forget it," he said. "I'll just tell them I quit the gum patch."

"You'll do no such thing," I said, "Like it or not, I am your pa and you'll do as I say."

He backed down and nothing more was said that day about the war. But the damage was done. The argument had trigged more painful wartime memories for me. I spent another sleepless night fighting a losing battle with my past.

This time the nightmare came to me as a jumble of battle scenes in which I strained to see through a pall of gun smoke. The hazy curtain lifted as if on cue, and I saw in my dream a column of Mexican soldados marching two abreast directly into my line of fire. Their marching band played the music from *The Barber of Seville* and their officers drove the peasant soldiers on with slashing sabers. As they drew closer, I took aim at their standard bearer and saw to my horror that he was Franciscan friar. Instead of a flag, he held in his upraised arms a golden monstrance containing the bone-white consecrated Eucharistic host. A stiff breeze blew the cowl off the friar's head revealing the melancholy face of Abner Winslow. The sun's rays gleamed off his monstrance, blinding me; and, in that instant, the soldados lowered their flintlocks and fired. I woke up on the floor beside my bunk bed.

"What's wrong this time?" Jessed groaned.

"Something bit me," I mumbled and, happily, he let it go at that.

The next morning, Jesse tried to run off. I tracked him down just in time at the recruiting station. He was taking in every word those blowhard recruiters had to say. They claimed our boys would send the Yanks home with their tails between their legs. With flags flying, drums beating and young ladies waving their hankies, one boy after another stepped forward and signed away his freedom; hoping in exchange, to win the red badge of courage—just a small flesh wound, proof of his valor as a loyal son of the victorious Confederacy. The biggest fear of those callow recruits was that the war would end before they could enter the fray.

I knew too well what those boys were thinking. I'd thought the same way when I was their age. But I also knew from bitter experience that many of them would rue the day they stepped forward and signed up. They'd die on some far off battlefield, and—if they were lucky enough—they'd be buried in a shallow, unmarked grave. Or, they would return home missing a limb, maimed for life or suffering from deep-seated anxiety, the invisible wounds of war. Same as me.

Jesse was just about to step forward when I came up behind him and took hold of the back of his pants belt.

"Take one more step," I growled, "and I will beat the living tar out of you right here and now in front of all your friends."

He stiffened, spun half way around and gave me a spiteful stare. "You can't tell me what to do." He tried to jerk free.

"I'm not telling you," I said. "I'm ordering you. Get your butt back to the cabin now." I yanked hard.

One of the recruiters, Jacob Muller, saw what I did and decided he didn't need any trouble with me.

"Well, boys," he said, "looks like it's time to call it a day."

The other recruiter gave Muller a puzzled look until he chucked his chin in my direction.

Jesse stood aside as the last of his friends came forward and signed up.

"Bully for you," Jesse shouted after them. "Give them blue bellies a good hiding for me."

They laughed back and said they'd be home in time for fall harvest.

Jesse and I didn't exchange another word for two days. When he wasn't working, he kept his nose stuck in one of his books.

CHAPTER THREE

I was reading the *Florida Sentinel's* account of the Confederacy's mounting troubles when the sound of approaching footsteps interrupted my thoughts. Jesse sashayed into the cabin whistling the tune to "The Bonnie Blue Flag."

"Guess what," he said with a smirk on his face. "Jeff Davis has announced that the army is going to replace volunteers with conscripts. Every able-bodied man 18 to 35 years of age will be required to serve."

His face flushed with excitement.

"Last I looked," I said, "you were only 16 going on 17."

"I'm tall for my age. I'll grow a mustache. They won't know the difference."

"They'll know the difference all right," I said. "They just won't care a copper if you throw your life away. Hell, you'd be volunteering to serve side by side with conscripts, men forced to fight. Draftees might as well be slaves."

"Slaves? Since when is a patriot a slave?"

"There might have been honor in volunteering to fight for the Confederacy," I said. "But there is no honor in being forced to do so. Those conscripts will feel a heap different about this row than those volunteers did; especially, when the draftees find out that any planter with 20 slaves is exempt from military service."

"Well, you don't own 20 slaves," he said. "So there is nothing to hold me back."

"You better read up." I waved the paper in front of him and added, "Jeff Davis still says that anyone who works in a trade critical to the war effort is exempt from the draft. You're staying right here in the gum patch."

He grabbed the newspaper, read the paragraph that I pointed out to him and flung it aside. The paper fluttered across the floor like a wounded bird. Jesse stormed out of the cabin.

Troubled by what had happened, I saddled up Mosey and rode into town to get Maureen's thoughts on dealing with my mulish son. As a school teacher, I thought she might have some insights about young boys, which she could share with me. Minny met me at the Foster's door and showed me into the library where I found Maureen slumped behind her desk, chin cradled in her hands, a dejected look on her face.

"What's wrong?" I asked. "Why so glum?"

She managed a weak smile then pointed to a textbook laying open on her desk. "This is what's wrong. It's the new arithmetic textbook that just came from Atlanta."

"Arithmetic isn't my favorite subject, either," I said.

"That's not what's bothering me," she said. "Read this."

She handed me the open textbook and I read:

If one Confederate soldier kills 90 Yankees, how many Yankees can ten Confederate soldiers kill?

Stunned, I had to read the question twice to absorb its full impact.

"There are many examples like that in the book," she said. "We are teaching our children to hate."

"Yes," I agreed.

"I can't teach this," she said.

"But you must," I replied.

"I'd sooner sew cockades for the soldiers' hats."

"I'm serious," I said. "You have to teach this lesson."

She looked at me with alarm.

"Don't you see?" I said. "Somebody has to speak the truth. This is the deadliest war in history. Today's sharpshooters are armed with rifles and minié balls. They can hit a six-foot target at 500 yards or more. Men are dying by the score without having a fighting chance. You can use this textbook to bring the truth to light. It's all in how you tell it."

"I can't even get my own brother to listen to me," she said. "Caleb is talking about enlisting."

"So is Jesse," I said. "I just had another big argument with him about it. That's why I came to see you."

"I'm afraid I don't have any advice for you," she said. "I pray this war will end before those boys are of age."

~

Gradually, things went from bad to worse. First, it was the damn foragers, like locusts, taking everything that wasn't nailed down. Then the Home Guard came, more or less conscripting young boys and old men to hunt down deserters who went on the dodge somewhere deep in the Everglades. They tried to get Jesse to join the Home Guard; claimed I didn't need him for such a piddly gum patch. But I wouldn't hear of it. I met that rag tag bunch at the cabin with my LeMat strapped to my hip and my rifle resting in the crook of my arm.

Their leader, Don Plunkett, was a former slave trader, who I knew from the faro table in the Salty Dog Saloon. Plunkett was a brute of a man with a shaggy, gray mane, bushy eyebrows and piercing black eyes. A mole over his right eyebrow made it appear to be perpetually raised, as if Plunkett questioned your every utterance. I'd seen him cower other men with his bleak, wolfish stare; but he was pushing 50 now; he had a paunch, and those days were long gone. The man to Plunkett's right was Jacob Muller, the local barber, an old coot accustomed to brandishing nothing more threatening than scissors and shooting off his mouth, urging the young men to enlist. On seeing my rifle, Jacob's face turned pale and mottled, the color of sour milk. The names of the other two geezers slip my mind, but I remember the look in their eyes when I cocked my LeMat—the most powerful handgun ever made, a pistol and a shotgun combined. It could fire grapeshot and nine .42 caliber bullets. Those geezers blinked faster than a shiver, a sure sign that they had no sand in them.

I was not about to knuckle under and let this bunch take Jesse.

"Gents, you're barking up the wrong tree," I said. "The boy stays right here."

Plunkett scratched a chigger bite and drew blood, then examined the tip of his finger before wiping it on his pant leg. Without shifting his gaze, he muttered, "There are four of us, Ed, case you can't count."

My voice dropped a notch. "I can count to ten," I said. "That's how many shots I can get off before reloading."

Plunkett and I glared at each other while the other mossbacks held their breath.

"You know," he said, "rumor has it you've been paying them niggers who work for you same as if they was white folk. If you was found to be a Unionist, all your property could be seized by us under the Sequestration Act."

"The Sequestration Act," I said, drawing out every syllable. "That's quite a mouthful, Don, and I'm sure it means something in Richmond. But, in these parts, possession is nine-tenths of the law. I like my chances."

Plunkett eyed my revolver and rifle, clenched the stub of the cigar smoldering in the corner of his mouth and said, "Have it your way for now."

Then he rolled his head to signal to the others. They reined their horses around and left without saying a word. None of that bunch wanted to tussle.

As soon as they were out of earshot, Jesse said, "I don't get it. You were ready to take on four men. But you won't let me join the Home Guard."

I said, "I've done enough soldiering for both of us."

"Tell that to all the townspeople, the ones who call me a chickenhearted slacker. You think I don't know they give me wooden stares and whisper behind my back?" he said. "I hate the way they look me up and down and cluck their tongues askin' why I haven't gone off to fight with their kinfolk."

"We've been down this road before," I said. "When are you going to learn it's a dead end? You're not going anywhere."

He gave me one of his defiant stares.

"And while you're at it," I said, "wipe that stupid frown off your face." I'd had just about enough of his guff.

He stomped into the cabin and I shouted after him, "Close that damn door behind you."

~

Jacob Muller's barbershop was a regular rumor mill. The man could put God Himself in bad repute. In no time, he and Plunkett noised about their version of what had happened at our showdown. My business slumped like a feed meal sack with a hole punched in it. One by one, most of the shipwrights, who bought my naval stores, made lame excuses then took their business elsewhere. None of them had the spunk to call me a scallywag to my face.

I took it as long as I could. I told myself my fighting days were over. I didn't want to go there again. But Muller and Plunkett wouldn't let up. Those backstabbers had no idea who they were messing with. Finally, it reached the point where something had to be done.

I told Jesse, "I'm going to pay Muller a 'friendly' visit at his barbershop and show him the error of his ways."

As God is my witness, I didn't mean for it to get so far out of hand.

I found Muller sitting in his barber chair, reading the newspaper. The bell over the front door jingled as I entered. Muller folded his newspaper and said cheerily over his shoulder:

"Shave and a hair—"

He glanced up and froze, his unblinking rabbit eyes fixed sideways on my image in the wall mirror. The newspaper slid from his lap.

"Morning, Jacob," I said without a smile. "Any news from up north?"

"Canfield," he stammered. "If it's news you're looking for, the telegraph office is just around the corner."

"Oh that's right," I said. "I forgot. You only deal in rumors."

He quickly slid out of his barber chair, palmed a pair of scissors and said, "You stay away from me."

Big mistake, those scissors.

I spun the barber chair around, using the footrest to take Jacob's legs out from under him. He hit the floor like a sack of potatoes. The scissors went flying. The parrot in the corner cage squawked and threw itself against the bars. I picked up the scissors and slapped them down on the sink with a loud click. Jacob flinched. I walked over to the table where he kept old newspapers for his customers, picked up one of the broadsheets and pretended to scan the page.

"Jacob, you need some fresh reading material."

"Come again?" His lower lip quivered.

I started shredding the paper into small pieces. "Some of your customers are spreading tall stories about something that happened in Key West way back in 1851."

"Stories?"

"Tall stories, Jacob. Rumors. Lies. Big fat lies." I started shredding faster.

His eyebrows winged up as if he were willing himself to take flight. "I wouldn't know about that," he said.

I kept on shredding. "Oh, I think you do. I think you know those stories aren't fit to line the bottom of your parrot cage."

He slid behind his chair again. "As God is my witness—"

That did it. I saw black. I stepped around the chair, grabbed him by the scruff of his neck, yanked his head back and dropped the paper shreds into his gaping mouth. He gagged.

"God hates a false witness, Jacob," I said. "He hates the man that speaketh lies. Proverbs 6:19."

Jacob coughed up the papers. I dropped him on the floor.

"Here's another proverb you'll want to study on: eating your own words can be a very unhealthy diet."

"Yes, sir," he sputtered. "I'll keep that in mind."

"Good," I said. "Don't bother getting up. I can find my own way out."

Satisfied that I had made my point, I stepped over Jacob and left him groveling on the floor of his shop while I went hunting for my next quarry, Don Plunkett. I found him pasting a recruitment poster on the side of the post office building.

"To Arms" the poster read in big, bold text, "Freemen of Florida Rally To Our Noble Cause. Join the Home Guard."

On seeing that sign, I snapped. Again. It brought to mind another recruitment poster, one proclaiming our nation's "Manifest Destiny," the big lie that had changed my life forever. I thought of all the young men who had believed that same lie; who had marched off with me to war, never to return from Mexico. I thought of all the Florida boys marching off to defend the slavocracy. Another big lie. My pulse started pounding like a drum. I lengthened my stride, closing the distance between Plunkett and me. I felt as if I were standing outside myself, watching myself, charge across the street just as I had charged across many a battlefield.

"Plunkett," I called out, "that poster is crooked; as crooked as the stories you've been spreading about me."

He spun around. Less than three feet separated us. I could smell his cigar breath.

"Canfield. This here's your chance to earn a bounty on every deserter you run to ground."

His eyes were blacker than the inside of a cartridge box.

"Here," I said, "let me straighten this out for you."

I brushed him aside, ripped the poster off the wall and tore it in two.

Plunkett brandished his paste brush as if it were a weapon. "Hey! That's government property you're destroying."

I laughed. "If I were you," I said, "I'd be more concerned about the private property dangling between your legs."

"Are you threatening me?" he asked.

"Forget what I said," I answered. "Just remember this."

The toe of my boot caught him squarely in the groin. He gasped, doubled over in pain. My right fist hit him in the kidney; my left connected with his jaw. He went down to his knees, his bucket of paste spilling across the ground. I hammered him again and again until he collapsed. Then I picked up his paste brush and swiped it across his face.

"Keep shooting off your mouth," I said, "and someone is liable to paste it shut."

I dropped his pistol in a horse trough and walked off. It felt good to get that off my chest. I took a deep breath to snuff out the flames burning in my gut. But I knew I'd gone off half-cocked. I'd given vent to my rage. I'd lost control.

And I had just added to my troubles. This wasn't the end of it. I would hear from the Home Guard again.

I headed for the Salty Dog Saloon to get a drink.

Later that day, Jesse met me at the cabin with an ear-to-ear grin. "I heard what you did to Muller and Plunkett."

"Good news travels fast."

"Word is you beat them to a pulp."

"They had it coming."

"Well, I'm glad you paid those boys a friendly visit. I'd hate to see what you'd do if you got angry."

I held up my swollen right hand. "The hell of it is I hurt my right hand. You're going to have to lend me a hand with my chores."

"I suppose I'll have to cut your hair now, too."

Jessie laughed; but not me. I'd seen how Plunkett gambled at the card table. When he lost, he doubled up on his next bet. The stakes were getting higher; this would end badly for one of us.

~

Early the next day, I paid Miss Maureen a visit at her home, hoping to share my version of what had happened before she heard it from someone else. I found her seated at a table on the verandah reading the newspaper. She looked upset by what she had just read.

"Morning, sunshine," I said. "You look like you could use a friend."

She looked up, wiped a tear from her eye and said, "Oh, good morning. I didn't hear you approaching."

"What seems to be troubling you?" I asked.

She unfurled the newspaper. "The paper has the casualty count for the latest battle. Two boys from Cedar Keys are listed."

"Who?" I asked.

She slid the paper across the table. "I can't bear to read it again."

I skimmed the article and saw the names of two local boys: Seth Hawthorne and Jimmy Duquesne. Both dead. Both under age. Jimmy had been shot by our own file closers, officers who ensured battlefield discipline by shooting any soldier who tried to desert.

"Plunkett is responsible for this," I said. "He's recruiting underage boys for the Home Guard. Before those boys know it, they're being shipped up north to fight."

On hearing me mention the Home Guard, Maureen looked up, pulled a loose strand of hair off her cheek and said softly, "I heard about what happened yesterday."

I held her gaze. "Just so you know," I said, "all I meant to do was reason with them."

"I believe you, Ed," she answered. "But you'll have to convince my father. He's heard a different version of the story."

"I'll stop by his office this morning," I said.

"If he offers you a cigar, please turn him down," she said. "He's been smoking like a chimney since the break-in at his warehouse and it's affecting his health."

I knew that a man of Peter Foster's prominence would not want his daughter to be seen in public with a brawler. After speaking with Miss Maureen, I set out for her father's salt works. It occupied a one-story wooden building next to the far end of the town dock. Behind the building stood several tall smoke stacks for the brick furnaces where huge kettles were used to boil the seawater until all that remained was the vitally needed salt. Foster's laborers worked from dawn to dusk cutting wood and feeding it into the furnaces that fired the 15 boilers. Then they bagged and weighed upwards of 50 bushels of salt a day and stored them in a warehouse until they could be shipped out. The warehouse was a windowless wooden building with a padlocked entrance. Shotgun-toting watchmen guarded the entrance around the clock to prevent another break-in.

I entered Foster's building and greeted his secretary, Cal Nordland, one of my drinking buddies from the Salty Dog Saloon. Ed was a clean-shaven man with long, gray hair combed straight back and tied so tightly in a bun that it made his head look too small for his body. Warm weather had brought him south; rheumatism had kept him here. But, as a young man, Ed had served in the Mexican-American War as an artillery officer, a position that left him hard of hearing and the rest of us wishing he didn't talk so loud. Unlike me, Ed often boasted about his battlefield exploits. In some ways, I owed my reputation as a local war hero to Ed's big mouth. At the start of the Civil War, he had urged me to start up a local company. I told him to put a cork in it.

"Canfield?" he asked at the top of his voice. "What brings you here?"

Peter Foster must have heard him because he called out from his office, "Canfield is that you? Come in."

He met me at the door to his office and gestured for me to have a seat across from his desk. His breath was foul and his clothes stunk of cigar smoke. I removed my hat and pulled up a chair that made a harsh, grating sound on the gleaming wooden floor. For an awkward moment, we both looked at each other as if one of us had just broken wind in church. Foster pursed his lips in what was supposed to pass for a smile and we both sat down. On the credenza behind his desk, I saw wooden models of his two sloops and several sailing trophies he had won. Symbols of better times, they now bore a dusting of cigar ash.

Foster was a stout man in his late forties with a leonine head framed by silken, white hair, axe-handle sideburns and a florid complexion. His eyes were blood shot and set close, creating the unsettling impression that he could bore in and expose your innermost thoughts. He leaned back toward the credenza and opened the lid of a humidor.

"Care for a Havana?" he asked. He offered me a cigar.

"No thanks," I said.

He paused while reading my expression, closed the lid slowly and smiled to himself.

"Yes, I know. They're habit-forming," he said with a half-hearted nod. "My daughter wants me to quit."

"She's concerned about your health."

"Yes," he said. He sighed and sagged back in his chair. "And I am concerned about her reputation."

Another awkward moment passed in which neither of us spoke.

"My daughter," Foster continued, "is a lot like her mother, my first wife, Helen, God rest her soul."

He gestured toward an oil painting of a very attractive women hanging on the wall behind his desk. The woman looked remarkably like Maureen: the same straight auburn hair, blue eyes and ready smile; only her complexion looked lighter.

"Helen was a very head-strong woman who did what she pleased," he said. "The doctor warned her about all the laudanum she took to achieve the coveted pale complexion of a well-bred woman of high estate. But Helen ignored the advice. She did not want the dark complexion of a field worker. She came to crave the laudanum and it eventually took her life."

"I'm sorry to hear about that, sir."

"Like her mother, Maureen does what she pleases," he said. "She may not be as fashion-conscious as her mother; but she is just as head strong; doesn't give a fig about what others might think. It was a mistake sending her to that teaching school. They put a lot of foolish ideas in her head. Now, she pays me no mind." He paused then added, "That's why I am speaking directly to you."

"And what advice would you have for me?"

He gave a slight cough, cleared his throat and said, "I want you to stop seeing my daughter."

My back stiffened. "Am I to know your reasoning?"

"Come, come," he said, "your reputation precedes you. By now almost every one in Cedar Keys knows what happened the other day. They also know why you haven't re-enlisted. It has nothing to do with running a turpentine still, does it? You were drummed out of the federal army."

Drummed out?

My head fell forward as if I had been rabbit punched. I had expected him to say something about my run-ins with Plunkett's men. This new rumor about my being court-martialed took me completely by surprise.

"First of all," I said, "the rumor mills forgot to separate the wheat from the weeds."

"Wheat from weeds? A bible lesson from you, Mister Canfield?"

"Call it what you want, but the truth is there is more to the story than you may have heard."

"Then you don't deny it?"

"Look, it happened way back in 1851. I was stationed in Fort Zachary Taylor at Key West and got into a card game in a bar."

"Gambling, too?"

"Yes, gambling. We're both gamblers. You and me. We gamble every day that we open our doors for business."

I could see that argument gave him pause for thought.

"In this case," I said, "it was a game of faro. I was losing big time when I caught the dealer using a stacked deck. I grabbed him by the wrist, felt his muscles tense, his hand tighten into a fist. He yanked free and went for his revolver. I swung wildly, cracked him on the jaw and lunged across the table to prevent him from shooting me. I can't remember what happened next. Everything is a blur in my mind. But, in the end, the dealer had a broken wrist, and he wouldn't be playing cards any time soon."

Foster looked puzzled. "What does this have to do with your—?"

"My court-martial?" I asked. "It turns out that I had just whipped a varmint by the name of Lieutenant Claussen."

"You struck an officer?"

"I allow as how it was not my finest hour in the service of my country. But, in my defense, the man was not in uniform so I had no idea who I was pummeling. Unfortunately, that argument didn't win over the judges in my court-martial hearing. They sentenced me to two years' hard labor at Fort Jefferson in the Dry Tortugas."

"That hell hole," he said.

"Yes. It's a God-forsaken, sun-bleached coral rock surrounded by water and infested with every contagion known to man or beast. It was the stiffest sentence they were willing to mete out, given the number of lives I had saved while fighting in Texas and Mexico."

His expression brightened. "So Nordland is right? You did serve in the Mexican-American War."

"That's right." For once, I was glad Cal had a big mouth.

"I did, too," Foster said. "Under whose command?"

As best I recall, we spoke for another hour or so about the campaigns we had fought in; the soldiers we knew in common; and what had become of them. He made no further mention of the rumors about me. Toward the end, we were both smoking Havanas. The cigars drew smoothly, burned evenly and held their ash for up to an inch. It was a satisfying smoke.

∾

After my meeting with Peter Foster, Miss Maureen wanted to know, "What did you and my father talk about—that is, between puffs on your cigars?" She wrinkled her nose teasingly.

"Mostly about the war, politics and women," I answered with a red face.

"Women?"

"About you and your mother."

"My mother?" She nodded and bit the inside of her cheek. "He's never gotten over her passing."

"Well, her portrait does hang right over his desk, a constant reminder of her. Do you remember her?"

"No. Not really. I was so young at the time and it was so long ago. I try not to dwell on the past."

"There is a striking resemblance between you and your ma."

"Yes. My father's second wife saw it right away," she said a little testily. "She took an instant dislike to me. I think that's why she sent me off to boarding school when I was ten."

"How did that make you feel?"

"Lonely. Scared, at first. I learned to stand on my own at a very early age."

"Why did your father go along with it?"

"She convinced him that the local school wasn't good enough for me. She wanted him all to herself."

"I didn't see her portrait in his office."

"You won't find one anywhere. It was a loveless marriage. I think the only reason my father married her was to have a son, something I could never be for him. Try as hard as I might to please him, I was still his little girl."

I gazed at her as if seeing her for the first time: her simple attire, the lack of jewelry, her unadorned hair, and her flawless complexion, free of any trace of make-up. In that fleeting moment, I understood her need to appear strong, invulnerable. She, too, bore invisible wounds.

"But it's obvious," I said, "that your father loves you."

"Yes, he does, in his own way; but Caleb is the apple of his eye."

"And yet, you get along so well with Caleb."

"Caleb and my two stepsisters are the only good things to come out of that marriage."

She gave a soft, trilling laugh that ended abruptly with her looking away, embarrassed at having revealed so much of herself. When she looked back, her expression was searching.

"What about you and your family?" she asked. "You never talk about them."

I paused, reluctant to share that part of my story; and, yet, she had been so open and trusting with me, I felt I owed her as much.

"I lost my ma and pa when I was 15," I said. "After that I was on my own."

"Didn't you have any kin who would take you in?"

"My nearest uncle had a daughter the same age as me," I said. "He didn't feel comfortable having the two of us sleeping under the same roof. So he took in my younger brother and sister and rented me out to a local farmer."

"He rented you out like a slave?"

That hurt. "I suppose you could look at it that way," I said, "but my uncle was dirt poor and I saw it as helping him pay for the rearing of my brother and sister."

"I apologize," she said. "I didn't mean to call you a slave. It's just that—"

"It only lasted a couple of years," I quickly added, "until my brother and sister could fend for themselves."

I didn't mention that I had lived in the slave quarters; that I'd seen black men whipped until their blood pooled at their feet; or that, I'd stood by watching slave traders tear families apart.

All I said was, "First chance I got I started a new life."

"Is that when you married Jesse's mother?"

"Soon after," I said. "Within the same year, I enlisted in the army. I guess you could say the army became my family."

"And now you and Jesse are back together—as a family."

"So long as he doesn't run off to war."

"I know what you mean," she said. "The Home Guard makes it sound like such a grand adventure."

"Believe me," I said. "It's far from that."

~

Once the Home Guard's stories about me started up, there was no stopping them. The rumors kept circulating like minnows in a mangrove tangle, spreading far beyond the circle of Muller and Plunkett. Most of the folks in our town sided with the secessionists. I still had my share of loyal friends—men like Adam Broady and Cal Nordland—but none of my buddies were shipwrights. My business continued to slump.

I was seated at the table in my cabin, trying to make sense of the sales ledger, when Adam Broady entered with a long look on his face.

"We just lost another order," he said. "If sales get any lower, we may have to look up to see bottom."

I closed the ledger, folded my hands over the cover and sighed. "I thought for sure sales would turn around by now."

"Well, they haven't," he said. He exhaled a low whistle. "Ed, I have a family to feed. I need this job."

"What's that supposed to mean?"

"Are you open to suggestions?"

Here it comes. A lecture on my drinking. "Sure."

"Lately," he said, "you've been spending a lot of time with that church lady, instead of working on the business."

I saw red. "Keep her out of this."

"It's just that ever since you started seeing Maureen Foster, you haven't been your grouchy old self. The Ed Canfield I know would be kicking up a ruckus, driving sales higher. But, no—you're walking around whistling church hymns."

I snapped. "You know damn well I tried to stop Plunkett. And you know that Maureen has nothing to do with the slump in sales. The two of us are just friends."

"Friends? Close enough that you share the same hymnal in the choir. Close enough that you walk her home after every prayer service."

"If you have any other ideas for turning things around," I growled, "let's hear them."

That's when Adam suggested we use my workboat to do some serious fishing. The gulf teemed with mullet, sea trout, sheepshead, whiting, grouper, flounder and pompano. Jesse and I would take the boat on early morning runs up the coast while Adam managed the turpentine still. We'd use a seine net to fish, salt and preserve the catch in barrels, then trade what we didn't eat for the vegetables of local farmers. The idea worked, too. Things were looking up until someone snuck onto the boat at night, took a knife to my seine net, and cut it to pieces. I was furious, bent on revenge. Broady tried to reason with me; he said I should go to the sheriff.

"With what?" I said. "We don't have any evidence. We can't prove Plunkett's boys did it."

I pictured Plunkett's gang having a good laugh at my expense. I totaled up all they had cost me, all the aggravation, all the time and expense. I went over it again and again in my mind as if taking a wet stone to the blade of my axe. I felt the urge to strike out.

I thought of how I'd seen Plunkett gamble and realized that I had to raise the stakes and force him to fold. But before I could up the ante, his men struck again. In the middle of the night, horsemen galloped into my gum patch with murder in mind. Broady's dog, Beau, heard them coming and started barking before they got past the cooper's shed. Jesse and I heard the dog's warning, bolted out of bed, hit the floor, loaded our firearms and returned fire. Hot lead filled the air. The horsemen skedaddled.

At first light, the brittle silence was broken by the sound of a shovel biting into the earth. I came out of the cabin to find Adam Broady digging a hole. The bullet-riddled body of his dog lay beside it. Adam paused when he saw me, his face flushed, his eyes red with rage.

"You were right," he said. "Damn and double damn those bastards." He started digging again. "I have to bury Beau right away. I can't have my boys see him like this."

"If it wasn't for Beau," I said, "that could have been us."

Jesse came up behind us, saw Beau and fell to his knees beside the dog.

I curled one arm around Adam's shoulder, and with the other arm I swept the entire bullet-strewn scene.

"Whoever is behind this," I said, "is going to pay."

I had a damn good idea who they were but I had to be sure. Too much was at stake. In the back of my head, I could hear Abner Winslow whispering, "Don't throw caution to the wind." But I wasn't listening.

After burying Beau, we scoured the ground looking for clues as to the identity of the gunslingers. I found some .577 caliber shell casings from Enfield rifles. Jesse found a piece of butternut-dyed linen that Beau had ripped from the shirtsleeve of one of the riders. The cloth was blood stained so the shooter's forearm had been bitten. Broady found a couple of brass rim-fired cartridge from a Smith & Wesson sidearm. It wasn't much to go on but it would have to be enough.

"Shouldn't we turn this evidence over to the sheriff?" Broady asked.

"What for?" I said. "He's just going to side with the Home Guard."

I told Broady and Jesse to stay behind in the gum patch, in case the riders returned. Then I reloaded my LeMat, saddled up Mosey and headed for the Salty Dog Saloon where cheap booze had a way of loosening lips. The rumor mill could work for me, too. I wanted the names of every last one of those nightriders.

I set off at a quick canter but Mosey soon sensed something was up. The horse felt the tension coiled up inside my body, ready to snap at any moment. The closer we got to

Cedar Keys the more skittish she became. She tried to shy away from the waterfront, fought the bridle, even reared up; but I talked her down and we entered Front Street where the morning sun masked the storefronts in somber shadows. A broom-sweeping shopkeeper saw me and backed into his store. A blacksmith paused; hammer in hand, until I passed. A woman dashed into the street and scooped up her child before I rode by. Word about what had happened at my place must have already reached town.

At the Salty Dog Saloon, voices spilled into the street in squeaks and squeals of laughter that sounded like someone was playing with a rusty water spigot. The jokes sputtered to a stop when I pushed open the batwing doors. A drunk sat passed out at the bar. The man on the next barstool glanced at my image in the mirror and froze with one hand in the peanut jar. To the right of the door, a clutch of men dressed in the butternut-dyed uniforms sat bunched around a table. Two blowsy barmaids draped themselves over one of the men, Don Plunkett. He whispered something to the women and they backed off. He snuffed out his cigar in an empty glass and glared at me with his poker face. The other men leaned forward, poised for action. They sat so close together I could take all of them out with a single shotgun blast from my LeMat.

"Canfield," the barkeep said with forced cheerfulness, "What will it be?"

"The usual," I said without taking my eyes off Plunkett.

"Aquardiente, it is."

He poured four fingers of rum. I reached for it while eyeing the butternut boys in the mirror. Lifting the glass, I turned to face them. "What are we celebrating, boys?"

"This here is official business," Plunkett said, "a meeting of the Home Guard."

"Business?" I said. "Well, I have one more thing to add to your business agenda."

"How's that?" The mole over Plunkett's right eyebrow ticked up.

"We had a little horseplay at the gum patch last night. One of the horsemen left something behind, a bullet from a Smith & Wesson sidearm."

"A clue?" Plunkett said. "Look who thinks he's the sheriff." He forced a laugh.

"Oh, I'm not going to trouble the sheriff about this," I said. "It would be no trouble at all for my LeMat."

Plunkett's face turned the color of tallow. He eased his right hand below the table where I couldn't see it. "If you're looking to be a hero, Canfield, enlist in the Confederate army."

"Now why would he want to do a thing like that?" another voice cut in.

We all spun around to see Peter Foster and Cal Nordland standing in the doorway. Both men were armed and wearing the battered forage caps from their days in the Mexican-American War. Nordland held an old-fashioned smooth bore flintlock waist high; Foster held an Enfield. They had come ready to fight on my side—veterans sticking together.

"Don, in case you've forgotten," Foster said, "the Confederate navy needs all the pitch and tar Canfield can produce in his gum patch."

Plunkett shrugged. "The way I hear it Canfield spends a lot of time fishing."

"That's not the way I hear it," Foster said. "I hear someone's been messing with his business, making it hard for him to sell his naval stores. You wouldn't know anything about that, would you?"

"Can't say as I do," Plunkett said.

"Well," Foster replied, "I'm sure you Home Guard boys have better things to do than sit around here shooting the breeze when you could be hunting down deserters."

Plunkett wasn't about to argue with someone as influential as Peter Foster.

"C'mon, boys," he said. "Let's go hang up some wanted posters."

"Be sure to hang them straight," I said sarcastically.

Plunkett glowered at me, shoved back his chair, and led the Home Guard past us and out the door.

"What is it between you and Plunkett?" Foster asked.

"He's recruiting underage boys for the Home Guard," I said.

"Well, when you see my daughter, you can tell her that Plunkett now knows where I stand."

Chapter Three

I left the saloon and headed straight for the Foster home where Maureen greeted me in the yard surrounded by her school children.

"I suppose," I said, "there's no point in telling you what just happened?"

"Let me guess," she said, "my father and Cal Nordland just saved your bacon."

"Ouch. That hurt."

She shook her head. "Somebody's got to watch your back."

"How in the world did you know what had happened last night?"

"That's easy," she said. "See that little blonde haired boy over there?"

She pointed to one of her students running around the yard.

"Sure."

"Well, that is Jacob Muller's son and he has inherited one of his father's less desirable traits."

"Meaning?"

"He has a big mouth. He's been bragging in the schoolyard about what the Home Guard just did to some scallywag. Sound familiar?" She paused and added, "Ed, when is this all going to end?"

"I wish I knew," I said.

When I got back to my gum patch, there was a wanted poster pasted on the side of my cabin. I ripped it down.

~

The rumors about me never let up. Business got so bad that I had to cut half my staff. It was a decision I struggled for weeks to avoid making. But, eventually, it became clear I had no other choice—four men had to go, including Caleb Foster. Of course, Jesse reacted strongly to the idea.

"You can't fire Caleb," he said. "He's doing a great job."

"He is also the last one hired," I said. "Besides, I'll help him find another job."

Before making the announcement, I thought it best to let Maureen know what I had to do and why. She had confided in me that the Fosters were struggling to make ends meet until Lloyd's of London paid off their insurance claim. Now she took the news of the layoffs harder than I had expected.

"But why Caleb?" she wanted to know.

"He's a smart boy," I said. "Too smart to be wasting his time in a gum patch."

Luckily, Caleb agreed. He told his sister not to worry. He said he'd find a better job in no time. But Maureen still fretted and I could sense she was beginning to wonder about me. I decided to smooth things over after the next choir practice.

"You were in fine voice today, Miss Maureen," I said.

She turned and said coolly, "Why thank you."

I began walking beside her as usual. "I see you're reading a book."

"Yes," she said, brightening. "I just shared it with Brother Storter. It's by a Danish philosopher, Sorem Kierkegaard."

"Can't say as I've heard of him." Philosophy books were not high on my reading list.

"Well," Maureen said, "Brother Storter really appreciated this passage."

She stopped, opened her book to a dog-eared page and read:

"'The tyrant dies and his rule is over, the martyr dies and his rule begins.' Brother says that we're the martyrs; the Yanks are the tyrants. Don't you see? That means the Confederacy will live forever."

She seemed positively elated at the thought of being a martyr. I wasn't so giddy at the prospect, and managed to put my foot in my mouth.

"Unfortunately," I said, "God marches with the biggest battalions."

"What do you mean?" She looked stunned. "God is on our side. We are winning."

"Actually, the Confederacy is losing. We're outnumbered," I said. "That's why we've been forced into drafting our soldiers."

Her eyelashes fluttered with the effort of seeing my point of view. "I can't believe I'm hearing this. Surely you don't think the South is in the wrong."

"What I think isn't going to make a difference one way or the other."

"And just what do you think?"

I should have hesitated long enough to think through my answer, but instead, I charged ahead as usual, saying:

"I think it was wrong for the draft to exempt from military service any one who owns 20 slaves. That makes it a rich man's war, and a poor man's fight. It also guarantees that there will be a greater demand for slaves."

The words were no sooner out of my mouth than I realized I had just dug myself into a deeper hole. Prior to the break-in at the salt works, Maureen's father had been one of the richest, most powerful men in town. But now he was deep in debt, and I had just added to his financial woes by firing his son.

There was an awkward pause in which I searched for the right thing to say, something to smooth things over, but nothing came out.

"As I see it," Maureen said, "the rich are paying a rather steep price in defense of our Southern way of life. Good day, sir."

She snapped the cover shut and, with her book firmly clasped to her breast, walked off with her head held high.

I was not about to make the same mistake I had made with my wife. I quickly sat down and began writing a letter of apology:

My Dear Miss Foster,

Please accept my sincerest apology for my thoughtless remark today. I meant no offense by it. I agree that this war has exacted a steep price from one and all, and I pray that we will soon see better days.

I paused to collect my thoughts before revealing the source of my deep-seated feelings about slavery. There was no avoiding it. She had to know. I dipped my pen in the inkwell and continued writing . . .

Though I love the South, I believe no society can sustain itself when nearly one-third of its population is held in bondage.

I got some sense of what it's like to be a slave when I lost my mother and father, and my uncle rented me out to a local farmer. The man treated his dogs better than he treated me.

To my way of thinking, slavery is a stain upon the Confederate flag. I pray that you can find it in your heart to make some allowance for my feelings on the subject, especially in light of the freedom that Minny enjoys in your household."

Respectfully,
your humble
and contrite servant,
Edward Canfield

I reread the note as the ink dried, folded it and put it in an envelope. Then I brought the envelope to choir practice, expecting Maureen to show up. When she didn't appear, I took the note the next day to the general store where I knew Minny did her shopping for the Foster household. Bright and early, Minny came around the street corner wearing a straw hat and a shapeless homespun dress, her bare feet kicking up a cloud of dust too slow to get out of her way. On seeing me, she stopped abruptly.

"Good morning, Minny," I said.

"Mornin', suh." Her response seemed guarded, as if she sensed I was up to something.

"Miss Foster wasn't at choir practice last night. I hope it's nothing serious?"

"She took to bed with dah vapors, suh."

"And how is she this fine day?"

"Tolerable well, suh."

From the way she said it, I could tell Minny knew who had upset Maureen.

"That's good to hear," I said. "I wonder if you would be so kind as to give her this note from me?"

"Yes, suh." She took the note and, without looking at it, slipped it under her straw hat. I stepped aside and watched her enter the store; then I left, hoping for the best.

Maureen showed up for the next choir practice and took her usual place beside me, acting as if nothing had happened. At first, we didn't speak or look at one another. We simply opened our hymnals and directed our attention to the choirmaster. He led us in song and I went through the motions scarcely able to focus on the page in front of me. I asked myself if I had made a mistake in exposing such strong views about slavery. I wondered if I had made matters worse. I couldn't read her mood. Finally, at a break in practice, I turned to Miss Maureen.

"I am glad to see you are feeling well," I whispered.

"Why thank you," she said without turning to look at me.

"Did Minny give you my note?"

"Yes," she said. "I read it."

"Only once?" I teased.

She was just as quick with her comeback. "Did you write it more than once?" She tucked a stray lock of hair behind her ear revealing the slightest hint of a forgiving smile.

"No," I said, "I only wrote it once, but I have relived those scenes more times than I care to count."

That answer seemed to affect her. "I'm truly sorry about what you had to endure on that farm. I'm sure your uncle meant good."

I nodded. "Nothing good came of it."

"I must confess," she added, "it gave me pause for thought about how easily we confuse good and evil."

"Then you make allowance for my indiscrete remarks?"

Before she could respond, the choir director tapped his baton to get our attention. "We could do with a little less whispering and a little more singing."

'Well?" I asked her again.

"Please turn to page 48," the choirmaster insisted. "Verses one and two."

Maureen smiled, turned to me and said, "If only you sang as well as you write."

"I'll take that as a yes."

We both laughed and began singing. Afterward, I walked her home. When we reached her house, she turned to me and said:

"Are you familiar with the story of *Macbeth*?"

"It's a play, isn't it?"

"Yes," she said, "a play written by William Shakespeare. It's the story of a rebellion in which good and evil are often mistaken for one another. I think you might enjoy it."

She loaned me a copy of Shakespeare's works from her father's library. I didn't much care for the way the Brit wrote but I read *Macbeth* anyway. I reckoned it would give me something to talk to Miss Maureen about besides the war.

~

If I remember rightly, it was about two weeks later that Caleb signed up as a drummer boy. Maureen didn't show up for choir practice that night, either. Afterwards, I went to her home with the excuse of returning her copy of *Macbeth.* Minny greeted me at the door with a long look on her face. I could tell she had been crying.

"Marse Caleb signed up," she said, "He done lied 'bout his age and signed up. Miss Maureen too upset to see y'all now."

"I'm sure Caleb will do his family proud."

"Proud? That boy coulda might get his self killed." Her eyes misted over.

I said something stupid like "He'll be home on furlough in no time. Just wait and see."

She shook her head and said, "That can't come soon 'nuf. Lordy, that can't come soon 'nuf. I wet nurse dat chile, I washt him, dresst him and fed him jes like my own. Now look what he gone and done."

"And you should be proud of what you have done," I said. "He's a fine, upstanding young man."

"Man?" she said. "He be still a boy. Blow away on a windy day."

"But once he made up his mind," I said, "you know, there was no stopping Caleb."

"Thas da God's honest truth," she said with a little chuckle. "Dat boy stubborn as a mule chewing on bees."

Minny started whimpering, bowed her head and stepped inside the house, closing the front door softly behind her. I didn't know what to do or say and left with a heavy heart.

By the time I got to the cabin, Jesse had heard the news about Caleb. To make matters worse, Caleb had told everyone who'd listen that they'd be reading all about his doings in the *Florida Sentinel.* He was a real talker.

Jesse actually thought his friend had lucked out.

"Banging a drum and parading around in a uniform in front of all the ladies, that's for me," he said. "It sure beats making barrel staves."

A few days later, I noticed Jesse was growing a mustache.

"Do you mind telling me what in hell you're doing?" I asked.

"What's eating you now?"

"What's that on your lip?"

"It's a mustache."

I could see he was proud of how much older it made him look. I also knew why he was growing it.

"Shave it off," I said. "It looks like you've got mice tails hanging out of your mouth."

~

The steady stream of bad news from the war front seemed to inspire Brother Storter in his search for new ways to attack our enemies from the safety and security of the redoubt that was his pulpit. Not content with attacking the Yanks, he started ranting about the blacks, too. He warned about the risk of a slave rebellion in a state where 44 percent of the population lived in bondage. He urged the faithful to keep the "darkies" in their place. I left that prayer meeting madder than a sack full of cats.

In one of his sermons on the Garden of Eden, Storter held up a newspaper photo of Abraham Lincoln and said, "We have to cut off the snake's head."

The man had a knack of turning violence into virtue so long as the killing was done in God's name.

Sure enough, that afternoon I caught Jesse using a picture of Lincoln for target practice.

That did it. I yanked the rifle-musket out of his hands and thrust my jaw to within inches of his face. "Finish your chores now."

He flinched but he didn't back down. The boy had some spunk. He braced his shoulders in defiance and said, "Lincoln is nothing but a black Republican."

"Careful who you call black," I said. "Lincoln wasn't the one slaving away, mucking out horse stables in Charleston."

"Do I look like a nigger to you?" he snapped back.

"How many times do I have to tell you?" I said. "It's Negro. And, as near as I can figure, that's exactly how you looked to that boy who whipped you."

"I'm not going to stand here and listen to this claptrap."

He pivoted and stalked off.

This time I got in the last word. "I liked you better," I shouted after him, "when you had your nose stuck in a book."

~

A couple of weeks later, Peter Foster pulled some strings to get Caleb transferred to Company F, Fourth Regiment, which was going to be billeted in Cedar Keys. I didn't take the news well. I figured the young ladies would be smitten with Private Caleb Foster and that Jesse would be hankering for some of that same female adulation. I expected another blow up with my son, but nothing like the one that followed.

I was sitting in my cabin, nursing a hangover with a few hairs of the dog that bit me, when Jesse burst inside, shouting at the top of his lungs.

"You were court-martialed!"

"Whoa," I said, cradling my aching head in my hands. "You'll wake the dead."

"You were drummed out of the army," he bellowed.

"What did you say?"

"What happened?" he snarled, his spittle flying into my face. "Did you desert another post?"

The room spun. I couldn't think straight. He stood over me, our heads almost touching. I rose, lifted an arm to fend him off. He slapped it away. Without thinking, I hauled off and hit him square on the jaw. He staggered back, gathered himself, roared and came at me like a raging bull, swinging wildly. I had no choice but to swing back, but I felt too woozy. I grazed him. He hit me. Hard. I fell to the floor. I was on all fours, when he raised a foot to kick me. I grabbed him by the other foot and yanked his legs out from under him. He fell back and hit his head on the floor with a loud *Thunk.* That took the fight out of him. He lay there stunned, sobbing, his chest heaving. I scooted over to him on my haunches and took a deep, rummy breath, trying to clear my head.

"Who's been talking to you?"

"One of Plunkett's men," he cried. "He says you couldn't cut it as a soldier."

"It's true," I said. "They court-martialed me, but not for ducking a fight. They threw me in prison for fighting the wrong man."

He wiped a sleeve across his face. "The wrong man?"

"A Union officer."

He nodded as if he understood the urge to rebel against authority, especially since I'd hit a Union officer. He propped himself up on one elbow, looked at me with his red-rimmed eyes and signaled for me to continue.

"We were playing a game of faro in a Key West bar," I said, "I was losing big, and I caught him cheating."

"What happened?"

"I beat that four-flusher to a pulp and they sent me off to Fort Jefferson in the Dry Tortugas. End of story."

"For how long?"

"Long enough."

"So that's why you didn't come back." His face brightened at the thought of my imprisonment.

"Something like that."

He sat up, tucked his knees into his chest, wrapped his arms around them and looked at me. I sat up, too.

"Ma said you were always bucking authority."

"Seems like it's a family trait." I was only half-kidding. That boy could start an argument in an empty house.

He jumped to his feet and extended a hand to help me up. I took it.

"So, you goin' to throw me in the brig one of these days?"

"Do as you're told and we'll get along just fine."

"Come to think of it," he said, "this place must be just like the brig. You locked yourself in and threw away the key. What are you punishing yourself for?"

"You don't know what in hell you're talking about."

He stuffed his hands into his back pockets and jutted his chin toward me. "You know," he said, "one of these days, I am going to enlist."

I ran a hand through my hair and felt a bump where he had hit me. I didn't let on that it hurt. I just turned my back on him, and said over my shoulder:

"You can go marching off when the angel Gabriel blows his horn. Until then, your butt belongs right here."

CHAPTER FOUR

I changed my tune on the morning of January 16, 1862. The day dawned bright and clear with no hint of what was about to befall the seaport of Cedar Keys. Jesse and I were using my new seine net on an early morning run when the Union gunboat, USS *Hatteras,* steamed into the harbor and, without warning, let loose her death-dealing cannons on our friends and neighbors.

At a distance, the heavy curtain of cannon fire sounded like approaching thunder, but on hearing the second barrage I recognized the metallic roar of naval ordnance.

"Haul in the net, boy," I called out to Jesse.

"Now?" He threw up his hands. "We just got here."

"Hop to it," I snapped. "We're heading back to Cedar Keys."

"But, we'll be heading straight into that storm."

"That's no storm. That's cannon fire. Cedar Keys is under attack."

Jesse gave a rebel whoop and started hauling in the net hand over fist. He was still a boy and didn't see war for what it really was. I wanted no part of this fight. My soldiering days were long over. But we had close friends in danger. We couldn't desert them.

If only half the things Brother Storter had said about the marauding Yanks were true—

I felt the first stirrings of anger, that all too familiar feeling smoldering just below the surface, ready to flare up in an all-consuming rage at the least sign of injustice. Left unchecked, the smoke and flames of fury could blind me in the heat of battle. I knew that from bitter experience. I couldn't let it happen again.

"Stand by to jibe," I shouted. "Jibe ho."

Jesse ducked quickly to avoid being hit by the boom sweeping across the deck as the stern passed through the eye of the wind. The mains'l snapped with a loud crack from the sudden rush of wind. Then we raced back to port on a broad reach as fast as the wind and waves would take us. The rigging squealed; spindrift stung my face. I clung to the tiller and listened to the Yankee cannons pounding away like the hammers of hell. I was wet, chilled to the bone, numbed by thoughts of what lay ahead.

The rumors had circulated for weeks, ever since the Yanks announced their blockade of southern ports. "Anaconda," they called it. The way I heard it they meant to destroy the harbor at Cedar Keys and our new railhead connecting the west coast and east coast of Florida. Without the trains, it would be harder to ship the cattle, fresh produce and salt that promised to make Florida the food locker of the South. The blue bellies meant to starve us into submission. Or, so they said.

The talk seemed far-fetched, but the railroad had persuaded the Confederate army to send a small force of 23 defenders from Company F, the Fourth Regiment, Florida Volunteers. Those fresh-faced recruits paraded through town with Caleb in front, banging away on his drum while the Home Guard brought up the rear. It was nothing much but for show.

Myself, I put no store by the rumors. The way I saw it, if the threat were real, they would have sent more troops to protect us. Besides, the Yanks had their hands full up North. There was no way they'd launch an attack this far south. At any rate, that was the other rumor.

Now a series of thunderous blasts rent the air, shattering any lingering doubts I might have had about "Anaconda."

"What was that?" Jesse asked.

"Sounds like thirty-two pounders," I said. "They mean to blow Cedar Keys to kingdom come."

I looked at Jesse for some reaction. To my surprise, he never flinched, never said a word; he just stood there, straight as a mast, his chin held high, fighting the wind, as if it were the Devil himself. Salt spray beaded his brow, peppered the front of his shirt. He was a Canfield, for sure.

"Weapons," Jesse shouted at me. "We have to get our guns from the cabin."

"We're not going to fight, not unless we have to."

"Not fight? What in hell are you talking about?" He looked thunderstruck.

"We're going to sail around the fighting and come in from the north side of town."

The boy gave me a look sharp enough to skin a coon.

"We can't just cut and run like cowards."

"Do I look like I'm running away?" I shouted. "Because, if I'm not mistaken, that's Seahorse Key and Cedar Keys' lighthouse ahead."

Being a Canfield, he didn't back down. "Damn it all, we have to stand our ground and fight."

"On whose side?" I shouted. "Answer me that. For all I know, some of those Yanks are men I served with in Key West; and, for better or worse, I know just about everybody in Cedar Keys. In this fight, I couldn't win for losing."

"And your loyal friends at Cedar Keys? The ones that have stood beside you—what about them?"

"God help them," I said.

"And, if He don't?"

"Look. We'll rescue who and what we can. I can't make it any plainer than that."

"What about Maureen? What about the Fosters?"

He hit a nerve when he mentioned Maureen. The hairs on the back of my neck stood up.

It would be just like Maureen to stay and fight.

But, I told myself, her father knew better than to resist overwhelming force. He would have made her see the light.

"Peter Foster is no fool," I said. "He knew it might come to this. He told me that, if there were ever an attack, they'd head south on one of his boats for a refugee camp he knew about."

"Where is this camp?" Jesse asked. "What's it called?"

"Damned if I can remember," I said. "I never thought it would come to this. But there's one thing I do know for sure. A refugee camp is no place you want to be, especially if you're a pretty woman."

"What if we find other women still in town?"

"We'll do all that we can to help any stragglers. Then, we'll go to the cabin for our weapons. And, if we have time, we'll save those naval stores. When the Yanks find them, they'll carry them off and torch the place. We'll have nothing to show for all our hard work. We have to get there before they do."

"Just so you know," Jesse said, "I'm not going to be dodging any Yankee bullets to save your naval stores."

Another barrage from the USS *Hatteras* sundered the air. Both of us fell silent and looked to the horizon as our boat plunged ahead, drawing us ever closer to the fighting.

Sound travels far over open water. As we approached Cedar Keys, the roar of battle reached a fever pitch, punctuated by the gut wrenching screams of shells that struck like lightning bolts. The thunderous explosions melded with the wretched whinnying of wounded dray horses and the blood-curdling cries of rebel soldiers. My heart pounded like a drum. The scream of hurtling ordnance set my ears to ringing.

Once we cleared Snake Key, I could see as well as hear the Yankee shells bombarding the blockade runners tied up at the Cedar Keys' wharf. I did a quick count—four schooners, three sloops and a ferryboat—but no sign of Peter Foster's sloop, *Journeyer*; it wasn't in the harbor. The Fosters must have sailed away in time. The remaining boats weren't so lucky.

The largest rebel blockade runner—a shallow draft schooner painted gray to appear on the horizon like a low-lying cloud—looked to be one of the newer boats being built in England. It drew the first fire. A tremendous explosion erupted amidships. It tore through the deck, toppled the mast and blew the cabin to pieces. The blast threw cargo out over the water, tumbling, twisting and churning through the air in what seemed like a slow motion descent into hell. The water caught fire. The angry flames leapt to the dockside barrels of turpentine then quickly engulfed the nearby cotton bales and spread to the sawmill, lumber shed, gristmill and livery.

"The wind is blowing onshore," Jesse said. "The whole port could go up like a tinder box."

Next, the Yanks brought their guns to bear on the harbor and, in rapid succession, their 32-pounders slashed through the air, blasted the quay, cratered the ground and threw up huge chunks of dirt and rock that spooked a flock of fleeing pelicans. The air was thick with smoke and screaming shells that slashed with random violence into Front Street. They battered the telegraph office and turpentine warehouse, destroyed the railroad's rolling stock and blew cavernous holes in the terminal. Huge clouds of dust and embers billowed out of the craters, obliterating the sun. With a hair-raising thrum, another series of shells buried themselves deep in the ships chandlery and the shipyard. They exploded with awesome violence, spattering the ground with bits and chunks of burning wood and metal. The carpenter's shop, cordage company and paint shop writhed in the riotous blaze.

I raised my spyglass and saw the rebel guard scatter like straw before the wind. Our rebel boys, outgunned and outmanned, never had a chance.

"They're fleeing without a fight," Jesse cried. "They're deserting."

"Take a good look," I said. "You won't find scenes like this on recruiting posters. None of those generals, the glory boys with pumpkin rinds on their shoulders, ever says a word about defeat."

A bunch of rebel soldiers raced across the waterfront, clambered into a flatboat, grabbed the poles and started poking as fast as they could. They never cleared the bay.

I heard a welcome break in the cannon fire.

"Reef the mains'l," I shouted. Jesse did as I said and a following wave brought us into a sheltering cove, a spit of land that jutted into the water like the barb of a fishhook. We tied up to a mooring post and waded ashore. Just as we reached the beach, I saw Yankee landing boats approaching a nearby section of shoreline. We were outflanked, forced to make our way through the middle of the town.

"Hit the dirt."

I didn't have to say it twice. We both dove for cover as the Yankee marines leapt from their boats into the foaming surf, sloshing ashore, low to the ground, their bayonet-tipped rifle muzzles pointed dead ahead. Twenty more paces and they opened fire on four rebels who raced for the protection of the pinewoods.

"Quick, Jesse," I said, "on your feet and start running."

I dodged behind some scrub brush and Jesse followed. In a half crouch, we circled around the waterfront where the surface of the bay shimmered like hammered silver with the bloated, floating bodies of mullet and minnows. The fish stink blended with the sulfurous stench of gunpowder hanging over the tidal flats. The hulks of sunken ships choked the harbor, their masts rising out of the water like burnt matchsticks. First Street had been completely demolished.

Further back from the waterfront, I recognized two intact landmarks, both shrouded in smoke—the Suwannee Hotel and the Schlemmer House Hotel where the wealthy plantation owners stayed when in town. The windows of the Schlemmer House were shattered, leaving them blind to the devastation. Just as well, I thought. Those windows used to look out on the Salty Dog Saloon and Gambling Hall where I had done most of my drinking. Now the saloon was flatter than spilt beer.

Turning the corner, we saw a mob of riotous Yankee soldiers coming out of Parson and Hale's General Store, their arms loaded down with looted merchandise. We ducked back out of the way and headed in the other direction.

We passed a two-story house built with tabby, a type of concrete made with oyster shells, lime, sand, and water. Smoke gurgled out of a gaping hole in its roof. A dead rebel soldier slumped over the railing of its front steps, his arms dangling between his legs, the rifle-musket lying beside him pointing out to sea. His red badge of courage had become a medallion of blood crusting over the peach fuzz on his jaw. Too young to shave, he'd been old enough to die.

Jesse picked up the soldier's firearm and examined it.

"It's busted."

"Looks like his nerves got the best of him and he rammed home too many charges," I said. "His musket backfired and the blow-by killed him."

Jesse dropped the firearm and I picked up the dead soldier's cartridge box. We came upon another smoldering house, a two-story wood-frame building, whose windows had been blown out by the concussion from a nearby shell burst. The bloodied and dismembered bodies of two more rebel soldiers lay beside the crater, one of them slack jawed and staring at his entrails as if he were a seer trying to divine his future.

I thought I saw someone peek out a window then duck back into the shadows. But, when I looked a second time, I saw a curtain blowing in the wind like the hankies that the young ladies had waved as the soldiers marched off to war.

The sound of nearby gunfire brought us up short.

We ducked behind a waist-high, crumbling stonewall and crabbed our way forward to see a clutch of Yankee soldiers leave Wilcox Gunsmith Shop, firing their newfound guns in the air. Their gunshots spooked a rebel out of hiding and he darted down the street only to be cut down by a fusillade. His arms and legs jerked every which way as if he were a puppet whose strings had been cut. He fell backwards into a horse trough.

The Yankees laughed.

"Good Lord," Jesse whispered. "That was Don Plunkett."

A damp chill ran down my spine. I despised Plunkett but this was no way to die. I smelt the odor of wet wool, the tang of wood smoke and death. I smelt my own funk.

"The good Lord wants no part of this," I said.

We dodged into the deserted home of Josh Stengel, the sparkie who ran the telegraph office. Outside the house, the Yankee soldiers sounded giddy with victory, whooping and hollering, their grisly laughter cutting through the air like the grim reaper's scythe.

Once it was safe, we snuck out the back door, cleared a picket fence and found ourselves on the street I'd been looking for. Two doors down stood the heavily damaged home of Peter Foster. I tried the front door; it opened. To my relief, the house was deserted. Foster and his family must have escaped on his sloop.

In the dining room, the breakfast dishes sat on the table. It looked as if the family was about to sit down to a meal of scrambled eggs, hominy grits and corn pone. A chair had been knocked over on its side. On the sideboard, I found a framed daguerreotype of Maureen posing with her students. I remembered the day the picture had been taken—the same day we had kissed for the first time. I removed the picture from its frame, and for a heartbeat, I relived the moment.

A broken window shutter banged against the side of the house, jerking me back to the present. I spun around in a half crouch. Nothing. I slipped the picture of Maureen into my shirt pocket and asked myself whether I'd ever see her again.

Where is that refugee camp her father had spoken about?

A hiss of frustration escaped my clenched teeth

"C'mon," I said to Jesse. "Let's get out of here."

A dead horse lay in the street, its tongue hanging out, its head already covered in bottle flies. Jesse saw it, too, started to gag, clamped a hand over his mouth and looked away.

Our town of more than 300 souls was laid out like a corpse, the waterfront a charred and smoldering ruin. The distant piping of a boatswain's whistle sounded to my ears like the keening of a grieving woman, her voice hollowed out by pain.

"We have to push on," I said, "Make our way back to the cabin and fetch what we can, then light out on our boat."

Jesse nodded, followed me around the edge of the town and down the old cattle trail that led to our clearing deep in the pinewoods.

~

The gum patch was deserted. Adam Broady and the rest of my crew had fled. Everything looked just as we had left it. I breathed a sigh of relief, if only for the moment. Despite the nearby bombardment, the air in the clearing remained heavily scented with the aroma from the slash pines—the smell of home.

Jesse was right; the cabin was a ramshackle excuse for a house—"Nowhere near as nice as Beecham's manse"—but it was paid for with the sweat of my brow. I hated to have to leave it now. I sucked in a lungful of memories then said:

"We have to leave now. It won't be long before a Yankee scouting party finds our still."

We stepped inside the cabin I had furnished with rough-hewn, sturdy, unpainted furniture. Sunlight barely filtered through the two windows shuttered to keep out the bugs. The floor looked more or less clean, empty rum bottles no longer lying in plain sight.

I moved one of the bunks, lifted the floorboards to get at our cache of weapons and ammunition and handed them to Jesse. Then we hitched Mosey to the wagon and began loading our tools, cooking utensils and the barrels of naval stores. Jesse insisted on loading his books, too. We made several trips from the cabin to the boat, taking the long way around. After using the dinghy to ferry everything to the boat, we returned to the cabin where I unhitched and unharnessed Mosey. She was a magnificent animal, a good 15 hands at the withers, and I watched with a heavy heart as she headed for the stable where I knew the Yanks would find her.

I took a last look around the cabin and was about to close the door, when I heard another horse nicker. Turning in the direction of Cedar Keys, I spied four riders move out of the shadows of the nearby tree line. I didn't recognize them, but their horses looked familiar, especially the bay gelding mounted by the lead rider. I had an uneasy feeling.

I reached for my holster, loosened the leather flap on the butt of my gun and shucked the LeMat. Then I flipped the lever on the end of its hammer so it could fire bullets. Holstering it again, I stepped outside.

"Let me do the talking," I said to Jesse.

The strangers rode heavy in the saddle, tight as a fist, cloaked in silence. One of them slumped over in the saddle, his head lolling back and forth, right arm hanging loose.

As they drew closer, I studied them, looking for clues as to their identity—rebels or federals? They might even have been deserters. Hundreds of them were said to hide out in the scrublands and glades, robbing and killing settlers. It was hard to tell just who these riders were because most of the rebel boys didn't wear the regulation army uniform. Hell, some of them didn't own shoes. The strangers' outfits were commonplace: forage caps and slouch hats, bedrolls slung across their shoulders, pistols jammed in their holsters, rifles swaying in their saddle scabbards.

I edged toward the cover of the corral and Jesse shadowed me. The horsemen saw us move, reined in their mounts then came on slowly, warily. Their horses were lathered, breathing hard. They shambled to a halt in a cloud of choking dust and pine needles. The rider mounted on the bay gelding kneed his horse forward. A bearded, stocky man, his face was begrimed by gun smoke giving his flesh the hard look of cast iron. His eyes were marble gray, just as cold and hard. He wore a sweat-stained slouch hat, a homespun shirt and knee-high boots. A Walker hung in his holster, an Enfield in the scabbard of his saddle. The make of the rifle told me he was most likely a rebel.

The rider eyed my LeMat, removed his slouch hat with his left hand and leaned forward, his saddle squeaking as if in warning. He gave a cautious grin, one that didn't reach his eyes.

"Name's McKenna," he said in a raspy voice. "Bill McKenna." He settled the hat back on his head.

I nodded. "Ed Canfield. This here's Jesse."

"You secessionists?" he asked.

It was a challenge, not a question. Before dismounting, he wanted to be sure we weren't pro-Union.

"We're rebels all right," I said. I just didn't mean it the way he'd take it. No sense looking for trouble.

He smiled, twisted in his saddle and barked an order to the other rebel soldiers—most likely these were the four men who had run for the pinewoods when the Yankee marines came ashore. As McKenna turned, I noticed the brand on the horse's flank, a circle D. They had taken these horses from Hap Doherty, my neighbor. Hap had let me borrow one of his geldings after I lost my first nag, Giddy Up, in a night of heavy drinking and faro playing. The army called what these soldiers had done foraging, not rustling. It really galled me the way they rewrote the rules to suit themselves. Then again, I had to admit, I had done the same thing in Mexico.

The other riders came forward slower than a fat pig in deep mud. McKenna dismounted, wiped the trail dust from his shirt and pants and made the usuals.

"This here's Private Fletcher, Hoagg and Pembrook."

I greeted them with a tight-lipped smile, a finger to the brim of my hat.

Fletcher gave me a wire-taut grin, barbed at both ends. Hoagg chewed on a quid of tobacco like a cow working its cud. Both men smelt of smoke and sweat, horse liniment and gunpowder.

The one called Pembrook was in a world of hurt. The right side of his shirt showed splotches of blood that dripped from the cuff of his shirtsleeve onto the flank of a horse the color of fresh tar. The other men dismounted then eased Pembrook off his mount and laid him on a poncho that they had spread on the ground. While they tended to their wounded friend, I told Jesse to water their horses at the creek. Meanwhile, I studied them.

McKenna had strapped his revolver to his leg in the way of a quick-draw gunslinger with the butt of the gun facing backward. The one called Fletcher was whip-lean. His face was all sharp angles and leather-tough, seamed by the sun, hardened by war. The other one, Hoagg, was shorter and blockish; a bull-necked, powerful man with porcine eyes, and a nose that looked like it had been broken more than once. His ears lay flat against his skull in the way of a dog that is about to attack.

The wounded soldier gave a loud groan that captured everyone's attention.

"He caught a miniê ball," McKenna explained.

The ball had struck Pembrook in the back of his shoulder. The soft lead, cone-shaped bullet would have spread on impact, tearing up his insides. A hastily tied tourniquet had not staunched the flow of blood. The man's brow was crimped in pain, his lower lip swollen and bleeding from the puncture marks left by his teeth. He shivered uncontrollably and his eyelids fluttered feebly with every shallow breath he took. He had soiled his pants. Out of the corner of my eye, I saw Jesse stop in his tracks, turn and take it all in before continuing, head down, toward the creek.

"Bring him into our cabin," I said.

The soldiers hesitated, glanced nervously in the direction of Cedar Keys and then toward Otter Creek. They nodded to themselves, carried him inside my sparsely furnished cabin. McKenna eyed the plank table, two chairs and two bunk beds that I had planned to leave behind; then he pointed to the bunk next to the cast iron washtub and signaled for them to lay Pembrook on the tick mattress. I opened the window shutters and lit a kerosene lamp.

The soldiers quickly unbuttoned Pembrook's shirt revealing the full extent of his wound. He screamed as they peeled the shirt off his blood-clotted shoulder. The bullet had ripped through his back and into his chest cavity, leaving behind a swollen glob of gristle, fabric and bone. There was no exit wound. No glory, either, in being shot in the back.

I propped up Pembrook's head and gave him a slug of water from my canteen. He managed to worry a little of it down, smiled at me weakly, mouthed a silent "Thank ye," coughed and turned away. He looked to be a young boy, younger than Jesse. Before the war, he might have been a drover, a cooper, a printer's devil, a shoemaker's apprentice—someone with a full life ahead of him.

"You got any ardent spirits to dull his pain?" McKenna asked.

I shook my head. My last two flasks were down on the boat. I gave the boy another sip of water. He tried to swallow but the water drizzled out the side of his mouth and down his chin. His breathing became more labored, each breath oozing another spurt of blood from the shoulder wound onto the tick mattress. The color drained from his face leaving gunpowder as his death mask. His eyes rounded and he looked at the ceiling, fixed for a moment on a vision that brought a grimace to his swollen lips. He gasped, exhaled slowly. The light left his eyes as easily as you might close a window shutter. I picked up his limp wrist, felt for a pulse, found none.

Without looking up, I said, "He's dead."

Everyone took off their hats and made a hurried sign of the cross. A moment of silence followed then I rose and turned to face the grim soldiers.

"Was he a God-fearing man?"

There was an awkward pause before Fletcher volunteered, "I believe he was a Mason."

Quick as a hair trigger, McKenna said, "We'll give him a Christian burial and let God sort that out later."

McKenna led us in a few mumbled prayers over the lifeless body then removed Pembrook's gun belt and boots. On a word from McKenna, the other soldiers picked up Pembrook's body and carried him out the door. McKenna followed behind with two of the shovels that I had been about to bring down to the boat.

The sky was pallid now, the color of bone. The windborne ash from Cedar Keys haloed the sun and drifted down, smudging the outlines of the nearby live oaks, cypress and longleaf pines. The cannonading had long since ceased. An unnatural stillness muffled the chattering of birds. The heat and humidity weighed heavily on us as the silent soldiers carried the lifeless body of their friend across the clearing.

"We'll bury him in the shade of that live oak," McKenna said, pointing to a moss-draped tree near our stream.

As they trudged there, I sidled up to McKenna. "Just so you know," I said, "that live oak's roots are close to the surface. It will be tough digging."

He hesitated and said, "Right" and ordered the others toward the clearing.

McKenna was clearly in command. I saw no sign of his rank, but that did not surprise me. When the bugles sounded and the lead started flying, Yankee sharpshooters aimed for the officers first.

"Are you an officer?" I asked.

"Just a private," he said.

"The other men follow your orders."

"I have more notches on my gun belt."

"Notches?"

"Before the war I was a bounty hunter."

At the gravesite, Hoagg and Fletcher stripped off their shirts revealing arms corded with muscle and torsos pale as a fish belly. Then they wielded the shovels, huffing and puffing, digging, scooping and dumping huge clods of the dirt, shells and marl beside the hole. Their heads and shoulders glistened with sweat, and from time to time they paused to catch their breath, wipe their foreheads with a kerchief and swat at the mosquitoes that descended on them. They constantly hectored one another about who would get which one of Pembrook's worldly possessions.

"I get his boots is all I'm saying," Hoagg said.

"They don't fit me none," Fletcher replied, "but his pistol with the pearl handle, that sure would feel good in the palm of my hand."

"Quit your jawing," McKenna snapped, "or there will be three more graves beside his." He glanced again in the direction of Cedar Keys.

When they had dug a deep enough trench, they tied Pembrook's legs together, folded his arms across his chest and lowered the body into the grave. Then they covered his head with a kerchief and shoveled dirt on top of him. The two diggers wiped their soiled hands on their pants while McKenna said another hurried prayer. Next he added a crude wooden cross with Pembrook's name carved into it. Seeing the name, I wondered who might be Pembrook's next of kin and whether they'd ever learn what had happened to him.

As they saddled up to leave, McKenna turned to me and said, "Them Yanks put marines ashore. If I were y'all, I'd skedaddle while I could."

"Much obliged," I said. I handed McKenna the cartridge box I'd gotten from the dead soldier in town. "Believe these are the right caliber for your Enfield."

McKenna grinned, took the cartridge box and raised a finger to the brim of his hat. Then Jesse and I watched him and his men ride off, heading south, the rider-less horse trailing behind them.

"I get Pembrook's saddle," Hoagg said.

"And I get his bridle and bedroll," Fletcher replied.

"I get his rain slicker."

We stood there listening to them dicker until their voices trailed off and they disappeared from view. Then, cloaked in silence, Jesse and I made one last trip to the boat. I had just touched the lucky horseshoe that I kept nailed to the mast when Jesse stepped aboard with his left foot first.

"How many times do I have to tell you," I said, "that's bad luck."

"Sorry," he said. "I just plum forgot."

"Well, sorry isn't good enough. Get off and come back on the way I taught you, right foot first."

He did as he was told, but that misstep troubled me. It was a bad omen.

The sun began its descent into the blue-black sea as we sailed away from the rack and ruin, heading for the open waters of Waccasassa Bay and beyond.

But how far beyond? Where was that refugee camp Peter Foster had spoken about?

~

I had the tiller and Jesse took the bow. With the wind at our back, we snaked around a reef and veered away from Cedar Keys, listening hard for the roar of cannon and the whistle of 32-pounders that might rain down on us at any minute. Without warning, the boat hit something large floating in the water, sending a shiver from stem to stern.

"What the hell was that?" I asked. "You're supposed to be paying attention."

I looked over the gun'l at what we had hit and was stunned to see a dead man floating, face up. With his chest bloodied and his eye sockets empty, the corpse stretched out his arms in a vain plea for mercy. Jesse peered over my shoulder and looked as if he might faint. His knees began to buckle and he grabbed the gun'l.

"Do you recognize him?" he asked weakly.

"Recognize him? No," I said, "but I've seen the look on his face a hundred times on a dozen battlefields."

The swollen, lifeless body drifted off into the dusk. I turned to Jesse and said, "Don't stand there gawking. Keep your eyes peeled for flotsam."

"On the starboard side," he shouted.

"Not so loud," I whispered. "The whole state of Florida will hear you."

But he was too nervous and his voice spiked the next time he called out.

"Son," I snapped, "what did I just tell you?"

"Shells on the bottom," he sounded, a little softer this time. I hauled on the tiller and we narrowly missed an oyster bed. Out of the corner of my eye, I saw Jesse give me a brief, approving look, then turn away without saying a word. Just like his ma used to do.

A few moments later he asked, "Where are we headed?"

"First stop is Mommer Wicks' place, back in the mangroves. We'll wait there until the Yanks are gone and the coast is clear."

"Mommer Wicks? The nigger who sold you this sloop? You gonna sell our naval stores to her?"

"It's Negro. N-e-g-r-o. And yes, the naval stores stay on board."

"What the hell for? They'll just slow us down."

"After we find Maureen," I said, "we're heading for Key West. That's where those naval stores will fetch the best price." I gestured toward the barrels of turpentine, pitch and tar stacked high on the floorboards of the boat.

"Key West?" Jesse objected. "The Yanks control Fort Taylor. They've turned Key West into a Union stronghold."

"True enough," I said, "but it's a bustling seaport where they'll pay top dollar for our pitch and tar to keep their ships afloat."

"But we'll be sailing into the naval base of the very devils that just destroyed our town. What about Fort Brooks at Tampa? It's in rebel hands and a heap closer."

Tampa was closer but the rebels would draft Jesse in a heartbeat. And without the gum patch, I'd have no excuse for holding him back. I sure as hell didn't want to risk losing my son for a second time. Maybe this time for good.

"Son," I said, "they're getting so desperate, they'd conscript you as soon as we set foot on the wharf."

"Great."

"Now you know that's not going to happen."

"Well, what about Fort Myers? We just can't sell out to the Yanks."

"Look," I said. "Truth be known, I'm an abolitionist. I rooted for Lincoln."

"I don't get it," he said. "Lincoln condemned your Mexican-American War."

"And he was right to criticize it," I answered. "That war made no more sense than this one. We're all going to have to pay the butcher's bill."

"We have to defend ourselves."

"We don't have to defend the slavocracy."

"Well, this ain't about the slavocracy," he said. "It ain't about the niggers."

"Watch your language," I snapped. I'd already warned him more than once about using that ugly slur.

"Well," he spat back, "call it what you like. I say it's about states' rights."

"Really?" I said. "I seem to recall Brother Storter saying we're fighting to protect the southern way of life, which just so happens to be based on slavery. Or, as he likes to say, 'servitude.'"

"It's God's plan for mankind," Jesse said.

"Tell me—how many slaves did God plan for old man Beecham to have?"

He blinked rapidly as if running a tally in his head. "Twenty, more or less."

"Ever see the overseer take a whip to a slave?"

"Sure. It's his job. What of it?"

"How did that make you feel?"

"Feel? I wasn't the one being whipped."

"But you did feel it when that farm boy took a switch to you."

"Not half as much as he felt it when I got through with him."

"But he was just doing his job when he whipped you, wasn't he?"

He sputtered out, "I'm no field nigger."

"Oh, that's right. I forgot. Your job was to clean out the dirty stalls."

"That wasn't my only job."

"Really?"

"Ma said my job was to clean the stalls and study hard so I wouldn't grow up to be a dumb-ass cracker like my father."

That hurt. "What else did your ma tell you about your pa?"

"She said you were a hard man. Hard as a hickory knot."

"Did she tell you how many times a Yank saved my life in Texas and Mexico?"

"So what?"

"So I'm not about to take up arms against the men I served with."

"That's crazy. They just attacked Cedar—"

"The South started this fracas when General Beauregard attacked Fort Sumter."

"But they'll shoot us or throw us in prison."

"Not a chance," I said. I held up two crossed fingers and added, "I saved Captain Brannan's hide once in a battle outside of Mexico City. He owes me."

I couldn't believe I had just said that. As a rule, I didn't talk about the war. I tried not to think about it at all. But many a night, when I closed my eyes, my thoughts circled back to it and I relived every bloody scene. The cavalry charges. The artillery barrages. The hand-to-hand combat. The killing. And, always, Private Abner Winslow calling out to me, "Don't throw caution to the wind." I'd wake up in a sweat, a silent scream on my lips. I'd go in search of a rum bottle, something to help me swallow the truth. Something that would help me forget. Something that would bring blessed oblivion.

"Yeah," Jesse said. "Well, that's ancient history."

"Maybe for you, but not for me. For me, it's as if it had happened yesterday."

I still felt as bitter and angry as on the day I had returned home from Mexico. I had tried to forget the fighting. I wanted to blend in and act normal. I wanted things to be the way they had been before the war. But I couldn't sleep at night without a lantern burning in the room. Night or day, the reminders were everywhere, ready to surface like a sambo gator rising up out of the muck and mire of fetid memories much as they had on a steaming hot July day in Charleston 16 years ago . . .

I had just passed a neighbor's place in Charleston, when the heat trapped inside his house caused his tin roof to start popping. To my ears, it sounded like gunfire. I whirled around, shucked my pistol and almost shot my friend as he stood there with nothing but a rake in his hand. I got good and drunk that day. But it didn't help. In the dead of night, the demons began beating the long roll while shouting, "Line of battle, boys, line of battle." I woke up on the bedroom floor in a pool of sweat while my pregnant wife screamed in fear.

The next day Jesse was born. Things went downhill from there. But I couldn't tell that to Jesse.

"What about the blockade?" Jesse asked. "There are hundreds of miles of open water between us and Key West. What about 'Anaconda'?"

"The Yanks don't have enough ships to make the blockade work," I said.

"Really?" he said. "Well, they did a fair job of making it work in Cedar Keys."

"We're not going to be a stationary target like those blockade runners in Cedar Keys' harbor."

"No sense arguing with you," he said. "You have an answer for everything."

"Stow it," I snapped back, but he had to get in the last word, even if it was muttered under his breath.

"You won't be satisfied until we're both dead and buried at sea."

The boy definitely had the Canfield temper. And, to tell the truth, if I had been him, I probably would have reacted the same way. We were a long way from the cover of the barrier islands and the Everglades. And, if a Union ship chased us, we couldn't get very deep into the glades with a boat as big as ours. But I couldn't see any other course of action. If we headed to the nearest Confederate army post, they'd draft Jesse. On the other hand, the federals had plenty of men in uniform and were not going to recruit, train and arm a loyal son of the South. Key West was the best choice of a bad lot.

My thoughts were preoccupied with scenes from the battle we had just left behind. In my mind, I could hear the dizzying screams of incoming shells, the whinnying of the horses, the whop of bullets chewing into human flesh and bone, the cries of the wounded. I could smell warm blood mingled with the rank odor of spent shell casings and burnt timbers. I could see Private Pembrook dying and that other slack jawed soldier gaping at his exposed entrails. I wondered how God could countenance such atrocities. I asked myself where was He in all this?

Did God even care?

Just thinking about it set my pulse to pounding. I lit a cigarette to clear my lungs of the smell of death. It didn't help.

Thunk.

"A cable just snapped," Jesse called out.

"Damnation!" One of the barrels of tar that Jesse had tied down had broken free of its bindings and had fallen to the deck. It was just a question of time before other barrels fell. We were near a large cove hemmed in on three sides by mangroves, cypress and willows. I tossed the cigarette overboard and turned the tiller to bring the boat about.

"No sense going out in open water until we lash down our cargo," I said.

Jesse nodded. "We'll have to anchor here until crack of dawn." His voice sounded drier than a creek bed in August.

We both knew that we hadn't gone very far and we were still in harm's way. If we were becalmed in the morning or didn't have a favorable wind, we'd be easy targets.

I had just lowered the anchor with a loud splash when a wave hit the side of the boat. Another tar barrel toppled over into the hold triggering a muffled groan.

A stowaway!

Stunned, I fell back against the gun'l as if struck by a bullet; then dodged behind some casks and fumbled with the leather thong that lashed my revolver to the holster. Jesse grabbed a shroud to balance himself and, in that same instant, I wheeled about to see a man crouching behind the fallen barrel, the pistol in his hand pointed straight at Jesse's chest.

Thickset, hair tousled, his face streaked with soot and his clothes singed and tattered, the stowaway looked like death itself.

"Come around with your hands held high," he called to me in a British accent.

I could hear Jesse cuss. "Son," I whispered, "let me handle this my way."

Jesse nodded.

"Quickly now," the stranger said, "or I put a new button hole in the lad's vest."

He said it like a man accustomed to killing.

I heard the click of his gun being cocked. A sharp, metallic sound, it left no doubt about his intention. A wave hit the side of the boat, her rigging groaned and she seemed to shiver with fear. I nearly fell.

"What is it you want?" I asked.

"I want you where I can see you. Toss out your weapon and come out where I can see you. Now!"

The boat rocked again; her rigging creaked in protest and I felt certain I was about to look death in the eye. I unholstered the LeMat, felt its cold, dead weight in my hand then skidded the revolver across the deck.

"That's better," the stranger said. "Now step out where I can see you with your back to me and your hands held high."

I stepped out and, as I sidled past Jesse, said under my breath, "The belaying pin. Grab hold of it as I pass. Then follow my lead."

I sidestepped toward the gunman, moving slowly so as to shield Jesse briefly from view. At that moment, Jesse grabbed the belaying pin and slipped it behind his back.

"We only have a few dollars, if that's what you want," I said over my shoulder.

The gunman laughed. "Money? Confederate graybacks won't be worth the paper they're printed on."

I took four more steps and the gunman said, "That's close enough."

I stopped and turned to face him in the fading light. My feet were spread wide to keep my balance on the rolling deck; my gaze locked on his. He rose with some difficulty, favoring his right leg, the one that must have been hit by the falling tar barrel. He limped across the deck toward my revolver and stooped to pick it up. At that moment, another wave rocked the boat, throwing the gunman off balance. His bad leg gave way and he staggered, slipped on some tar, and fell. I saw my opening and took it.

I threw myself at the man, grabbing his pistol hand, twisting it backward. The gun went off with a roar that sent birds flapping into the smoldering sky. The two of us tumbled across the deck in a heap. Jesse lunged at him and swung wildly with the belaying pin. He missed. I slammed the man's gun hand on the floorboards; the pistol fired again, just missing me. The bullet blew a hole in the gun'l. I fell back, my ears ringing from the sound of the gun. Jesse wrenched the pistol away. I spun around and hooked the man with an elbow to the head. He swung back. I slipped the punch, saw his exposed chin and put all I had into a shot that snapped his head back. I followed up with two more quick rights. Again and again. The man groaned and went limp. The fight went out of him.

"Enough! You win. I surrender." He let out a strangled gasp.

"Damn right," I huffed. My knuckles hurt. "If he moves a muscle, son, clobber him."

I gritted my teeth and holstered my revolver while Jesse held the belaying pin at ready. Then I examined the man's gun. It was a Remington .44 and must have set him back damn near a month's wages. Lying there spread eagled on the deck, he no longer looked so threatening. His chin was bruised and cut, and blood trickled from his mouth and mixed with the soot on his neck to make it seem as if he had gills. His breath came in the short, ragged gasps of a fish out of water. There was a powder burn in his frock coat but no sign of blood.

I grabbed him by his coat collar and pulled him into a sitting position. "Who in hell are you? And why were you stowing away on our boat?"

"I'm fleeing the Yanks," the stowaway said, wiping his bloody nose with his sleeve. "Just like you."

"Fleeing?" I laid the barrel of the smoking gun against the man's cheek. "Well, you are going to flee this world for good if I don't get some straight answers. Who are you?"

The stowaway eyed the gun barrel. "Smith . . . the name is Matthew Smith."

The name meant nothing to me. And I could see it meant nothing to Jesse. I knew just about everyone in the town, but this man apparently was a newcomer. I took him to be about 30 years old, heavier than I was, dressed in an ill-fitting double-breasted claw hammer coat that emphasized his girth. He was clean-shaven with short-cropped hair and a firm jaw. A weak eye gave him the distracted look of someone who's told so many tall stories he can't tell tuther from which.

"Empty your pockets," I said. "Let's see some proof of who you are."

Smith emptied his pockets of a watch, some gold coins, a pencil and a soggy piece of foolscap that had been folded over several times. I unfolded it, struck a lucifer and scanned the paper. The ink had begun to run, but in the dim light I could still make out a list of ships sailing out of Cedar Keys, the names of their owners, when they departed, and when they returned to port. To my amazement, our boat, the *Dead Reckoning*, was listed there, too.

How did this newcomer know I was the owner?

I had bought the sloop in the past year—before everything went to hell in a hand basket.

"What's this all about?" I asked.

Smith's expression stiffened the way leather does on a cold day. He hesitated, unsure how to answer. "It's a list of vessels."

I raised his revolver as if to club him. "Don't play me for a fool," I said. "I can read. What I want to know is what's it for? Are you a Yankee spy or a rebel turncoat?"

Smith's eyes widened, his bruised jaw went slack. If he were a spy or turncoat, both sides would want to hang him. And, if they caught him on our boat, I realized, they might hang us right along side him.

"You're wrong," Smith stammered. "I'm nothing of the kind. I'm the new agent for Lloyd's of London. We insure most of the ships on the gulf coast. That's my list of ships we insure or want to insure."

Jesse and I looked at each other. It sounded so far-fetched it might be true. He did have a British accent. And Peter Foster had been expecting someone from Lloyd's of London to settle his insurance claim after the break-in.

But why would a Brit hide out on our boat?

He read the puzzled look on my face and said, "Unfortunately, the Yankee cannons can't tell a Brit from a rebel."

"Since when does an insurance agent pack iron?" I wagged the Remington .44 beneath his nose.

"You're a fisherman," Smith said. "Why are you packing a LeMat?"

"You'll have to do better than that," I said.

"I carry a lot of money," Smith said. "I need the gun for protection. Look at my gold coins. Whose image do you see on them?"

I picked up one of the coins and turned it over in my hand.

"It's a gold sovereign with Her Majesty's likeness on it," Smith said.

"Given the cotton trade with England, you could have come by this anywhere."

Smith shook his head, looked away. "Good Lord, man, there's an embargo on all trade."

Suddenly, his head snapped back and he pointed at something in the distance. "Look," he said, "behind you. They're coming."

I spun around to see what had caught his attention. In a panic, flock after flock of egrets, white ibises and herons took to the air, their faint silhouettes outlined by the fading sunlight. One after another, they rose above the salt marsh in undulating waves that rushed toward us like the flood tide. Below the birds, I saw the glimmer of pine knot torches darting back and forth as if they were blobs of pulsating, ghostly light. Then I heard the menacing sound of men crashing through the scrub brush and the scratching and croaking of critters fleeing ahead of them.

Yankee marines heading our way, blocking our escape route.

The bottom dropped out of my stomach.

"They must have heard those pistol shots," Jesse said.

I tossed Smith's revolver to Jesse and he caught it with both hands.

"Don't shoot unless I do," I said.

I quickly lashed Smith to a ringbolt. "One word out of you," I said, "and you're fish bait."

The Yanks advanced slowly, cautiously, giving us time to furl the sails. Then I ducked below, got our rifles and hunkered down next to Jesse to wait for the oncoming marines. I counted the torches and figured there were at least twenty of them, more men than we had bullets in our firearms.

"Quiet," I hissed at Jesse. "Keep your prayers to yourself."

He swallowed his words in mid-sentence. As the Yanks drew closer and closer, the sun remained a stubborn blood-red smear on the horizon. An onshore breeze rippled the water's surface and stirred the cordgrass. The leaves trembled as if with fear, and the brackish water gave off the fetid scent of bird droppings, leaf rot, mold and decay. The smell of death accompanied the high-pitched keening of the tree frogs and the moan of flying insects.

The marines were less than 100 yards away now, close enough that we could get glimpses of their torch-lit silhouettes through the undergrowth, hear their muttering and cursing as they stumbled over black needle rush, cordgrass and downed trees. In the gathering darkness, cypress trees and thick undergrowth screened our boat from view.

"Keep a sharp eye, lads," I heard their lead officer bark. "This is where those shots came from."

His Irish brogue sounded as hard and gritty as crushed shells, and the waters of the cove amplified it. He might as well have been standing next to me, breathing down my neck. I wanted to swat at the mosquitoes that bit me, but the sudden motion and sound might have given our location away.

"Well, whoever fired them must have taken off when they saw us coming," another marine said. "We'll never find them in this Godforsaken marsh."

Just then another gust of wind and water rocked the boat and her decking creaked.

"Wait. What was that?" their leader asked. "Did you hear that?"

An eerie silence followed in which all that could be heard was the spooked birds flapping their wings. I didn't breathe. My mouth felt bone-dry.

"It was just some bird," another man volunteered.

"More like a banshee," said another.

More silence. Another gust of wind, another wave, another creak from the decking could reveal our position at any second.

"I know how to flush them out," their leader growled in frustration. He fired wildly into the undergrowth and trees. Leaves and twigs rained down on our deck, birds took to the air and a creature of the night leapt from the shoreline into the water with an enormous splash. I pressed my hand down on Jesse's shoulder to keep him from jumping up and returning fire. I could feel his heart doing double time.

"What was that?" one of the men yelled.

"Look—a cottonmouth snake," someone shouted. "They're poisonous."

They started backing off. "Let's get the hell out of here."

They beat a hasty retreat. But, just as I thought we were safe, their leader stopped.

"If we can't flush them out," he snarled, "we'll burn them out."

With a maniacal cackle, he threw his pine knot torch into the air and took off in a mad dash. Three other soldiers followed his lead. I watched their torches soar above the crown of a sand live oak and plunge into the salt marsh grasses beside our cove. The flames sputtered, then sparked and, fanned by a breeze, licked at the parched black needle rush and cordgrass. The flickers of fire danced across the tips of the grass and leapt to the winter-dry scrub brush just beyond the sand dune. Slowly but surely, the flames spread to the hardwood hammock where they ignited the ferns, creepers and sphagnum moss hanging from the oak trees. The onshore wind whipped the swirling flames into a fury. Swirling embers reached out to distant pines, igniting the highly combustible creosote in the upper branches. It looked as if the trees were torches, lighting up the sky with angry yellow flames.

We used wet rags to extinguish the hot cinders that drifted down on the boat and waited for the rising tide to snuff out what remained of the fire. Then we weighed anchor and pushed off from shore a short way and dropped anchor again. We were safe for the time being. But in the morning it might be a different story. If the marines returned, we would no longer have the cover of darkness and dense foliage to conceal us.

~

Somewhere around midnight a squall rolled in off the Gulf. It seemed to me as if the heavens were weeping over the fate of Cedar Keys. But, instead of dampening our spirits, the brief downpour cleared the air and cheered us. With Smith lashed to a different ringbolt, we hunkered down under the upended dinghy, lay down on top of some old patched sails and covered ourselves with the cheesecloth we used for mosquito netting. There was nothing more to do until the morning.

Tired as I was, sleep did not come easily. I dared not light the lantern I always burned at night to keep my demons at bay. In this uneasy state of mind, I kept hearing the challenges that Jesse had flung at me:

"We can't cut and run," he'd said. "We have to stand our ground. We can't sell out to the Yanks."

No one had ever accused me of backing down from a fight. Here was my own son giving me grief for not standing my ground. I rolled out of my bedding and fumbled in the dark until I found the makings of a smoke and a flask of rum.

Eventually, the rocking of the boat lulled me into a drunken stupor. I fell into a fitful sleep only to be jerked awake at first light by the screams of what I thought was a terrified woman. I threw off my mosquito netting and sat bolt up right so fast that I felt woozy. In the dim light of dawn, I groped for my pistol.

"Take it easy, Captain," I heard Smith say.

The Brit's voice brought me to my senses. I turned toward him, rubbed the salt from my eyes, exhaled.

"It was just a red tailed hawk," he said.

"A screech owl, more likely," I insisted.

He nodded and gave me a clamshell grin as if to say I was wrong.

I kneaded the back of my neck and tried to clear my head.

"You were talking in your sleep," Smith said.

Another nightmare.

Only this time the nightmare wasn't about what had happened in Mexico. This time I had dreamt about the attack on Cedar Keys and the Yankee shells that had rained down on the port, each barrage falling closer and closer to Maureen's home.

"Marines," he said. "You kept talking about the marines."

Wrong. I'd been dreaming about Maureen. I turned my back to Smith and reached into my shirt pocket for the makings of a smoke; but instead, I pulled out the picture of Maureen that I had found earlier in the Foster's home. Even in the dim morning light, I could see the sparkle in her eyes. I looked to the northeast where smoke rose off the blackened, burned out marsh. I glassed the distant ruins of Cedar Keys where the only signs of life were the vultures circling above. On the waterfront, I saw the bombed out shell of a warehouse, ships chandlery and livery. Behind them stood the building where Maureen and I had sung in the choir. Staring at what little remained of the place, I couldn't help but wonder what might have become of her and her family.

Smith saw the picture of Maureen in my hand and realized his mistake. "If it's Maureen Foster you're wondering about," he said. "I saw the Foster's boat escape."

He knew Maureen? Then again, he knew his ships. He must have had dealings with Peter Foster.

"Was she heading south?" I asked.

"As fast as the wind would take her."

I breathed a sigh of relief and went in search of a nautical chart.

Jesse came up alongside me and said, "What's with you?"

"Nothing. Why?"

"I don't know. You look a little flummoxed."

He was right. I was a little surprised at how much the Brit seemed to know. It felt a little spooky. I blinked to clear my head and asked, "Is everything tied down now?"

"Yes. And I've weighed anchor and hoisted the sails."

"Good." I looked to the bone-white sky and said, "We're setting sail for Mommer Wick's place, and if need be, every refugee camp between here and Key West."

"I wouldn't do that, if I were you," Smith said.

We both turned to look at him.

"Wouldn't do what?" I asked.

Smith crooked his head slightly as if sighting me over the barrel of a rifle. "Wouldn't sail for Key West in this sloop."

"And why in hell not?"

Smith returned my stare without blinking. When he spoke, his voice had the crisp air of a man of authority. "Because it's my business to know the history of a vessel and this one has a questionable past."

"What are you saying?" I asked with a sweeping gesture that took in the entire boat. "The *Dead Reckoning* is a workboat for hauling naval stores and fish. Nothing more."

"True," Smith nodded. "She is a workboat now, but before you bought her, she was a blockade runner."

I scoffed at the idea. "She's too small and to slow run the blockade. A steamer could easily overtake her."

"Small enough to escape notice for a long time, big enough to carry a precious cargo," Smith replied.

Precious?

"What kind of cargo are we talking about?" I asked.

"Counterfeit currency," Smith replied. "Thousands of dollars in bogus bills that aren't worth the paper they were printed on. She used to run down to Havana with a load of turpentine and return with stacks of graybacks printed in England."

"Confederate currency?" Jesse muttered. "That's treason."

"Running the blockade is a dangerous game," Smith said. "Not everyone who risks it is a loyal son of the South. Scrape off that paint and you'll see what little might be left of her real name, the *Sea Ranger*."

"But, if her cargo was counterfeit graybacks," I said, "that would weaken the Southern economy and aid the North. Why would the Yanks want to sink her?"

"At the time, the Yanks had no idea what she was smuggling," Smith said. "She was inbound from Cuba with a load of bogus bills, when they tried to take her as a prize and haul her down to Key West. But her master ran her aground and fled with his crew into the mangroves. Before the Yanks could haul her off, a storm came up and they abandoned her."

"But, given her small size, what led them to think she was a smuggler's craft?" Jesse asked.

"Spies, young man. The gulf coast is rife with spies."

Suddenly, it occurred to me that most of the other ships in Cedar Keys had been blockade runners. Now those wrecks were most likely going to be hauled back to Key West as salvage. The Yanks must have been looking for us, too. That early morning fishing run may have saved our lives.

"Why are you telling us this?" I asked.

"You could have thrown me overboard last night," Smith said. "But you didn't, not even after I pulled a gun on you. I owe you one, Captain."

I chewed on that for a minute. "And if we ignore your advice?"

His eyes were slits, his voice sandpaper gritty. "You'll be pressing your luck."

Luck?

Some seamen, including me, believe it is bad luck to change a boat's name. Mommer Wicks and her boys must have changed the sloop's name when they repaired the stove-in section of the hull. Sure enough, ever since I'd bought the renamed boat, I'd had a string of bad luck.

"If I were you," Smith said, "I'd make my own luck and head for a secluded refugee camp between here and Key West."

"And just where would this secluded refugee camp be?" I asked.

"You've heard of Charlotte Harbor?"

"Sure. It's right here on the chart: 26 degrees, 42-1/2 minutes north. That's not exactly secluded."

"True. But it's a large bay with five inlets, the safest being Boca Grande, and several rivers empty into it."

"How deep is this Boca Grande?"

"At least three fathoms. There is a shoal in the middle but with a two-fathom passage through it."

"Once we clear Boca Grande, what then?"

"We head south through Pine Island Sound toward Punta Rassa."

Punta Rassa.

I didn't like the sound of that. Before the war the cracker cow hunters made a fortune shipping longhorn piney livestock out of Punta Rassa to Cuba. But now Yankee gunboats patrolled that coastline, cutting off all trade.

"I know what you're thinking," Smith said. "But we're not stopping at Punta Rassa. That's where we head up into the Caloosahatchee River. The refugee camp lies two miles from the gulf."

"Maybe two miles as the crow flies," I said. "But we'll be tacking around sandbars, dogleg bends and the overhanging branches of trees." I could imagine us beating for twice that distance at half the speed and with three times the effort.

"The main channel is broad enough and deep enough much of the way," Smith said.

But that still left the glades with their mangrove tangles and flooded grasslands.

"Your dinghy can take us the rest of the way," Smith said. He gestured toward the dinghy upended on the fore deck. It was barely big enough for the three of us.

"How is it you know so much about this camp?" I asked.

Smith hesitated as if reluctant to reveal a closely guarded secret.

"I know some chaps who camp there," he said. "They're Quakers and don't believe in war. They took refuge in the camp at the start of the hostilities. The camp has grown over time."

I scratched the bridge of my nose and gave it some thought.

Jesse read the expression on my face and said, “Well, we are going to need fresh water and provisions and you did say you’d stop at every refugee camp.”

The boy definitely did not want to sail into Key West harbor any time soon.

“If it’s not the camp you’re looking for,” Smith said, “we can simply weigh anchor and ghost away.”

“I don’t know,” I said. “I’m not familiar with the upper river.”

Smith strained against his lashing and said, “I can recognize the landmarks and pilot you around the reefs and shoals that have claimed many a shipwreck. I can find the camp.”

“Pilot this boat? You mean untie you?” I asked.

Smith hiked his shoulders. “Look, with me having this bum ankle and you having that LeMat on your hip, I’m no threat to you. I can be your leadsman while you man the tiller and the lad handles the rigging.”

I took it all in and weighed our options. Jesse was right. We would need to stop for provisions. If Smith tried anything fishy, there were two of us against one, and we were armed. The Yankee blockade was a sieve. And, if the refugee camp was as safe as Smith said it was, what could be the harm? I might even find Maureen there.

“Smith, you better know what the hell you’re talking about,” I said. ”Untie him, Jesse.”

Jesse looked none to pleased with my decision to untie Smith, but all he said was, “This is passing strange.” Then he did as he was told.

We set sail, caught a stiffening breeze and ghosted away from shore. The *Dead Reckoning* seemed to come alive at the prospect of a long voyage. She was a handsome sloop, single-masted, gaff rigged with a short bowsprit that resembled a sailfish breaking water. Her steam-bent white oak ribs were double-planked with Honduras mahogany and her keel, deck, planking and beams were made of Georgia longleaf pine. Her strakes spread out from the bowsprit like the wings of a bird taking flight. Mommer Wicks and her boys had given her two coats of white paint. There was a large cargo space amidships and a white canvas canopy that covered a hold wide enough for barrels of fresh water and food, and four storage compartments. The dinghy mounted over the fore deck provided shelter from the weather. But, like all flat-bottomed boats, she rolled in a beam sea; and the added weight of the turpentine barrels would test her mettle. And mine.

CHAPTER FIVE

We sailed down the coast on a broad reach with the wind coming over a rear quarter and both sails pulling smartly. Crystal River was soon abeam and in due course the inlet to Homosassa Springs was put astern. I kept a wary eye out for Yankee gunboats and here and there spotted evidence of their marauding in the form of a burned out salt works.

Smith never missed a chance to point out a landmark and tell us about some ship run aground or sunk by a storm. His mind was a regular catalog of misery. I think he enjoyed putting the fear of God in Jesse.

"Do you know what a falling barometer means?" Smith asked Jesse with a gleam in his wandering eye.

"Of course I do," the boy replied, eager to put him in his place. "It means a change in the weather—a change in air pressure."

"Ay, it does indeed," Smith said. "It means a change in pressure. Can you feel it in your bones, matey?"

He grabbed Jesse by the arm, his fingers like talons, both of his eyes now focused on my son. Jesse yanked away and a loose button rolled across the boards.

"Foul weather lies ahead," Smith said.

"Cut the boy some slack," I said, half in jest. Smith's tall tales were a welcome break in the monotony of the long voyage so I didn't press the point.

"These are troubled waters," Smith continued. "Captain Kidd and Jean LaFitte prowled this coastline. To this day, the ghost of Jose Gaspar, the last of the buccaneers, prowls this coast in his phantom ship, the *Floridablanca*."

"I don't believe in ghosts," Jesse said.

"You'll believe in this one soon enough," Smith said. "Gaspar was a Spanish bloke accused by a jilted lover of trying to steal Spain's crown jewels before fleeing to these shores. Along the coast of Florida, he became feared as the blood-thirsty pirate, Gasparilla."

He paused then added in a disquieting voice, "The fiend plundered over 400 ships, never showing mercy to the poor buggers."

Smith seemed to delight in the telling.

"What became of him?" Jesse asked of me.

I shrugged and said, "They claim a federal gunboat sunk his bark. But Gasparilla refused to be taken prisoner. He wrapped an iron chain and anchor around his neck, and still holding a cutlass in his hand, jumped into the sea never to be seen again."

Smith laughed and added, "Except by those who dare to enter these waters where his treasure lies buried."

"You don't scare me none," Jesse said.

Smith gave a fiendish laugh and said, "In these waters, lucky blokes make the best sailors."

~

Late in the day the sun descended toward the horizon like a molten fireball, reducing the clouds to sifted ashes. The *Dead Reckoning* was nicely making way at six knots when we passed a burnt out section of the coast.

"Mooncussers," Smith said.

"Who?" Jesse asked.

"Mooncussers," Smith repeated. "They're cutthroats who wait for a moonless night to light false beacons on the beach. The lights draw unsuspecting ships onto the reefs. Then they plunder the cargo and kill the ship's crew and passengers."

"It's a myth," I said to Jesse. "The fire was probably set by hunters trying to drive game into the open."

"Well, that ship is no myth," Smith replied.

I looked aft and spied a ship steaming out of the bay we had just passed. Shrouded in smoke, she appeared like a low-lying storm cloud, a gray specter, her course laid across our bow.

"Hand me the spyglass," I said to Jesse.

She was a three-masted, square-rigged ironsides flying the Union ensign. She had auxiliary steam power, a large quarterdeck, four whaleboats hanging from her davits and gun mounts bristling with cannons. I took her to be roughly 145 feet long with a 22 foot beam, which would give her a draft of somewhere around 7 to 8 feet. She couldn't follow us into the shallows. But first we had to get there.

"She's a Union gunboat," I said.

"What should we do?" Jesse asked.

"The wind is in our favor," I said, "and we have a good head start, enough to beat her to the shallows."

"But she has a full head of steam," Smith said. "She's twice as fast as us."

"With the sun setting," I said, "her master won't risk running aground."

"And just who made you an authority on steamships?"

I ignored Smith's jibe, handed the glass to Jesse and hauled on the tiller, steering for the nearest shallows.

It quickly became apparent that I had misjudged the gunboat's speed and the daring of her master. When I looked again, she was closing fast, her bow pointing right at us, her paddle wheel churning through the water, turning it as white as shark's teeth. She threw off spume with the violence of a feeding frenzy.

"Let me have a look," Smith said. Without so much as an if-you-please, he snatched the glass from Jesse and studied the fast closing ship. His jaw muscles tightened and he said, "It's the *Argonaut.* She's armed to the teeth. Gun crews at stations. She's on the Devil's errand."

"Well, we're about to give the Devil a run for his money," I said.

"You must be daft," Smith said. He stood there looking as if he had been struck by lightning. "You can't possibly expect to fight a gunboat."

"Hold your tongue," I barked. I was not about to lose my boat and my naval stores to those Yanks. Besides, I thought we could outmaneuver the bigger ship and avoid a pitched fight.

"You bloody minded fool," the Brit added. "This sloop is no match for a gunboat. Her cannons can blow us out of the water, and her crew is most likely armed with repeating rifles. They can load on Sunday and shoot all week. We don't stand a chance."

I knew better than to engage in the kind of pitched fight he was describing. My Springfield might hit a stationary target at 500 yards, but not on the pitching, rolling deck of a boat. My LeMat and Jesse's Remington .44 were meant for close-in fighting. We were outgunned and outnumbered.

I knew that. But, I also knew that I wasn't about to back down.

"Jettison four of the turpentine barrels," I yelled.

"That's not going to lighten our load enough," Smith snapped.

"Don't stand there gawking," I growled. "Do as I say and heave those barrels overboard now. There's no time to lose."

Jesse and Smith looked at me, dumbfounded; but they obeyed my order. Using hand axes they chopped the cables that secured four of the barrels then heaved them one by one into the sea where they bobbed to the surface.

Just as the last barrel hit the water, one of the *Argonaut*'s cannons fired. A puff of smoke was followed by a loud report that shattered the stillness of the dusk.

"It's just a warning—no shot," Smith said. "If we don't hove to now, the next one will be loaded with live ammunition."

She was within a half mile of us now, putting us well within range of her guns. But, with darkness descending, we were becoming harder for her gun crew to sight.

"She won't try to sink us," I assured the others. "Her commander will want to take us as a prize to the Admiralty Court in Key West."

The words were no sooner out of my mouth than the *Argonaut* fired another shot, this one filled with live ammunition. I saw the puff of smoke, heard the roar of her cannon, felt the shock wave as the ball of iron blew a hole in the air and soared past us. It plunged into the sea in a huge geyser just a few yards beyond our bowsprit. The after shock sent a shiver through our sails. And down my spine.

"Open another barrel and this time torch that turpentine," I shouted.

"Are you mad?" Smith cried. "You'll set the whole boat ablaze."

He had a point. Turpentine is highly flammable and burns with a dense, acrid smoke. But it is also lighter than water and will float. That's what I counted on. I needed a diversionary tactic that would buy us some time. I reached into my shirt pocket for lucifers and handed them to Jesse. He cracked open another barrel and lit the turpentine, sending a cloud black smoke billowing into the air behind us. A roar went up from the deck of the *Argonaut.*

"They think they've hit us," Smith said.

"And that's exactly what we want them to think," I replied.

With a firm hand on the tiller, I steered the *Dead Reckoning* through the waves, adding a wall of smoke to the darkening gloom that lay between our small craft and the Yankee gunboat.

Once the master of the *Argonaut* realized he'd been duped, he sent another shot past our bow. I refused to hove to.

"She'll soon lose sight of us," I told the others. It couldn't happen fast enough to suit me.

The *Argonaut* sent a third cannon ball thundering past our mains'l, this one missing by a narrower margin. Her crew was good. Very good.

The *Dead Reckoning* raced for the whitecaps that indicated a shoal and beyond that the safety of the shallows. But first I had to make sure she cleared the shoal. I could hear the demonic hissing of the windblown spindrift, the rumble of the combers, deep and low, like the beating of a heart. The turpentine fumes made my eyes water and I struggled to see clearly as I pointed her bow straight for the foaming cauldron.

"You'll run us up on that bloody shoal," Smith protested.

"I've sailed these waters before," I snapped back. "I know what I'm doing."

Smith backed off in sullen silence. Jesse threw the lead again and again, anxiously calling out the depth as we drew ever closer to the shoal. Behind us, the huge warship plowed its way through the smoke. I could hear her paddle wheels churning the water. She was so close her crew started firing their rifles blindly into the wall of smoke.

"Two fathoms," Jesse shouted.

We were about to go up on the reef.

"Jibe ho," I cried out. I hauled the tiller toward the leeward side and the three of us ducked, shifting our weight to the center of the boat just as the *Argonaut's* cannon fired again. The shot grazed our starboard side. Splinters, shards of planking and bits of tarp filled the air. The *Dead Reckoning* shuddered as if in pain. I brought her around on a steep leeward roll. Her stern turned through the wind, just clearing the shoal, leaving in her wake an oil slick from a burst turpentine barrel that had fallen overboard.

"Quick, jettison that burning barrel into that oil slick," I shouted.

Jesse and Smith heaved the burning barrel overboard into the oil slick created by the other turpentine barrel. Tongues of fire briefly flared and danced across the water's surface in front of the oncoming gunboat. Another roar went up from the *Argonaut*'s crew.

"Take the tiller," I shouted to Jesse.

He took hold and I grabbed my rifle.

"Don't shoot," Smith cried out. "They'll hang us for sure."

I loaded my weapon and rested my elbows against the gun'l. Then I waited for the crest of the next wave to give me a clear shot at the nearest floating turpentine barrel. It was no more than 50 yards away. I held my breath, sighted it and squeezed off a shot that struck the barrel, igniting the turpentine in a fireball that set the other barrels ablaze.

The *Argonaut's* coxswain must have been blinded by the smoke and distracted by the flames. He turned her wheel too sharply and brought her up on the shoal with a tremendous, bone-jarring, grinding crunch. A following wave hammered her stern and she struck the shoal again with a force that sent her blocks squealing and tumbling across her deck. It jarred one of her cannons loose and threw the lookout from the crosstrees into the water. Pandemonium broke out on the gunboat's deck.

Concealed by the billowing smoke and darkening sky, we sailed behind a hardwood hammock and were hidden by a wall of trees.

In the next instant, I heard Smith cry out, "The boy has been hit."

I spun around to see Jesse lying on the deck, holding his right leg, his face contorted by pain, his pant leg crimson with blood. My heart leapt. My stomach flip-flopped like a fish out of water. My reckless rage had gotten the best of me. Once again. But this time, my son was the one being punished by the demon that was my fury.

"Judas Priest!" I said. "Don't move. Lie still." I fell to one knee beside Jesse.

"It hurts something awful," he moaned.

"Let's have a look."

I saw a large bloodstain spreading across his right pants leg, half way between his knee and hip, close to a major artery.

"How bad is it?" Jesse asked. His eyes focused on the bloody stain.

Smith quickly lit a candle and I used my Bowie knife to cut away the pant leg and examine the wound. A large wooden splinter had pierced Jesse's leg, embedding itself deep in his muscle. The entry point was an angry, purplish, bleeding mass of tissue, sinew, blood and bits of cloth. A few inches higher and it would have hit a major artery. Jesse would have bled out. Without thinking, I jumped to my feet and kicked the gun'l, taking all my anger out on the top-most plank, the splintered devil's seam. One or more of the Yanks' wild rifle shots had torn a chunk out of the boat's side. It was as if she and Jesse had both been wounded by the same shot.

"He needs a tourniquet," Smith said.

"Right, right." I took a deep breath and got hold of myself.

"You took a hit in the thigh," I told Jesse. "It's a flesh wound, a bleeder, but no broken bones."

I tried to sound reassuring. But I'd seen enough of what wounds like this one could do and I knew that, if a man survived the wound, he could lose a limb or his life to gangrene. Jesse's wound had to be treated quickly. I washed his leg with water from my canteen, then poured turpentine on the deep gash and tied a tourniquet to stop the bleeding. But that was all I could do for the time being.

"We'll tend to your wound as soon as we get out of harm's way," I said.

Jesse nodded stoically, closed his eyes and said, "Smith was right. These are troubled waters."

"You going to be okay?" I asked.

"Yeah."

As I turned away, he grabbed me by the sleeve. "Pa," he said, "you were amazing."

That was the first time he had called me his father.

I lowered my eyes and said, "Get some rest. If you need anything during the night—anything at all—call me."

I took the helm again and Smith took the lead as the *Dead Reckoning* eased away, inching along the inner channel in the darkening gloom, desperately trying to put distance between the *Argonaut* and us.

Lady Luck was with us as we felt our way along, using only our jib and the lead line. We'd gone little more than a mile when we heard gunfire coming from the direction of the *Argonaut.* It sounded like the ship was under attack. Rebels must have been encamped nearby.

We headed for deeper water and tacked away under a blood red moon. Once in the Gulf, the boat danced across the waves, expecting no favors from the elements. I looked to the sky where the first glimmer of stars appeared like a sprinkling of diamonds on a black velvet jeweler's cloth, I decided to press my luck and sail by the stars.

"Get some sleep," I said to Smith, "and I'll wake you when it's your turn to take the helm."

~

Throughout that long night, every time Jesse moaned in his sleep, I recalled what had happened and why. I couldn't bear the thought of him losing his leg or his life because of my recklessness. Slowly, I came to the realization that defying the Yankee gunboat had little to do with saving the boat and naval stores. It had everything to do with proving myself to my son.

The next day we made good headway and were soon abeam Anclote Key, the first of the 320-mile chain of barrier islands straddling Florida's gulf coast. I asked Smith to take the tiller while I checked on Jesse. He was half-awake, his face flushed and puffy, his eyelids drooping, his forehead showing the strain, each crease another silent scream. When I touched his leg, he let out a low moan.

"I'm sorry, son," I said, "but this has to be done."

He nodded and shut his eyes and I worked swiftly, removing the bandage as gingerly as I could. The bleeding had stopped but his thigh was badly swollen and discolored and the shard of wood had buried itself deep in his thigh. I touched his forehead; found no fever; a good sign. I changed the bandage and said:

"Mommer Wicks' place is close by. I'm going to have her take a look at this."

"Look at what?" Jesse said. "My leg? Hold on! Whoa! No Nigger woman is—"

"Negro," I broke in. "Negro woman. And, yes she is going to look at your leg."

"I want a white doctor," he demanded, "a white, male doctor."

"Well, like it or not, you're going to get a female black woman, a Santeras."

"A who?"

"Mommer is a Santeria priestess, a conjure woman, a healer."

"Black magic! She's not going to poke her big, black fingers inside me."

"If she doesn't you'll die of gangrene."

"Lord, I'm as good as dead anyway."

"If you keep talking like that, I'll see to it that you are."

I pivoted and walked off.

~

The wind ruffled our sails and our rigging nickered as if the *Dead Reckoning* were a warhorse chomping at the bit. I took the helm again and Smith moved to the bow to keep a weather eye. With full canvas set, we captured every breath of the wind and raced down the coast on slate gray waters. From time to time, we had to head up to avoid a coral reef but we pressed on.

Soon the constant pounding of the waves began to take its toll. The boat started leaking at the devil seam.

"We're shipping water," Smith called out.

I lashed the tiller in place and came back to have a look. "You're going to have to patch it and bail," I said.

Smith repaired the damage as best he could while we continued coasting along. But he couldn't completely stop the leak. We had to make it to Mommer Wicks' place where we could repair the boat and tend to Jesse's leg wound.

After checking my charts, I tacked toward the coast where we rounded a barrier island; then I steered the boat into a broad channel fringed with mangrove trees. The further up the channel we sailed the harder we worked to tack back and forth. As we tacked, the branches of willows, bald cypress and live oaks bent heavy with rain, stooped low, ready to reach out and tear our mains'l to shreds. In the play of light and shadow, spectral figures seemed to appear, transform themselves into moss or vine-covered tree limbs and vanish in the lush underbrush. Alligators and snakes moved silently through the brackish waters. Raccoons darted in and out. Otherworldly sounds came from everywhere in the canopy of endless green. Every log seemed to hold a turtle, frog, snake, otter or raccoon. There were birds by the hundreds.

Rat-a-ta-ta-tat.

The sound of a woodpecker startled me and for a second I thought we were under fire. I scanned the shoreline as we rounded a bend and entered a wide expanse of water. On our port side, a hammock loomed in the distance. Once the home of hundreds of nesting birds, now the hammock's trees looked forlorn, their gnarled branches clawing at the sky as if keening a loss, their trunks coated ghostly white by the droppings of frightened birds, shot at close range. That sound I'd heard wasn't from a woodpecker after all. It was the small arms fire of plume hunters.

A wounded bird thrashed desperately in the water. In nearby trees, crows watched and waited, somber as pallbearers, as if secure in the knowledge that their black feathers weren't worth the shot. Vultures hovered overhead and bright-eyed raccoons peered out of the shadows, eager to take a turn at gorging themselves. More gunfire sent the critters scurrying for cover.

"That gunfire would be Mommer Wicks' boys," I said to Smith.

"Plume hunting?" he asked fretfully.

"Not likely," I said, trying to ease his mind. "They're probably hunting for food."

"How can you be so sure?" Smith asked. "From what I hear, New York milliners pay seventy-five cents a feather to keep big city ladies dressed in the height of fashion. That makes the plumes of some birds worth more than their weight in gold."

"True enough," Jesse said, eager to show Smith a thing or two. "But only during spring when nesting birds are in their nuptial plumage."

"That's when plume hunters are wary of strangers like us," I added. "With so much money at stake, they're quick to shoot, slow to ask questions.

"Just who is this Mommer Wicks?" Smith asked.

"She's a Cuban black," I said. "Mommer Wicks isn't her real name. Folks just call her that because of all the candles she burns as a Santeria priestess."

"Can she be trusted?"

"Mommer doesn't care who wins this war as long as she's left alone," I said. "The glades are full of people like Mommer and her boys. I met more than my share when I worked as a surveyor. They're deserters, runaway slaves, outlaws, predators, men and women on the dodge. They take on a new name; hide out on mosquito-infested hammocks, protected by alligators, panthers and poisonous snakes."

I hauled on the tiller to clear a half sunken cypress and, as we rounded the next bend, I called out Mommer Wicks' name. We heard no reply.

We shortened sail to slow the *Dead Reckoning* just as Mommer's boys emerged from behind a huge cypress only twenty feet ahead. The sun shone in my eyes and I could only see their silhouettes and the glint of light on the barrels of their Flobert rifles, the kind of small caliber firearms supplied by feather merchants. Those guns were deadly accurate at this distance, but slow to fire. We'd have at least three-seconds to react—the time it took for the trigger to spark the priming cap, ignite the powder and fire.

A finger of sweat ran down my spine.

A breeze blew and a shaft of sunlight cut its way through the trees to fall across the boys' faces. The one on the right, Leroy, was a huge, no-neck man-child in a sweat-stained cotton shirt cut off at the sleeves and bib coveralls with one suspender missing. A leather juju pouch hung from his neck and his head was cocked back like the hammer of his rifle.

The other brother, Cleatus, was shorter, thinner and taut as a coiled spring. He wore a dirty rag as a sweatband and ill-fitting coveralls that looked to be hand-me-downs from his bigger brother. Both men were shoeless, their brown feet coated with the dust of crushed seashells.

Cleatus raised his rifle waist high, pointed right at me and licked his lips in the way that a snake smells its prey.

Leroy squinted and said, "Whatchall want?"

The threat in his voice was unmistakable. It was obvious from their reaction that the boys had no idea who I was. Not that I could blame them. We'd only met once, close to a year ago, when I bought the boat from their Mommer. Both of them were too drunk at the time to see straight. They looked drunk now.

"Let's not go getting buck fever," I said. "It's me, Ed Canfield. You remember me. I bought the *Dead Reckoning* from your Mommer last year. This here is that sloop."

They both squinted at the boat. I took off my hat and stepped onto one of the turpentine barrels so they could see me clearly. To put them at ease, I made a show of my empty right hand. Leroy nodded and said something to Cleatus who simply shrugged his shoulders. We were almost abreast of them.

"Whas in dem barrels?" Cleatus asked, gesturing with his rifle at our naval stores.

"Naval stores," Jesse volunteered. "We run a gum patch."

I shot the boy a quick sideways glance of rebuke. "Not any more." The less said about our business, the better.

The two brothers laughed and Leroy said, "Gum patch? Lordamighty, we thought y'all wuz foragers. Coulda might have got yoself killed, yes."

"Dat for damn sure." The smaller brother chuckled and gave the tight-lipped smile of a man with crooked teeth. He hawked up a dark quid of tobacco and spat. "Three of dem confedrit sodjers come tru tothr day when we gone. Took our plumes and most victuals. Dey ain't nothin' but robbin', murderin' heathens, yes."

Jesse and I exchanged knowing glances. It sounded like McKenna and his bunch were still foraging.

"I know what you mean," I said. "A while back foragers ransacked our cabin."

A black-and-white spotted catch hound with a broken tail emerged from the brush and ran toward Leroy. On seeing us, the dog dropped a dead curlew that had been dangling from his mouth and snarled. Leroy rubbed the dog behind the ears and whispered something that calmed down the critter. Cleatus lowered his rifle.

"We need help," I said. "A gunboat tried to take our boat as a prize. She needs some patching up. So does my son. He's wounded in the leg."

Jesse shook his head to signal that he wanted no part of this type of healing. But the brothers ignored him; they were more concerned with what I'd said about the Yankee gunboat.

"Dem devils track y'all here?" Cleatus asked. His eyes were the color of a slick, peeled onion; they skittered back and forth, trying to see who or what might be trailing us.

"No," I said. "We put paid to their plans."

"Y'all done beat a gunboat in dis here boat?" Out of the side of his mouth, Cleatus said something to his brother in Gullah, the language of the Cuban blacks.

Reading his expression, I knew he didn't believe me. "It's the God's honest truth," I said.

Leroy lowered his rifle, grinned in a lopsided, sly way and responded to Cleatus in Gullah. The only word I recognized was "Mommer."

Leroy paused as if searching his mind as to what to do next.

"I'm willing to pay," I said.

That did it.

"Bring yer boy inside," he replied. "Give Mommer an offering fo' her majik."

Money talks in every language.

Jesse gave me a panicked look. If he could have, he would have jumped up and run off. His eyes widened and he muttered something under his breath. I'd seen that same look on his mother's face whenever I came home drunk.

We tied up to their rickety wharf, jury-rigged a stretcher out of broken tree branches, a tarp and some rope; lifted Jesse onto it and carried him ashore. It took a few minutes to get our land legs and cross the clearing to Mommer Wicks' place, a nut brown, one-room shack hunched over buttonwood posts like a field worker on all fours. A stick and mud chimney spewed out a meandering plume of smoke. The windows were screened with canvas flaps to let air in, keep critters out, and the door was a flour sack that had been dipped in cement. Wooden gutters diverted rainwater through downspouts to a lichen-mottled cracker barrel that had been turned into a cistern. Next to the shack, a makeshift lean-to served as a barn that stood empty. The entire scene was wreathed in ground-hugging smudge pot smoke that snaked out and around the stunted trunks and limbs of nearby trees like tendrils of Spanish moss.

Leroy went ahead of us, the lifeless curlew dangling by its neck from his big fist. As he passed by me, I saw a scar on his right cheek, a grayish mass glistening with sweat, in the form of the letter R. He had been branded as a "runaway" slave at some point in the past. Cleatus brought up the rear.

To the right of their shack, a double-fluted ship's anchor leaned against the trunk of a strangler fig. A gumbo-limbo tree shaded the other side of the shack, its twisted trunk and limbs red and peeling like a man who has been in the sun too long. In the side yard, a rain puddle engulfed a garden of milkweed, wild geranium, horse nettle and other weedy looking medicinal plants.

At our approach, a scrawny calico cat ran beneath the house and a red-throated skink darted between the slat boards. Leroy opened the door and signaled for us to enter a room that contained an odd assortment of wicker and hardwood furniture, most likely flotsam from shipwrecks. Candles lined the mantle of an open hearth, their feeble light casting dancing shadows on the walls. Judging from the looks of the place, the boys drank or gambled away their profits from plume hunting. The air in the room was dank and heavy with the scent of tallow, sweat, smoke, bark juice and the aroma of the squirrel and cabbage stew that simmered in an iron kettle on the back wall.

Next to the hearth, I saw Mommer, a gaunt, old hag, stoop shouldered with nappy gray, close-cropped hair and a face that could have been carved from mahogany. The bags under her eyes sagged as if she had seen more than her fair share of misery. She wore a loose-fitting, multi-colored tunic with an open collar that revealed a shell necklace and a juju bag.

Leroy grinned. He seemed pleased with himself—like a cat laying a dead bird at someone's feet. He gestured toward me and said something in Gullah that I took to mean I was the man who had bought the *Dead Reckoning*.

Mommer looked up briefly, gave me a stare as cold as a frog's behind, one that gave way to a toothless, wary grin. Just as suddenly her brow puckered and she mumbled something in Gullah to Leroy. She returned to her cooking, dipped a ladle in the kettle and sampled her stew with a satisfied smack of the lips.

Leroy said, "Mommer say y'all can't have yo money back. A sale be a sale."

"I don't want my money back," I said. "I like the boat. All it needs is some quick patching up."

Leroy said something under his breath to Mommer and she nodded appreciatively and signaled with her spoon for us to step forward.

"Much obliged, Ma'am." I smiled and wiped my feet on the threshold, an elaborate show of respect that I could see took the old black woman by surprise. Smith followed my lead.

Mommer wiped her hands on her apron, came and bent over Jesse, rolled her eyes and tsked, tsked. "He looks none too good, yes."

"He's wounded in the leg," I said.

"I'll be fine," Jesse stammered. "No need to trouble yourself."

The old woman nodded to me and gestured for us to lay Jesse on a bed with a threadbare tick mattress in the corner of the room. Jesse had a look of disbelief on his face.

"There has to be a better way than this," he said.

I tried to distract Mommer from Jesse's antics. "Is this a statue of Saint Francis?" I pointed to a table that held a candlelit shrine with an unfamiliar, red and black religious statue.

Mommer Wicks snapped. "Dere be no saints here!"

"Dis be Mommer Wicks' macumba," Leroy added as he raised the wick on a lantern.

"I can't believe I'm hearing this," Jesse whispered to me.

"Dat be Eleggua," Mommer said with a touch of pride. "He de guardian of crossroads. Punish dem that no respect him. All healing begin by honoring de trickster, Eleggua."

"Just so long as my son gets better."

She pointed to another shrine that held a framed image of what she said was Chango, the God-devil, and a picture of the Virgin of Caridad. Next to the pictures stood two small statuettes, one adorned with a cowry shell-studded crown, the other with a calabash headdress that held an inverted mortar and pestle. An offering of tobacco leaves lay before the altar. I reached into my pocket for a coin, pulled out Smith's sovereign and laid it next to the tobacco leaves.

"An offering for my son," I said. I glanced over at Jesse.

Mommer Wicks stiffened, raised one eyebrow and stared at me. "Santeria de way of blood."

I picked up the sovereign, swiped it across the dressing for Jesse's wound and placed the bloodstained coin back on the altar.

Mommer Wicks nodded. Then, over her shoulder, she spoke to her boys, ordering them to put down their rifles, which they did most reluctantly.

Mommer turned back to Jesse, knelt by his side and examined his wound. I shot a quick prayer heavenward. As her boys moved closer to see the ceremony, I wedged myself between them. The old lady knit her brow, closed her eyes, fingered her juju bag and began to mumble to herself in Gullah. After several minutes, she straightened up, took the dead curlew from Leroy and brought it over to a table where she slit the bird open with a knife and removed its entrails, all the while mumbling to herself, as if in a trance. Then she placed a small cup of the bird's blood on the altar, tied a knife to a stout stick and poked the blade inside the glowing embers of the fireplace.

When the knife blade glowed red hot, Mommer removed it from the fire and poured water over it. The blade hissed like a snake. Jesse recoiled. Mommer smeared the curlew's blood on his forehead and told us to take hold of his arms and legs. His skin felt clammy, his face was as gray as sifted ashes and his breathing came in short, raspy gulps as if he were drowning in his own bile.

"I need a shot of moonshine," he said.

Leroy gave him a couple of pulls on a jug of bark juice and we waited for the color to come back into Jesse's face. Then Mommer knelt down beside Jesse, took a shallow breath and with two swift cuts laid open the wound. Jesse moaned through gritted teeth, then nodded for Mommer to continue. She probed with the blade until she felt the shard of wood then gingerly removed it and handed it to me.

The wood was as thick as my index finger and had splintered on impact. It was coated in blood and warm to the touch.

Mommer said something to herself in Gullah and smiled.

I heard myself exhale and realized I'd been holding my breath.

Jesse grimaced in pain, but Mommer wasn't done yet. She poked the blade back in the fire, waited for it to get white hot and signaled for us to hold on to Jesse again. As soon as we had a firm grip, she laid the flat of the blade on Jesse's wound. The hiss of burning flesh abruptly turned into a howl. Jesse's piercing scream tore through the cabin and up into the canopy of trees, then ceased abruptly. He had passed out. Mommer cleansed the wound with water, smeared a poultice of medicinal herbs on it and bandaged the leg with a clean cloth.

"Smells something awful," Smith whispered.

"Not half as bad as gangrene," I said.

For the next ten minutes, we listened, more or less respectfully, as Mommer said more gibberish and chants over Jesse and worked herself into a frenzy. I'd never seen the like. When she finished, she removed a set of dice from her apron pocket, blew on them and tossed them on the floor. Then she read the dice for a sign, nodded appreciatively and let a smile spool out on her face.

"Yo boy be up to traveling t'morrow," she said.

One look at Jesse's leg told me the old lady had swallowed too much bark juice. There was no way Jesse would be up to traveling in the morning.

On a signal from his mother, Leroy said, "Y'all kin share our victuals and spend de night."

"Much obliged," I replied.

Jesse came to and we made sure he was comfortable; then Smith and I worked hard at patching the holes in the boat as best we could. Later, we sat down to talk with Leroy and Cleatus about the best way to avoid the Yankee gunboats near Egmont Key. They drew me a map showing where the federal ships patrolled.

Meanwhile Mommer fried up some corn pone to go with her squirrel and cabbage stew. I fed Jesse then ate with the boys. Later, Leroy got out his mouth organ and began playing. The man couldn't carry a tune in a bucket. But we sang along to songs like "Sugar in the Gourd" and "All Around the Chicken Roost." The singing put me in mind of Abner Winslow and the way he used to sit around the campfire at night singing and playing his squeezebox. Abner could surely sing.

At dusk, clouds of mosquitoes arose from the mist to form the ghostly shapes that Mommer's boys called "swamp angels." We swatted them away as best we could and finally gave it up for a lost cause. Then, we carried Jesse down the oyster shell path that led to the boat where I made sure he felt comfortable.

"I'll be right over here, if you need me," I said.

He nodded and shut his eyes. As darkness closed in, I lay down on some sails and pulled a mosquito net over my head. My thoughts were as black as the starless sky. I fell into a troubled, nightmarish sleep in which I thought I heard the gravelly voice of the leader of the Yankee marines, the same man who had set fire to the salt marsh.

"They're in there," I thought I heard him bellow. "Open fire!"

Bullets whipped and whined through the air. I threw off the bed sheet, grabbed my pistol, cleared the hold in a single bound. More bullets, thick as hornets, ricocheted off the mast and deck, tore chunks out of the gun'l. I fired blindly into the night, leapt to the wharf, raced for the woods, darted around a line of trees and scrub brush. Just as I jumped over a fallen log, someone hit me from behind.

I fell to the ground, rolled over on my side, ready to fire when I saw Smith lying there.

"Lay low," he said.

Before I could take the next breath, a bullet hit Smith in the face, just below his right cheekbone. The bullet spun him around and splattered me with his blood and brains. He dropped his rifle, gave a strangled moan and fell over in the mud like a load of cordwood. My heart in my mouth, I crawled to him on my belly and turned him over. With a start, I realized I wasn't looking at Matthew Smith, but at the face of Private Abner Winslow. His eyes wide open, he looked off to the side as if afraid to stare death in the face. I closed his eyelids, picked up his rifle and turned toward the Yanks.

"Don't throw caution to the wind," Private Winslow moaned.

I spun back around in disbelief. Surely, he was dead. I had just seen him die. I had seen him die in Mexico. I had seen him die a hundred times in my sleep. He couldn't be speaking. When I looked the second time, Winslow had once again become Smith. Tears welled up in my eyes so that I could hardly see. I wiped them away, grabbed a charge, tore it off with my teeth, poured it into the barrel and tamped it down with the ramrod. Then I returned the ramrod, set the primer and rolled back on my belly. With the rifle butt against my shoulder, I cocked, took careful aim and waited for the first man to raise his head.

That's when I felt a hand grab me by the shoulder and wrench me from a sweat-drenched nightmare. With a gasp, I sat up and blinked into the blinding light of a storm lantern held inches from my face. I squinted, rubbed my eyes and saw Smith. I reached up, grabbed him by the shoulders.

"You're alive?"

"You were having another bloody nightmare."

I nodded, as breathless as if I had run through the woods, grateful to be alive. Embarrassed, I mumbled, "Better rest up. We have a long day ahead of us."

He nodded and returned to his berth. I lay back down, laced my hands behind my head and closed my eyes.

~

The next morning I awoke with a gasp, too groggy to recall yet another nightmare that had torn me from my sleep. When I checked Jesse, I was astonished to see he looked a heap better. Mommer Wicks had been right. I changed his dressing again and brought him a breakfast of salt pork and grits that Mommer had cooked up.

He sat up, took the plate and said, "Damn but I'm hungry." He paused, a forkful of food inches from his mouth and said. "And that Negro woman don't get any credit for doctoring me. I was already on the mend."

"You're half right," I said.

"Meaning by that?"

"Meaning that for once you used the word Negro, instead of Nigger. There's hope for you yet."

I found Mommer and gave her two of Smith's coins. She bit them and nodded. The grayish cast to her one good eye took on a hard sheen as if it were a crystal ball in which she had foreseen that I would pay in gold.

I went down to the wharf and made sure everything was shipshape. We were about to cast off when Mommer Wicks approached, carrying a small bundle. She gave me a sideways smile as she handed it to me.

"This here be in case he gets da fever ag'in."

The bundle contained a mass of squirming maggots.

"Jes put them on dah wound," Mommer said, "and they clean it up right quick." She paused then added, "Dat camp y'all be lookin' for? Furst y'all gots to find duh wreck of duh *Island Skipper.* It be pointing duh way."

I thanked her again and we shoved off.

As we sailed away, Jesse said to me, "You ain't putting those maggots on me."

I ignored him, held up the brothers' hand-drawn map and shouted back at them:

"Thanks for your help. Thanks for the map."

For our sake, it had better be accurate.

~

CHAPTER SIX

On a rising tide, we left the inlet behind and were soon sailing down the coast on a beam reach, a light breeze stirring, our billowing sails huge and white against a cloudless cobalt sky. I took the tiller, Smith had the weather watch and Jesse lay by the mast, resting his leg. The sun hung low in the sky, the air felt cooler now and so crisp and clear I could see for miles. The repairs to the boat held and it was smooth sailing.

To port, I saw legions of mangroves and cypress, silent sentinels lining the shore. Their trunks were veiled in wisps of morning fog, their foliage shivered in the chill morning air. To starboard, I saw nothing but gentle swells of two to three feet and an occasional island. In the distance, I could see sea gulls hectoring fishing boats.

At one point, the sound of a distant steam whistle reached my ears and I glassed a smoke-belching side-wheeler, leaving the mouth of a bay under the Confederate flag in defiance of the embargo. She was asking for trouble and we gave her a wide berth. Hour after hour, we sailed with no sign of Yankee gunboats.

Later that day, the wind slackened, the sea turned to glass, our sails went limp and the sun beat down on us savagely. With Smith at the tiller, I sought shade beneath the canopy. In the sultry heat, my mind drifted back to Cedar Keys and to the death and destruction I had witnessed. The more I thought about it, the less sense it made and the angrier I got at God for letting it happen. I couldn't let go of it. It was Mexico all over again. I looked up at the sky and asked myself where was God when you needed Him.

I thought of how close Jesse had come to losing his life and felt a pang of guilt with every breath I took. I couldn't deny the fact that I had acted recklessly. I asked myself how

I might make it right with my son. I walked over to where he was lying and sat down on my haunches.

"How you feeling?"

He wiped his brow, arched one eyebrow and looked at me as if I had just asked the dumbest question ever. "Some things you just can't shake," he said.

"I can't get Cedar Keys out of my mind, either," I said. I pulled a flask out of my pocket and offered him a swig.

He shook his head, leaned forward and looked me right in the eye. "Do you feel guilty?" he asked.

"About what?"

"About not fighting at Cedar Keys. About surviving."

"Which is it? Not fighting or surviving?"

"We're lucky to be alive," he said. "I mean if we hadn't been fishing, we would have been in the same fix as everyone else."

"Chalk it up to pure luck."

He had a far away look in his eye. "There was no way those rebel soldiers could have defended Cedar Keys, was there?"

"Not a chance," I said. "All that drum beating and parading around in town was just for show. The army is stretched too thin. Why else would they send only one lieutenant and 22 privates to defend a key port?"

"You knew that all along; didn't you?"

"Nothing the army does would surprise me."

He nodded.

"I wonder what became of Caleb?" he asked. "You think he's okay?"

"He was probably on his pa's boat when the Fosters took off."

"I suppose you're right."

"I'm sorry about this," I said, pointing to his wound. "How does it feel now?"

"Tolerable." He paused and added, "I take back what I said about Mommer Wicks."

"Want me to get you one of your books?" I asked. "Reading might take your mind off things."

"Thanks, but I'm not up to it right now."

"Let me know if you change your mind." I cuffed Jesse on the shoulder then stood and went back to the helm.

Somehow, in some way, it helped to talk like that. It was one of the few conversations we'd had that didn't turn into an argument.

~

Shortly after midday, while taking another swig of rum, I saw Smith hobble over to the port side, use his right hand to shade his eyes and scan the shoreline. Seeing me out of the corner of his eye, he held onto the gun'l and limped toward me. I put the flask away and nodded at him. The swelling on his face had gone down, his eyes looked clear and bright and he didn't favor his bad leg as much.

"Won't be long now," he said with a crooked smile.

I was in no mood to talk but, just to be polite, said, "See you're looking a tad better."

"Actually, I'm feeling bloody awful," he said. "I could use a smoke."

I reached into my pocket and handed him the makings. "Looking forward to meeting up with your friends?" I asked.

"Friends?" He frowned.

"You know, your Quaker friends."

"Oh, right," he said. "The chaps who I visited in the refugee camp."

"Quakers don't believe in war; do they?" I asked.

"No," he said. "They're pacifists." He took a deep drag on the cigarette and let the smoke leak out of the side of his mouth. His weak eye seemed to drift off, too.

"What about you?" I asked. "What do you believe in?"

A tight-lipped grin curled the corners of his mouth. "Me? I'm what you'd call a free thinker, a realist. What about you?"

"Baptist," I said. "You believe in God?"

He chuckled. "Many a man has become a true believer in the heat of battle."

"What happened at Cedar Keys wasn't a battle. It was a bloodbath."

"Yes, it was beastly."

"It's going to get a whole lot worse, too," I said. "Those gold braid glory boys are following military strategies from

Napoleon's era. Well, Napoleon's troops didn't have to charge repeating rifles firing miniê balls that could kill a man at 500 yards. While those generals sit on their mounts above the fray, as if posing for statues, all about them their soldiers are dying. Those poor boys blindly follow orders only to be mowed down like grass before a scythe.

He nodded. "Still going on to Key West?" he asked.

"Soon as we can get some provisions and find who I'm looking for."

"You'll be pressing your luck," he said. "The Key West harbor is full of prize ships like yours just waiting to be auctioned off."

"You sound like Jesse."

"He's a smart lad. If you change your mind and stay at the refugee camp," he said. "I might have a business proposition for you."

"What kind of proposition?"

"Let's just say that a chap with your ability at the helm could do well under the right circumstances."

He clapped me on the shoulder then stepped around me and limped back to Jesse. The two of them spoke briefly then Smith shook his head and shambled off. Jesse limped his way to the stern, a look of concern on his face.

"Has Smith got you all riled up?" I asked.

"Why don't we just stay in the refugee camp where it's safe?" he asked. "Why push on to Key West?"

"Refugee camps are cesspools of disease," I said. "You wait and see. We're just staying long enough to get provisions."

"But the camp can't be more dangerous than Key West."

"And just what do you know about Key West?" I asked.

"I know the Yankees captured it; made it a northern port. That's enough."

"It also happens to be the richest city in the South," I said. "Those Key West Conchs live high on the hog, salvaging ships run up on the reefs. While we're making do with chicory and baking 'secession bread' with rice flour, they're eating steak off gold plates and smoking fat Cuban cigars. They'll pay top dollar for our naval stores."

"Maybe so, but I still say it's selling out to the enemy."

"The enemy?" I said. "Answer me this, Jesse: who does God consider the enemy?"

His chin was only inches from mine. "What's your point?" he said. "God is on our side, the side of the righteous."

"Really?" I snorted.

"Really."

"What if both sides think they're righteous? What if both sides think that God is on their side? Don't Abe Lincoln and Jeff Davis pray to the same God? Don't they both pray for God to smite their enemy?"

Jesse didn't back down. "I'd have to go along with what Brother Storter says. He's a man of God."

"You would?" I asked. "That's interesting because the preacher isn't going off to war. He isn't marching off to the tune of 'The Bonnie Blue Flag'. He isn't taking up arms. He's hiding behind his pulpit and selling out boys like you."

"Hey, the Yanks took up arms against us. They're the invaders. In my eyes, that makes them the enemy."

"Well, just so you remember, when we dock in Key West, I don't want to hear you whistling 'The Bonnie Blue Flag'."

"We'll both be whistling a different tune if your army buddy doesn't remember you."

"He'll remember."

"Remember what? What happened in Mexico? I have a right to know, Pa."

I let out my breath in a long rummy sigh and said, "I suppose you'll hear soon enough from one of the Yanks. You might as well hear it from me."

My tongue loosened by rum, I started speaking in a raspy voice about what had happened outside Mexico City. I relived every moment just as I had on that swelteringly hot day and on many a night since then in my troubled sleep . . .

"Santa Ana's army had barricaded itself in Chapultepec Castle on the outskirts of the Mexican capital. Our orders were to storm that heavily fortified position. I was in the thick of the battle. They pinned us down on the Belen Causeway with a hailstorm of lead and artillery fire. We took a god-awful pounding; lost most of our guns, horses and close to 130 good men. Four times that number were wounded. A mortar dropped a canister right near me, cutting a gun crew to pieces. I was covered in their blood. I looked to First Lieutenant Brannan, lying there unconscious, broken, bleeding. I thought he was dead."

"Isn't Brannan your army buddy?"

"Yeah. But it turns out he wasn't dead. I took one look at him and I figured, if we stayed there, we'd all be killed. I snapped. I couldn't take it any longer. I couldn't kneel there waiting for the next ball to take my head off. I jumped up, yelling for Private Winslow and the others to cover me."

"You charged?"

"I screamed at the top of my lungs. I cussed a blue streak. I ran, leaping over bodies, ducking, dodging in and out of the stone archway of the aqueduct that ran right down the middle of the causeway. I headed straight toward the dug in soldados. A bullet knocked my hat off. A ricochet nicked my neck. Another one grazed my shoulder. But I kept charging ahead."

"Is that how you got those scars?" Jesse asked.

I looked at him, surprised by the interruption; then fingered the ever-present reminders of that day. "Right."

"What happened next?"

"A roar went up from our boys. They charged after me, running in a half-crouch, under the cannon fire, shooting at will. The greasers turned tail and ran. We breached Belen Gate, a major artery leading right into the heart of the city. But I didn't stop. I ran down those cadets, and fought my way into their citadel."

"You charged a citadel?" Jesse asked.

"Yeah. Five of us stormed into the citadel and made our way up the tower."

I swallowed hard.

"I've never told anyone about this part," I said. "But you might as well know the truth about your old man."

"The truth?"

"The stairway of the tower was steep and dark. The air was thick and heavy with gun smoke. I couldn't hardly see. Just as I cleared the top step, a young cadet with a rapier lunged at me from the shadows. I dodged; he missed; I clubbed him from behind with the butt of my musket and he fell head first out of the turret."

My voice strained with the effort of dredging up the next memory.

"I heard a sharp noise to my right. I spun to face my attacker, and in the same motion, I thrust home with my bayonet. Too late, I saw it wasn't a greaser. I had just bayoneted Abner Winslow by mistake."

"Private Winslow? One of the men who were supposed to lay down cover for you and the other men?"

I nodded. "Yeah. Private Winslow. Only in camp, no one called him that. We called him 'Caution' because the boy was so reckless. He always slept in what the army called 'battle line'—in his uniform, a loaded gun by his side, his haversack nearby—ready, willing and eager to fight. Caution was only 16 years old, scarecrow-thin with a cowlick that stood straight up as if every inch of him was primed, cocked, ready to go off. Small as he was, he could draw a ramrod, tear a cartridge and pull a trigger quick as the best of us. The last reckless thing Caution ever did on a battlefield was disobeying my order. It cost him his life."

"He died?"

I nodded. "My bayonet hit him in the thigh. It punctured an artery. He bled out on the floor of the tower."

"Lordamighty," Jesse whispered. He looked at the wound on his own thigh.

I paused, then added, "When the killing stopped, General Winfield Scott said, 'You have been baptized in guts and blood and come out steel.' *Baptized?* Baptism is supposed to wash away your sins, isn't it? This baptism left me with an indelible stain."

"It was an accident," Jesse said. "You weren't to blame for what happened."

"Happened? You know what happened?" I sighed. "They patched up my shoulder and my neck; sent me home early with Brannan, who was also on the mend. That's how the two of us became good friends. They gave us Certificates of Merit, promoted me to Corporal and made Brannan a Brevett Captain. They paraded us around like heroes. He went back, but they discharged me, sent me home to be there when you were born."

"You were a hero," Jesse said. "You saved your men."

"Not all of them. I sent that Certificate of Merit to Winslow's mother. Told her that her son was the real hero. That he had died with his face to the enemy."

"Meaning you?"

I nodded.

"Is that when you started drinking?"

"It's one way to deal with the pain."

"Ma says you were drunk when you re-enlisted."

"Yeah," I said. "I was drunk. But the truth is, I wanted to get away, leave the past behind me. Key West is as far away as you can get."

"Get away from who? From ma and me?"

"No. From the killer I had become."

Hearing me say that took his breath away. He pursed his lips as if to say, "Oh," but nothing came out. We stayed there for several minutes, the only sound coming from the rippling of the boat's wake, the snapping of the sails. The wind began clocking around to starboard and I adjusted the tiller. We sailed on in silence as the sun sank into the sea.

~

At dawn, the sky was overcast, the humidity insufferable, and dark, foreboding storm clouds formed an impenetrable wall on the horizon. With every stitch of sail aloft, the *Dead Reckoning* cut through the water on a broad reach, holding firmly to her course. She made a good six knots per hour until late in the day when the wind intensified and the waves mounted. We trimmed our sails and took a spanking from the sea for several hours. By nightfall, the squall had passed and we settled down for a much-needed rest, swinging at anchor under a moonlit sky, relieved that we had seen no federal gunboats that day.

On the following day, the town of Punta Rassa appeared on the horizon, hugging the shoreline with a hodgepodge of wooden buildings, saloons, a hotel, several large livestock pens and a wharf. Shadowy figures moved in and out of the buildings. We sailed on with an eye peeled for Union gunboats and entered the mouth of the Caloosahatchee River, a two-mile wide expanse where the water ran several fathoms deep and mangrove islets made passage difficult. Several miles upriver, I spied the wreck of the *Island Skipper*, a Bahamian smack hung up on an oyster bed, her bow stove in and her broken mast pointing toward an almost invisible break in the wall of mangroves. A wisp of smoke rose above the distant trees and I called out to Smith. He came over, studied the shoreline with me then bobbed his head up and down and pointed to an inlet.

"The refugee camp is in there."

"Raise the centerboard to quarter-down," I said, "and let out just enough sail to allow the jib to goose wing."

Smith did as he was told. I turned the boat to port, and we kept an eye out for sand bars and oyster beds as we made our way slowly upriver. We tacked back and forth making little headway and eventually reached a point where I felt the boat could go no further.

"We'll anchor here," I said, "and wait for a rising tide."

"The camp is just around the bend," Smith complained.

Maybe so, but the risk of running aground was too great. I sat down, reached for my flask and took a swig of rum as I studied the river current.

"This is no time for ardent spirits," Smith complained.

He may have been right but I was not about to let the limey's comment pass. "Do yourself a favor," I said, "and stow it."

After a few more pulls on the flask, I could see there was no point in waiting for high tide. It was time to lower the dinghy. I held the boat by a chain at the bow while Smith held it at the stern. Jesse got in only to have his bad leg buckle under him. He pitched head first into the mucky water and came up gasping for air, his head covered in weeds and mud. He was such a sorry sight that Smith and I started laughing. But only for a heart beat.

On the far bank, the tall grass stirred and something massive slid into the dark water with a mushy, gurgling sound that snatched the breath right out of my mouth.

Jesse tried to climb back into the dinghy only to lose footing in the muck and mire, once, twice. To my horror, the head of a sambo gator surfaced within a few yards of him. Jesse saw it, too, and spun the dinghy around to keep it between him and the gator. The beast hissed, snapped its tail spraying all of us with water.

I shouted—what, I don't recall, except that it wasn't a prayer. I had only seconds to react before the gator submerged, came at Jesse from below and dragged him under in a death roll.

I shucked my LeMat and fired. The beast shuddered but didn't stop. Jesse lunged for the boat. The gator lunged, too. I fired again. The bullet missed. The gator grabbed Jesse in its jaws, dragged him backward into the black, scummy water. With a violent shake of its head, the beast tore something off. It flew through the air. Jesse's boot. For a split-second, he was free. He squealed like a rusty wagon axle and thrashed about.

I fired again. This time my bullet ripped through the gator's eye and exploded in its brain. A violent spasm ran from its head to its tail. Rolling over on its back, it slid backward and got hung up on a submerged log.

Jesse scrambled to his feet and we hauled him into the boat. His face looked as white as the gator's belly; his boot was missing. But he was alive. We all laughed insanely.

Jesse hugged me, pounded me on the back and said, "That was one helluva shot."

I knew better. At such close range, I should have killed that gator with one shot. But I'd been drinking and my aim was shaky. I shuddered to think what might have happened if I had been drunk.

Jesse looked at me as if seeing me for the first time and hugged me again.

I stiffened and said, "Let's take a look at your leg."

He sat down and I examined his leg to see what damage the gator had done. Weeds and muck covered the leg. I removed the dressing and washed the leg with fresh water from my canteen. To my surprise, there were just a few nasty puncture marks where his boot had been. For the most part, the gator had missed. I cleaned out the puncture marks then pulled a flask of rum out of my back pocket and poured some alcohol over the wound. Jesse never flinched. After redressing the wound and making sure he felt comfortable, I walked over to the gun'l with the rum flask in hand.

I held up the pint-sized, oval shaped flask and watched the sunlight glint off the images embossed on the rose-colored glass. The flask bore the bust of General Zachary Taylor and the words "General Taylor never surrenders." Thousands of these flasks had been made to commemorate the victory over Mexico. I received my flask at my farewell tribute banquet. I'd held onto it all these years because each swig I took from it somehow made it easier to swallow what I'd done. It was the salve I applied to an invisible, open wound.

General Taylor never surrenders. What about me? What had I been doing for 16 years?

I leaned over the gun'l, uncorked the flask and watched the last of the rum bleed into the water. Then I cocked my arm and threw the flask as far as I could. The splash spooked a clutch of black moorhens. They flew off, cackling among themselves about my awkward toss. I had taken my last swig of ardent spirits.

~

We got into the dinghy and I began rowing. Jesse and I grew excited and bantered back and forth as we neared the refugee camp; Smith seemed to withdraw into himself. I just assumed his bad leg was acting up.

Rounding a bend in the channel, we saw a large encampment in a burned out clearing. There must have been a hundred tents and some ramshackle shanties and stick hovels huddled together like frightened sheep in a slaughterhouse pen. The walls of some of the shacks were slat boards chinked with bousillage, a mixture of mud and Spanish moss. Several small boats and dinghies had been hauled up on land and converted into shelters. Smoke rose from chimneys and from smudge pots stuffed with kerosene soaked rags, their fumes blanketing the squalid scene in a gray pall. I wrinkled my nose at the smells from the open latrine and from the heaps of rotting garbage spread throughout the camp. I swatted at mosquitoes that seemed big enough to saddle and ride. A puny breeze tugged at the nearby palms making their leaves rattle like dead men's bones. The only sign of life was a dun colored dog that kept growling and backing off at our approach.

"I don't like the look of this," Smith said.

"Me neither," Jesse agreed. "I smell trouble."

"That's not all you smell," I said.

As the dinghy drew us closer, the sky opened and it began to drizzle. I could hear the distant sound of singing, the soft, melodious voices of men and women blending together in a chorus that rose above the treetops in the bittersweet lyrics of a hymn.

"Listen," I said. "Singing. They're singing 'Abide With Me', the funeral hymn. Someone has died, would be my guess. They're probably holding a service."

I climbed out of the dinghy, waded ashore and tied the painter to a tree. Then I found a piece of driftwood that Jesse could use as a crutch and helped him wade ashore. The three of us followed the sound of the singing down an uneven path, stepping over rain puddles and around downed tree limbs, making our way to a small clearing. In the center of the clearing, dozens of people stood beneath umbrellas, their heads bowed, the men wearing black armbands, the women dressed in black, their heads covered with black lace mantillas. They stood in a semi-circle beside an open grave, one of a number marked by simple wooden crosses. A pine box coffin sat beside the open grave.

I recognized the closest umbrella-clutching mourners as refugees from Cedar Keys. They must have escaped on other boats while we were still fishing. We stayed back at a respectful distance, hidden by the trees and sheltered from the rain by their overhanging branches.

In front of the assembly, and leading them in song, stood a lean man with the erect bearing of a preacher, someone accustomed to talking down from a pulpit, having people heed his every word. One of the mourners held an umbrella over the preacher's head so I could not get a good look at him. But, when the preacher slowly turned to take in the entire assembly, I recognized Brother Storter. Despite the rain, he remained the very image of pompous self-righteous rectitude. I chuckled to myself at the thought of how Caleb Foster had mimicked Storter, pounding an imaginary pulpit and quoting from the Bible in a voice that rolled like thunder over the heads of his transfixed congregation.

The funeral hymn having been sung, Brother Storter made a show of wiping his wet eyeglasses with a kerchief as if to make certain he would be able to see things that were not revealed to other, lesser mortals. Then, placing the spectacles back on the bridge of his nose, he opened his Bible and read a passage from Samuel, ending with the verse:

"And the victory that day was turned into mourning, unto all the people."

He closed the book, scanned the assembled mourners and began in words that I had heard at so many of his funeral services that, still to this day, I recall the gist of what he said . . .

"On this sad day of mourning, yet another of our dearly beloved soldier boys has become a sacrificial lamb at the hands of the murderous Yankee invaders. Our spirits are heavy burdened and our minds can scarcely conceive how this great calamity befell us and, in particular, this devout, God-fearing, righteous family. But we draw comfort, yes comfort I say, in knowing that we can look forward to a new day, yes a glorious new day, when God will smite our enemy and the forces of evil will be driven from our beloved South."

It was one of his player piano sermons with minor changes to the notes. I just couldn't bring myself to join the other mourners shouting "Amen." But the preacher didn't need much in the way of encouragement. He pounded his Bible in the very manner that Caleb had mimicked. Actually, I liked Caleb's version better. The boy was a hoot.

Storter went on for another five minutes as first one woman and then a second one fainted in the sultry heat. Seeing he was losing the attention of his audience, Storter began his usual wrap up with a flourish . . .

"Yes," he said, "we weep today for a young hero whose life has ended far too soon. But this beautiful man is closer to God now. He's resting in the bosom of Abraham. He has the Lord's ear. And you can be sure that, when God hears what these Yankees have done, those devils will taste the salty tears of defeat forevermore. They are the Devil incarnate and it's only a question of time before they are put to rout by our loyal sons of the South. God's vengeance will be swift and sure."

Storter closed his Bible, stepped forward and whispered in the ear of someone who appeared to be the dead soldier's kin. The man approached the pine-box coffin with his back to us, his head bowed beneath his umbrella. Something about the way he carried himself troubled me. The man knelt, placed a single flower on the coffin and rose in place. Then a woman stepped forward, clasped him by his trembling shoulders and they returned to their places. Both heads remained bowed as the coffin was lowered into the grave. The first shovelful of dirt landed on top of the coffin with a hollow *Thunk.*

On a hand signal from the preacher, the young woman began singing in a voice as pure as a nightingale's, a voice I thought I recognized. Maureen Foster's. An umbrella and a black mantilla concealed the singer's face and her voice was quickly lost among the singing of the other refugees so I couldn't be sure. Yet the young woman did sound like Maureen.

The mourners turned as a body and started filing past the grave, heading toward us as they sang, heads bowed low in grief beneath their umbrellas:

"For all the saints, who from their labors rest,
Who Thee by faith before the world confessed,
Thy Name, O Jesus, be forever blessed.
Alleluia, Alleluia!"

My heart pounded in my chest and I strained to see the nightingale's face beneath her umbrella and mantilla. The closer they came the more certain I felt. It had to be Maureen. On Sunday after Sunday I'd stood beside her in the choir hearing her angelic voice. Surely, there could only be one like it.

"Thou wast their Rock, their Fortress and their Might;
Thou, Lord, their Captain in the well-fought fight;
Thou, in the darkness drear, their one true Light.
Alleluia, Alleluia!"

They were almost upon us when I heard her voice again, carrying the melody beyond the range of all the other singers.

"O may thy soldiers, faithful, true, and bold,
Fight as the saints who nobly fought of old,
And win, with them the victor's crown of gold.
Alleluia, Alleluia!"

Maureen!

Without thinking, I stepped out of the tree line, bringing the entire wide-eyed, slack-jawed procession to a ragged, silent halt. Jesse and Smith moved forward on either side of me. I saw Maureen first, then her sisters, Kate and Helen.

"Miss Maureen," I said.

She raised her umbrella, looked at me, wan and teary-eyed. Then she glanced nervously at the man in front of her, Peter Foster. His red-rimmed eyes burned like a furnace. One look from him and Maureen turned away from me.

Suddenly it occurred to me that the dead soldier might be Maureen's brother, Caleb. But it couldn't be Caleb. He was so full of life, always laughing, horsing around and doing sidesplitting imitations of pompous people like Brother Storter.

"Caleb," his father would scold, "you watch your tongue. One of these days you're going to trip over it."

Could Caleb actually be dead?

"These men have no business here," Peter Foster said in a smoldering voice.

"But they're refugees like the rest of us," the preacher said.

Peter Foster jabbed an accusing finger at me and at Jesse. "Those two are nothing but sum-bitches. They have no place at my son's funeral."

His son's funeral! Caleb was dead.

The mourners shrank back as if we were lepers. I wanted to say, "You're wrong." But I knew it would be pointless.

"Please," Brother Storter said as he turned to the others, "do not let this disruption mar the solemnity of this sacred occasion. Let us proceed." And with that, he turned on his heels, began singing again and led them off.

Head down, Maureen started to glance back at me, but the man next to her wrapped a protective arm around her and swept her away. I recognized Jack Pemble, one of the three-man crew who ran the lighthouse before it was put out of commission. The "wickies" rotated on and off the beacon with two men always tending the light while the third man went on shore leave. When Pemble took his leave, he showed up at choir practice where the ladies fawned all over him, eager to hear his stories about the lives he had saved in the line of duty. The man was so full of himself it's a wonder his uniform fit. But, to give the Devil his due, Pemble was definitely a ladies' man: six feet tall with fair skin, piercing blue eyes, wavy brown hair, and a pencil-thin mustache. He could also sing better than me.

"Peter," I called after Maureen's father, "I am truly sorry to learn of your loss. Please accept my most heartfelt condolences."

"How dare you, sir," Foster shouted back.

"Pray tell, what was that about?" Smith asked.

"It's a long story," I said. I glanced over at Jesse and saw him questioning one of the stragglers, another boy his age. When he turned toward me, angry red splotches had spread across Jesse's cheeks. I knew I would have some explaining to do, but before I could say a word, another voice cut in:

"Well, I'll be dipped in shit and rolled in bread crumbs, if it ain't Ed Canfield."

I turned to see the two shovel-totting gravediggers walking our way: Ned Boyle and his son, Malachi. They were Conchs, the nickname given to Key West natives, men who'd fight at the drop of a hat and drop it themselves, if need be. Ned and Malachi had left Key West for Cedar Keys soon after the Yanks seized Fort Zachary Taylor.

Ned was a blockish, powerful man who wrested a living from the Everglades. When he wasn't digging graves, he used an axe and handsaw to cut buttonwood trees and rick them for charcoal. That kind of backbreaking work put a sharp edge on the man's appetites. His grizzled beard bore traces of moonshine, grease and tobacco juice; his face was sandpaper rough; his soiled cap had a broken bill; and he smelled of sweat, smoke and mold.

Malachi was a stumpy version of the father, hard-muscled, tanned and squinty-eyed, mule-strong. I thought of him as the village idiot, a man with a skull too thick to leave much room for a brain. But it was the eyes that gave most folks the willies. They were red-rimmed, like the eyes of a young osprey, always looking for trouble. He kept a Colt .36 jammed into his belt and seemed too eager to use it. The army had rejected him on account of his clubfoot.

"Gave you up for dead." The older Boyle chortled. I got the feeling he was sizing me up for a coffin. His black eyes glowed like hot stove lids at the thought of his own joke. He planted the blade of his spade in the muddy soil and cupped his hands on the top of the handle, his elbows forking outward. Malachi laid his well-muscled forearms across his chest like a stack of cordwood and eyed me. We hadn't been on speaking terms since the day I caught Malachi whistling at Miss Maureen. At the time, I let it pass because Malachi wasn't right in the head.

I cocked my head in Jesse's direction and said, "Jesse was wounded but he's alive and well. So are we."

"Y'all may be alive, but y'all ain't well," Ned said as he shook the rainwater off his hat. "We got us unionists, rebels, runaway niggers, pacifists, spies, moonshiners, Bible thumpers and randy refugees living cheek by jowl, fighting over every scrap of dry land and every morsel of food."

I thought it odd that he hadn't mentioned Quakers but I let him ramble on.

"When someone dies," Ned said, "they auction off his lousy tent to the highest bidder. This here refugee camp is the closest thing to hell this side of the Mason Dixon line."

"I believe we just had some brimstone thrown our way," I said.

"You mean old man Foster?" Ned asked. "He's clear out of his mind about what happened to Caleb." Ned gave me a big, conspiratorial wink.

"What happened?" Jesse blurted out.

Boyle smiled. He enjoyed this. "Someone—I ain't sayin' who—but someone paid Caleb to sign up for him when them recruiters came the second time around. The boy did it for the money on account of his family being on hard times after your pa cut Caleb loose from the gum patch."

"Who told you that?" Jesse demanded.

But Boyle kept right on beating his gums. "Old man Foster didn't know about his boy signing up until Caleb became drummer boy. Caleb is the one what warned the town about the Yankee warship. Took a piece of shrapnel for his trouble. Happened right outside the Foster house. They carried him onto the family's boat, but when they hit the reef, Caleb was too weak to swim to shore."

Jesse shot me a fierce, knowing look.

I tried to change the subject. "Thank God the others survived."

"Thank Jack Pemble," Boyle said. "He's the one who pulled them out of the surf."

"How many people managed to escape the Yankee attack?" I asked.

"Hard to say," Boyle replied. He lifted his rain-soaked cap and scratched his head again. "Folks like y'all still streaming in. We ain't got but half enough to eat as it is."

"What happened to the other people buried in that graveyard?" Jesse asked.

"Let's see," Ned said. "We've buried twelve so far, ain't that right Malachi?"

Malachi nodded. "Four killed by Yanks. Eight killed by fevers."

Boyle shot his son an angry look. "Malachi is a little teched in the head. Don't hardly know what he's yammerin' about."

"What kind of fevers?" Smith insisted.

Malachi ignored his father's rebuke. "Dysentery, pneumonia and maybe the yellow fever."

"Yellow fever?" I asked. "Are you sure? This isn't fever season."

"In this here swamp anything is possible," Ned admitted reluctantly. "Doc Raymond says it's the miasma, the poisonous vapors in the air."

"Yeah," Malachi said. "Doc says we could might raise the flag, the yellow jack."

Yellow fever. We had just sailed into the middle of contagion.

~

CHAPTER SEVEN

Jesse and I left Smith behind, got back in the dinghy and I rowed in stony, rain-splattered silence back to the boat. Once we were aboard, Jesse turned to me with tears in his eyes, his crutch held high as if it were a cudgel.

"You paid Caleb Foster to take my place, didn't you?" In the gray rain, his face had taken on the sheen of forged steel.

"They're taking boys your age now."

"Answer my question." His voice was rough as a rasp, each word pronounced as if it were an obscenity.

I shook my head. "Put that crutch down. I never meant for it to come to this."

"Of course not. You just wanted me to slave away in your lousy gum patch." He flung the crutch at the barrels of tar. It bounced off harmlessly.

"Before you jump down my throat listen to what I have to say. Business was so far off, I knew you wouldn't be considered exempt any more. The recruiters would snatch you right up."

"Tell me," he asked. "How much did you pay Caleb to take my place?"

A ragged sigh escaped my lips. "All right, I paid him. Yes, I paid him. But I didn't put a gun to Caleb's head and force him to sign that paper. I paid him $300 to sign up and another $15 a month until his father got the insurance money. If I hadn't done it, he would have taken someone else's money. He would have signed up for someone else, instead of you. You heard Boyle say it—Caleb's family needed the money."

"Boyle doesn't know what the hell he's talking about. Peter Foster is a rich man, a helluva lot richer than you."

"On paper, maybe. But the break-in at the salt works left him deep in debt."

"The break-in?" Jesse rubbed the back of his neck. "I thought Caleb said it was covered by insurance."

"Right. But Lloyd's of London wasn't paying up. Meanwhile, the Fosters were just getting by."

"But why would you pay Caleb to sign up? Why not just pay him to stay in the gum patch?"

"One way or the other the recruiters were going to take him in six months. This way I got some money to the Fosters when they needed it—without embarrassing Maureen's father."

"Does Maureen know what you did?"

"I didn't have to tell her. Caleb went and bragged to his family. I think Maureen understood it wasn't my doing. She'd heard her brother talk about signing up. But old man Foster had a conniption fit. He was mad as hell at me. I tried to explain that Caleb had lied to me—that the boy claimed he had his father's permission—but Foster wouldn't listen. He told Caleb to return the money. I tried to get them to tear up the piece of paper but they said it was out of their hands."

"Judas priest," Jesse muttered. "You have a real talent for messing up."

"Look," I shot back, "you're my flesh and blood. I had to protect you. Like it or not, if I hadn't done something, you'd be the one lying in that grave right now. Thank God you're alive."

"Thank God? Thank God? You missed your calling," he said. "You should have been a preacher."

He spun around and went below deck where I could hear him crying. The sobs came in great hiccups of grief that sounded as if they were torn from the depths of his soul.

He was right. I had messed up again and what's more I knew that no amount of talking would make things right. I should have held out, found someone bigger and stronger to take Jesse's place. I should not have let Caleb talk me into it. But what that boy lacked in size, he had made up for in gumption and fast talk.

"I'm gonna kill me some Yankees," he'd boasted.

Hell, the uniform—what there was of it—didn't even fit him.

Caleb was a sight, that's for sure. Now he was gone.

The rain let up and I sat on deck mulling over something else that deeply troubled me. Something I hadn't shared with my son. The mere mention of yellow fever brought to mind what had happened when my mother came down with the fever and they quarantined us. I could still see my father standing at the front window, staring out into the empty street, day after day, hoping and praying someone would come to our aid.

Dad was a stonemason, as solid and unshakeable in his Christian ways as the walls he built for the rich. But his faith was sorely tried when those rich plantation owners turned their backs on us. They claimed we were "white trash, no better than niggers" and they didn't lift a finger to help us.

As strong as he was, dad was no match for a foe like yellow fever. If it weren't for two free blacks, Nat and Sue Corcoran, all of us might have followed ma to the grave. Those blacks were the only ones who gave two hoots and a holler. They didn't cut and run.

They say that the contagion doesn't affect most blacks. I wouldn't know. But what I do know is those two caring souls shared with us their meager sustenance. It was just enough to help us get by. Yet, at my mother's funeral, those two kind-hearted Negroes had to sit in the back pew of the church. The white folks sat upfront.

After the funeral, dad got drunk and rode back into town with a cartload of stones. Before they could stop him, my father—a God-fearing man, if ever there were one—had broken every window in their lily-white church. They said it took four men to wrestle him to the ground, hog tie him and drag him off to jail.

With my mother dead and my father in prison, they auctioned off everything we owned to pay our debts. Then my younger brother and sister went to live with my uncle and I was rented out to that farmer until I decided to make my own way in the world. That's when the fire began burning within me, always simmering just below the surface, ready to flare up and explode in a volcanic outburst against any perceived injustice. The army was the one place where my passion found free rein. They paid me for my explosive rage and they got their money's worth; that is, at least until

I turned it on the big brass. When they felt the full force of my wrath, they called it "soldier's heart." After serving time for the fight with Lieutenant Claussen, they drummed me out of the service.

Now I felt that same righteous wrath building up inside. I knew I had to do something for the refugees who were trapped here like my family had been. I had to do something to make things right. What—I didn't know.

Then I remembered what Ned Boyle had said about food being scarce and I knew what I had to do.

~

The next morning I told Jesse I was going hunting, took my rifle and started making my way past the mangroves and scrub brush and through the pinewoods in search of game for the refugees.

I had covered close to a mile, when the sound of thunder reached my ears. Looking to the sky, I expected to see signs of a brewing storm, but instead, I noticed a dust cloud rising above the tree line. The cloud grew, the ground trembled beneath my feet and the rumble became more distinct. I knew without thinking that at any moment a herd of cattle would clear the trees at the far end of the glade. The drovers had to be working for a blockade runner. They had to be daring and dangerous men. Instinctively, I took cover behind a buttonwood tree.

An outrider appeared first. He wasn't outfitted like the cowboys I had seen in Texas and Mexico. Out west, on the open plains, the cowboys used lassoes and saddles with pommels to herd and rope the cattle. In Florida's dense tall grass and scrub brush, lassoes were useless in driving free-range cattle, many weighing more than 600 pounds and brandishing huge three-foot horns. Instead, this cowhand had a large whip dangling from his saddle. He was a cracker cow hunter, so-called because his kind used the crack of their whips to drive cattle.

The outrider made right for the nearby stream. Next, a chuck wagon pulled by four oxen clattered into view, staying upwind of the dust from the oncoming herd. The lead steers cleared the tree line, their heads down, tongues lolling, staring dully at the ground. They must have smelled the water.

Their pace quickened. Their pounding hooves drove the other creatures of the glades before them in panic and pandemonium. Grackles, white-eyed vireos and limpkins took to the air. Raccoons dove for cover in hollowed-out logs. Insects rose from the glade in filmy clouds.

A rangy hound loped along beside the lead cows, keeping his head close to the ground. Then the rest of the herd came into view, driven by cow hunters on stocky cow ponies. My instinct to hide had been right. This bunch looked as if they were on a first name basis with Old Scratch.

The trail boss in the lead was whipcord lean with broad shoulders that hunched forward as he rode. His ash-gray slouch hat hung low over his brow; a bandoleer cartridge belt hung from his shoulder and a carbine swayed in a scabbard. The grip of a Colt Navy revolver protruded from his tied down, quick draw holster. It was the kind of sidearm he might have "borrowed" from a Yank.

Halfway back, on the flanks of the herd, rode two swingmen in high-crowned, wide-brimmed hats, leather vests, long-sleeved, collarless shirts and chaps. Both had revolvers slung from their hips and one had a single-shot, breech-loading carbine. They looked to be trail-hardened. Behind them rode a leather-tough flanker who was also well armed. A drag man—the greenhorn in the bunch—brought up the rear. He had a bandana around his face to ward off the choking dust, a pistol on his side.

The trail boss turned the herd toward the fresh-water creek. The dog took a quick drink, spun off from the wagon, started circling back and forth, heading toward me, getting closer and closer, his head hanging low to the ground, the fur on the back of his neck standing up. I cocked my rifle.

The dog got within 30 feet when he spotted me and bared his fangs. I tried to shoo him away but he kept on coming. Twenty feet. Ten. He snarled and attacked. I fired a warning shot in the air. The dog bolted.

Spooked by the gunshot, the cattle backed, milled, snorted, hooked and lunged into each other in trying to turn away. The stunned cowhands spun their horses around, not sure at first where the shot had come from. The trail boss wheeled his horse around again. In the same instant, he saw me. He whipped out his pistol.

Suddenly the lead cow broke into the open, stampeding the rest of the herd in one furious rampage. The crackers and their dog lit out after them.

The wagon stayed behind, one wheel hung up on a downed tree. Now it was just the roundup cook, his sidekick and me. They had no idea I was there. They cussed the dog, climbed down from the wagon and examined the wheel. Something told me to stay silent.

"I'd swear I heard a rifle shot," the cook said.

"You've been on edge ever since Cedar Keys," his sidekick answered.

"Yeah, well, stealing the salt was supposed to be easy money," the cook said. "Until those damn bags of salt burst and clogged the bilge pumps."

"At least salt is a helluva lot easier to spend than worthless Confederate scrip."

Salt? Could they be talking about Peter Foster's salt?

I edged closer.

"But now we have blood on our hands," the sidekick said.

"Captain Quill had no choice," the cook said. "Once that damn insurance adjuster started snooping around, he had to kill him. What's done is done."

I'd heard of Quill. Captain Damien Quill. He was a ruthless British seaman hired by the steamship owners to run the blockade with smuggled goods. That large, gray blockade runner that the Yanks sunk in Cedar Keys' must have been his ship. Quill must have stolen Foster's salt to line his own pockets only to have the salt clog his bilge pumps and force him to limp back into port. I pressed closer to hear more. The cook cracked his whip, the oxen responded and the wagon wheel came free.

"Imagine the look on the faces of them Yanks," the sidekick said, "when they figure out the man they found floating in the bay isn't Quill; it's Matthew Smith, the claims adjuster."

They both laughed.

Quill must have shot Smith. He must have switched clothes with the dead man to throw the Yanks off his tracks.

That would explain why Quill's clothes didn't fit. It would also explain why Peter Foster hadn't received his insurance money.

No wonder Smith—or rather, Quill—didn't want to go to Key West. He had made up that story about the Quakers so we'd take him to the Caloosahatchee River where he could meet up with this gang.

In the distance, I could see the outrider returning. I didn't like my odds with these gunslingers. I backed off quietly and made my way to the boat where I found Jesse on deck. He was on all fours with a bucket of water and a holly stone that he used on the deck, scrubbing away with both arms as if trying to remove the stain of Original Sin itself. He looked up when he heard me approach. I could see his face still looked flushed, his eyes red with tears.

"You're going to open that leg wound again," I said.

"I'll do as I please," he snapped back.

"Have you seen Smith?" I asked.

"No."

"Well, it turns out Smith is not his real name."

Jesse stopped scrubbing, gave me a sideways, puzzled look and straightened up slowly. Then I told him about the cracker cow hunters and what I'd overheard about Smith's real name being Damien Quill. I told him that Quill's men had stolen Peter Foster's salt and that some salt bags had broken up and had fouled the bilge pumps in Quill's ship, the gray blockade runner we had seen the Yanks sink in Cedar Keys.

Jesse nodded, wiped his sweaty forehead with his shirt and said, "I'd heard the English were building blockade runners and using their own naval officers to captain them."

"Quill was pretty convincing as an insurance agent," I said.

"What are we going to do about him?"

"Do? I think we've seen the last of Captain Quill. Chances are, he's long gone by now."

Jesse stood and hobbled over to the gun'l.

"What about you?" I asked. "Are you going to stick around?"

"Me take off?" He paused with the slop bucket held waist high. "Believe me, I thought about it."

"But you're still here."

"Yeah, well, you can stir up more trouble than John Barleycorn. Someone's got to clean up your messes." Then he threw the dirty water overboard.

~

Later that day I was fixing to hunt again, when Brother Storter paid us a visit on a horse-drawn wagon he must have borrowed from one of the other refugees. He called out to the boat and, when I looked up, he gave me his practiced smile, stiff as his preacher's collar.

"Hello, Ed," he said. He climbed down from the wagon and met me on the beach with his right hand raised as if in absolution. I smiled but kept my distance, not out of disrespect but out of fear of the contagion.

Storter clasped his hands behind his back and said, "After the funeral service, Doc Raymond pulled me aside and told me that six more refugees have come down with something. He says it sure enough looks to be yellow fever. If necessary, he will quarantine the entire camp. From that point on, no one will be able to enter or leave until the disease runs its course. We'll be trapped here and many of us will die, no doubt. I took myself for a ride along the river to pray about it and came upon your boat. I believe you are the answer to prayer."

The answer to prayer? That was a first for me.

The preacher pointed to the barrels of pine tar, turpentine and rosin stacked on the boat's floorboards. "Those are from your gum patch, aren't they?"

"Yes. What of it?"

"Doc believes that burning rosin and pine tar will help suppress the contagion," he said. "Your cargo could help save lives."

Well, I knew Brother Storter could exaggerate when he wanted to make a point; and I had only laid eyes on Doc Raymond once. For all I knew, he could be a quack. So I did hesitate to respond. After all, those barrels were all I had left to make a fresh start.

"Who is this Doc Raymond?"

"Doc used to be a ship's surgeon. When his ship sank off Key West, he set up practice there."

"Then what's he doing up here?"

"He made the mistake of treating a nigger who had been tarred and feathered. That just about ended his practice."

"I know the feeling. How many barrels are we talking about?" I asked.

"How many lives are you willing to save?" he replied.

That did it. In the back of my head, I heard my father's cry for help as my mother lay dying. The memory felt as sharp as the business end of my Bowie knife.

"Brother Storter," I said, "give us a hand offloading this cargo."

We worked quickly offloading the barrels and stacking them on the dinghy, then ferrying them to shore and to the preacher's borrowed wagon. Next we covered them with a tarp so as to not alarm people, and hauled them to the doctor's tent. All the while I hoped to see Miss Maureen and warn her about the yellow fever.

In a show of gratitude, Brother Storter gave Jesse a pair of pants and down-in-the-heel boots that looked to be his size. The preacher had taken them off a man he had just buried. Before the war those boots might have sold for $3.25. Now, Storter claimed, they were "worth more than $20." Of course, that was $20 in worthless Confederate scrip.

As I left Storter's tent, I caught sight of a lithe, young girl with golden brown hair and a milk white complexion. It was Maureen's little sister, Kate, carrying a bucket of fresh water to one of the other tents. At that moment, a hand from inside that tent opened the flap for her and I got a glimpse of Jack Pemble patting Kate on the head. I made a mental note of the tent's location so I could return later that night.

On my way back to the boat, I noticed a number of rough-looking, heavily armed men cutting down trees on the edge of the camp. They weren't your typical refugees. But at the time, I had other things on my mind.

~

Back at the boat, Jesse tried on the pants and boots, which fit; then said he needed to rest up. I took my rifle and went hunting. This time, I got lucky. I'd only gone a short way when I came across a flock of turkeys. I clucked and purred those gobblers into range and bagged a couple. Then I used my Bowie knife to field dress the birds, bundled them up in a sack and headed back to the boat.

On the way, I began mulling over what to make of Maureen's family living in the same tent as Pemble. Boyle had said that Pemble rescued the Fosters when their boat broke up on the reef. I wondered if there were more to the story than that. Once at the boat, I tried to rouse Jesse but he was fast asleep. So, with the turkeys in hand, I headed for the camp by myself. With dusk descending, I used a storm lantern to light my way.

My thoughts focused on Maureen and what I would say to her and her father. I hadn't spoken to her since shortly after Caleb had enlisted in Jesse's place. Peter Foster had forbidden her to see me, and this time, to my regret, she had gone along with her father's wishes. She quit the choir and after a few weeks so did I. Hell, I couldn't sing anyway. Now I had to speak with Maureen and her father. I was within a few yards of Pemble's tent when I heard someone moan in pain.

"Her fever is rising," I heard Peter Foster say. "Get us more cold water for Minny."

Minny was sick. At Minny's age, any fever could take her quickly.

A lantern flared and the silhouette of a woman appeared on the wall of the tent. She picked up a water bucket and, in the next instant, pulled back the tent flap and stepped out into the night. In the glow of her lantern, Maureen's face looked drawn, pale and dark circles shadowed her eyes. She moved swiftly in the direction of the river and I followed in her footsteps, closing the distance between us. She cleared the last row of tents and made her way down the embankment.

Suddenly a large, blockish figure leapt from behind a tree, grabbed her and threw her to the ground. Her storm lantern fell, Maureen screamed, darkness engulfed them. Stunned, I stood there for a second not fully grasping what I had seen.

"Hey you," I shouted. "Leave her be."

I dropped the turkey sack, charged at the dark figure, leapt on his back and grabbed him in a chokehold with my free arm. But he was too strong. He broke my grip, spun around and punched me in the jaw. My storm lantern went flying. My knees buckled, I staggered backward and fell to the ground. I heard him take off in an ungainly, lurching run, disappearing into the night.

I turned to Maureen, lying beside me on the ground. The fall had knocked the wind out of her and she struggled for air. I could feel her warm breath on my cheek.

"Are you all right?" I wheezed then picked up the sputtering lantern so she could see me.

"Ed, it's you," she gasped.

"Yes," I said. "You're safe." I moved a strand of hair off her tear-stained cheek.

She threw her arms around me and I felt her tremble all over.

"Thank God you were here. He was going to—"

"Who was going to?" I asked. "Did you get a look at him?"

"No," she said. "It all happened so fast. Did he hurt you?"

"I'll be fine," I feigned. Two of my teeth felt loose. "It's you I'm worried about. You have to get out of this place. It is too dangerous."

"But we can't leave now," she said. "Minny has come down with a fever. She is too sick to leave."

The thought of the Fosters providing such comfort and care for their slave took me back. Despite what they said about defending the Southern way of life, deep down the Fosters thought more like the Yanks than they cared to admit to themselves. They loved Minny and treated her like a member of the family.

"Maureen," I said, "this camp is filled with dangerous riff raff. Besides, the whole camp may soon come down with yellow fever."

"Yellow fever," she gasped at the thought. "Land sakes, Ed Canfield, what makes you say such a dreadful thing?"

"Brother Storter says six people are showing symptoms now."

Her eyes widened. "Six? Surely, you don't think Minny is one of them."

"Not likely," I said. "For some reason, Negroes are less likely to catch yellow fever, but she could have caught something just as serious."

In the next instant, I heard another voice shout, "They're over here."

"I see him," Maureen's father bellowed. "Don't let him get away."

Turning, I saw a half dozen torch-bearing men scrambling down the embankment right at me.

"Grab him," another man shouted.

"Don't," Maureen called out. "Don't hurt him."

I tried to get to my feet, but they tackled me, held me on the ground, punched and kicked me. I covered my head and protected myself as best I could.

"You have the wrong man," Maureen screamed. "He didn't do anything."

"What? What's that you say?" Peter Foster cried out. He huffed and puffed, and tried to catch his breath.

"He saved me," Maureen said. "The other man attacked me. He ran that way." She pointed in the direction of the woods.

They stopped and got off me. I sat up and saw the man who had been pummeling me the hardest—Jack Pemble.

Maureen's father asked, "Are you all right, Maureen?"

"Yes," she answered. "Just a little shook up."

Foster gave a sigh of relief then saw my face in the light of the torches. "It's Ed Canfield," he said. "What are you doing here?" He shot a quick glance at his daughter then back at me.

"Be quick about it," Jack Pemble said. "Explain yourself, Canfield."

I wanted to crack Pemble on the jaw. But I knew better than to start another row. "Never mind me," I said, "While we're standing here, he's getting away." I pointed toward the pinewoods.

"Who was it?" Peter Foster asked.

"I'm not sure," I said. "All I know is he ran with a limp."

With one voice, they said, "Malachi Boyle. After him."

They started to run off. I picked up the water bucket only to have Peter Foster rip it out of my hand.

"As for you, sir," he said, "if I were you, I'd make myself scarce. It's dark out here and you wouldn't want to be mistaken for Malachi Boyle a second time." Then he turned to his daughter and said, "Maureen, you best go back to the tent and lie down. I'll get the water."

I spied the loaded pistol jammed into Foster's waistband and backed off, all the while looking at Maureen and she at me. I raised my lantern, pointed at the turkey sack and said:

"There is some fresh meat in that sack." Then I pivoted and walked off.

Back at the boat, Jesse stirred when he heard the dinghy come alongside. He took one look at me and said, "What in the world happened to you?"

"I got in a tussle with someone who tried to take advantage of Miss Maureen. The next thing I knew I was fighting off a half dozen men who mistook me for him."

"Who did it?" Jesse asked. "Did they catch him?"

"I'm not sure. It was too dark to get a good look at him. I think it was Malachi Boyle but he got away."

"That dimwit? What makes you think it was him?"

"Whoever it was ran with a limp."

"If they catch him, they'll hang him from the nearest tree," Jesse said. "How is Miss Maureen?"

"She's pretty shaken up but she'll be okay."

"And you?"

"My jaw hurts. I have a couple of loose teeth. How about you?"

"I'm too tired to talk," he said. "Let's get some sleep."

Jesse got under the mosquito netting and went to sleep, but I was too sore. I needed a smoke.

A drop in the temperature and a steady breeze held most of the mosquitoes at bay but the dark night throbbed with the sound of hoot owls, the ceaseless chatter of crickets and cicadas, the muted flap of wings and the raucous croaking of frogs. The moon bathed the glades in a ghostly gray light too dim to penetrate the shadows, yet bright enough to reflect off the red eyes of gators. The howl of a panther spooked a wild hog from beneath a saw palmetto. A crashing sound in the underbrush warped into a choked off scream.

Suddenly lights appeared on the edge of the glade. Three, four, five of them, weaving, ducking and dodging. I tossed the cigarette aside and reached for my rifle.

"They're coming!" I bellowed. In the same breath, I fired a warning shot above the nearest light.

Jesse woke with a start, took one look at the eerie lights and roared with laughter. "You're shooting at fox-fire," he said. "That's swamp gas."

I stared in disbelief as the lights vanished in the night. My heart pounded in my chest; my breathing came in uneven gasps. I lowered my gun and slumped down on the deck, my chin resting on my chest.

"Who'd you think it was?" Jesse asked.

"Those cracker cow hunters," I muttered.

He laughed again. "They have their hands full rounding up all those cattle you managed to spook."

He lay back down, pulled the mosquito net over his head and went back to sleep.

I rolled myself a smoke and sat there watching a meteor shower blaze across the vault of the sky. It soared overhead the way a rocket flare arcs high above a battlefield, its brilliant light illuminating the heavens until it gradually fades to nothingness, its burnt embers plunging to the earth below. It put me in mind of what had happened in Mexico. I thought about Abner Winslow and how, when we carried him down the stairs of the citadel, we left a trail of bloody footprints behind. If only I could retrace the steps I took that day.

Why did Abner have to die? Why couldn't it have been me?

I sat there for more than an hour until I heard Jesse moaning in his sleep. I lit the storm lantern and tried to rouse him. I could see he was flushed, sweating and feverish to the touch. He started babbling like a drunk. I wiped him down with a cool cloth. I told him he'd be just fine, but I had a strong hunch what he was up against. This was how it had started for my mother.

Yellow fever.

For many of its victims—people like my mother—yellow fever was a death sentence. Those lucky enough to survive were often too weak to fight off the other tropical diseases like dysentery, dengue fever, cholera, malaria or small pox.

I couldn't let that happen to Jesse. I stayed up with him through the rest of the night and prayed to the Almighty as my son's condition worsened.

~

At the crack of dawn, I got Jesse on his feet and into the dinghy. Then I rowed back to the camp, threw his arm around my neck and carried him to Doc's tent. I pulled back the flap and saw men, women and children lying curled up on cots, shivering and sweating, their faces flushed, their skin swollen and appearing as if it were chapped. The smell of the kerosene lanterns mingled with the rank odor of vomit and fecal matter. The sounds of coughing and moaning blended with retching and mewing cries for help.

Doc sat on a nail keg beside a patient's cot. He looked up, gave me a glassy-eyed stare over half-moon spectacles. He looked to be in his fifties with thinning gray hair, sunken cheeks and red-rimmed eyes, heavy-lidded from lack of sleep. I had seen him briefly the day before when I delivered the barrels of pine tar and pitch. I could tell he recognized me, too, but couldn't call my name to mind.

"Ed Canfield," I said.

"Doc Raymond," he replied. He took one look at Jesse and grumbled, "We don't have any more cots. He'll have to share that one." He pointed to an occupied cot.

I laid Jesse down on the cot next to a small boy whose skin looked shriveled and leaden colored. His hair was damp from perspiration. He bled from his eyes and ears. His teeth chattered. Seeing his parched lips, I bent over a nearby water bucket, dipped a sponge and squeezed a few drops at a time onto the boy's cracked and thirsting mouth. He thanked me with a silent blink of his eyes and, in that moment, I realized I knew him: Zach Wetherby, the ten-year old son of the ships smithy in Cedar Keys. The boy liked to trail Jesse and Caleb around town. Zach's father was a pacifist and had no part in this insane war that had claimed his son as a casualty. I felt the boy's pulse; it fluttered weakly. He stared vacantly into space in a way that sent a chill down my spine. I wiped Zach's feverish brow and looked at Doc.

Doc saw my discomfort, shook his head, wiped his dirty hands on a towel and said, "Didn't recognize him, did you? Well, he don't recognize you, neither."

"Where are his parents?"

"Gone. Both of them."

"He's in a bad way, too," I said.

Doc blew through his nose to express his frustration. "So is most everyone else in here."

"How long has he been like this?"

"Two days."

"Will he make it?" I took a shallow breath and waited for an answer.

Doc pursed his lips and looked up as if the answer was written on his forehead. "Hard to say. Some recover. Some don't. If their vomit turns black, and they slip into a coma, half of them will never wake up."

Ma's vomit turned black three days before she slipped into a coma and died.

I turned and spied another familiar figure lying on a nearby cot: Bill Mulroney, the cabinetmaker. He lay there in sweat-drenched clothes, his teeth chattering as his wife wiped his sweat-beaded brow.

"He came in last night complaining of a fever," Doc said. "It isn't yellow fever but God only knows what else it might be in this swamp."

I turned in a circle, slowly taking in the hellish picture of small children, women and men in desperate need of relief from their misery.

"How can I help?" I asked.

"Just don't inhale the vapors."

"There must be something more we can do for them?"

"Sure there is," Doc said, rolling his eyes. "All we need is some quinine, Peruvian bark, calomel, sugar of lead, nitre and tartarized antimony. That's all."

"Where do we get all that?"

Doc gave a dismissive chuckle. "Nearest place I know is Key West, more than a days' sail from here; that is, for anyone fool hardy enough to try."

I thought again about what it had been like for us when my mother died of the fever, deserted by the rich and powerful. I remembered my father throwing up his hands and crying, "For God's sake, won't anyone help?" I remembered feeling like a caged animal. I felt myself trembling once again with rage at the memory of being totally abandoned. I couldn't let that happen to Jesse. To Maureen. To her family. Or, to any of the other refugees for that matter.

"I'll do it," I said.

"Do what?"

"Run the blockade. I have a sloop, a good size one. She's 40-feet long with an 13-foot beam and a flat-bottomed centerboard."

"You're not actually thinking about doing this?" Doc asked.

"I don't see anyone else volunteering, do you?"

"Of course not. It's too dangerous, especially in a beamy flat-bottom boat."

"She handled the chop between here and Cedar Keys."

"You did that?"

I could see that impressed him. "Me and my son."

"Without his help, you'd be tempting fate."

Quill had said much the same thing. We'd be crazy to sail to Key West, he'd said. And that was with a three-man crew. Sailing single-handed on a boat the size of mine would be very dangerous. But I could see no other choice.

"I said I'd do it and I will."

"Mister, let me feel your forehead," Doc said.

"What the hell for?"

"To make sure you're not feverish, half out of your mind."

He felt my forehead then tugged at the waddle under his chin and grunted, as if disappointed to find me healthy.

"Satisfied? Now, who do I talk to in Key West? Where do I get these supplies? How do I pay for them?"

Doc eyed me over the rims of his spectacles. "What's your name again?"

"Ed Canfield."

"And is he your son?" He jerked a thumb in Jesse's direction.

"Yes."

He leaned forward so that Jesse couldn't hear him.

"Well, Ed, you may be a good father, and I'm sure you mean what you say, but there's no sense in both of you dying."

"Jesse is not going to die."

He folded his arms cross his chest as if wrestling with an idea. "You ever been out in a real blow in that flat-bottomed boat?"

He didn't say what he meant by a real blow but I knew from first-hand experience. In a northern, the fetch coming across the gulf builds tall, squared-up, breaking waves that can capsize a boat like mine in a heartbeat.

"Yes," I said.

He nodded, taking it all in. "Well, at least hurricane season is behind us. That's to the good."

There was a long pause before he said, "Ever sailed to Key West?"

"There's always a first time."

"And a last time," he snorted. He scratched the back of his neck and started muttering to himself. "Roughly 125 nautical miles, give or take . . . winds out of the east at eight, maybe ten, knots." He paused, eyed me again and said, "Charts? You have good charts?"

"Look, if he says he can do it," Jesse cut in, "he can do it."

"Son," Doc said, "we're talking about the graveyard of the sea."

"And we're talking about my pa," Jesse said.

Coming from Jesse that meant a lot. I turned and we exchanged looks. His face looked feverish and stippled with sweat but his eyes were as hard as flints. I knew that he meant what he had just said and it felt good. Real good.

Doc eyed Jesse, then me.

"What's the answer? Do you have good charts or not?" he asked.

"Yes." They'd have to be good enough.

The knot in Doc's forehead unwound. "Come to think of it, if you stayed here, you'd probably die of the fever. So what's the difference?"

"The difference is this way we have a fighting chance."

"Have it your way." He knelt down on one knee and pulled a steamer trunk from under his own bunk. He opened the lid, removed a bundled up Union flag, stood and handed it to me.

"I thought this might come in handy some day. Be sure to run it up before you enter open water."

"Much obliged," I said.

He fumbled in his shirt pocket for a scrap of paper, pulled a pencil from behind his ear and said, "There's a man in Key West by the name of P. J. Cornelius. He owns half the town. He'll know where to get what we need."

Then Doc quickly jotted down a note to Mister Cornelius and said, "Give him this. Tell him they're for me, Doc Raymond, and he damn well better move heaven and earth to get them."

He reached into his pants pocket and pulled out a wad of greenbacks. "You'll need this, too," he said, handing it to me. "Just in case you're not as persuasive as I am."

I didn't count the money; just slipped it into my pocket.

"Hold on," Doc said. "Put that money in your boot where it belongs. Key West is a den of pick pockets and thieves."

I did as he said then shook his hand. He held onto my hand and drew me closer so that only I could hear.

"Remember—there are two bouts of the fever," he said. "Just when they start to feel good, the second fever sets in. That's the one that can kill them. If you want to save your son and the others, you need to be back before that happens."

I turned to face Jesse and saw he had propped himself up on one elbow. He had a stoic look on his face but I knew what he was thinking. I had never sailed south of here by myself. The coastline's treacherous shoals and oyster beds had claimed the lives of many a seaman, most of them more experienced than me. It was a job that called for a leadsman and a helmsman, and on top of that, I'd have to keep a hawk eye out for Yankee gunboats. Sailing solo into a busy harbor could also spell trouble.

Jesse stared at me as if memorizing every crease and wrinkle in my face. He started to say something, but I cut him off.

"Don't say a word."

He saw the cast of my eyes, shook his head and grinned. Then he reached in his pocket and pulled out the wood chip that had wounded him. "I was only going to say, 'Take this for good luck.'"

We both knew I would need all the luck I could get. I took the wood chip, smiled and stepped back, but I kept my eyes on Jesse, knowing we might not see each other again. As I turned and started to leave, he called out, "Be sure to step on the boat deck with your right foot first."

I laughed a little too loud.

"Keep a hawk eye out for the jetties just outside the harbor entrance," Doc said. "They're treacherous."

"I'll follow another ship in," I replied.

Doc reached out and took my hand. "Good luck."

Luck. There's that word again.

I left the tent and headed back toward the boat. The ghostly silence of the camp was broken by a sharp metallic chink and a grinding crunch. I looked in the direction of the sound and saw four men with pick axes and shovels laboring at the edge of the pinewoods, digging a large open pit, which I took to be a mass grave. The man with the pickaxe grunted as he drove the blade into the gritty, unyielding soil. The thought of what might happen if I didn't make it back troubled me all the more. I remembered the mass grave my mother had been buried in. Lost in thought, I didn't hear Maureen coming up behind me.

"Ed," she called out. "Wait. I have to talk to you."

I spun around and saw her coming toward me, the wind in her hair, her cheeks flushed. Her dark brown camp dress—sullied and missing a collar button—revealed the nape of her swan-like neck. Glistening, jewel-like beads of perspiration ran down her throat to disappear behind the collar of a dress that strained to contain her ample bosom. My gaze settled on her smiling lips and those big, blue eyes.

"Miss Maureen." I searched for something to say but couldn't find the words.

Soft as a kiss, she said, "Thank you for coming to my rescue last night."

"Any man would have done the same," I said. "Did they catch Malachi?"

Her eyebrows winged up, her voice had an edge. "No. The cad is still out there somewhere. He and his father took off in the middle of the night."

"Be sure and stay close to camp," I said.

"I will," she said. "Jack says he won't let me out of his sight."

"Jack Pemble?"

"Yes," she said, her expression brightening, "The lighthouse keeper. He rescued us when our boat ran aground."

"Is that his tent you're staying in?"

"Yes," she said. "He managed to get one. He's been such a comfort to our family I don't know what we'd do without him. If you got to know him better, you'd really like him, Ed."

Like him? I'd like to throttle him.

There was an awkward pause in which neither of us knew what to say. Then Maureen filled the void that separated us, speaking in a somber tone of voice.

"You were right about Minny," she said. "Doc says she doesn't have yellow fever. But it's just as bad. It's dengue fever."

Dengue fever.

The symptoms were a high fever, aching joints, a rash and fluid build up in the lungs. I had seen it take people younger than Minny.

"She has taken a turn for the worse," Maureen said. "She's half out of her mind. Keeps repeating the same strange word over and over again: Eleggua."

"She's praying," I explained. "Eleggua is the Santeria God of crossroads."

"Crossroads? You don't think—?" She started to ask, but stopped in mid-sentence. She couldn't bring herself to say that Minny might die. Her distress was obvious. I wanted to take Maureen in my arms.

"I'm sure she'll be okay," I managed to say.

"We can only pray."

"And, say a prayer for Jesse, too. He just came down with yellow fever."

She gasped. "Oh no. What does Doc Raymond say?"

"Doc needs more medicine," I said. "And I'm going to Key West to get it."

"Key West? But what about the Yankee blockade?" she asked.

"I'll just have to chance it."

"By yourself?" Her eyes widened and she put a hand to her mouth.

"Today is the 16th of the month," I said, "my lucky day."

She wasn't fooled. "Wait. What about Jack? He could help."

Jack was the last person I'd want to have set foot on my boat. "He's been in the same tent with Minny," I said. "I can't risk that he might come down with the fever, too."

It was a flimsy excuse but the best one I could come up with on the spot. I could see she wasn't buying it.

"Have you ever sailed those waters by yourself?" she asked. It was her schoolteacher's tone of voice.

"No," I said. "But I have good charts, a compass and a sturdy sloop."

"You'll need more than that," she said.

"I'll need your prayers," I replied. That answer seemed to affect her.

"Ed Canfield, you know most assuredly I will pray for you." Her voice was firm, resolute.

We stared at one another for several seconds then I took her hand in mine, kissed the back of it, turned and strode off.

"Godspeed," she called out.

I waved at her over my shoulder and, when I turned back, I nearly collided with Pemble. He walked past me, heading toward Maureen. We exchanged challenging sideways glances and I saw that he wore his lighthouse keeper's uniform. I wore the same clothes I had slept in for days.

But I had no time to waste on such thoughts. The idea of sailing the *Dead Reckoning* by myself was reckless, even crazy, but the sooner I set sail the better my chances of reaching Key West by midday when the fishing boats would be out to sea and the harbor would be less crowded, easier to maneuver.

~

Just as I reached the dinghy, I heard a voice from behind shout, "Freeze, Canfield."

I froze with my arms held high and turned to see Ned and Malachi Boyle, their eyes darker than bootblack, their pistols pointed right at my chest, an Arkansas toothpick hanging from a scabbard on Ned's belt. Malachi's face bore scratch marks.

"Get his firearm," Ned said to his son.

Malachi lurched over and took my gun, then cracked me on the jaw with the butt end. The move was so quick I didn't see it coming. I staggered and fell, my lip split and bleeding.

"That's for last night," he said.

"Y'all ought not to have laid blame off on my boy," Ned said. "They would have lynched him if'n they got their hands on him."

I spat out a trickle of blood. "What are you going to do now?"

"Well, seeing as how we don't know these waters," Ned said, "y'all gonna steer your boat down the coast until we come to a safe harbor. Then we'll decide what to do with the likes of you."

He poked his pistol into my ribs and signaled for me to, "Get a move on."

We took the dinghy to the boat, weighed the fore and aft anchors and set sail under a brooding sky.

~

Storm clouds moved in over the treetops, flexing their muscles, scattering the somber light. I knew that Florida has more thunderstorms than anywhere else in the country, but in the winter, storms are infrequent. I thought this one would blow over. Besides, the tide was with us and I was eager to clear the channel and reach blue water as fast as possible.

The Boyles just sat there on the taffrail, guns drawn, watching me until I said: "I could use one of you to act as leadsman, the other as watchman."

They looked at me in disbelief, then at one another, and laughed scornfully.

"That is," I said, "if you don't want me to run this boat aground."

That got their attention. They swallowed their laughter and agreed. I quickly showed those two landlubbers what to do. It was high tide and by keeping to the middle of the twisting channel, we cleared the shallow spots. Then, holding the tiller in one hand and the main sheet in the other, I brought the bow around and watched the sails fill before lowering the centerboard to full down position and heading into open water.

"A Yankee gunboat," Ned called out.

I spied the ship in the distance and, no doubt, her lookout in the crosstrees saw us, too. But with the stars and stripes flying from our mast, the lookout must have taken us for a Yankee vessel. The other ship didn't change course; but, just to be safe, I did.

As the boat tacked through the wind, I shifted my position and reached for the sheets. The sail filled on the new course, the wind took hold and the *Dead Reckoning* responded in a series of leaps and bounds. With the wind astern, we sailed wing and wing, making good headway. Both Boyles held on for dear life. Seeing their ashen faces gave me an idea: if my two captors became seasick, I could overpower them.

I saw flashes of lightning in the distance and heard the rumble of thunder. Instead of steering clear of the storm, I let it overtake us—an insane move in a beamy boat, but at this point, I had nothing to lose. As the storm drew closer, the wind intensified, the seas began to build and the storm clouds gathered like a clenched fist aimed right at the *Dead Reckoning*. The Boyles turned green around the gills.

I trimmed the sails to spill excess wind and widened the sheeting angles. A white cap crashed across the bow and both Boyles went to the gun'l retching. That's when I made my move. I lashed the tiller to take the waves at an angle and rushed Ned Boyle. He was over the side heaving his guts out when I whipped his pistol out of his holster, grabbed his Arkansas toothpick and hauled him back on the deck. He felt too sick to say or do anything and collapsed in a pitiful heap at my feet. Malachi turned to face me and I chopped him on the skull with the butt of the gun, knocking him senseless. We were even. In a matter of minutes I had both men disarmed and lashed to the mast.

Now I had to get us out of this rapidly deteriorating situation. I had underestimated the speed of the onrushing squall that roiled and churned the water. It had quickly overtaken us, walling out the sun behind a black, ominous shelf cloud. The wind shifted in a heartbeat. Salt spray cross-stitched the surface of the water. Gusts of wind sheared the tops off waves. Spindrift the size of buckshot tore at the sails. The sea steamed with white spume that hissed and lashed out at the writhing sails and rigging. I scrambled to reef the mains'l, felt the boat shudder with each pounding wave.

The *Dead Reckoning* plunged up and down great chasms of water, now teetering at the top of a crest, now diving into the yawning black maelstrom. I struggled to change course only to hear her rigging mock my efforts in a squealing chorus of demonic voices. The boat pitched and rolled as she struggled to come about. Suddenly, a monster wave knocked her so far down that green water cascaded over the gun'l and surged across her deck. It raked her rigging, tearing loose a mad tangle of ropes and blocks that whipped and slashed across and around and over everything in its path. Barrels, equipment and debris careened back and forth, sliding and crashing into the sides of the boat and anything that got in the way.

I heard Ned Boyle cry out in pain: "You idiot. You're going to drown us."

"Shut your trap," I shouted back. "Hell, you're not going to drown. You were born to hang."

With my head down and my eyes crusted over with salt, I squinted into the maelstrom and took the worst of the storm. The boat responded to every move of the tiller and gradually we made our way out of the heavy seas. But I couldn't relax. The storm had cost me precious time.

The sun fought its way through the cloudbank then sank into a blood red bed for the night. I sailed into the darkening sea with only a binnacle light and compass to guide me. Soon a shaving of moonlight turned my wake into a glistening strand of phosphorescent pearls. An occasional mullet broke the water's surface in a silvery streak and clusters of glowing jelly fish lit up the otherwise inky blackness. Overhead, the mains'l muttered to itself like a man talking in his sleep. As the night wore on, the endless hours at the helm took a heavy toll on my body. Salt spray stung my cheeks and crusted my bloodshot eyes. My hands and shoulders ached from wrestling with the tiller. I felt my energy draining away. I needed to rest. Drowsiness overwhelmed me, my eyelids drooped, and my head slumped forward over the tiller. I was about to fall asleep on my feet.

Suddenly I heard the rumble of the surf crashing on a reef. I bolted wide-awake at the helm. With my heart pounding in my chest, I hauled on the tiller, trimmed her sails and put the reef behind us. The Boyles were too seasick to say anything.

~

At sunrise, I rubbed my eyes and scanned the horizon. The storm clouds had cleared and the dawn sky had turned from black to pearl gray. With my glass, I could see the silhouette of Florida's keys in the distance. There was no sign of the Union blockade. I made a quick inspection of the boat and saw that she had lost some rigging, which would have to be replaced at the ships chandlery. The devil seam next to the scuppers bled water again and I patched it as best I could with some oakum and a maul.

I shared some guavas and hard tack with the Boyles and called it breakfast. Then I adjusted the sails and let the *Dead Reckoning* run before a light and balmy wind. Soon, I passed several wreckers heading out to their stations where they hoped to salvage any ships that might have run aground during the storm. But I saw no other vessels that morning.

Now the *Dead Reckoning* moved swiftly and easily, scarcely stirring a whisper of white riffles where her prow peeled back the pale underside of the opal colored sea. A squadron of lumbering pelicans flew past in formation, skimming the gilded surface of the water. I had more than made up for lost time.

CHAPTER EIGHT

By mid-morning, I saw the first signs of Key West—the 86-foot tall lighthouse and two 65-foot tall wooden towers from which lookouts glassed the reef, always on the alert for shipwrecks. Next I spied the stark, forbidding silhouette of Fort Taylor, an enormous three-story brick structure, built in the shape of a trapezoid with sections of it still under construction. Its five-foot thick walls bristled with Rodman and Columbiad cannons capable of firing shells three miles.

The Spanish had called the four-by-two mile key "Cayo Huesa," the island of bones. The grinding molars of the surrounding coral reefs had chewed through the hulls of so many ships that these waters had become known as a graveyard of the sea. And yet, the waterfront had a festive look. Located on the northwestern section of the island, the town had many small cabins lining the shore, many of them whitewashed and their doors and shutters painted in bright colors salvaged at random from doomed ships. These were the homes of the fishermen, spongers and seamen, known for generations as Conchs. The Boyles were Conchs, but for some reason they had not become seamen.

I steered away from the fort and rounded the bony flank of the breakwater where I dropped anchor and waited to see how other boats maneuvered their way past the jetties. In a nearby flat-bottom boat, two men spread shark oil on the water's surface, the better to see the sponges they would harvest from the sea bottom. Another man rowed past in a dinghy weighed down to the gun'l by a large overturned leatherback destined for the turtle kraals and the cannery.

A gruff voice hailed me and I turned to see a fisherman at the helm of a Bahamian smack. He was craggy-faced with doleful eyes and a great shaggy beard. His mate stood a head taller than him but stooped over as if his sinewy arms were too heavy for his frame. The fisherman took quick note of the two Boyles lashed to my mast in their yellow oil slicks and looking for all the world like trussed up chickens.

"This here is a busy channel," the fisherman said. "It's no place to anchor."

"I'm new to these waters," I said. "Mind if I follow you in?"

He gave me a sideways look, starting at my feet and working his way up my trunk until our eyes met. "We'll take you as far as the wharf at the foot of Whitehead Street," he said. "You'll have no trouble mooring there while the wreckers are out to sea."

"Much obliged." I weighed anchor and followed him into the Key West bight. We kept to the leeward side of a slow moving boat and entered a harbor where the flags of many nations flew from the masts.

The clang of iron, the belching of boilers and the staccato drumming of caulking hammers tinkered with my memory. I had forgotten what a large, vibrant city this was. The Key West air smelt of soot, tar, oakum and seaweed as well as the pungent odor of dead fish and sponges drying in the sun.

A steamship snorted a cloud of insolent black smoke as its hoist lowered huge stacks of lumber onto the wharf. Her rumbling engines were a death knell of sorts for the smaller, slower sailing wooden vessels that rode idly at their moorings. They simply could not compete with steamers on the open seas. One by one, the tall ships of a bygone era were being turned into coal barges towed around by their noses. Nearby, empty handcarts and wagons stood aside, their nags looking forlorn in the shadows of the warehouses.

On the wharf, a mountain of coffee bean sacks towered above the heads of the stevedores laboring to load another steamer. Barrels of molasses were stacked three high. Two men with shotguns stood guard as stevedores carried huge bales of bird plumes from South America up the gangway. The sides of the bales had been stenciled with the name and address of a New York feather merchant. The ship's captain craned his neck over the railing to make sure the valuable plumes were safely aboard.

The busy port echoed with the sound of English, Spanish and French shouted and cussed by sweating seamen, all in counterpoint to the hearty Jamaican sea shanties sung by the black stevedores. Squeals of delight caught my attention and I turned to see bare-chested boys diving off a pier to retrieve coins tossed by the passengers of a schooner. The foppish fashions of the passengers reminded me of how Jesse had dressed when he first arrived and about how much he had changed in the meantime. I had to make things right for him. I couldn't screw up again.

As the *Dead Reckoning* approached the wharf, I put out the fenders, scandalized the gaff-rigged mains'l and back winded the jib to slow her down and glide up to the open berth. She thumped against the pilings and came to rest next to a large schooner with a cargo of New England ice packed in sawdust.

The fisherman, who had piloted me into the harbor, pointed at the Boyles and called out: "If y'all have anything to declare besides them two chickens, the Customs House is on Duval Street."

"Much obliged," I said.

He waved and continued on his way past other fishing boats tugging at their anchors as if eager to sail off. The sight reminded me of something an old fisherman had once said about a 90-pound redfish I had caught:

"Mind what I say, that fish wouldn't have gotten into trouble, if it had kept its big mouth shut."

In this city rife with spies and counterspies, I would have to guard my tongue.

I tied a clove hitch to the mooring post and flaked the sails, when I heard footsteps from behind. Turning, I saw a gaunt, middle-aged man dressed in knickerbockers, a tweed jacket, and a straw hat striding briskly toward me. A trim mustache and sideburns accentuated the sharp plains of his face. He walked stiff-legged, bent forward at the waist as if going uphill, his head hanging low over hunched shoulders, a walking stick in hand.

"This berth belongs to me," he said brusquely. He was a scarecrow of a man with a voice as dry as thatch.

"But that fisherman said—"

I swallowed my words on seeing the fisherman sail out of earshot. I'd forgotten how easy it was to run into trouble in a big city like Key West. I was also tired, not thinking clearly and never questioned the man's claim.

"I'd be much obliged," I said, just to be rid of him, "if I could rent your berth for a day."

I reached into my boot and pulled out some of Doc Raymond's money. The curmudgeon grimaced at seeing where the money had been kept then plucked it out of my hand with two fingers as if holding a dead mouse by its tail. He glanced at the two Boyles, then back at me, and said:

"Twenty four hours is all. This is the berth for one of my wreckers and, after yesterday's storm, I expect her back in port any day with a prize ship."

He stuffed the money in his pocket, wiped his hand on his pant leg and, with a wave of his walking stick, turned on his heels and stalked off.

"Welcome back to Key West, Canfield," Boyle chortled.

I climbed onto the *Dead Reckoning* where the Boyles were lashed to the mast. Their rain slickers dripped puddles on the deck, their hair was matted and they smelt doggy. I released them one at a time but kept their hands bound in front of them.

"Let's go, gents," I said with a wave of my revolver. I had to put this behind me and find P. J. Cornelius fast.

"My leg hurts," Ned said. "I need help."

"Give your pa a hand," I ordered Malachi. The two men struggled to their feet and staggered for a moment until they got their land legs. Ned screwed up his face in a look that was two parts spite, one part puzzlement.

"You're crazier than a coot, you know that," he said. "When y'all get through telling your side of the story to the sheriff, we're going to have our say. Then, it's our word against y'all. Two against one. Two Conchs against one sum-bitch."

Both of them laughed.

"I'm trembling in my boots," I said derisively. But in the back of my mind, I felt a little uneasy. It seemed to me that Ned and Malachi had grown cockier as we approached Key West. I hadn't counted on the fact that they were natives of the island, Conchs. Now I wondered what kind of reception I would get. I prodded the two men in the back with the barrel of the LeMat and said, "Let's go."

Malachi was the first one off the boat. Ned limped along behind him, struggling to keep up as we made our way down Whitehead Street. We passed a ship that had been hauled up on rails to repair her storm damage. The shipwrights scurrying about their business paused and fell silent as we passed. Small boys darted in and out of fences and shrubs to get a better view of my prisoners.

"What y'all lookin' at?" Ned snarled at the rubbernecking boys. "Ain't your ma taught you no good manners? It ain't polite to stare."

"No more gawking, kids," I said. "Run along home."

Just as we reached Jackson Square, a church bell tolled: 10:30 A.M.

In front of us stood the imposing county courthouse and jail. The jail was a steep-roofed, two-story brick building with a wooden annex in the rear for the prisoners' cells. The front door of the building opened onto a lobby where a secretary sat behind a desk. The secretary took one look at the Boyles, smiled in recognition, and disappeared behind a side door that bore the sign "Monroe County Sheriff, D. B. Cappelman." Moments later we were ushered into the sheriff's office. He looked up, took his boots off the top of his desk and shook his head.

Cappelman was a hawk-faced man with salt and pepper hair, a handle bar mustache and a forehead creased by a perpetual scowl. He rubbed his eyes, stretched his arms, cleared his throat and said, "I hope this ain't gonna require paperwork." His drawl was as thick as molasses.

Ned Boyle was quick with an answer. "Nothing to trouble your head about, D.B."

A wry smile tugged at the sides of the sheriff's mustache. It was the cool-eyed smile of someone who saw irony where others saw misfortune.

"Why Ned Boyle," he said, "I ain't seen you in ages."

I did not like the sound of that greeting, no sir, not one bit. Cappelman pushed back his chair and stood. He was tall, solidly built, packing a Remington. The grin on his face snagged when he was half way out of his chair. His raptor eyes focused on me, his probing gaze making me aware of how scruffy I must have looked.

"And just who might y'all be?" he asked.

"The name is Ed Canfield."

Cappelman's gaze shifted to my LeMat. I holstered the gun and laid the Boyle's guns and knife on his desk. Then he folded his arms across his chest, leaned his haunches on the edge of the desk and crossed his legs.

"What's this all about, Ned?"

"Nothin' that the boys and me can't handle—"

"Malachi tried to force himself on a woman," I cut in. "I saw him do it. Then the two of them tried to draw down on me."

The sheriff glanced at me then back at Ned and Malachi. "What have y'all got to say for yo'selves?"

"The man is a bold faced liar," Malachi said.

"He's a nigger lovin' scallywag, too," Ned added.

Cappelman's eyebrows narrowed. He pinched the corners of his mouth with his thumb and index finger.

I gave Ned a fierce stare and leaned forward. Anger twisted my voice into a plaited, coiled whip. I lashed out. "I should have thrown you two skanks over board when I had the chance."

"Easy stranger," Cappelman said. "Y'all got any witnesses to back up your charges?"

He moistened his mustache with his lower lip.

"Not down here. Up at the refugee camp," I said.

"The refugee camp? And just where would this refugee camp be?"

"Up the west coast near Punta Rassa."

I could see where this was going. Nowhere.

Cappelman eased his haunches off his desk, stuck his hands into his back pockets and bowed his head in thought. "Ed, it's Ed, right?"

I nodded but inside I fumed. I had no time for this tripe. I had to get back to the camp.

"Let's you and me talk about this in private." He motioned with his head for me to join him in the inner office, beyond the hearing of the other men.

Out of the corner of my eye, I noticed Ned nudging Malachi as if to say, 'I told you so.' I wanted to hit him over the head with a two-by-four.

Cappelman opened the door to the inner office, a cramped room furnished with a table, two straight back wooden chairs and several filing cabinets. A Union flag stood in one corner, its stripes yellowed from the smoke of countless cigarettes. The jalousies on the street side admitted slats of indifferent light as well as droning mosquitoes. He straddled one chair and gestured to the other. I didn't sit.

"Ed, we got ourselves a little problem here." He threw a hand out as if he were showing a winning poker hand. In this deal, I figured, the cards were marked.

"A problem?" I folded my arms across my chest.

Cappelman scratched a mosquito bite on the back of his neck. "First off, I ain't sure this happened in my jurisdiction. For all I know, y'all might be talking about something that happened in Manatee County. Second, it's your word against theirs. They win two to one."

Ned Boyle had been right. "But," I protested, "he tried to have his way with a young woman by the name of Maureen Foster."

"Maybe so, but without her testimony, my hands are tied."

I shook my head. "You can't be serious."

"Serious as a circuit preacher. Even if it happened in Monroe County, y'all don't have a victim. Y'all don't have any evidence and y'all don't have no eyewitness to back you up."

I thought this kind of crap only happened in the army.

"And to think," I said, "I let those two buzzards live."

Cappelman folded his arms across the back of the chair he straddled. "Since y'all can't back up your charges, I'm going to have to let them two boys go, and when I do, y'all may want to make yourself scarce. They have lots of friends hereabouts and those Conchs stick together like tobacco and spit."

I glanced at the clock on the wall. It was already 10:45 A.M.

"I'm leaving soon enough," I said, "but first I have to find a man by the name of P. J. Cornelius."

"Mister Cornelius?" Cappelman stood slowly; his eyebrows winging up as if seeing me for the first time.

"What business would y'all have with the likes of him?"

"I was told he could provide the medicines we need in the refugee camp."

Cappelman shook his head. "Cornelius can get his hands on just about anything he wants. He owns an auction house, a ships chandlery, four schooners and two wreckers, all sailing under the Union flag. The bastard. "

"Where might I find him?" I asked.

"That's easy," Cappelman said. "Same place he always is—in his office, counting his money. The man's one of the richest people in town, but he'd steal the pennies off a dead man's eyes."

~

Cappelman gave me directions to Cornelius' auction house. I gave him the Boyles' guns and Ned's Arkansas toothpick. Then, bone-weary and disgusted, I left and headed down the street, searching for the auction house.

Turning a corner, I passed a tangerine colored Cuban bodega where idle, old men sipped sherry, puffed on fat cigars, played cards and most likely passed the time of day talking of winds, tides and currents, of fish they'd caught, and of fish that got away. The hot Key West sun had blistered and peeled the bodega's colorful paint leaving it looking as if it were covered with fish scales. In the next alleyway, a gaggle of sweaty men wagered on a cockfight, the birds penned in a small ring leaping at one another with razor sharp talons, wings outstretched, hackles up, pecking, slashing, clawing to the death. The killing put me in mind of the bloodletting at Cedar Keys and I lengthened my stride.

A few doors down, a black woman leaned out the window of her small shack to haggle in Haitian patois over the price of the ewe that a man held by a rope. Two small boys played hoops in the street. Older boys played mumbly peg with their knives. A baby cried. A rooster crowed. It all looked and sounded so insanely normal I couldn't stand it.

I wanted to shout at them, "What are you doing? How can you act so normal? Don't you know people are dying of yellow fever?"

Directly ahead of me I saw a large tin-roofed, unpainted, two-story wood-frame building that seemed to sag under the weight of all its wares. A verandah fronted its street side, and on the other side, weathered planking led down to a splay-legged wharf where a large hoist loomed over the waterfront. The hand-painted sign above the door read: P. J. Cornelius, Auctioneer. I opened the tin-sheathed door and entered a cavernous space that smelt of seaweed, cork, hemp and mold. In the flickering light of oil lamps I saw row upon row of crates, huge bales and naval stores that had been salvaged from sinking ships. Rats scurried in and out of the shadowed rows.

"The auction doesn't start for another hour," a voice barked.

I turned to see a bear of a man step out of the shadows with a shotgun cradled in his hairy arms. I took a step back.

"I'm not here for the auction," I said. "I have urgent business with Mister Cornelius."

The man's black eyes narrowed to slits and I could see the unspoken question in his face: What business would Cornelius have with the likes of me? Then I remembered what Sheriff Cappelman had said about Cornelius' grasping nature.

"I know where there are seven wrecked rebel ships just waiting to be salvaged."

The man's expression softened and he gestured with his shotgun toward a staircase that led to the second floor.

"All right then but be quick about it."

I climbed the stairs two at a time, opened the pebbled glass door and saw a sallow-faced male secretary seated behind a dark mahogany desk. He looked up from his paperwork, raised a disapproving pencil-thin eyebrow and sniffed as if he were a ferret taking my scent. His hair was parted in the middle and pomaded. His white shirt looked crisp and starched and his tie was knotted so tightly around his neck that his lips seemed bloodless.

"Good morning," I said. "Would you tell Mister Cornelius that Ed Canfield is here to see him?"

The man stiffened. "Canfield?" He pronounced the two syllables in my last name as if they were separate words and examined his desk calendar. "I don't show an appointment for a Canfield. How did you get past McSwain?" he asked.

I didn't have time for this officious little paper pusher. But I figured he meant the guard downstairs so I played along. I told him I knew the whereabouts of seven shipwrecks.

"Humph. Wait right here." The secretary spoke as if he were sucking on a piece of horehound candy, pushed back his chair, rose behind his desk, chin in the air, and retreated down a side corridor. I watched him open a door, stick his head inside and speak in a muffled tone to its occupant.

The secretary abruptly turned on his heels and marched back down the hallway.

"Mister Cornelius will see you now." Without actually looking at me, he clicked his heels together, bent at the waist and gave a sweeping gesture toward the office door.

"Thank you." I brushed past him and walked down the corridor. Cornelius greeted me at the door, and with a start, I realized he was the same man who had just charged me for using his berth. He recognized me, too.

"You again," he scowled, blocking the door. "I thought this was about some shipwrecks."

"That's right, seven shipwrecks," I said.

He spied the LeMat on my hip and paused. Then his greed got the best of him and he opened the door slightly. I stepped into an office that must have been the size of my cabin in Cedar Keys. Behind a huge desk sat an armchair with damask upholstery and next to it a pair of floor-to-ceiling bookshelves stacked with leather bound volumes.

The desktop was clear except for a green blotter, ink well and pen, a brass desk lamp, a file folder and an ashtray. The walls were studded with oil lamps. It looked as if Cornelius was accustomed to burning the midnight oil. The hardwood floor gleamed. To the left of the door, an oriental accent rug lay beneath a couch and an ottoman. Above the couch hung an oil painting of Cornelius and an older man, possibly his father. The older man had the same beak-like nose and hooded black eyes as Cornelius.

"You have a splendid office, sir," I said.

"Trappings of the trade," he replied matter-of-factly.

His nostrils flared and he reached into his vest pocket, removed a silver box and put a pinch of snuff in his nose to mask the smell of my clothes. "Now what's this about seven shipwrecks?"

Apparently, he was not a man given to small talk. Just as well. I needed to get back to the camp. As he sat down behind his desk, a small black dog leapt from the kneehole onto Cornelius' lap. He stroked the dog and eyed me. In the stony silence, I could hear the dog licking its paws.

Two upholstered visitors' chairs sat in front of the desk and between them stood an etched glass globe on a brass stand. Without thinking, I spun the globe to find the outline of Florida's coast.

"Careful," Cornelius snapped. "That's a genuine Waterford crystal." He paused for effect. "Imported from Ireland."

I stopped the spinning globe. "Mister Cornelius," I said, "I do know the whereabouts of some shipwrecks but first I have more urgent business to discuss with you."

He arched an eyebrow. "More urgent business?" What I said had peaked his curiosity. He stopped stroking the dog and gestured for me to have a seat. I remained standing.

"Just what brings you here?"

"Doctor Raymond sent me to see you," I said.

Cornelius stiffened. The dog's ears perked up.

"What is Don Quixote up to this time?" he asked with an air of exasperation.

"Who?"

"My brother-in-law, Doctor Raymond."

Brother in-law? Doc must have been the ship's surgeon on one of Cornelius' ships.

"What windmills is he tilting at these days?" Cornelius hitched his chair up closer to the knee well of his desk.

"I don't know anything about any windmills," I said. "But your brother-in-law's life is in danger. He is in a refugee camp near Punta Rassa where yellow fever has broken out.

On hearing me say "yellow fever," Cornelius stiffened, and squirmed back on his chair, but I kept on talking.

"Doc is trying to treat the sick and dying but he's running low on medical supplies."

I reached in my pocket for the note from Doc. "He said you could lay your hands on what he needs."

Cornelius' boney fingers crabbed across the desk and picked up the note. He shook his head, adjusted his gold-framed reading spectacles on the bridge of his nose and read. Watching him, I got the distinct impression that he was the kind of man who couldn't sleep well at night unless he'd gotten the better of someone that day.

He removed his glasses and asked, "Do you have any idea what these supplies go for on the black market?" His voice spiked and the dog leapt off his lap and hid under the kneehole.

"No, sir," I said. "But Doc Raymond said you would move heaven and earth to get them."

"He would say that." He smoothed the corners of his mustache, looked at me and said, "How did you get here from Punta Rassa?"

"I ran the Union blockade."

Cornelius' eyebrows winged up. "You ran the blockade? You and who else?"

"Just me and my LeMat." I patted the butt of my revolver.

"What about the Boyles?"

He just let slip that he knew the Boyles.

"They tried to shanghai the wrong man."

"I see," he nodded. His black eyes clouded over. He sighed and added, "Very well. Be at my house at five this evening and you will have your supplies, Mister—"

"Canfield. Ed Canfield. There's just one other thing," I said.

"Yes?"

"I'm going to need some supplies for my boat, too. She took some damage during the storm."

"What sort of damage?" He rolled his eyes.

"She needs some caulking, some shrouds."

"And you expect me to supply them just because I own the ships chandlery?"

"Like I said, sir, Doc Raymond—"

"Yes, yes," he muttered, "Doc Raymond. You'll have your supplies. Now what's this about seven shipwrecks?"

"I just came from Cedar Keys where the Yanks sunk seven blockade runners in their berths."

"Cedar Keys," he snorted. "I know all about Cedar Keys. My sources told me about it before the attack began."

Sources? More likely spies.

"Where do you think my wreckers are now?" he asked.

I shrugged. No sense irritating the one man who could help me.

"Very well," he said with a dismissive wave of the hand. "Go. Go to the ships chandlery and speak to Peter Kearns. Be at my home at five o'clock sharp for your medicine. And not a word of this to anyone."

"Thank you," I said. I wiped my hand on my shirt and reached out to shake his hand, but he ignored the gesture and stuck Doc Raymond's note in his pocket instead.

As I turned to leave, I noticed that the back of Cornelius' office door held a full-length mirror in which he could see himself while seated at his desk. All the while we had been talking, he had been observing his own performance in the mirror. He was a man accustomed to playing many roles, a chameleon of sorts. His kind weren't fussy about the truth.

What kind of hold could Doc Raymond have on his cagey brother-in-law?

Once out on the street, I put the thought out of my mind, squared my shoulders, threw back my head and lengthened my stride, heading for the local newspaper, the *New Era*. I had to know what had happened after I left Cedar Keys.

~

The newspaper said most of the damage to Cedar Keys occurred in and around the harbor. It did not mention my still. I sighed and turned to another big story: *Deser-*

tions Spike In Confederate Ranks. Upwards of 11 percent of rebel soldiers were running off; and some were hiding in the Everglades where they preyed upon civilians. I had my doubts about the story because the *New Era* was pro-Union, but I kept my thoughts to myself and asked the publisher to recommend a place to eat. The last thing I had tasted was a belch but I wanted to avoid my old drinking holes and the temptation to get liquored up. He directed me to the Green Parrot tavern.

As I approached the tavern, I saw two men seated in front of it, slouched down on a slat board bench, taking in the sun, talking to each other out of the sides of their mouths while watching passersby like hawks. One of the men smoked a corncob pipe; the other whittled a stick. Seeing me approach with a LeMat on my hip, they fell silent as gravestones, their eyes fixed straight ahead as I crossed the street in their direction.

From inside the tavern, the sound of music and laughter and hoots and loud oaths reached my ears. I figured some wreckers were celebrating the taking of another prize ship, possibly the one being auctioned off by Cornelius in an hour. One drunk led the others on his banjo in a hearty rendition of a wrecker's song:

"When we come long-side to find she's bilged,
We know just what to do—
Save the cargo that we can,
The sails and rigging too."

The place exploded in raucous laughter, shouts and hollers and calls for another round of drinks. I reached the wooden sidewalk in front of the tavern and was about to enter when the batwing doors blew open and out flew a drunk. He stumbled out into the street and fell head first into a puddle. The two men on the bench slapped their knees and laughed. I decided to eat somewhere else—in a place where Trouble didn't hang his hat.

I'd gone less than a block when it started to rain. I ducked inside the Mooring Post, a wind-weathered two-story tavern that had obviously been cobbled together with the flotsam from numerous shipwrecks. On the first floor, a twenty-foot long mahogany bar with a brass footrest and brass spittoons ran along one wall. To the right of the bar, a beaded curtain covered the entrance to the kitchen and the staircase that lead to a second floor. A sign on the wall read, "Rooms rented by the hour." Five greasy oil lamps cast their turbid light across the card tables in the rear of the tavern. Further back, the sawdust-covered floor canted like the deck of a listing vessel. There were only two windows—both too small to throw a body out—straddling a door that opened on stairs that led down to the wharf.

As they drank, the listless men on the barstools kept one eye on the reflections in the cracked mirror above the bar. They looked up furtively at my image in the mirror then went back to their drinking. The air in the tavern was hot and muggy. The place reeked of Cuban cigars, stale beer and sweat. The cigar smoke drifted neck-high around the customers, forming currents and eddies on the surface of the conversations like spawn on a scummy pond. The smoke burned my eyes.

Rain hammered the tin roof and the wind rapped its fingers on the windowpanes. The seamen raised their voices to be heard above the din. I made my way to the bar, looking to get something to eat.

"Dadgum, here he is now," I heard a familiar voice say above the noise.

I glanced at one of the card tables and saw Ned and Malachi Boyle sitting there, glowering at me. My heart skipped a beat. Ned knocked back his drink in one, quick gulp, laid his cards on the table and cracked his knuckles.

The man behind the bar saw what was about to happen and signaled anxiously for the piano player to start banging out the "The Star Spangled Banner." No one stood at attention. The musician shifted seamlessly to "God Save the South." Still, no one stood.

I should have bolted then and there, but for some reason I didn't. Maybe I was just too tired to run. Maybe I was feeling a little too cocky after getting the best of the Boyles on my boat. Maybe it was just knowing I had the LeMat on my hip. Whatever the reason, I turned to face the two

Boyles, one of my boots hitched on the brass footrest, both elbows leaning on the bar, the fingers of my shooting hand brushing the grip of the LeMat.

The barkeep wiped his hands on his apron and said, "Fellers, no one wins if the sheriff is called."

Ned ignored him, belched, and patted Malachi on the knee as if to say he could handle this by himself. Then he pushed away from the card table, hitched up his pants, and came toward me, still limping. He was shorter than me but twenty pounds heavier, most of it muscle. I started to have second thoughts about this. It brought back memories of all the scrapes I had gotten into in saloons like this and how they always had ended up with me in trouble with the brass. I had no time for this. I had to get back to the refugee camp. I began to edge toward the door, when someone grabbed my shoulders from behind and shoved me toward Boyle.

"Well, well, well," Ned said to the entire room, "I do declare. If it ain't Ed Canfield."

All eyes snapped toward us. Several gamblers pushed away from the table and Malachi stood on the seat of his chair to get a better look.

"Please fellers," the barkeep said, "Not in here. Not another fight."

Ned came closer. The pianist played "Dixie". The barkeep tried to distract Boyle.

"Hey, Ned," he said. "Have one on me." He reached across the bar and handed a bottle of rum to Ned.

Boyle grabbed the bottle by its neck and turned it upside down, as if it were a club; then held it out so that the rum slopped onto the floor, forming a sawdust slurry. With Boyle distracted, I used the toe of my boot to ease the brass spittoon into his path.

"Canfield," he said, "you and I have some unfinished business to attend to. How's about we settle it now?"

The room erupted in cheers from the other men. They immediately started wagering.

"How's about we don't," I said.

Boyle rushed me with the rum bottle poised to strike, tripped over the brass spittoon and stumbled, face forward, flailing at the air. My first punch caught him on the nose; the second drove wrist-deep into his gut. He dropped the bottle, staggered backward, holding his nose and slipping on the wet sawdust. I sprang at him, driving another fist deep into the man's exposed gut. I felt the whoosh of his boozy breath; saw the white of his eyes. I swung for his gut again but this time I hit something hard, unyielding—a belt buckle. White-hot pain shot straight through my fist. I grabbed my hand.

Boyle hammered me in the jaw. I stumbled back, lost my balance. Boyle hit me again and I fell. He leapt on my back, strangling me with his huge, callused hands. I gasped for air. My neck muscles bulged with the effort to breathe. I couldn't break the heavier man's grip. I brought my head back sharply and cracked Boyle squarely on the jaw. He fell off me. I rolled over on my back just as he regained his feet and pounced. I caught him in mid-air with a straight leg to the rib cage. Something cracked. Boyle groaned, his face turned ashen and he fell to the ground, clutching his stomach, gasping for air, puking.

I jumped to my feet just as Malachi threw back his chair. Out of the corner of my eye, I saw the barkeep cock his arm as if to throw something. A shot glass. In the split second it took for me to think, "He's done this before," he chucked that glass with all his might. Right at my head. Everything went black.

CHAPTER NINE

It began with a headache, a throbbing, pounding, mind-numbing *rat-a-tat-tat* that felt like the beat of a drum. I struggled to find my way out of the mental fog of pain, opened my eyes, blinked and lifted my head. My blood-matted hair stuck fast to the mattress. When I pulled away, a searing pain spiked through the side of my skull. I moaned, eased myself into a sitting position, feet on the stone floor. I felt the back of my head. My hand came away bloody. I wasn't dreaming.

The drumming grew louder. I looked around for its source and saw and *smelled* that I was in the brig, not in the county jail, but in the brig. I thought I must be dreaming but the headache felt all too real. I was in one of two holding cells just inside the main gate of Fort Zachary Taylor. Three uniformed cellmates stood on their tiptoes, craning their necks to see out a barred window abuzz with flies drawn to a slop bucket in the corner. I rose slowly and, with one hand on the clammy cell wall, made my way to the window and peered out through the bars toward the parade ground. The rain had stopped. There were no puddles. I must have been out for awhile. The scene in front of me put me in mind of the first time I had been locked up in here . . .

It was the summer of 1859, six months after I'd been posted to Key West. The rotgut food in the commissary was so wormy that I held a one-man protest in which I grabbed the cook by the scruff of his neck and shoved his head into a pot of what he had called boiled mush. My commanding officer did not appreciate my table manners and sent me to the brig. It would become a familiar haunt.

Now, on the parade ground, the drumbeat warped into the sound of a military band playing the "Dead March". I looked on as a small procession filed past my window, led by a doleful looking, Bible-clutching parson dressed in black. In the unforgiving Key West sun, he sweated profusely.

Next, a prisoner in leg irons shuffled into view, his shadow lagging behind him. Two soldiers followed him, their rifles on their shoulders. Behind them came pallbearers carrying a coffin, which looked to be an empty rifle box. The solemn group made its way between a large number of Yankee soldiers formed up in an open square. They stopped within view of my cell.

My mental fog lifted as I realized I was about to witness an execution. I remembered Quill's warning about what might happen if I was caught in Key West. I wondered what had become of Captain Brannan. I thought of the Yankee gunboat that I had drawn onto the shoal. I asked myself what kind of punishment I might expect at the hands of the Yanks.

When the prisoner reached a wooden post, the provost cantered into view, mounted on a skittish black stallion. The music stopped. A shiver of sweat wormed its way down my spine. The prisoner turned to face the mounted officer. A twelve-man firing squad stood at parade rest, their rifle butts on the ground, their barrels inclining slightly backward against their right shoulders, hands crossed on the gunstocks. To their side stood a sergeant, his sword touching the ground, his left hand cupped over the right.

The provost read the charge—spying for the Confederacy—and asked the prisoner if he had anything to say.

The condemned man replied:

"Yes, I do. I am ready to die for the Confederacy. But facing my Maker as I do, I realize that duty and honor are not enough to attain eternal glory. I must rid my heart of all rancor and desire for vengeance. So I forgive you blue belly Yankee bastards. Step closer, men. Aim straight and true. Don't make a mess of it."

The man's courage stunned me.

The chaplain approached with his Bible, spoke for a moment, stepped back. A soldier came forward, rope and mask in hand. The prisoner was blind folded, tied to the post. The sergeant ordered the firing squad to, "Shoulder arms." Then, without a moment's hesitation, he barked the command:

"Ready, aim, fire."

Twelve rifles roared in unison, their bullets slapping into the prisoner's frail torso. His body jerked, he cried out in pain, his moan swallowed up in the sound of gunfire echoing off the walls of the fort. His knees buckled and he slumped to the ground at the foot of the post.

"Order, arms," the sergeant snapped.

The firing squad brought their rifles down to their sides. The tang of gunpowder burned my nose. I glanced at the sergeant and saw him smirk. A doctor stepped forward, placed a silver-plated stethoscope on the man's chest and declared him dead. Then the doctor backed away and nodded to the commanding officer. On a signal from him, the pallbearers came forward, untied the dead man and placed him in the coffin.

"Right face, march," the sergeant bellowed.

The firing squad marched past the lifeless body as the band struck up a dirge. The entire assembly followed in their footsteps.

I was so intent on watching the grisly spectacle that I didn't hear the jangling of a key ring, the clunk of the turning lock and the groan of the rusty cell door yawning wide.

"Damn it, Canfield," a gruff voice said, "You got cotton in your ears?"

I turned to see a duty guard holding open my cell door.

"Let's go," he said.

I took two steps toward him, staggered and he grabbed me by the elbow. I wobbled then stiffened and steadied myself by leaning on the duty guard until I got my legs under me.

"My head hurts something fierce."

"That may be the least of your worries," the duty guard said as he handcuffed me and nudged me through the cell door.

"Where are we going?" I asked, not sure I wanted to hear the answer.

"You are going to Commander Hill's office," the guard said.

Commander Hill? Not Brannan?

"What for? I'm a civilian, not a soldier."

"You'll find out soon enough."

My mind reeled with the possibility that I might face a firing squad, too. I tugged on the handcuffs and reached in my pocket to finger the lucky wood chip Jesse had given me. Stooping, we entered a tunnel-like passageway lit only by flickering lanterns. The slimy cobblestones felt slippery underfoot; the rank air burned my lungs; cobwebs brushed my face. A few feet outside the passageway, the duty guard stopped in front of another private. They exchanged salutes.

"He's all yours," the duty guard said.

"Very good," the new private replied. He was a raw-boned, hatchet-faced man with leathery skin, blood shot eyes and the haunted look of a man who's "seen the elephant," the soldiers' term for a heavy battle.

He opened a door to the outside and said, "This way." As soon as the door closed behind us, his expression changed and he looked me over, head to toe. "Canfield, you wouldn't be any relation to Ed Canfield, would you?"

Surprised, I said, "One and the same."

"Well, as I live and breathe." He squinted at me with rheumy eyes, the color of pond water. "That's what I thought. It's just that your face is bruised and swollen. I'm George Ramsey. Remember me? I was garrisoned here with you after the dust up in Mexico."

I looked at him again but couldn't place the face. Heavy drinking had erased many a memory of those days. He saw the confusion in my eyes and said:

"No matter, I still remember you and some of your antics." He chuckled at some private memory and added, "You were one crazy sum-bitch."

"So they say." I scratched the back of my ear.

He laughed again and said, "I can still see the look on Will Claussen's face when you caught him cheating."

Will Claussen.

Now that was a name I remembered. I still had his teeth marks in my knuckles.

Ramsey motioned for me to continue walking. "You must be crazy as ever to sail in here on a rebel boat."

"I'm no rebel, leastways not that kind of rebel."

"Well, who or what are you fighting for?"

"The people in the refugee camp near Punta Rassa. They're fighting yellow fever. I came here to get the medicine they need."

"And you were going to go back into that contagion?" He shook his head. "Like I said, you must be crazy."

"What time is it?" I asked.

"Close to 1500 hours," he said. "But I wouldn't bother my head about the time, not in here."

We turned a corner and he led the way across the parade ground of the fort. The slanting rays of the sun skimmed the surface of the fortress walls to cast a murky shadow over the massive casements. Off to my left, I saw soldiers responding to recall from fatigue duty. Geese, ducks and chickens scurried to get out of their way.

On the right, I saw three soldiers being disciplined in a way that was all too familiar to me. They were gagged and seated on the ground with their hands and feet bound, their knees drawn up, their arms passed around them. A rod had been inserted, horizontal to the ground, between the arms and backs of the knees. It was called the buck and gag.

Private Ramsey saw the men, too, and said, "It's an easy way to dry out the drunks."

"Easy on who?" I said.

Ahead of us, a small stand of fruit trees had been planted in the center of the parade ground to provide welcome shade as well as fresh fruit. We cut through the trees and I picked an orange and stuffed it my pocket. I wanted to rid my mouth of the sour taste of my own blood. A small boy saw me pluck the orange and ran off to tell someone.

"One of the officers' kids," Ramsey grumbled. "The snot-nosed monsters think they can order us all around."

He pointed out some of the newer features of the fort, the ones that had been added after I was drummed out of the service.

"That there's our new barracks off to the right," he said. "Enlisted men on the second level, officers on the third."

"Where is Brannan?" I asked.

"Long gone. He's a Lieutenant Colonel now," Ramsey said, "in charge of the Department of the South."

My heart sank. "He isn't here?"

"Hell no. None of them commanders stays for long. Since Brannan left a year ago, we've had French and Hill. Far as I'm concerned, no one should be expected to stay here more than six months. If yellow fever, malaria or dysentery don't kill you, the heat most surely will."

"What about you?" I asked. "You were here when I was."

"Just my luck," he said. "They sent me back here after I was demoted."

"Demoted?"

"They said I was a straggler on account of my not being in a big hurry to die. I got three months to go." He pointed to another building and said, "That there's the new sutler. The man's crooked as a dog's hind leg. Charges whatever price he damn well pleases for victuals so long as the officers get their cut."

We turned to the left and proceeded past the stable, smithy, the magazine, artillery shed and a cistern.

"Still only two fresh water wells on the island?" I asked.

He jerked a thumb toward the cisterns. "The fort now has 40 cisterns to capture the run off during the rainy season. We have to make sure it lasts all year. Trouble is some of the cisterns are taking on salt water. That stench you smell comes from the tidal flush latrines. They don't work none too good during low tide. I tell you this place is a real shit hole."

"Tell me about it," I said.

We entered a narrow passageway in the fortress wall and he opened a door. I followed him into the room and he shut the door behind us. It was a small, windowless space with a desk, two camp chairs and a wooden filing cabinet. A side door led to an inner office and, after telling me to have a seat, he disappeared into the other room. Moments later the inner door opened and Ramsey said:

"Someone else is with the commander now. You'll wait in here."

I stood, walked past Ramsey and entered a rectangular-shaped office, an unkempt workspace with a large, file-stacked desk, a brass spittoon sitting on the floor and three deck chairs that must have been salvaged from a shipwreck. The only light and air came from an iron-barred window that opened on the interior of the fort. A telescope stood in one corner to the right of the desk and a parrot cage in the other. The parrot announced my entrance with a loud squawk. The soldier seated at the desk looked up; Private Ramsey handed him some papers and left.

The nameplate on the desk read, "First Sergeant Wheaton." He was a short, rotund man, the wrong physical dimensions for the standard issue army uniform, which came in only two sizes. His blouse strained at the buttonholes and his double chin chafed at the wool collar where a heat rash mottled his sagging flesh. His kinky black hair was parted in the middle and bristled at his neck like a hog's back. He waved a weary hand toward a chair and mumbled something that I took to mean 'have a seat.' I remained on my feet. The parrot squawked as if in surprise at my refusal to obey an order.

While Wheaton studied my papers, his prickly eyebrows moved up and down with astonishment. He pulled at his lower chin with his thumb and index finger and glanced up several times.

"You actually volunteered to run the blockade by yourself?" Wheaton asked.

I was amazed that he knew that about me but simply said, "Yes, sir."

He shook his head and chuckled to himself. "You're in a peck of trouble."

He gazed at the papers again while nonchalantly opening his desk drawer to remove a piece of hardtack, which he held up in his hand. The parrot cocked its head, hung upside down from his cage and took the food in his beak. Wheaton rested his elbows on his desk and steepled his fingers. The parrot squawked and Wheaton held up another piece of hardtack, this one just beyond the bird's reach.

"What do you say?"

A brief pause and then the parrot squawked, "Worm castle. Worm castle."

With a porcine laugh, Wheaton gave the parrot the hardtack. "Even he knows this hardtack ain't fit for human beings." Then he picked up a file folder, fanned himself and said, "But you know all about the wormy food here. Ain't that right?"

I was about to say something when the door behind Wheaton flew open and Ned Boyle stepped out. His face was brick red; his bulbous lips the color of mortar. His right eye was black and his nose was swollen. We exchanged angry glances. He sneered and stormed off, leaving me to wonder:

What in hell was Boyle doing in there?

Wheaton hauled himself out from behind his desk and disappeared into the office that Boyle had just left.

Moments later, Wheaton stuck his head out the door and signaled for me to enter Commander Hill's office. To my surprise, the room was sparsely furnished, Spartan-like. Just a desk, several cane bottom chairs, a plank table, a few filing cabinets and a Union flag.

Commander Hill did not see me enter the room. He and a soldier stared out the window at the parade ground where the man had just been shot for spying.

"Do you suppose, sergeant," Commander Hill asked, "that the man ever learned he had traded his life for counterfeit graybacks?" His dentures lent a mechanical sound to his speech, each phrase ending with a click as if a bullet had been chambered.

"All we know, sir," the officer replied, "is that we caught him selling the plans for 'Anaconda.'"

"What a waste of a human life."

Hill reached over and closed the window shutters. The two men turned to look at a large map spread out on the commander's desk. Hill was a block-jawed man with a well-trimmed goatee, broad shoulders and the erect military bearing of someone who has his eye on a higher office. The marine was shorter, leaner with a spade beard and thick sideburns. Hill looked upset by what he had just witnessed.

"'Anaconda,'" Hill said. "That's what Winfield Scott calls his paper blockade. I call it folly." He jabbed an angry finger into the hollow of his palm.

"Yes sir," the soldier replied.

"Tell me Sergeant Murphy," Hill continued, "how is the navy supposed to blockade the entire coast of Florida—1,200 miles of coastline, not to mention,106 rivers, inlets, islands and the Godforsaken Everglades? Tell me how are we supposed to do that with only 79 steamers and 42 sailing ships?"

Sergeant Murphy shook his head and answered in a thick Irish brogue:

"Jeff Davis and Stephen Mallory are mocking us, sir. *The New York Tribune* is calling us a laughing stock." He paused as his lip curled into a mongrel's sneer. "But they'll eat their words after they hear what we did to Cedar Keys."

I saw black. I recognized the sergeant's gravely voice. He was the same man who had set fire to the hammock, the same man who had given the command to shoot the spy. I sucked in a quick breath of fresh air to snuff out the fire burning in my chest.

"The British are behind this," Commander Hill said. "I'm told there are more steamships flying the rebel flag in Liverpool's harbor than in any southern port."

"We'll catch the limey bastards, sir," Sergeant Murphy said.

Hill pounded the desk with his fist. "Really? What about Damien Quill? I was told you had killed the man at Cedar Keys and now this."

Murphy squirmed. "We sunk his ship in her berth, sir. But he managed to escape. The man is a cat. He has nine lives."

"And his present whereabouts?"

"Somewhere near Punta Rassa."

"Yes, and he's replaced the blockade runner you sank with one of our own, the *Argonaut.* I want the man captured and hung from the highest yardarm as a pirate. Is that understood? Do I make myself plain?"

"Yes, sir."

Hill sighed, shook his head, looked up and saw Wheaton and me. Several seconds passed while he took my measure. With a wave of his hand, he dismissed Wheaton, who snapped a salute, clicked his heels, spun around and left the room. Hill slumped down in his chair and fixed me with a steely gaze. My head ached so much I had trouble meeting his stare.

"So you're the one who Boyle accuses of being a blockade runner."

I felt as if I'd been clubbed from behind.

He laughed and winked at the marine. He was toying with me. "Well, you did have the audacity to sail the *Sea Ranger* into my port."

"My boat isn't a blockade runner," I said. "She flies the stars and stripes and her name is—"

"Sir," he said. "When you address me, you will use the word 'sir'. Is that understood?"

"Yes, sir. It's a workboat by the name of *Dead Reckoning*. Ask anyone in Cedar Keys. They'll tell you."

"Cedar Keys has been wiped off the map," Murphy said.

I loathed the man but my expression never changed. I wouldn't give him the satisfaction of seeing how I felt.

Hill leaned forward in his chair, his arms folded and resting on his desk, watching for my reaction. "Let's cut to the quick," he said. "Your reputation precedes you. I know all about your war record and how many lives you saved in Texas and Mexico. But then you ran amuck down here and got yourself court-martialed. If it had not been for Brannan's testimony—"

"They would have thrown away the key," I said.

"True enough. Brannan also said you were fearless and would wear a bright red shirt into battle."

"If I took a bullet to the chest, I didn't want the enemy to have the satisfaction of seeing blood on my shirt."

"Yes, and you made yourself an easy target, too. Tell me, Canfield, do you know the difference between being fearless and reckless?"

"Sir?"

Hill's eyes narrowed. "Ned Boyle tells me you're the one who lured the USS *Argonaut* onto a sandbar."

Hellfire and damnation! Boyle was selling more than charcoal.

"Your reckless actions endangered a Union warship and the lives of her entire crew." Hill paused then added, "I consider that an act of war."

"It seems to me the *Argonaut*'s master was the reckless one," I said.

Hill gave a scornful sideways glance to Murphy who hitched his shoulders as if flinching.

"As I see it," Hill said, "you ran her aground where she would fall into rebel hands."

"Rebel hands? That wasn't my doing."

"Really? What a strange coincidence." Hill leaned back, looked out the window then spun back to face me. When he spoke, his words were as hard as forged steel. "After you ran the *Argonaut* aground, rebels drove off the ship's crew, repaired the damage and sailed her down the coast where they met up with your friend, the infamous Captain Damien Quill."

Friend?

"Ned Boyle tells me you and Quill sail together." The commander's eyes turned stone cold.

"I knew him as Matthew Smith, not as Quill. He was a stowaway on our boat. He said he was from Lloyd's of London."

Hill whisked the air with his left hand, dismissing this explanation as if it were a pesky mosquito. "Where is Quill now?" he demanded.

"I have no idea," I said. "He took off as soon as we reached the refugee camp."

Hill pushed back his chair and came around the front of his desk. He stood within three feet of me.

"Ned Boyle also tells me that you had a falling out with Quill and that you stampeded a herd of cattle that he was about to ship to Cuba."

"Boyle has been swilling too much bark juice," I said. "I stumbled on the place where the rebels board their cattle for Cuba."

"So you did stampede them?"

"By accident."

"And that would have been somewhere near Punta Rassa, correct?"

He glanced at Murphy who nodded.

"Right," I said. "Near Charlotte Harbor." No sense telling them the exact location.

"Ned Boyle is unable to pinpoint the location on this map, but he says you can."

Hill pointed to the large map on his table.

I looked at the map and said, "It isn't on any chart, but I can find it. I have to find it. That's where the refugees are."

"Quill knows that section of the coast like the back of his hand," Commander Hill said. "He's been sailing in and out of the Everglades whenever he wants. Now the limey has command of a steamship and there is no telling what he'll do."

"Those are treacherous waters, especially for a ship that size," I said. "He has to be an able seaman."

Sergeant Murphy rankled at my statement, widened his stance and clasped his hands behind his back.

"We're not talking about some swashbuckling romantic war hero," Murphy said. "Quill isn't fighting for the South. Our spies tell us that he is running cotton, tobacco and cattle down to Cuba and returning with a boatload of geegaws, fancy hats, perfume and rum. He's told his crew of cutthroats that cognac commands a higher price than the chloroform needed for the soldiers."

"Quill is a ruthless freebooter," Commander Hill added. "When you stampeded his cattle, you made yourself a dangerous enemy. He is just as fearless as you are and he has a long memory."

"He should be returning from Cuba any day now," Sergeant Murphy said. "We want to put our marines ashore and set a trap for him. To do that, we need you to lead us to his camp."

"Hold on," I said to Hill. "I've seen enough blood shed."

"Sir!" Commander Hill barked. "You will address me as 'sir'."

"Sir," I stammered. My head hurt too much to be playing these word games. "All I aim to do is reach the refugee camp with the medicine the doctor needs while there is still time."

"On one of our steamers, you will reach your destination safely," Commander Hill said. "Without our help, you run the risk of being sunk by us or by Quill. Of course, if you don't cooperate, there is always the possibility of being charged as a Confederate blockade runner or even as a spy."

Spy!

I thought fast. If I said yes, I could be caught in the crossfire between the federal warship and Quill's *Argonaut.* If I said no, I could be hung or shot like the spy I had just seen executed on the parade ground. I had to make them think I would cooperate. I had to get the medicine back to the camp.

"How fast can you be ready?" I asked.

Commander Hill flashed a well-satisfied smile at Sergeant Murphy then looked back at me. "I'll speak to the Admiral McKean this very day. We'll have a ship coaled, provisioned and her crew mustered and ready to sail as soon as possible."

"Good," I said, knowing full well, I would be long gone by then. If I left early the next morning, they wouldn't be able to overtake me before I reached Florida's Ten Thousand Islands. Along that section of the coast, the shallow waters favored a smaller, flat bottom boat like mine.

They removed the handcuffs and I used a pencil from Commander Hill's desk to draw a circle on the map around a section of Boca Grande. "That's where we're headed," I said. But, of course, it wasn't. I was steering them toward the shallows.

"Now if you'll excuse me," I said, "I have to get some supplies and provisions."

The clock on the wall read 4:30 P.M. I had to meet Cornelius within thirty minutes. Out of habit, I knuckled a salute and left quickly, escorted across the parade ground by a guard. This time I noticed another soldier spread-eagled and tied down to a wagon wheel. He was burning in the hot sun like a pig roasting on an open pit, another reminder of how the federal army dealt with its prisoners. The slightest misstep and that could be me. Again.

~

After leaving the fort's main gate, the sally port, I reached into my pocket for the orange I had plucked from the tree. I peeled and ate it as I crossed the huge wooden causeway that connected the fort to the island. A gust of wind brought the fetid smell of the tannery on the edge of town to my senses. I wrinkled my nose, turned downwind and soon came upon a rutted, white-shelled street called Johnny Cake Row.

The street was fronted by whorehouses built in the style of shotgun shacks with a long hallway running from the front door to the back and small rooms on either side. Most of the shacks were as shabby and derelict as their owners. A drunken sailor slept in an alley and in the middle of the street a mangy dog chased its tail in circles. A rooster crowed. A floozy stepped out of the shadows, coyly twirled her tattered parasol and cracked a toothy smile. Sin was getting an early start on an evening's work.

"Say there, sailor," she slurred in a whiskey voice, "you look like you could use some horizontal refreshment." Her beeswax had already begun to melt in the hot sun and her skin appeared to be gelatinous, peeling away to reveal the ravages of pox. A small girl in a soiled flour sack dress, stood behind her, sucking on her thumb, silent as a shadow. The whore offered me her opium pipe but I stuck my hands in my pockets, shook my head and stepped aside. She flipped me a mock salute in anger and I continued on at a fast pace to the respectable part of town.

I soon reached a neighborhood where the homes were more substantial and enveloped by a wide range of exotic tropical plants, fruit-bearing trees and colorful vines. Huge banyan trees dangled their prop roots from thick, gray limbs; graceful palms trees swayed in the sea breeze which had bent and twisted them over time; banana trees held out their luscious fruit; multi-colored bougainvillea, wisteria and other flowers wove their way up the sides of verandahs to impart a welcoming fragrance.

I turned onto Front Street, alive with the sound of farm wagons, surreys, buckboards and vendors; then I walked two blocks to the east. The homes in this section were large, rambling structures painted stark white, many of them two stories high with verandahs and captains' walks on their roofs. They had been built by ships' carpenters, rather than by architects, using mahogany stripped from countless shipwrecks, and in a gingerbread style unique to the island. Some of these homeowners had grown wealthy by renting their slaves to the government for building the very fort in which Union soldiers now held sway over their island. Many of them flew Confederate flags in defiance of the Union occupying force.

I wove my way in and out of the pedestrians, and down streets where chickens wandered freely, unfazed by the passersby. Reaching the corner of Green Street, I continued on to William Street, and then headed east for a block until I came to the address Cornelius had given me. I paused at his white picket fence to collect my thoughts and take in the imposing two-story wood-frame house. It stood back from the street on coral pillars, its front entrance wreathed by red bougainvillea and violet wisteria. The ornate columns trimmed with intricately carved wood molding supported wrap-around porches on both levels. The roof was steeply slanted to shed the semi-tropical rains; its wood shingles protruded over the upper windows as if frowning down on my ragged appearance.

When I crossed the footpath to the house, a peacock squawked a warning at my approach, then turned its tail in a sweeping arc and walked off slowly, majestically with an air of stiff-necked indifference that might have bordered on disdain. The steps to the front porch squeaked under my weight.

Chapter Nine

A dog growled inside the house. I knocked. Another growl. Another knock. A sudden yelp followed by hurried footsteps that clicked across a hardwood floor.

A cautious black hand pulled back the drapery on the front window affording me a brief glimpse of a drawing room furnished in dark wood, brocade chairs and an upright piano. I smiled at the stern looking black woman inside.

"What y'all want?" the woman called out. Her voice held enough starch for a week's worth of laundry.

I stepped back into the afternoon sunlight the better to be seen from the window. "I have an appointment with Mister Cornelius."

A pause. Then the front door opened a crack, the chain link lock still in place. Shadows concealed all but the black woman's suspicious eyes. "Who be calling?"

"The name is Ed Canfield."

Her eyes looked as black as a root cellar and just as cold. She removed the chain link lock and opened the door just wide enough to admit me.

"Wait here, suh." Then she turned and disappeared down a hallway. I took a shallow breath and eyed myself in the ornately framed wall mirror. The light from the crystal chandelier hanging above my head revealed every bruise on my face. My right eye was swollen and my cheek was black and blue.

To my left, I saw a paneled gaming room in which an enormous antique tapestry hung above an intricately carved mahogany sideboard. A scale model of a clipper ship sat on the sideboard along with a large, carved elephant tusk. To its right, stood a card table, and to the left, of it a grandfather clock that seemed to tsk-tsk softly as if scolding me for my rumpled appearance. Or was it my tardiness? The hands of the clock read 5:05 P.M.

Before I could take in the entire scene, I heard the woman's footsteps returning.

"Marse Cornelius say he see y'all now. He be waitin' out back da manse."

I followed her past a dining room in which the walls had been stenciled in a pale green and pink floral pattern.

The ceiling above the dining table bore a colorful fresco of fruits and vegetables cascading out of a cornucopia from which hung an ornate brass chandelier. My boots clicked on the dark hardwood floor of the hallway. Laid with hearts of pine, its heavy resin content made it dense and impenetrable to termites. Only a well-to-do man like Cornelius could bear the expense of such costly flooring.

As we passed another door off the hallway, I heard a small dog scratching at the other side, snarling at me. We turned a corner and the black woman stopped and pointed to a door leading to the backyard. I stepped through it and turned to see where she had pointed. When I looked back, the door had already shut. The hinges hadn't squeaked.

I walked down the back stairs, across a limestone path and around the back of a tall hedge. Turning the corner, I came to a stop, surprised at what I saw. A lush garden encircled a yard fragrant with the sweet scent of tropical flowers. The names of most of the plants escape me now. But it seems to me I saw to my right a huge fichus tree with numerous trunks that seemed to wall out the rest of the world. In the corner, a thatch palm shimmered in the breeze, exposing the silver underside of its dark green leaves. Beside it, and to the left, stood two fish fuddle trees and next to them I saw wild tamarinds, bay cedars and a sabal palm.

A Negro gardener doffed his straw hat and pointed me toward strange, exotic and beautiful foliage of all shapes and colors. In silence, I followed a serpentine path of crushed, white sea shells until I came upon Cornelius standing with his back to me in front of a large pigeon coop. He opened the coop door and released the birds in a dizzying flutter of powerful wings. They were homing pigeons, the kind the army used to send messages here in the Florida Keys where telegraph service didn't exist.

Why would Cornelius need homing pigeons?

Cornelius turned to follow the flight pattern of the birds and stopped when he saw me.

"They'll be back," he said. "I only reward them with feed after they return."

"Return from a mission?" I asked.

"So you've served in the military," he said.

"Yes."

"And in this war," he asked, "where do your loyalties lie—North or South?" He shrugged his shoulders as if speaking of a trivial matter.

"I have friends on both sides."

"And enemies as well, it would appear." He eyed the bruises on my face.

"Right now," I said, "I'm more concerned about my friends in the refugee camp who are counting on me to return with the medicine."

"Of course," he said. "Have a chair, Mister Canfield. I was just getting to that." He pointed to a wrought iron table with two chairs. The table held a potted plant, a wooden box and a small brass bell.

I took a seat and brushed up against a four-foot tall plant with blue and orange blossoms resembling an exotic bird. I'd never seen the like.

"It's the bird of paradise," Cornelius said. "Imported from South Africa."

"It's beautiful."

The words had scarcely cleared my lips when he said:

"The fruit is poisonous."

I nodded, not sure why I needed to know that.

"Most of these plants," Cornelius added, "are as dangerous as they are beautiful. Take this plant, for instance . . ."

He leaned over the strange looking potted plant sitting between us on the table. Its green and red leaves consisted of two lobes facing each other, both rimmed by tiny hairs.

"Flying insects search for this plant," he said. "They hunt for its rich, gooey nectar as eagerly as some men hunt for salvation. But Key West is not the New Eden."

He paused, tapped the contents of an envelope—a housefly—onto the plant. Instantly, the plant's leaves snapped shut on the bug.

"Despite its beautiful appearances," he said, "the Venus Flytrap, is a carnivorous plant. In a heartbeat, the unsuspecting hunter becomes the prey."

He raised his head, fixed me with his beady eyes and said, "Mister Canfield, no one is to know where you got the medical supplies you've been hunting for. Understood?"

The threat was unmistakable.

"If it's all the same to you," I said, "I'd like to conclude our business. I have to make some repairs to my boat before I set sail."

Cornelius blinked and, when he opened his beady eyes, the glint was gone.

"Our business?" He stressed the word business. "I'm glad you put it that way. You see Mister Canfield, my brother-in-law, Doctor Raymond, seems to think I run a charity. He fails to recognize that I am, first and foremost, a businessman. As such, I extract a price for every service I render."

Doc Raymond had prepared me for this show of greed. I reached into my boot and pulled out the wad of money.

On seeing my stash again, Cornelius wrinkled his nose and shook his head in a condescending manner. "In this particular case," he said, "I have something other than filthy lucre in mind."

He seemed to take delight in my befuddlement.

"Information, Mister Canfield," he said. "I trade in information. After you have delivered your medicine, I want you to report back to me on everything you have seen. I want to know the name of every federal steamer, schooner, sloop and smack you encounter. I want to know the location of every revenue cutter and blockader."

He licked his lips as if savoring the aftertaste of his vile speech. The man was asking me to spy for him. He wanted the kind of information that I'd found in Captain Quill's pocket when I caught him hiding on the *Dead Reckoning*. The homing pigeons were Cornelius' way of communicating with his spies up and down the coast.

"Follow my meaning?" Cornelius asked. His eyes narrowed to chisel points.

"Yes," I said, "you made yourself perfectly clear. Now, about that medicine—people are dying and there is no time to lose."

"Be that as it may," he said, "I've received word that the wrecker whose berth you are using has been delayed. You can stay there until the Union ship is fully coaled."

My stomach clenched.

How did Cornelius know about my naval escort?

"Yes. And I have a lot to do between now and then," I said.

Cornelius pointed to the wooden box sitting on top of the table. "Your medical supplies are in that box."

I took it and said, "Much obliged."

He picked up the small brass bell that had been sitting next to the box and jingled it. "Mabel will show you out."

~

After talking with Cornelius, and listening to his proposition, my head spun. I had a tremendous urge to drink. Every fiber of my being craved the taste of rum. Just one drink, I told myself. Four fingers of Aquardiente. That's all. Something to take the edge off. Something to help me relax. I was too wound up, I thought.

Without making a conscious decision, I found myself heading in the direction of an old haunt. But as I turned onto Southard Street, I came across Cornelius' ships chandlery. The enormous wooden building was all that stood between a drink and me.

"Don't throw caution to the wind," I heard Abner Winslow say in the back of my head. "One drink will lead to two and the next thing you know—"

I swallowed hard, crossed the street and stepped inside the ships chandlery, a dimly lit, dusty space with 14-foot beamed ceilings decked with all types of nautical supplies. Standing in the doorway, my view was partially blocked by displays of buckets, anchors, chains and buoys. I moved toward the front counter and spied a clerk with a fly swatter poised to strike. He whacked the top of the counter, killing something, then called out in a scratchy voice to another clerk in the back of the store.

"That's twelve today. Let me see you top that."

Seeing me, he limped over, his right sleeve empty and flapping at his side like the broken wing of a bird. He laid down the fly swatter and adjusted the finger-smudged glasses that had slipped down the bridge of his nose. Rail thin, pale as a conch shell, he smelled of tobacco. The years had rounded his shoulders.

"What can I do for you, sailor?" He had a voice like a crow.

"I'm looking for Peter Kearns," I said.

"That would be me." He spat a quid of tobacco juice at a nearby spittoon and missed.

"I'll be needing some supplies," I said.

I handed him my list of supplies—some shrouds, a caulking iron, oakum, cotton, tar and odds and ends. He read the list, nodding and poking at it with his index finger like a solitary heron working the shoreline.

"And just how are you planning on paying for all this, mate?" he asked as he rubbed the back of his neck.

"Mister Cornelius said there would be no charge," I replied.

Kearns looked at me in disbelief. "You're the one who ran the blockade?"

I nodded as he took my measure assaying every bump and bruise on my face.

"And you're thinking of going back out there?"

"I am going back."

He gave me a penetrating look. "Have you been drinking?"

"I'm as sober as Sunday."

He shook his head, gave a small asthmatic cough. "You're still as crazy as ever."

"Do I know you?"

"Ex-Private Peter Kearns," he clucked as if the name should mean something to me. On seeing it didn't, he cracked a gap-toothed smile, revealing teeth the color of winter corn. "You might not remember me, but I remember you, all right. You were fearless. We served together before this happened." He patted his empty sleeve. "If you hadn't attacked the citadel and turned that howitzer on the greasers, I wouldn't be here today. I thought for sure you would make colonel one day. What happened?"

"It's a long story," I said. "Too long. I'm in a real hurry."

He chuckled to himself, recalling something from the past. "You were always bucking authority, questioning orders. You marched to a different drummer, lived by your own rules."

"Guilty as charged," I laughed.

Leaning forward and lowering his voice to a conspiratorial level, he added, "Ed, you could be headed for trouble. This is an island of divided loyalties. Spies are everywhere, selling information to the highest bidder. They change colors faster than a chameleon. Hell, they even make up stories about their neighbors just to curry favor with the federals. By the time you cast off, word will have spread. No telling who may be laying in wait for you out there."

"Right now," I said, "my only worry is those supplies. After that, I want to get a bite to eat, buy some clothes and get some much needed sleep."

Kearns fixed me up with the supplies and said, "Good luck. Once you clear the harbor, you'll be on your own. Don't expect the Union navy to protect you. The whole fleet has problems with broken pumps, leaky boilers and such. A third of the ships are in for repairs right now."

I took Kearn's warning as good news. With so many ships needing repair, it was less likely they could spare a vessel to track me down.

After hauling the supplies back to the boat, I headed for a mercantile store on Duval Street that Kearns had pointed me toward. Purdy's General Mercantile Emporium occupied a squat, one-story whitewashed wood-frame building. A bell over the front door jingled as I stepped inside.

"We're closed for the day," a man called out from behind a curtained doorway in the rear.

"This will only take a minute," I said. I scanned the shelves for the pants and shirts I needed. "And I'm paying with greenbacks."

"Very well then," the man said. "What can I do for you?"

I turned to see a short, lean man wearing a crisp, pressed white jacket, black stock, striped pants and a smile that had been painted on. He was as stiff as a starched collar; his face as pale as a cue ball and his thinning brown hair was pomaded and parted in the middle. Thick spectacles gave him an owlish appearance and his head tilted to one side as if he were perpetually eavesdropping. A tape measure hung around his neck. His handshake felt limp, cold as a fish.

"I need some clothes," I said.

"Don't we all?" he chuckled.

When I didn't laugh at his little joke, he rubbed his hands together nervously. "Yes, well, what did you have in mind?"

"A pair of work pants," I said, "and two shirts. Red shirts."

A short while later, as I left Purdy's emporium, I saw a bodega with a hand-written sign: "Fresh-Brewed Coffee." It had been a long time since I'd drunk anything but chicory. Bitter chicory. A cup of coffee would only cost me a few minutes and might clear my head and lift my weary spirits. So I sat down at the bodega for a steaming cup of coffee while reading an old copy of the *New Era* that someone had left behind.

The front-page headline immediately caught my eye:

Union Claims To Have 264 Ships In Blockade.

That was a much bigger figure than I'd heard in Commander Hill's office. But a quick reading revealed Peter Kearns was right. Most of the ships in the blockade were converted fishing smacks, ferry boats, private yachts, harbor tugs and barnacled schooners; many were wanting repairs. They were a motley lot, but on the other hand, the blockade runners dared not fire back for fear of being considered pirates.

Another story reported that someone by the name of Lindsey, a member of the British Parliament, was building shallow draft blockade runners that made Yankee steamers look sluggish. The blockade was lucky to catch one out of six British-built ships. By that point, their owners had made a fortune buying cotton at six to eight cents a pound and selling it at $1.00 a pound in England. Then, they used those funds to buy guns, gunpowder and ammunition that they sold to the South at exorbitant prices. The more mercenary blockade runners didn't bother with shipping heavy munitions; instead, they hauled high-priced, lighter-weight luxury goods such as perfume and rum.

The article mentioned Captain Damien Quill by name.

I tore that page from the paper, folded it and stuffed it in my pocket, thinking it might become useful later.

Buried on an inner page was news of the first noteworthy Confederate loss of the war: the Battle at Fishing Creek, Kentucky. Despite outnumbering the Yanks, the rebels were whipped and forced to retreat.

The two sides were so far apart they couldn't even agree on a name for the battle. We called it the Battle of Fishing Creek; the Yanks called it the Battle of Logan's Crossroads. Surely, the men who fought there called it hell on earth.

Another article reported that, at a recent auction:

1,608 packages of heron's plumes were sold, the average package weighing 30 ounces for a total of 48,240 ounces. At a bid price of $30 an ounce, the total value of the sale was $1,447,200.

I knew it took about four birds to make an ounce of plumes. That meant, more than 180,000 birds had been slaughtered in their nests and maybe three times as many chicks or eggs had been destroyed—close to 700,000 lives sacrificed on the altar of the gods of fashion.

Little did I realize at the time that close to 700,000 soldiers' lives would also be sacrificed on the altar of Mars, the god of war.

And that's not counting the wounded and maimed or those—like me—who bore the invisible wounds of war. Later, it would be learned that the second most common diagnosis made by doctors during the war was "soldier's heart." But the condition affected thousands of civilians as well as soldiers. I can vouch for that.

I tossed the paper aside and headed for the boat.

~

CHAPTER TEN

With little more than two hours of daylight remaining, I wasted no time in making repairs to the boat. But just as I drew my hammer back to strike another blow with the caulking hammer, I heard a moan. I paused, looked about, saw nothing. I struck again. Another moan, this one louder. I looked toward the next boat slip.

"Damnation," a man cussed. "What in hell is going on now?"

I lowered the caulking hammer as the man's head rose just above the gun'l of the vessel tethered next to mine. His hair and beard were a rumpled mass of gray, his skin a shade lighter than beef jerky and his eyelids—swollen by sleep—protruded like a turtle's. He had a rum bottle in his right hand. When he stood, I saw his pants were held up by a rope and were cut off at the knees revealing spindly legs.

"I beg your pardon?"

"Well, you can beg all you like," he slurred, "but you ain't pardoned. I'm tryin' to get some sleep over here."

"I didn't see anyone on that boat."

"Smack," he hiccupped. "She's a smack."

"Right." She was a Bahamian smack; about 30 feet long.

"You're in a heap of trouble, son," he said. "Wait 'til P. J. Cornelius finds out you is using his slip."

"Mister Cornelius knows."

One eyebrow ticked up. My answer seemed to impress him. His expression softened. "What time is it, anyway?" he asked, rubbing his eyes with the palm of his free hand.

"You've slept the day away."

"Sleep? How in hell can a man sleep with all the racket you've been making?"

"I just got here," I said. "I don't know what you're talking about?"

"Well, who in hell was that making all that racket?"

"What racket? When?"

"Damn it all," he said. "How should I know? It's your boat and your crew."

"I don't have a crew."

"Well, whoever it was, he was hammerin' away to beat the band on your bowsprit."

My bowsprit?

Someone must have tried to damage the *Dead Reckoning*.

"Wait right there," I said.

I scrambled to the bowsprit and examined the damage. He was right. Someone had taken a blunt tool to the fittings. Whoever had done it, must have expected the bowsprit and jib to be carried away in a strong wind, leaving a hole in the bow where she'd take on water. There was no way I could fix it before sunset.

"I didn't do it," he said nervously. "Whatever it is, I didn't do it. You be sure and tell Mister Cornelius I had nothing to do with it."

The waddle of flesh under his chin trembled like the throat of a lizard in the heat of day.

"Did you get a good look at who did it?" I asked.

"No. The feller leapt from the deck onto the wharf and took off yonder. From behind, he looked about your height, more on the heavy side, maybe, and older, maybe. But I can't be sure. I didn't get a good look at him."

The description more or less fit Ned Boyle. It would be just like him to sabotage my boat. "Much obliged, Mister?"

"Neally," he said. "Gus Neally, best damn seaman in the harbor."

"Name's Ed Canfield," I said.

"Glad to meet you, Ed. Any friend of P. J. Cornelius is a friend of Gus Neally."

I took another look at his boat, the *Shore Thing*, and an idea surfaced in my mind. She seemed to be a seaworthy, ketch-rigged smack, smaller than the *Dead Reckoning*, which would make her easier for solo sailing. There was a cockpit, a large live-well forward with a hatch and ample room on deck. Dozens of fishing boats like her anchored in the harbor. She could pass unnoticed under the watchful eyes of the Yanks who'd be on the lookout for the *Dead Reckoning*.

Besides, with a name like the *Shore Thing*, she just might be my lucky break.

"That's a right smart looking boat you have there, Gus," I said. "Is she seaworthy?"

"Tight as a frog's ass," he said. He took a swig from his bottle.

"Have you ever considered chartering her?" I asked.

"How's that?" He belched.

"Meaning would you consider chartering your boat to me?"

He wiped his mouth with the back of his hand and gave me a hard squint. "Now why would I want to do a thing like that?"

"I'd return her within a week," I said. "Meanwhile, you can hold this sloop for collateral."

He eyed the *Dead Reckoning* and pulled on his nose.

"She's wanting a lot of work."

"That's why I'd like to charter the *Shore Thing* for a week."

He scratched the back of his head. I could see he enjoyed haggling. "A week is a long time."

"There's easy money in it for you."

He responded with a slow nod.

"Cash upfront and no graybacks," I said. "Agreed?"

His left eye twitched. "What say we talk a spell?"

He hitched up his sagging pants and invited me onboard his boat. After inspecting her, I dickered with him over price for several minutes before reaching into my boot for the money that Doc had given me. I handed him the agreed upon sum and watched him count the bills one at a time.

"Gus," I said, "if you could skin a flea, you'd tan the hide and sell it."

"Jes put your scribble here," he said, handing me a piece of paper to sign, "in case some gator gets hold of yuh."

I signed it, handed it back and he stuffed it in his pocket.

"And be sure," he said, "to put in a good word for me with Mister Cornelius."

Neally gave me a hand moving my gear over to the *Shore Thing* and I made sure I took the Yankee flag, just in case.

Then Neally took off for Johnny Cake Row with the money I had given him burning a hole in his pocket. Before leaving the *Dead Reckoning*, I opened a box of carpenter's tacks and sprinkled them all over the deck. Later that night, I lay down on the *Shore Thing* with my boots on and the LeMat by my side.

About three in the morning, I thought I heard a sound on the deck of the *Dead Reckoning*. Reaching down, I grabbed the revolver, cocked the hammer and rolled over on one elbow with the gun barrel pointed toward the sound. I heard a deck plank creak softly once, and then twice, followed by a series of pain-filled, muffled cries. The intruders had found the carpenter's tacks. They cussed under their breath and I bolted up, gun in hand just in time to see Ned and Malachi leap off the deck and pound down the wharf and into the night.

After that, sleep came in snatches. Nightmare thoughts and images engulfed my imagination. I could hear Peter Kearns warning me over and over again about spies. In my semiconscious state, I saw myself as a drummer boy marching across a smoke-choked field, stumbling over lifeless bodies, marching right into the line of fire laid down by enemy marksmen. The miniê balls were thick as the holes in a player piano roll. Cannon balls roared overhead to gouge huge holes in the ground. I stumbled and fell flat on my back into a crater. When I rolled over on my side, Caleb Foster was lying beside me.

I woke with a start, unable to breathe. The heat was stifling. My shirt clung to my clammy skin; my hair was matted with sweat. For a moment, I wasn't sure where I was. Charleston? Mexico? Cedar Keys? Then a dog barked, calling me back to the present. I exhaled, threw off my mosquito netting, sat up and cradled my head in my hands. A church bell tolled in the distance and I counted the peals. Six in the morning. I threw off my sweat-soaked shirt, rummaged through my duffel bag until I found my new red shirt and put it on.

High time I got going.

I quickly cast off the dock lines, stowed the fenders, hoisted my sails and struck out for the refugee camp. The harbor stirred with the boats of reef fishermen heading out after the snapper and king mackerel, which they would sell in the local market. The small flotilla made it easier for me to slip undetected past the harbor watch.

Leaving the Key West bight, I cleared the sea wall heading northeast, following the fishing boats past Boca Chica Key, Stock Island, Big Coppitt Key and the Sugar Loaf Keys. To the West, sea gulls and brown pelicans wheeled and danced on the thermal updrafts, signaling the location of drift fishing boats after snapper, grunt, grouper and tarpon. Occasionally, the water's surface would boil as halfbeak ballao and small flying fish skimmed out of the sea ahead of marauding kingfish. Seeing the life and death struggle playing out before me, I couldn't help wonder whether I was the kingfish or its prey.

At Big Torch Key, I changed my heading and set sail for the Florida Straits. For much of that day, it was clear sailing with nothing to mark my passage but the thrumming, snapping staccato of the shrouds and stays and the walloping of the waves against the bow of the boat. I made five to six knots an hour sailing on a broad reach through turquoise waterways and emerald straits, past sun-dappled shoals of sand and coral. Sweat blistered my brow and ran down my neck in thin rivulets that pooled in soggy patches on the back of my shirt. My lips cracked and I moistened them from time to time with a swig of water from my canteen.

Every now and then, the boat would attract the attention of a school of playful dolphins, which would surf in her wake. At one point, I spotted the dorsal fin of a huge mako shark, a monster weighing at least 500 pounds. It made several passes at the boat before losing interest and disappearing. I passed a number of fishing boats and commercial steamers and kept a hawk eye out for federal gunboats and blockade runners. They both meant trouble. I made my way north without any problems and set a course for the Ten Thousand Islands and the mangrove hammocks that line the coast.

But my luck didn't hold out. The wind turned against me and I was forced to spend an extra night at sea. Then, while passing Pavilion Key, I heard a strange thumping sound coming from the area of the mast. Quickly checking the shrouds, I discovered one of them had just snapped; its loose ends were flogging the sail. Gus Neally had said the smack was tight as a frog's ass. He hadn't said anything about her shrouds.

If the shroud next to the broken one also snapped, the mast would become unstable, lean to the lee side and possibly capsize the boat. I quickly changed my tack to let the good shroud take the pressure. Then I grabbed the loose shroud in my hand and saw where it had worn through. At first, I considered splicing the damaged shroud the way an old salt had taught me; but then I remembered what he'd said—"Every splice weakens a rope by one eighth." I didn't want to press my luck. So I tied a line to the broken shroud and ran the new line to the block on the gun'l where the old shroud ended. Then I tacked back to my original course, trimmed my sail and continued on at a slower pace.

By sunset, I could barely make out the faint outline of Cape Romano in the distance. As the sun dropped, the temperature fell, the wind picked up and the seas began to build. I put on my rain slicker, covered the medicine box with another slicker and stored it in the cockpit. Then I dropped the sails, sheeted them and weather cocked into the wind.

Dark, towering cumulonimbus clouds soon stretched across the horizon, bringing heavy rains. Powerful gusts of wind, accompanied by deep, booming peals of thunder, shook the small boat. Lightning scorched the sky and I took a pounding from the waves. The wind-lashed sea hurled ropes of spume across my bow like a dragnet pulling me down. The salt spray stung my face and the waves wrestled with me for the tiller. The *Shore Thing* had her bow about fifty degrees to the wind, when—without warning—the wind shifted and a real 'pounder' roared up from the depths, grabbing her in its fist. With bone-jarring force, it slammed her down, bow-first. Coming out of the trough, I fought to keep her bow near the wind but I over-corrected. The wind caught her broadside, and her rigging moaned as she strained to come around. At the crest of the next wave, her bow was headed too far to starboard and—*Boom*—the boom slammed down to port, grazing my shoulder and nearly taking off my head. I lay there in the cockpit dazed and shaken.

After several seconds, I struggled to my feet on the pitching, rolling, spray-slick boat and took hold of the tiller again. Every timber creaked and groaned with the boat's effort to stay afloat. A sudden gust lifted the bow and my legs went out from under me.

"Lordamighty," I cried.

I fell backwards, slamming into the taffrail. I felt as if I were a rogue buoy in a squall, reeling back and forth with nothing to hold onto. Gasping for air, I struggled to my feet and took hold of the tiller again. I dared not let go. The thunderclaps were no more than three minutes apart; meaning the worst of the storm was still a few miles off.

At the crest of a wave, I saw an opening in the coastline where storm-lashed combers pounded a sandbar, and beyond that, the flickering lights of what appeared to be a small fishing village, maybe a dozen shacks sitting on stilts at the water's edge. But the lights soon died out in the rain.

For what seemed like an eternity, the boat swerved and lurched about like a drunken sailor as the storm spent its full fury. To my astonishment, the stout little craft managed to right itself again and again. Then, as fast as it started, the storm died away. The wind and waves fell off and the *Shore Thing* somehow found her feet, stayed afloat.

I spent the night in my rain slicker and damp clothes, chilled to the bone, teeth clicking, shivering uncontrollably as the temperature dropped. Unable to sleep, my mind lurched back and forth trying to make sense of the last few days. I asked myself why God had allowed the killing to happen. Maybe He just didn't care. Maybe He figured we had it coming to us. Like Sodom and Gomorra. The North and the South.

Maybe it's the Day of Reckoning that Brother Storter squawked about.

Even now, all these years later, it's as if I'm still standing there, leaning over that gun'l, blinking hard to hold back the tears.

If I wasn't in hell, I was in limbo. I started counting the stars in the firmament and gradually drifted off to some place between sleep and wakefulness. I began hallucinating. In my nightmare, I saw myself surfacing from the depths of the sea only to be ensnared in a floating bed of kelp. Beside me, another man lay face down in the seaweed. I nudged him, looking for some sign of life, when—to my horror—he raised his head, and pulled off a strand of kelp, making his face clearly visible.

Private Abner Winslow.

Still dreaming, I gasped, tore at the kelp and started swimming away as fast as I could in heavy seas. Winslow seemed to follow me effortlessly, dragged along by the kelp that bound us together. At the crest of a wave, I saw in the distance wind-lashed combers racing along a beach, their spume thrown to the wind like the white manes of wild stallions. If I could just reach those horses, I thought. But first I had to make it through the surf. Each new wave that broke upon me drove me down, forced me to fight for a foothold in the undertow. Finally, exhausted and gasping for air, I staggered ashore and collapsed on the beach. When I caught my breath and rolled over, Winslow was gone. So were the white stallions.

I woke with a start.

At first light, the warming rays of the sun brought welcome relief and dispelled my darkest thoughts. I rose, rubbed the salt from my eyes, stretched, worked my stiff muscles and looked about. I glassed the shore and spied sandpipers running back and forth on the edge of the surf like dance hall girls performing their routines to the clap, clap of the surf's applause.

To my surprise, no fishing village appeared on the coast where I had seen lights the night before. Someone had lit fires on the shore and, lucky for me, the rain had doused the flames. But who—hunters or mooncussers? I couldn't say. I glassed the shoreline again, looking for signs of any threatening activity and spied several well-armed men stalking the shoreline, heads down, as if reading sign.

That broken shroud may have been a lucky break. If I hadn't stopped to fix the problem, I might have sailed right into trouble.

I quickly inspected my craft. Gus Neally's smack was no longer "tight as a frog's ass." The cockpit was a shambles, nearly everything in it lost to the storm, including the chronometer. Both the running rigging and standing rigging were damaged but repairable. The keel was intact; the tiller and rudder were in working order; and the box containing the medicine was high and dry.

I repaired the damage as best I could. Then I hoisted the sail, leaving the sheet slack, and weighed anchor; the bow fell off the wind and I sailed away. It was only when I reached for my charts that I discovered they were missing—lost to the storm. I would have to sail the rest of the way with nothing more to guide me than memory and gut instinct: dead reckoning.

In the distance, I spied three dagger-like, fast moving waterspouts heading straight for my boat. I knew that old seamen considered their appearance a bad omen. I also knew that any one of them could easily destroy a small craft like mine. I veered away from the threat, nearly broaching, but quickly trimmed my sails and maintained steerage. When I looked back, the waterspouts were still following in my wake. They hovered above the water like three witches on broomsticks—like the witches in Maureen's book, the one about *MacBeth.* "Fair is foul, and foul is fair," the witches had proclaimed. They had convinced Macbeth that good was evil and evil was good. I did not want to make Macbeth's mistake. I changed my course by three points and watched the waterspouts unravel and collapse under their own weight.

In the tumult of war, where both sides made their own rules and proclaimed that God was on their side, I would follow my own moral compass in choosing between good and evil. I would use dead reckoning to find my way through the roiling waters of whatever this war would bring.

~

I felt my way up the coast, passing one barrier island after another, most of them little more than hammocks of mangroves, pines, sea grapes, gumbo-limbo, and Jamaican dogwood. Herons, egrets, roseate spoonbills, wood storks and rails would take to the sky as I passed. Occasionally, a mullet would leap from the water in a silvery flash and a porpoise would surface to blow. Further north, I passed through brackish and freshwater marshes, with small upland hammocks where gumbo-limbos, live oaks and slash pine thrived.

I thought of Mommer Wicks and the way she had prayed, rambling on in her own Gullah lingo, reciting a chant that had somehow made a difference for Jesse. I found myself repeating over and over the names of the refugees who counted on me, as if by chanting my own solemn litany I could somehow make a difference in the outcome. I remembered what Quill had said about all the shipwrecks lining the coast and that maniacal laugh of his. I kept wondering whether I had remembered to step onto the deck with my right foot first. I recalled what Quill had said about making my own luck.

From time to time, a distant sail gave me a start and I lowered my sail until the other ship ghosted away; then I continued northward until, finally, I entered the mouth of the Caloosahatchee River. In the distance, I could see the silhouette of a familiar wreck, the *Island Skipper*, her broken mast pointing like a witch's forefinger in the direction I had to sail. The tide was with me and the *Shore Thing* cleared the shoal and entered the inlet sending ribbons of water coursing through the roots of the mangrove tangles.

The *Shore Thing* proved only slightly easier to handle than the larger *Dead Reckoning* had been. I strained to bring her around each new bend in the channel but I had no choice. I had to push on before the winter sun began its early descent.

Late in the day, the glades come alive with strange, forbidding cries, croaks, screeches and gurgles. I spied a raccoon eating a horseshoe crab. A barred owl swooped by on wings as silent as death, a helpless snake writhing in its talons. Alligators slithered past the smack's hull. On this day, the cooler temperature seemed to subdue the frogs, cicadas and crickets; it kept the sand flies and mosquitoes from boiling up in choking, blinding clouds.

With a sign of relief, I spied the camp ahead. I had made it back alive in one piece. I hoped I wasn't too late. I thought for sure someone in the camp would spot the boat and alert the others. I expected them to come running down to the beach to meet me. But then I realized the *Shore Thing* was unfamiliar to them.

All I saw were two little, brown-haired girls playing beneath a tree. As I drew closer, I recognized them as Maureen's sisters, Kate and Helen. They were smoking a beehive, trying to get some honeycomb. When they saw the unfamiliar smack, they gave me a hard squint and froze. I raised my arm in a friendly wave only to have them back away, turn and rush off, disappearing like changelings in the shadows and smoke from the smudge pots and cook fires that wreathed the distant tent rows. I shrugged it off, dropped anchors off the fore and aft deck, and ducked into the cockpit to get the box of medicine.

When I looked up, I saw a shadowy figure darting in and out of the trees, hurrying toward me on unsteady legs. As he came near, I recognized the man: Doc Raymond.

Where are all the others? Are they sick? Dead?

My heart pounded in my chest.

Doc held back at the tree line, obstinately waving for me to come to him. Wearing a broad smile, I held the medicine box up for him to see and threw one leg over the gun'l. Then I eased myself into the water feet first, making sure to keep the medicine high and dry as I made my way onto the beach. It felt good to be on firm ground. But Doc seemed agitated and waved me on again. Puzzled and worried, I crossed the beach to where he stood hidden among the shadowed trees, breathless and flushed in the face.

He took the box from me and gasped, "Thank God you made it back." He took a deep breath and added, "What happened to your face? Were you able to get everything? Did Cornelius charge you for these?"

"Slow down," I said. "One thing at a time."

He opened the box and hurriedly counted the supplies as if he had expected Cornelius to shortchange him. I asked myself again what kind of hold did Doc have on his brother-in-law? Satisfied that everything was there, Doc looked up and noticed the *Shore Thing*.

"What became of your sloop?"

"I'll fill you in later. Where is everyone? Where is—"

"Take it easy," Doc said. "Your son is back at the camp with the others."

"What about Maureen Foster?"

"She's been a big help to me."

Maureen was alive! "Great. Let's go."

"Hold on. You can't go to the camp just yet."

"Why in hell not?"

"Those little girls weren't after honey. They were my lookouts watching for you."

"Lookouts? What do you mean?" I asked.

"This camp isn't what you think it is," Doc said. "It's a hideout for deserters and smugglers led by Damien Quill. The refugees from Cedar Keys stumbled into it without realizing what we had gotten ourselves into."

"Where is Quill now?"

"His gang attacked and seized that gunboat you ran aground, the *Argonaut*."

That must have been the gunfire we heard after making our escape.

"While you were gone, Quill sailed her into a nearby bay. Now he's using her to run the blockade with the cattle he rounded up after you stampeded his herd."

"Good riddance."

"Not so fast," Doc said. "Quill shanghaied the five most able-bodied refugees for the *Argonaut*'s black gang. They're stoking the boilers on his run to Cuba and back. The rest of us are being held hostage. They're using us to negotiate a prisoner exchange for the soldiers captured at Cedar Keys."

I couldn't believe my ears. Everyone in the camp was at risk. Maureen. Jesse. Everyone. My guts started churning.

"The Yanks aren't about to negotiate," I said. "Trust me. When their cannons get through shelling this camp, it will be lower than a gator hole."

"There is nothing we can do. We're under guard at all times."

"How many men did Quill leave behind?"

"There are three men guarding us in the camp and five in the other bay building a cattle pen and a wharf they can use to offload and load cargo."

Eight men. My mind began racing.

"And how many men do we have?"

"Healthy? Just a handful, including your son.

"But you say there are only three men guarding the camp?"

"Yes, but they're holding our firearms. There is no way for us to put up a fight."

"Where are the rebel guards now?"

"One is always on guard duty; otherwise, they stay clear of us because of the contagion."

"Let's go," I said.

"Hold on," Doc said. "You can't go sashaying into camp. Those rebels know you stampeded their cattle. They think you're a damn Yankee. You could wind up like Jack Pemble, or worse."

"What happened to Pemble?"

"He made the mistake of mouthing off to the one of them and got himself pistol-whipped."

"Where is Pemble now?"

"He's tied up," Doc said. "They gagged him and bound him hand and foot on the ground with a rod passing between the arms and backs of the knees."

"The buck and gag," I said. "Well, what do you suggest?"

"First off," he said, "we can't leave that smack here in plain sight. We have to anchor it, step the mast, hide the sails and rigging and camouflage it so it looks like just another wreck thrown up on the shoal."

"Well," I said, "she's already taken some damage in a storm. Let's see what we can do to make it look like the stranded hulk of a real wreck."

We worked feverishly for several hours camouflaging the smack with mud, marl and broken tree branches. As we worked, Doc filled me in on conditions in the camp. Five more people had succumbed to diseases of one kind or another, including Minny, and at least that many more were sickened by yellow fever. Maureen had not fallen ill, but she was heartsick over the loss of Minny. To make matters worse, her father was one of the men impressed into Quill's black gang.

"I don't know how she does it," Doc said. "But she's holding up."

My pulse pounded like a drum. I couldn't wait to get back to camp.

~

Just before dusk, Doc said, "C'mon. We have to get to my tent before someone reports me as missing. There are spies everywhere."

Within ten minutes, we cleared the tree line that rimmed the camp. I saw rosin and pine tar barrels burning between the rows of tents, their black fumes blanketing the entire scene. I could taste the air I breathed. I could hear people hacking and coughing. The pall of gritty smoke—that was meant to purify the pestilent air—lent a menacing funereal gloom to the melancholy scene.

Yellow jack flags hung limply above two large, gray hospital tents on the edge of the camp. When we reached the first tent and I pulled back the flap, the first person I saw in the light of the kerosene lanterns was Jesse, sitting up on his cot. On seeing me, he hauled himself to his feet and staggered toward me. His face looked pale and haggard and he had lost weight, but he had re-grown his mustache. He looked a lot like my old man.

"Look at you," I said, "alive and well." That was a slight exaggeration. But I saw a spark in his eyes that gave me some hope.

"And look at you," he said, "You look like you were ridden hard and put up wet." We embraced, then he stepped back, eyed my red shirt and nodded. "I knew you could do it. How did the boat handle?"

"It took some damage," I said and quickly explained what had happened and why I had returned on the smack.

"Listen up everyone," Doc said. He clapped his hands to get their attention. "Ed made it back from Key West with the medicine we need."

He held the box up for all to see.

"I knew he could do it," Cal Nordland called out.

A muted cheer went up and Doc signaled for the men to hush up. I scanned the tent for young Zach Wetherby and saw him sitting up on a cot near Jesse, still shadowing my son wherever Jesse went. Zach had made it this far. I choked up. Then I watched as Doc dispensed the quinine and other medicine.

Once Doc had treated every patient, he and I switched into dry clothes and sat down on a cot, surrounded by the refugees. They wanted to know what I had been up to and I told them. They listened closely, especially when I confirmed what Jesse had already told them—Quill was running the blockade to line his own pockets and those of his investors in England; he had masterminded the break-in at the salt works; and he had killed the agent from Lloyds of London.

"We should have used him for fish bait," Jesse muttered.

"But fill me in on what has been happening here," I said.

"Remember those rebels we met up with at the gum patch?" Jesse asked.

"You mean Bill McKenna and that bunch?"

"Right," he said. "They came riding in here right after you left."

"Are they part of Quill's gang?"

"It doesn't look that way. But, with Quill on his way to Cuba, McKenna took right over. He thinks he can arrange a prisoner exchange for the rebels that were captured at Cedar Keys and those of us who side with the Union. Then he expects to escape on the *Argonaut* with Quill. His men are guarding us while the rest of Quill's gang finishes a cattle pen and wharf in the next cove."

"He's talking through his hat," I said.

The tent flap flew open and Maureen ducked in. Her face looked haggard, her shoulders were rounded and she wore a black dress. A knitted shawl protected her from the chill of the night. On seeing me, she dropped the shawl, rushed over and hugged me in front of the other men. I could feel my face flush with embarrassment.

"Kate and Helen were right. Thank God you are alive," she said. Then, realizing what she had done in front of the others, she drew back. "The rebels mustn't know you made it back."

"I'm safe for now in this tent," I said. "They won't set foot inside it for fear of yellow fever."

"That's true," Doc said. "They don't know that the worst has passed."

"How can you say the worst has passed?" Maureen protested. "You know they're torturing Jack Pemble and they've shanghaied my father and the other men."

"I was speaking about the fever," Doc said lamely. He handed Maureen the shawl she had dropped.

Doc was right. I could see that half the men were already on the mend. We just might have a fighting chance with this group. Maureen turned back toward me, her eyes searching mine for some glimmer of hope.

"Where is Pemble tied up?" I asked her. I had felt Pemble's punches and knew he could pack a wallop. We could use him in a showdown.

"Right next to their tent," she said.

"Don't even think about freeing him," a voice from behind said. "You'll get us all killed."

The foul words hung in the air like swamp gas. I turned to see Trent Oakland, a no account, ferret-faced fisherman, who had hung out at the Salty Dog Saloon, cadging drinks from the rest of us. He had thin, windblown hair and a weak chin hidden behind a straggly goatee. His complexion was as pale and thin as a snake's shed skin. Half the time, he was tighter than the bark on a tree; but drunk or sober, you could always count on Trent to do or say the wrong thing.

"We're going to free everyone in this camp," I said.

"Oakland's right for a change," said Brother Storter. "They're heavily armed. They'll run roughshod over us. Pemble was a fool to shoot off his mouth. You're not going to catch those weasels asleep."

"I agree," said Josh Stengel, the telegraph operator from Cedar Keys. He held up a hand as if warding off a blow and added, "Once you start down that road, there ain't no turning back. Y'all may be able to take out McKenna and his bunch. Y'all might even beat the five men working on the wharf. But, like as not, when Quill returns, it will be a different story."

"Damn right," Oakland said. He pivoted on his heels, nodding his head, seeking agreement from the other men. "We got women and children to think about. This is no time to throw caution to the wind."

"What did you just say?" I snapped. "What did you say about caution?"

Oakland shifted the quid in the corner of his mouth and gave me a knife-edge stare. "Ain't you the slacker who got his self court-martialed?"

"Court-martialed?" I grabbed him by his throat and lifted him off the ground with one hand. His eyes bulged like a toad's. "I'm the only man here," I said, "who risked everything to bring back that medicine."

"Don't do it, Ed," I heard a familiar voice say. "He ain't worth it."

I turned to see Adam Broady.

"He's right, Pa," Jesse added.

I wrestled with myself, struggling to get my temper under control. Then I dropped Oakland in a heap on the ground and turned to face the other men. They stood there gawking at me, not sure what to make of what had just happened.

"Any one else care to call me a slacker?"

No one said a word. They were good men, but so gaunt and wasted by the fever their clothes looked like they hung from a wall peg. The blank look on their hollowed out faces told me arguing was pointless. The attack on Cedar Keys had cost them everything. Now the only flag they saluted was yellow jack.

"Ed, there is no way we can fight," said Josh Stengel. "Not now, not after taking quinine. It blurs the vision." Before I could muster a reply, he added, "It's just too risky. I say we wait for the prisoner exchange."

"Speak for yourself," another man growled, his voice flat and anvil hard. When he stepped out of the shadows, I saw Nick Savarese, a shipwright from Cedar Keys. "My son is one of the men impressed on that black gang; and, if Quill ain't helping the Confederate cause, I mean to get my boy off that damn steamer."

Savarese was a swarthy, barrel-chested man in his early 40s. He had shoulders the size of ham hocks and a neck as thick as his head. Nick was the kind of ornery cuss I'd want on my side in a fight, but right now he looked a mite yellow around the gills.

"Count me in, too," another man said. It was Tom Perry, the sawmill operator from Cedar Keys. "My brother was impressed on the *Argonaut.*"

Perry had served a stint in the Second Seminole War and knew how to handle a firearm.

"You're both insane," Brother Storter chimed in. "Go ahead and kill yourselves, if that's what you want. But don't do it here and now—when the rest of us might pay the price for your folly."

An argument erupted with both sides trading insults.

Finally, Maureen could no longer countenance such behavior.

"Listen to you," she raged, "bleating like lost sheep while one of your own is being tortured and the others have been shanghaied."

Maureen's red-faced outburst shamed us men into silence for the moment. It was so quiet you could hear yourself breathe.

"What do you think is going to happen to all of you," she added, "if they can't arrange a prisoner exchange?"

Oakland tried to weasel his way out. "There are three of them, Miss, all battle-hardened men, and all we have is one gun."

"Not just any gun," I said. "A LeMat can take out three men with one shotgun blast."

Oakland rolled his eyes, swiped at a pesky bee.

"Where are they keeping the guns they took from you?" I asked.

"Under lock and key in their tent," Jesse answered.

That complicated things. But seeing Oakland swat at the pesky bee gave me an idea. "We may have another weapon, one they couldn't take away."

That got a rise out of them. They all turned to me looking for some explanation.

"Earlier," I said, "I saw Helen and Kate using a smudge pot to smoke a beehive so the girls could gather honey."

The men nodded, not sure where I was headed.

"Well," I continued, "we can smoke that hive to put the bees to sleep then throw the hive into the rebels' tent. When the rebs scramble to get out of harm's way, we can take them out."

"And just who is going to throw the hive into the tent?" Storter asked, playing to the other skeptics. They all took a sudden interest in their fingernails. Pleased with himself, Storter grinned like a cat.

"I will," Maureen said firmly.

Caught off guard, everyone turned in silence to look at her. Maureen's eyes blazed. Her hands were on her hips, her elbows jutting out in a show of inner strength.

"This is a man's business," I said.

"That's very gallant of you, Ed Canfield," she said in a tone of voice I hadn't heard before. "But it is also precisely why I have to be the one to do it. They'll never suspect me. I'll put the hive in a bucket as if I'm hauling water from the creek. The sentry will let me pass and when I reach their tent, I'll open the flap and throw the beehive inside. They won't know what hit them."

She paused and added, "The rest is up to those of you who are man enough to fight."

Jesse and I looked at each other in amazement. I hadn't realized what a polecat Maureen could be. The other men murmured among themselves.

"But what about the sentry?" Doc asked. "He'll come running when he hears gunshots."

"There won't be any gunshots," I said. "The only thing the sentry will hear is the whooping and hollering from inside the tent. When he comes running, we'll jump him."

"How do we handle the five men working on the wharf?" Savarese asked.

"They're too far off to hear anything," I said. I was making it up as I went along, hoping I was right.

"But we still have to overcome them," Savarese said. "And they always have a vedette posted."

"We'll disguise ourselves as McKenna and his men," I said. "By the time the vedette recognizes us, we'll be on top of him and it will be too late."

"What then?" Doc asked.

"After we capture them," I said, "we move the *Shore Thing* and one of the other boats from the camp into an inlet where Quill can't block our escape."

"Escape?" Savarese said. He pounded a fist into the palm of his hand. "I'm not leaving here without my son. We have to rescue the men on the black gang."

"The *Argonaut* is due back any day," Storter said. "Are you going to throw a beehive on the ship's deck, too?"

"Once she docks," I said, "she'll be vulnerable. They'll have to start swaying off her cargo of Cuban gimcracks and geegaws to make room for the new shipment of cattle that Quill expects any day."

"We can attack at dusk," Jesse said, "when they have a skeleton crew posted."

"Nonsense," Brother Storter said. "You'll never make it past the gangway."

"We don't have to," I answered. "We'll draw them off the ship by setting fire to the cargo on the wharf. When they see those flames, they'll come running."

"They'll come running alright," Storter said. "Straight at you with guns drawn."

"We'll be wearing the uniforms of the rebels we capture in the other inlet," I said. "When Quill's men see the flames, they'll run right by us. And while they're fighting the fire, we'll slip aboard and free the black gang."

"Let's see. You're going to set the cargo on fire, free the black gang, fight your way off the ship and outrun the rebel bullets?" Storter asked. "You've been reading too many penny dreadfuls."

His gallows humor—if that's what it was—fell flat. The other men were not amused.

"We may draw gun fire," I quickly agreed, "but after their first hurried volley, they'll be shooting in the dark and into a wall of smoke."

"Smoke? That's not exactly a solid breastworks," Storter said.

"Not just smoke," I countered. "We'll have the steamship between us and them. We'll leap off the back side into the water where our boats can sail around, anchor and fish us out."

"Just supposin' you pull this off," Wilcox, a gunsmith from Cedar Keys, cut in. "How would you escape? The *Argonaut* is twice as fast as the sailboats. She'll overtake you."

"Maybe not," Savarese said. "The copper sheathing on an ironside only extends to the water line. Below that, her hull is wood—just like any other ship. If we blow a hole in her hull and take out the bilge pumps, her furnace will flood and she'll be dead in the water."

Nordland, the ex-artillery officer, jumped in. "And I'd know just where to put the explosive charge."

"Maybe so," Wilcox answered. "But it will take a helluva blast to blow a hole in that warship."

Nordland was quick to shout him down. "There's more than enough coal dust in the *Argonaut's* hold to do the job."

Once again I was glad he had such a loud voice.

A moment of murmuring followed then Broady laughed out loud and slapped me on the back. "It's such a simple, straightforward plan," he said. "Hell, it just might work."

"But, promise me, please," Maureen said, "that you'll rescue my father and the other men in the black gang."

She turned in a semi-circle while establishing eye contact with each man in the tent. Oakland turned away.

"When Quill steams back into the bay," Brother Storter said, "it will be every man for himself and the devil take the hindmost."

I shook my head and said, "Let's have a show of hands. How many are willing to make a stand?"

Seven hands shot up. That was all. Besides my son and me, there was Savarese, Perry, Nordland, Broady and Doc.

All but Doc were rough and ready gladesmen, willing to fight because they had family working in Quill's black gang. I still felt uneasy.

"I'd feel better," I said, "if you were healthier."

Broady was the first to speak up. "Hell, I couldn't look the missus in the eye if I didn't try to save her brother."

The others quickly agreed. But I still thought they looked a little shaky on their feet. I remembered what Doc had said about yellow fever: there are two bouts of the fever; just when the victims start to feel good, the second one sets in. That's the one that can kill them.

Yet, looking at our small group, I saw no fear. The men appeared resolute. I rubbed my hands together in the same way you might scrape a flint stone with a knife.

"That settles it," I said. "We have twelve fighting men."

"Twelve?" Jesse asked. "I make it seven?" His gesture took in the five volunteers and the two of us.

"You're forgetting," I said, "we already have five men aboard their ship."

"And Jack Pemble," Maureen added.

"That's right. Make that thirteen," I said with some hesitation.

Thirteen is an unlucky number.

"And one fighting woman," Maureen added. She stood there steady as a hickory plank.

Stunned by her spunk, all I could say was, "Fourteen."

Adam Broady whispered in my ear, "I take back what I said about her being just another church lady."

We both chuckled. But my mind quickly turned to more sobering thoughts. We were outnumbered and outgunned, and some of us looked as flat as stagnant pond water. But we had the advantage of my military training, and the element of surprise on our side. It would have to be enough.

Storter, Oakland and the other men drew back into the shadows and left the rest of us standing in a tight-knit circle. We got down on our haunches and spent the next half hour studying a map that Broady drew of the camp in the dirt. I noticed Jesse kept rubbing his eyes and pulled him aside.

"What's wrong?" I asked.

"Stengel was right," he said. "The quinine blurs your vision."

"Well," I said, "it sure doesn't blur your thinking. You knew straight off that we had to attack at night."

"I got that idea from one of my books."

"A book? What kind of book?"

He nodded. "The story of Jason and the Argonauts."

"The Argonauts? *The USS Argonaut?*"

He laughed. "It's a book of Greek mythology. The Argonauts were seamen. Quill's ship is named after them. At one point in the story, they get lost at sea and return at night to the same place they just left. In the dark, they think they've reached a hostile shore and start killing one another."

"It's a myth?"

"Maybe, but one that could mean a happy ending for us."

"Let's hope so," I said. "First we have to take on McKenna and his bunch."

We agreed that Jesse, Maureen and I would slip out of the tent in the morning. She would make her way to the beehive while Jesse and I headed for the rebels' tent. Savarese would keep an eye out for the sentry and give a bird whistle if he saw him coming. Broady and Perry would make their way toward where the rebel horses were hobbled and tie them up to a tree and cut off that escape route. Doc and Nordland would stay behind to make sure Oakland and his bunch didn't sneak out to warn the rebels. Once all the details were worked out, we called it quits for the night.

As Maureen started to leave, I said, "Wait. I'll walk you back to your tent."

She turned and looked at me, her expression a mixture of concern and relief. "Are you sure?" she asked. "It could be risky for you."

"At this hour of the night," I said, "the sentry is probably asleep on his feet."

She hesitated and I clicked my heels together, bowed slightly from the waist and pulled back the tent flap with one hand. As she ducked past me, the scent of rose water washed over me and for a moment it seemed as if we were once again walking down the street in Cedar Keys without a care in the world. I followed her out into the moonlit night and, to my surprise, Maureen took my hand.

"I'm so grateful you made it back," she whispered.

"And, I'm truly sorry about Caleb, your father and Minny."

"Thank you," she said, squeezing gently.

We turned toward her tent, walking side by side, only inches apart. There was so much I wanted to say but I didn't know how to put it into words.

"It's hard to believe any of this has happened," she said.

"I know what you mean," I answered. "It feels like a nightmare and that, at any moment, we'll wake up and everything will be the way it used to be."

"Some things can be," she said.

"Like what?"

"Like our friendship," she said.

My heart leapt in my chest. "I'd like that," I said.

"It was very courageous of you to stand your ground in there," she said.

"Me? You're the brave one. You shamed those men into volunteering."

"I just can't let those renegades get away with this," she said.

"We'll put paid to their plans tomorrow," I replied.

She pecked me on the cheek, then stepped back, a look of alarm on her face. "Your skin feels hot," she said. "Are you running a fever?"

"I'm just worked up," I said. "I'll be fine."

"Are you sure?" she asked, the worry apparent in her eyes.

"I'll have Doc check it out," I said. But I didn't really mean it. I didn't have time to be sick.

"Please do," she said.

"Good night, Maureen," I said in my most reassuring voice.

Then she pursed her lips, pecked me on the cheek and ducked inside her tent.

I was a little light-headed, confused, not sure what to make of what had just happened.

She kissed me. Twice. But what about Pemble? Had she kissed him, too?

I was still puzzling over what had happened, and making my way back to Doc's tent, when I heard a soft, muffled sound and ducked behind a cypress tree. A stealthy figure slipped out of Doc's tent and headed straight for the rebels' tent on cat's feet. We had a spy in our midst. I undid the strap on my LeMat, cocked the hammer and waited for the man to pass my tree. In the pale moonlight, I made out who was skulking off—Trent Oakland. I stepped out from behind the cypress, right arm raised, the barrel of my revolver inches from the head of this white trash.

"That's as far as you go," I said.

He stumbled backward and said, "Canfield! What's this all about?" His head pivoted to the left and right as if looking for a quick exit. "I was just going to relieve myself."

"The latrine is the other way," I said.

"I plum forgot."

"Turn around with your hands up where I can see them and head back to the tent."

"I got turned around in the dark," he said. "I'm confused is all. I've got the flux."

"You're sick all right," I said, "and if you don't get a move on you'll die of lead poisoning."

I poked him in the back with the barrel of the revolver and he reluctantly retraced his steps, grousing every step of the way. Then I pulled back the tent flap and told him to get inside. At the sound of my voice, several people sat bolt upright on their cots.

"What happened?" Jesse asked, rubbing his eyes.

"I found this peckerhead sneaking over to the rebel tent."

"A turncoat?" Doc asked.

"Quick! Tie and gag him," Nordland said. "I see the sentry coming."

I threw Oakland to the ground before he could call out. He raised an arm to ward off my next blow and exposed a bandage on his wrist—in the same place that Beau had bitten one of the nightriders. It was too much. I kicked him in the stomach and he doubled up in pain.

"That's for Beau," I said.

He gasped for air. Then we bound and gagged him and laid him down on his cot until the sentry's footsteps came and went.

Later, we sat up on our cots and talked about what to do with Oakland. In the end, we decided to leave him trussed up for the night and give him a chance to rethink where his loyalties lie.

I tried to catch some shut-eye but I soon began to sweat. This time it wasn't the night sweats. This time I fretted about the here and now. I lay there for what seemed like hours, tossing, turning, unable to get any rest. My mind whipsawed back and forth with thoughts about what the dawn would bring and about my being the only one with a gun. It felt as if everything rested on my shoulders. Perspiration clotted my blood-red shirt.

CHAPTER ELEVEN

Some things you never forget. Every detail of what happened next is forever etched in my mind.

With the arrival of dawn, adrenalin began to take hold. I rolled out of the sack, answered nature's call and returned to the tent to find Jesse waiting for me.

"I see you have an extra one of these," he said, holding up my other red shirt. "Mind if I borrow it?"

We looked at one another for several seconds before I could clear my throat. "Wear it in good health," I said.

He laughed and slipped the shirt on, and to my surprise, it fit.

"You'll do your mother proud," I said.

"I'm not so sure she'd agree. Those are rebel boys we're taking on."

"Renegade rebels," I pointed out. "They're not fighting for the South. They're fighting for themselves and for Quill."

Maureen entered our tent with an empty water bucket and a smoker for the beehive. She wore a long sleeve blouse, gloves, a straw bonnet and a lace mantilla to protect her from bee stings. She looked pale and frail and I could sense her unease, but she tried her best not to let on how she felt.

She looked at me and asked, "You feeling okay?"

"Sure. This is just my ornery side showing. How 'bout you? Nervous?"

"I've got the jitters," she replied, "and a sour stomach."

"It's not too late to change your mind."

"And miss out on all the excitement?" she said. It was the kind of half jest her brother Caleb used to make.

"You're amazing," I said.

"Are you going to stand here talking all day?" She held up the bucket and gave me a tight grin.

Our heads were almost touching. I could inhale her breath, her spirit.

Jesse cleared his throat to get our attention then said, "Everyone's ready."

I looked about the tent one last time. The other men were all grim-faced, but determined.

"Okay," I said. "Let's go."

Each man took up his assigned position. At the bend in the creek, Maureen disappeared in the direction of the beehive. Jesse and I made our way stealthily across the campground, heading toward the tent of the sleeping rebels. The faint glow of the rising sun lit our path but the light also threatened to expose us. A dog started to snarl and we backed off and went another way.

Savarese whistled and we froze. I glanced back at him and he signaled with his hands. The sentry was only sixty feet away. Sunlight gleamed off the bayonet on the sentry's rifle barrel. He pivoted, turned in our direction and I recognized Private Fletcher. In 30 strides, he would be upon us. I picked up several stones and tossed them behind Fletcher's back. They hit the ground with a clatter that brought Fletcher to a halt. He spun around, his rifle lowered, his eyes straining to locate the source of the noise. I threw two more stones.

"Who goes there?" Fletcher called out.

I threw another pebble, this one further than the rest.

"I say, who goes there?" Fletcher started edging his way toward the sound.

As soon as he went behind the row of tents, I threw a pebble at a nesting pelican and the bird took to the air, stirring up an entire flock. In the chaos, Fletcher rushed back, confused and distracted, his attention focused on the birds. I tapped Jesse on the shoulder and then I darted across the last tent row. Jesse stayed on the other side and made his way up the row of tents. I waved my kerchief in Maureen's direction and saw her start toward the rebel's tent with her bucket in hand. My heart pounded in my chest. I wished I hadn't let her talk me into giving her such a dangerous role. But it was too late for second thoughts. The sound of her footsteps crunching on the crushed seashells broke the stillness of the dawn like the sputtering of distant rifle fire. The sound caught Fletcher's ear and he spun around, his rifle aimed at Maureen. I reached for my revolver.

"Halt," he ordered. "Identify yourself."

"It's just me. It's Maureen Foster," she smiled, calm as can be, "filling up our water bucket. Someone else has come down with the fever."

On hearing word of the fever, Fletcher shook his head, backed off and turned away. "Be quick about it," he said over his shoulder.

Maureen took fifty more paces, reached the rebels' tent, lifted the flap and threw the beehive inside. Then she dashed away.

The reaction from inside the tent was almost instantaneous. The angry bees went berserk. The two men started whooping and hollering in pain, slapping and jumping, bumping into each other. Hoagg threw back the tent flap and scrambled out on his hands and knees. I kicked him hard enough to knock him senseless. On hearing Mckenna's shouts, Fletcher came running. He never saw Jesse. He never knew what hit him. Jesse clobbered him and sent him sprawling in the dirt.

But McKenna fooled us. He crawled out the back side of the tent, took one look at what had happened and lit out just as a crowd came running to see what all the commotion was about.

"Out of the way," I shouted.

They fell back. But the morning light was dim and I was too wound up to shoot straight. I held my fire for fear of hitting someone else.

McKenna grabbed young Kate by the neck and spun her around in front of him, her small body shielding him from my revolver. She screamed in wide-eyed panic and tried to pull away but McKenna clasped her tightly to his chest. His face was no longer begrimed by gun smoke, his beard had been trimmed and his deep-set, gray eyes looked as hard as concrete.

"Go ahead," he snarled, "shoot and she dies, too."

Maureen rushed to my side, her lower lip trembling. "Don't shoot," she cried.

Chapter Eleven

The three of us stood ten feet apart, neither side knowing what to do next. But little Helen did. She saw McKenna grab Kate and rushed to her big sister's aid. Before any one could stop her, Helen threw a rock that hit McKenna squarely in the head. Stunned, he released Kate and staggered back into the arms of the angry crowd. They wrestled him to the ground, pinned him there and pummeled him senseless before I could stop them.

Maureen untied Jack Pemble and he pushed and shoved the crowd aside. He seethed with anger, tried to get at McKenna until I wrapped him in a bear hug.

"Easy does it," I said. "They're worth more to us alive than dead."

He looked at me for a second as if seeing a ghost. "You made it back."

"Yes."

He sucked wind and straightened up. "We can always kill them later."

I was about to chew him out when Maureen appeared at Pemble's side. "Thank God, you're okay," she said. Then, in what seemed like an after thought, she turned to me and added: "Now we have to free the men on the black gang."

"I want to help," Pemble said.

"Believe me," I replied, "you'll get your chance."

We redistributed the weapons that had been seized, and then questioned each of the rebels separately, trying to learn as much as we could about Quill's operation. The threat of being thrown back in the tent with the beehive loosened their lips just enough for us to learn what they'd been told by Quill's men.

As best I recall, they said Quill had close to 45 men on the *Argonaut* and that the next cattle drive was well under way and would soon reach our section of the coast. Quill planned to off-load his Cuban cargo and hide it in the glades; then make another quick run with a new shipment of cattle his other men were rounding up. We'd have to strike quickly or we'd get caught in a pincer attack from Quill on our front and the cracker cow hunters driving the cattle toward our camp.

I did most of the questioning until McKenna said something that set my teeth on edge.

"You're not going to get away with this, you know," he said. "Quill is on his way back with enough men and weapons to blow this entire camp to smithereens."

"That's where you're wrong," I said. "He isn't running the blockade with guns and ammunition."

McKenna smirked and said, "You don't know what you're jawing about."

"The limey doesn't care who wins this war," I said. "All Quill cares about is making a profit. He's bringing in silks, perfume, liquor, quinine, chloroform, bonnets, food, clothing—anything that's lightweight, scarce and highly profitable. Weaponry weighs too much."

McKenna looked at me with disdain. "You make about as much sense as a pea hen."

"Think about it," I said. "The only way he can outrun the Yankee man-o-war is by lightening the *Argonaut's* load. In fact, by now he has most likely sold the *Argonaut*'s cannons in Cuba. They're too heavy and useless on a blockade runner. One shot from those cannons and he's considered a pirate and can be hung from the highest yardarm."

McKenna wavered for a split second then held firm to his view. "Sell them to Cuba? Quill wouldn't do that. The South needs every cannon she can get."

"When the *Argonaut* steams into that bay," I said, "there will be no cannons on her deck."

"I'll believe that when I see it," McKenna said.

"If seeing is believing," I said, "read this article from the Key West newspaper."

I reached into my pocket and pulled out the news article about Quill that I had saved only to discover it was sopping wet and unreadable. McKenna laughed. I figured his mind was closed, and dropped the subject, knowing we would both know soon enough who was right.

We had just finished questioning our prisoners when Brother Storter approached us. Dressed in black and followed by a small group of men, he put me in mind of a shark followed by pilot fish. He clasped the lapels of his frock coat in his fists and, in his most moralizing tone of voice, said:

"We've taken a vote and we have decided that it is foolhardy to stay. We are leaving the camp with the sick, elderly, women and children, and heading into the Everglades this afternoon." He gestured over his shoulder toward the men who had followed him.

"Suit yourself," I said. "We're not going to abandon the men on the black gang."

Storter's lower lip jutted out. "Yes, well, I suppose it is better that a few should fight on instead of putting all the people at risk."

Damned if that wasn't just like what Storter had said in his speechifying. He'd said that Caiaphas, the Jewish high priest, had justified killing Jesus by saying: "It is better for you that one man die for the people than that the whole nation perish."

What a hypocrite. Never troubled by a pang of conscience.

"Take some of the medicine with you," Doc said.

"We'll need weapons and ammunition, too," Storter replied.

He was right. The Everglades crawled with gators, snakes, wild boars, panthers and bear. Storter's group wouldn't stand a chance without firearms. But what galled me was the fact that the preacher knew we'd do the Christian thing. He knew we'd give them the guns, even though we needed all the firepower we could muster for the upcoming battle.

I looked about and saw all the anxious children clinging to their mother's skirts. I saw young Zach Wetherby standing off by himself, unsure what to do next. I told Stengel to take a quick inventory of our makeshift armory and leave with whatever we could spare. Then I asked Broady to make sure Stengel took only what they'd need. Within a half hour, most of the tents had been struck and a line of horse-drawn wagons was forming up on the edge of the camp. The men staying behind with me were the last to bid goodbye to their loved ones. As I watched Adam Broady hug and kiss his wife and boys, I asked myself if I was throwing caution to the wind. Adam still looked a little sickly; yet, he had volunteered to fight to free the black gang. I put the thought out of my mind. The cluster of wives and children slowly unraveled until only Maureen remained. She stepped forward, a pistol in her hand.

"I'm staying," she said.

I got a lump in my throat, stepped forward and gently took the pistol from her hand.

"Maureen, you've done more than anyone could expect," I said. "But your little sisters are going to need you to watch after them."

"My father—"

"Your father would want you to take care of Kate and Helen."

Tears welled up in her eyes and trickled down her cheek. I wanted to wipe them away and tell her everything would be all right but I couldn't bring myself to do it.

"Your sisters need you," I said. "Go."

She knit her brow, took a deep breath and sighed. Then she turned and walked away, glancing back several times. Zach Wetherby trailed off behind her.

"She's an amazing young woman," Pemble said.

"She sure is," I replied.

"Why don't you tell her that?" he asked.

"Come again?"

"Tell her how you feel about her."

Dumbfounded, I looked at Pemble. "What are you saying?"

"I'm saying it's obvious that the two of you are in love and high time you told one another how you feel."

"I thought—"

"That she liked me?" he asked. "I'm a little too buttoned up for her. She seems drawn to the stubborn, mulish type—men who defy convention and refuse to go along with the crowd. Sound familiar?"

"She told you that?" I asked.

"Not in so many words, but I got the message. Go on," he said, "while you still have time. Tell her how you feel." He smiled broadly and gave me a nudge in the direction Maureen had taken.

I grabbed Pemble's right hand in both of mine, pumped it up and down and thanked him. Then I rushed to catch up with Maureen. She heard my footsteps coming from behind and spun around, a look of puzzlement on her face.

"Let me help you pack," I said.

"But we can only take a few things," she said. She searched my eyes for a better explanation.

"I know," I said. "But there's something I don't want you to leave without."

"Like what?"

I pulled back the flap of Pemble's tent and we both ducked inside where no one else could see us. The scent of her rose water filled the air and I took a deep, intoxicating breath. She must have seen the change in my expression because she looked at me and asked once again how I felt.

"I've never felt better," I said. I paused, took another deep breath and hesitated, wanting to choose my words carefully.

"What is it then?" she asked.

"There's something I want you to take with you," I said.

"Ed," she said, "for mercy's sake, say what you mean. We have to pack in a hurry."

I put my hands around her waist, drew her to me. She didn't resist. Our lips met. I felt her tremble. We drew back and I said, "I mean, I love you."

Then I kissed her full on the lips. Hers were soft and full and yielding. Before she could react, the tent flap flew open, light flooded in and Helen and Kate rushed inside. Maureen and I stiffened and stepped back. She smoothed her wrinkled dress.

"Were you two kissing?" Helen said. "Yeck."

Kate frowned to make known her disapproval. When she spoke, her voice sounded frosty. "Brother Storter says we have to pack right away."

"We were just saying good-bye," I said, and I gave each of the little girls a peck on the cheek as if that was how I had been saying goodbye to their older sister. In the next few, hurried minutes Maureen and I packed their things. Just as they were about to leave, I stole another kiss.

"Take care of yourself, Ed," Maureen whispered. "Take care of my father, too."

"I will," I said. "But where will you go? How will I find you?" I asked.

"Brother Storter says there is a church nearby where he has done some preaching. He says we can board a ship there and head for Key West."

"But that's a northern port," I said.

She nodded. "Brother says the Yanks may command Fort Taylor, but they can't command our spirits."

True enough. But, returning to Key West after what I had done posed serious problems for me. First off, I had disobeyed Commander Hill's orders by leaving the harbor on the *Shore Thing*; and, second, with any luck, I was about to do battle with the USS *Argonaut* for the second time. Then again, I wouldn't be welcome in a Confederate port either—not after attacking the rebels and Quill. If any of Quill's men were to escape, it would be their word against mine and I already knew how that would play out. Yet, the gambler in me knew that I had to play the hand I had been dealt.

"I'll make it back to Key West," I said. "Somehow. Some way."

She blew me a kiss just as a breeze stirred. The folds of her dress ballooned out like the sails of a ship leaving port. She gathered the dress in her hand and raised the hem so it wouldn't drag on the ground then turned to leave. I wanted to rush after her but I knew I couldn't. I had to stick it out in the camp with the other men and watch her ghost away.

Maureen, her sisters and young Zach joined the clutch of other refugees leaving for deeper in the glades. I sure couldn't blame them. It didn't look like we had much of a chance against Quill. The line of refugees rode off, heads bowed low, silent as pallbearers. Oakland, having been untied, gave me one final pinch-faced look before cantering off. After the last wagon had disappeared into the glades, I turned and went to find Jesse.

~

An eerie stillness now hung over the nearly deserted camp. When I found Jesse and the other men, my son gave me a searching look and said, "You sure you're up to this? You look tuckered out."

I shook my head and said, "You ought to know me better than that by now."

He grinned and said, "Figured you wouldn't quit."

"Your old man doesn't know the meaning of the word," Broady said.

The rest of the men nodded in agreement.

"Okay," I said, "Listen up. We'll wait until dusk before taking on the five men at the wharf."

I decided that three of us would lead the attack on the crew that was building the wharf. I would dress as McKenna; Jesse would dress as Fletcher; Pemble would dress as Hoagg. The others would lurk behind and attack on a signal from me.

Two hours later, I turned to Jesse and Pemble and said, "Time to go."

We made our way through the woods to the other inlet and hid behind a bald cypress tree while we reconnoitered the rebel camp. I glassed the scene to see what we were up against. The river at this point was about a half mile across; the inlet was a half moon-shaped stretch of sandy beach skirted by mangroves and fed by a creek that flowed past a campsite. At the mouth of the inlet, the rebels had built a large wharf straight out into deep water to make it easy for the ship to dock and sway off its cargo. An empty, makeshift cattle pen stood near the shoreline. Four of the rebel soldiers were putting the finishing touches on the wharf while a fifth man, a vedette, sat a horse overseeing the approach to the wharf from land and sea.

We pulled our hats low over our heads, tightened our gun belts and stalked out of the woods, straight for the shoreline and the wharf. I held in my gloved hand a rag soaked in turpentine. Our eyes were riveted on the vedette and his powerful, black steed. The other four men were so intent on their job, they didn't look up.

We were within fifty feet of the vedette when he reined his horse around and took a closer look at us. I waved and called out "Howdy" and he seemed to relax. We kept walking.

"If y'all are healthy," he said, as he kneed his horse in our direction, "we can sure enough use more hands to finish this here job on time."

We were within ten feet of the rider. The horse sensed something. His nostrils flared and he shied away. His rump passed in front of me. I lifted the tail and swabbed the genitals with the rag soaked in turpentine. The horse twitched, snorted, bunched its muscles, coiled and sprang. The rider jolted into the air and hit the ground. The horse kicked out and thundered down the wharf, stomping and jumping, trampling and banging, crashing into lumber, nail kegs and anything else in its way.

The stunned rider tried to get to his feet but I thumped him good with the butt of my pistol.

"Loose horse! Loose horse!" I cried out.

The four rebels on the wharf turned, saw the horse galloping straight for them, dropped their tools and dove head first into the water with the horse right behind them. We raced down the wharf and, when they surfaced, they were staring right into the barrels of our guns.

"Looks like we caught ourselves a mess of fish," I said to Jesse.

Pemble gave a hearty laugh. "Catfish, if you ask me."

We ordered the rebels out of the water and tied them up while Perry and Nordland got the horse. After all the prisoners were secured in one tent, we brought the *Shore Thing* around, loaded her with the remaining barrels of turpentine and brought them to the wharf where we stacked them next to sawdust and kindling from the construction site. Then I had Doc and Pemble move the *Shore Thing* and another boat from the camp to a nearby inlet where they couldn't be seen by anyone on the *Argonaut.*

~

Later, we all cleaned our weapons, a painstaking process that took up to a half hour. The guns had to be washed with hot water. Then the six chambers in each revolver had to be reloaded with a combustible cartridge and seated firmly with the loading lever. Next, percussion caps had to be placed on each of the six nipples in the rear of the cylinder and covered with tallow.

Afterwards, we sat around a campfire talking about what the next day might bring. We knew we were greatly outnumbered and would have to rely on cunning, stealth and luck.

Lots of luck.

One by one we fell silent, lost in our own thoughts. With the fire still blazing, Doc dispensed more medicine, passed around some pencils and paper and asked each of us to write letters to our loved ones. The hope was that the letters would be found in our pockets and delivered, if we didn't make it back.

I took the picture of Maureen out of my pocket and focused on it in the light of the campfire. Seeing her posing with those students, I couldn't help thinking what a great mother she would make and whether I would live to be the father of her children. Then I wrote a brief letter to her in which I said:

To Miss Maureen Foster,

Somewhere in southwest Florida.

Though we are far apart tonight you are ever present in my thoughts.

I hope that all goes well tomorrow and that we will soon be reunited. But, if my luck should run out and you receive this letter, I pray that you will treasure these sentiments from an ardent admirer who feels privileged to have known you. With great affection and concern for your wellbeing, I remain to the end your devoted servant.

Edward Canfield

The letter was a little stiff and stilted, I admit; but I figured someone else would be reading it, too. So I kept my innermost feelings to myself and hoped Maureen would be able to read between the lines. As I slipped the letter into my pocket, Doc sat down beside me.

"Your son and Cal Nordland are right," he said. "You're a helluva soldier."

"I did what I had to do; nothing more," I said.

"I saw a look come over you today that I've seen before."

"A look?"

"The same haunted look I've seen on the faces of other veterans." He paused and added, "Mind if I ask you something?"

"Sure. So long as you don't mind if I don't answer."

"I'm thinking," he said, "that you still deal with what happened the last time you were in uniform. I'm thinking you still have nightmares about what happened in Mexico."

He threw a stick into the campfire and sparks leapt into the air.

"War changes a man," I said.

"Some more so than others. Has anyone ever told you that you might have 'soldier's heart'?"

"What of it?" I said.

"Well," Doc said, "backtracking gets a man nowhere. You have to move forward with your life. When this fracas is over, I'd like to sit down with you and have a long talk. There may be some things you can do about it."

I'd heard that before. More than once. "Right now," I said, "I'm more concerned about the next twenty-four hours."

Doc stood up, dusted the seat of his pants and walked off. I was too unsettled to sleep and moved over to sit on another log next to Jesse. Together, we gazed in silence at the dying embers of our campfire.

"Red sky tonight," he said after a few minutes. "A lucky omen." He gestured to a sky clotted with crimson tinted clouds.

"I'd feel luckier," I said, "if we had a few more good fighting men on our side."

"I know what you mean," he said. "Savarese and Broady were confused and were having trouble keeping up with us today. A second bout of fever may be coming on."

"The others don't look that strong, either."

"What about McKenna?" Jesse asked after several long seconds. "He seemed to waver for a second when you told him about Quill's cargo. Think he and his bunch would throw in with us if they saw what Quill was really up to?"

"Same thought crossed my mind," I said. "If the *Argonaut* steams into the bay without her cannons, McKenna just might believe I was telling the truth."

We let it go at that and before long the mosquitoes got too pesky. We returned to our tent, turned in and pulled the netting over our heads.

This time all it took was the soft cooing of a nearby chuck-wills-widow to shatter my sleep. I heard the trilling as the whistle of incoming rounds, the flutter of wings as the sound of artillery shells just before impact. A breeze stirred, rattling the palm trees and I heard the sound as if it were grape shot chewing through the night, searching for me. I saw myself running in a panic through a forest of denuded, splintered trees, dodging in and out of the choking, blinding gun smoke. It smelt like brimstone. Like hell. The crackle of the dying campfire warped into the sound of a military band playing the "Dead March". Above the din, I heard a voice cry out, "Ready, aim, fire." And when the smoke cleared, I saw Private Winslow tied to a tree, head hanging down, and blood oozing from his chest. He raised his head, looked up at me and said, "Don't throw caution to the wind."

The vision jolted me awake in the middle of the night and I lay there in a cold sweat, shivering and wondering if I'd ever live down what I had done.

~

Shortly after first light, we all rolled out of our bedrolls. The morning sun fought its way through a gunmetal gray cloudbank to revive our spirits. An onshore breeze caused the grass to shiver as if in anticipation of what the day held in store for us. We yawned, stretched as though it was just another day; then slipped into our itchy, ill-fitting woolen Confederate uniforms.

No one said a word until Doc broke the brittle silence.

"An army travels on its stomach," he said. "Come and get it."

He had built a fire and had rustled up some salt pork 'n drippins. I sat on a tree stump, taking in the aroma of that grub, thinking about how my mother used to get up every day, stoke the fire and cook us up a breakfast of cornbread, grits, greens and gravy. I wondered if I'd ever taste another home-cooked meal. I wondered what Maureen would be eating for breakfast and whether I'd ever see her again.

Doc handed me a cup of fresh-brewed chicory and a plate of the grub. I took a sip of the chicory—bitter, but bracing. Nordland rolled a cigarette with one hand and lit up. The smoke reached me and sucked my appetite away. I put my food down, walked off.

"Hey," Nordland shouted after me, "if you ain't gonna eat that—"

"Help yourself," I said.

Jesse joined me several minutes later down on the wharf. I heard him come up behind me, recognized the sound of his tread, but was surprised when he put an arm around my shoulder. We stood there in silence for several minutes.

"Jittery?" I asked.

"Some."

"Once the shooting starts, you'll be fine."

"How about you? You look pretty limp."

"These last few days have been rough," I said, "but I'll be okay."

A few hours later, a rope of smoke cleared the tree line. The *Argonaut* appeared at the mouth of the inlet about a half-mile off. In these shallow waters, a ship that size could easily run aground, but with the tide in her favor and Quill in command, she proceeded slowly and steadily upriver. I had to admire his seamanship.

I stood stock still as the *Argonaut* drew closer then glassed her to make sure there were no cannons on her deck. Sure enough, Quill had done just what I'd suspected he would do. He'd sold them.

"Wait until McKenna sees this," I said. I turned and headed back up the hill.

"Where are you going?" Jesse called out.

"Goin' for reinforcements," I shouted back.

I raced to the end of the wharf, mounted the vedette's horse and high-tailed it back to the camp where Doc was feeding the prisoners. I dismounted on the run, hitched the horse to a tree and came to a stop in front of Bill McKenna.

"McKenna," I said. "You didn't believe me when I said Quill was in this for the money. You said he'd never sell his cannons in Cuba when the Confederacy needed them, right?"

"What of it?" he asked.

"Well, the *Argonaut* just steamed into the bay without any cannons on board."

"To hell you say," he muttered to himself. I could see he was shocked to the core. Setting aside his grub, he looked to the men on his left and right. Fletcher and Hoagg shrugged their shoulders as if to say his guess was as good as theirs.

"On your feet," I said. "You're about to see for yourself."

I had Doc untie McKenna's feet, while I kept him covered. Then I prodded him from behind with the barrel of my pistol and directed him toward a huge live oak at the edge of the camp.

"Start climbing," I said as I handed him my spyglass, "and take a gander at the *Argonaut.* Tell me what you see, or better yet, what you don't see."

McKenna climbed the live oak until he could see over the surrounding trees then trained the spyglass on the ship, which approached the wharf. I saw him adjust the focus several times in disbelief before letting out a sigh that trailed off into a curse. He lowered the spyglass and shook his head.

"The limey shit bucket sold the cannons to the Cubans just like you said he would."

"He's done more than that," I said. "He's run down to Cuba with enough cattle to feed a rebel regiment and he's returned with a cargo that has nothing to do with winning the war."

McKenna scrambled down from the tree.

"And you can forget about exchanging the hostages for the prisoners of war, " I said. "All McKenna will want for the hostages is money."

McKenna handed the spyglass to me and said, "I've seen enough. How can I help?"

I holstered my pistol and said, "We need you, Hoagg and Fletcher to help us take on Quill and his men."

"My men will do whatever I say."

"Good. There's no time to lose."

We told Hoagg and Fletcher what had happened, untied them, broke out more weapons and armed them.

"What about them?" Fletcher asked. He pointed to the five other rebel prisoners, the ones who had been working on the wharf.

"Their Quill's men," I said. "They stay put."

The four of us made our way on foot to the other inlet where the *Argonaut* had already docked and was about to sway off her cargo. Jesse met us with a wry grin but the other gladesmen were not smiling.

"What the hell are they doing here?" Pemble demanded. His jaw jutted out at McKenna's men. The veins in his neck bulged with venom. The palm of his hand rested on the butt of his pistol.

"They've seen that Quill has stripped the cannons from the *Argonaut.* They've come around to our way of thinking," I said, eager to defuse a tense situation. "They're throwing in with us."

Pemble shook his head, but before he could say anything, Adam pulled him aside and calmed him down.

"How do we know we can trust them?" Nordland bellowed.

"You don't," Fletcher snapped back. "Any more'n I know I can trust y'all."

"Look," McKenna said, "we don't like what Quill is doing same as y'all. We aim to stop him."

"That's enough jawing," I said. "Gather round everyone while I go over the plan one more time for the benefit of our reinforcements."

I got down on my haunches and drew a map of the shoreline in the dirt while McKenna, Fletcher and Hoagg looked on. The gladesmen stood behind us, craning their necks to see how the soldiers would react to my plan. If these trained military men didn't go along with what I said, I knew the gladesmen would lose heart.

I had to win over McKenna's team. They listened intently as I explained how my team would set the cargo on fire to draw the rebels off the ship; then McKenna's team would free the black gang and blow the ship. We'd all escape on the sailboats. When I finished, there was a moment of intense silence while I held my breath and waited for a reaction.

Broady broke the tension with an attempt at humor. "They have us outnumbered three to one. The poor bastards."

McKenna grinned, turned to his men and said, "The bastard I want to get my hands on is Quill."

I had won over McKenna. But Fletcher and Hoagg were slower to come around.

"What if it rains?" Fletcher asked, "What if you can't start a fire? What then?"

"It's winter," I said. "The dry season. There's scant chance of rain, not after the gushers we had last week."

"There are a good twenty yards of open ground between the tree line and the wharf," Hoagg said. "All it would take is one sharp-eyed sentry—just one—and we're done for."

"It will be nearly dark," I said. "With the rebels' clothes on our backs, they won't suspect anything."

Some thing else troubled Fletcher. "Are your boats big enough for all of us to escape on?"

"Odds are all of us won't be making it back," I said.

I watched as all of them absorbed the impact of what I had just said.

McKenna spoke up again. "Hell, Fletcher, you've been wanting to use your fancy new pistol, the one you took off Pembrook. Here's your chance."

But Fletcher still held back. "Let's say we take them by surprise and somehow actually win and escape. Where are we headed after we win—north or south?"

"We'll sail for Fort Myers where the rebels can disembark," I said. "After that, anyone who wants to stay onboard the *Shore Thing* can head for Key West with me and Jesse."

"I want to hear that from the rest of you," Fletcher said, "in case Canfield here isn't one of the men who make it through this fracas."

The others agreed. Fletcher glanced at Hoagg and McKenna for some reassurance. Hoagg gave a half shrug as if to say, "Don't look at me. He's in command."

Fletcher looked at McKenna, hesitated and nodded that he was satisfied. Then I reminded everyone that we were outnumbered and outgunned. We had to make every shot count.

"If you're packing a Remington .44," I said, "be sure to carry more than one fully loaded cylinder. That way you can reload six shots at a time."

"Don't shoot for the head," McKenna said. "Shoot for the waist. Let the gun's recoil raise the trajectory of your bullet."

"And be sure," Hoagg said, "that the hammer is set between the live chambers so the gun doesn't go off while you're running."

Fletcher quickly added, "After every shot, cock the hammer and raise your arm so the dead cap falls off; otherwise you'll jam your gun."

It was basic stuff any gladesman would know but a sign that the soldiers were uneasy about fighting beside men who were not battle-tested.

I told everyone to double check his weapons one last time. Then we waited in the tree line for the sun to start declining. The gulf breeze picked up and the temperature dropped steadily. I began to feel woozy again. My sweat-stained wool uniform clung to me. I moved deeper into the cooler shadows where I heard a soft rasping sound close by. Turning, I saw Broady bent over and retching. He heard me, looked up, embarrassed and wiped his feverish face with his sleeve. His vomit was black

"Don't say anything," he said. "I'll be all right."

I nodded, but in the back of my mind, I thought the black vomit meant only one thing. The medicine wasn't working.

Adam might not make it.

I think Broady sensed the same thing. The spark had left his eyes.

He blinked slowly as if to say, "Do what you have to do."

I nodded, turned toward the others and heard myself say, "All right men, let's go. The elephant is waiting."

We split into our teams. I led the gladesmen and we made our way around the tree line on the side of the wharf where we had left the barrels of turpentine. The ship's crane had already swayed off most of the crates and boxes, which were stacked near the turpentine barrels. Half a dozen men worked on the wharf and all of them packed pistols. In the dying light, I saw one of them eyeing the barrels of turpentine with suspicion. He said something to another man, who scratched his head and shrugged his shoulders. I thought of what Fletcher had said: it would only take one sharp-eyed rebel to do us in. There was no time to lose. We stepped up our pace, using the tree line for cover.

We were just about to come out onto the flats when something caught my attention and I signaled to halt. We dropped to the ground, hidden by the tall grass and the saw palmettos. Every one except Broady. He staggered ahead, half out of his mind with fever. Seconds later, I saw what I had heard: a sentry trudged past a copse of trees, not twenty feet from Broady. The soldier leveled his rifle and glared at him.

"Halt," he said. "Friend or foe."

Broady mumbled something incoherent.

"Damn it, man, you drunken bastard give the password."

The sentry cocked his rifle. I motioned for the others to stay put, unsheathed my Bowie knife and crawled through the underbrush.

"I'm only going to ask you one more time," the sentry barked.

I came up on him from behind. The sentry heard me. He spun around just as I lunged. I caught him off balance, knocking him to the ground. The two of us disappeared in the thick grass. Moments later, I emerged from the undergrowth, wiping the blade of my knife on the side of my pants. My temple pounded. My hat felt three sizes too small.

"Broady," I hissed. "Why didn't you drop when I ordered you to?"

But I knew why. I knew he was sick. I saw the hurt in his face. I felt like an ass for speaking that way to my sick friend. Turning aside, I said softly to Perry, "He's not up to fighting."

Perry nodded. "Leave him with me. I'll cover your backs as best I can. I'll make sure he gets to the boats if I have to drag him every step of the way."

I had no choice but to agree. Broady could put all of us in jeopardy. I stepped forward and embraced my good and loyal friend and said, "You've done all you can here."

Broady nodded and said, "Give them a shellacking for me." Then he stepped aside.

On a signal from me, Pemble and Doc spun off for the cove where the two boats were hidden. My team was now down to Jesse, Savarese, Nordland and me.

"I don't like the way this is going," Nordland said.

I cut him off. "From this point on," I said, "there will be no hiding. No retreating. Spread out and move out."

Nordland, the old veteran, stiffened and came to attention, despite his rheumatism. We headed across the open grass and made our way down to the wharf where the rebels were manhandling huge stacks of cargo. I could see Captain Quill leaning over the gun'l to oversee the offloading of the crates. The work detail labored so hard they scarcely took note of us. Those that did see us must have thought we were part of the work detail. Savarese and Nordland headed toward the gangway; Jesse and I strode toward the ship's stern.

Up close, the *Argonaut* looked enormous. Its boilers and smoke stacks throbbed and steamed as if the ship were a living, breathing monster. The yellowed portholes gleamed like huge, unblinking serpentine eyes that glared at us and dared us to challenge its ferocity. I felt dwarfed and lost in its shadow and wondered whether we could truly disembowel her. All I had brought to the fight was my LeMat and two other revolvers jammed into my belt.

"Where in hell y'all been?" a rebel asked me. "We got our hands full here."

I waved him off and we made our way back to the turpentine barrels. As I cleared one of the packing crates, I saw the seaman who had questioned the turpentine barrels. He was now squinting at Jesse and me the same way. He was about to call out to someone else when a hand reached out from behind a crate and yanked him out of sight. Moments later, Savarese ducked his head around the corner, looked both ways, gave us a thumbs up and disappeared again. Jesse and

I moved behind one of the shipping crates stenciled with the words "Cuban Rum: 151 Proof."

Highly flammable stuff.

"We start the fire here," I said. "When the flames from the sawdust, kindling and turpentine find the bottles of rum, the alcohol will explode as if a bomb went off."

We broke open and tipped over the first of the turpentine barrels and watched it slosh across the surface of the wharf and onto the crates of rum. I struck a lucifer and was about to set the fuel on fire when a rebel on the deck of the *Argonaut* looked over the gun'l.

"Hey," he shouted," what in hell y'all think you're doing?"

I dropped the lucifer into the kindling and sawdust and jumped back. *Whoosh*! The flame took hold, the turpentine exploded in a fireball that singed my hat, sucked the breath out of my lungs and lit up the sky. We were clearly visible to the rebel. We jumped behind the packing crates just as the rebel opened fire, his wild shot ripping into a crate of Cuban rum.

The greedy flames licked at the rum and raced across the wharf igniting more of the cargo.

"Run," I shouted. "The rum will explode any second."

We whipped out our guns and raced down the wharf, firing at the stunned men in the work detail. Other rebels started firing at us from the ship's deck.

I heard Quill shout, "Kill them! Kill the bloody bastards!"

Perry opened fire and the rebels ducked for cover, giving us the opening we needed. We reached the foot of the wharf just as the rebels came rushing down the gangway in headlong pursuit.

I turned and fired a shotgun blast from the LeMat into a crate of rum bottles at the foot of the gangway. The crate exploded with deafening, fiery force just as the rebels reached the wharf. The flying shards of wood and glass cut them to pieces. In the smoke and debris, I saw McKenna and his men rush up the gangway and onto the ship, Savarese and Nordland were right behind them.

Jesse and I put in our best licks as we raced down the beach, zigzagging back and forth. A swarm of angry bullets whizzed past our heads, gouging geysers of sand from the tidewater flats. My heart pounded. My head throbbed. I could hear my labored breathing, feel my steps faltering. Exhaustion took hold of my body. I staggered, then collapsed, landing headlong in the sand, too weak to go on.

Jesse turned around and rushed back.

"Keep going," I gasped. "Don't stop for me."

"Are you hit?" Jesse asked.

"No. Just keep going," I said again. "That's an order."

He grabbed me under both arms and hauled me to my feet. "That's a stupid order," he said.

I looked at him, but said nothing. He started dragging me toward the *Shore Thing* and the other boat. The boats were anchored just off the beach, not 20 yards away. I could see Pemble and Doc urging us on. I could see Perry taking careful aim at our pursuers, their silhouettes framed by the setting sun. He squeezed off another round, hit one rebel and brought the others to a halt. They dove for cover behind some cargo and returned Perry's fire. We waded into the water and reached the *Shore Thing* unscathed; then we opened fire, giving Perry the cover he needed to drag Broady to the boat. After Perry and Broady were aboard, we weighed anchor with Pemble at the tiller and Doc following behind in the other boat. I was weak and winded and had to lie there next to Perry until I caught my breath. I could hear the sound of heavy gunfire coming from the *Argonaut.* McKenna's men had run into stiff resistance.

I hauled myself up, staggered to the helm and took the tiller from Pemble. Then I brought us about, heading for the steamship while the other gladesmen reloaded their guns. Just as we neared the *Argonaut,* I heard what I took to be Nordland's three warning shots. The men had only ten minutes before she blew. They had to free the black gang and get everyone on deck and over the side of the ship. There was no time to spare.

We plowed our way through the floating, flaming debris from the wharf. Suddenly a huge explosion erupted inside the bowels of the *Argonaut,* just below her waterline. Something had gone wrong. She had exploded too soon. She roared like a wounded beast, her smokestacks groaned and gasped with pain. She slowly began to keel over in a sea of angry flames. Pandemonium ran wild on her deck.

Her crew couldn't escape down the burning gangway. They had to jump overboard into the fiery water. They started throwing hatch covers, deck chairs, doors and crates into the water to disburse the flames before diving in. Several of them surfaced, saw us coming and started swimming toward the *Shore Thing* and the other boat. Pemble fired a warning shot and they quickly turned and swam for the beach. As we came around the stern of the *Argonaut,* I spied Hoagg and several men from the black gang. McKenna and Fletcher were nowhere to be seen. The water on this side of the *Argonaut* looked clear of debris and flames.

"Jump!" I shouted. "Jump!"

Hoagg climbed up on the gun'l and spread his arms as if about to leap. At that moment, Quill appeared on deck, a pistol in hand. He shot Hoagg in the back of the head at point blank range. Hoagg jerked, spun around and fell into the sea. In the next instant, Peter Foster struck Quill a crushing blow to the back of the skull with the flat of a shovel. Quill collapsed on the deck. Suddenly McKenna and Fletcher reached the deck, guns blazing. They fired at the rebels and covered the backs of the black gang as the men dove overboard. But Quill's men kept coming and backed Fletcher and McKenna into a corner. If they dove in now, the renegades could easily pick them off in the water. They fired again, dashed to the other side of the deck, leapt headlong into the water and swam for shore. The rebels shot at the swimmers and we let loose with a salvo that made the gunmen duck for cover.

Fletcher reached the beach first. Ducking and dodging, he made his way across the ground as bullets whistled through the air. Just as he leapt over a pile of debris, a bullet hit him in the thigh. He staggered and sank to his knees like a punctured balloon, a look of astonishment on his face. Clutching his thigh, he stared at the red stain and tried to get to his feet. A second bullet wiped the disbelieving look from his face. He collapsed in a puddle of standing water. McKenna paused just long enough to see whether his friend was dead or alive; then he raced down the beach, plunged into the surf and swan to our boat.

We quickly fished our men out of the water. I could see Peter Foster thrashing about. It was clear that he wasn't a good swimmer and would not make it to the boat. But I couldn't maneuver any closer amid all the flotsam. Stripping off his boots, Jesse dove in and reached Foster in twenty strokes.

Foster panicked, flailed about and, when Jesse told him to hold on, started dragging him down. Jesse dove deeper, came up from behind Foster and hit him in the head with a piece of flotsam. Then he dragged Foster's limp, unconscious body to the *Shore Thing*. Pemble pulled them into the boat and shouted, "Let's get the hell out of here."

I did a quick head count: Jesse, Pemble and Perry looked exhausted but unhurt; Savarese bled from his ears; Nordland had a lacerated forehead; Broady was retching over the gun'l; Peter Foster lay unconscious on the deck; McKenna was holding his side. Three more of the black gang were onboard the other boat, huddled together, looking shell-shocked and terrified.

"Fletcher and Hoagg are dead," I said to Jesse. "We're still missing two men from the black gang."

"We can't desert them," Jesse said.

There was that word again. Desert.

I was not about to desert them. We called out the names of the missing men, our cries lost in a maelstrom of our own making. I tacked back and forth through the fiery flotsam. Each explosion from within the *Argonaut* sent another wave across our bow, threatening to swamp us. Gradually, the flames died back and the lifeless renegades, who bobbed in the water, slipped silently below the surface. The only sounds that remained came from the men on the wharf and beach. They had scattered like wind-borne ash.

"There's nothing more we can do here," I said to Jesse. "Let's head out to sea before the renegades on the beach regroup and attack us."

As we pulled away from the *Argonaut,* her timbers groaned and her metal sheathing buckled under the repeated blows of internal explosions. She gave a deep, guttural moan and exhaled a cloud of soot.

~

CHAPTER TWELVE

We each took an assigned station on the *Shore Thing* and the other boat and sailed away from the devastation, heading for the mouth of the bay. It was too dark to tell where the sea met the sky but Lady Luck steered us clear of the shoals. Venus and the first of the sentinel stars stood watch as we sailed off to the drum roll of the waves pounding against our hulls.

None of us had the strength to express our troubled thoughts. We were too injured, too weak, too dispirited over the loss of good men to voice our true feelings. It didn't feel like a victory.

"What happened?" Peter Foster called out. "Where am I?" He sat up, raised his head, blinked his eyes and looked about.

"You're safe now," Nordland said. "You were drowning until young Jesse here risked his life to save you."

Foster rubbed the back of his head and gave the rest of us a befuddled look. In the gloom, the salt water and coal dust had mixed to give his face the look of a tintype. He was about to say something but Broady started hallucinating, shouting and thrashing about on the deck. Doc gave Broady some laudanum, which took several minutes to affect him. Gradually, he stopped babbling feverishly, closed his eyes and lay back.

We approached the mouth of the bay with a series of close hauled legs to beat a course upwind.

Suddenly Savarese called out, "Running lights!"

I looked to the south and spied the running lights of a large ship sailing under auxiliary steam power less than a mile away, cutting off our exit from the bay.

"It's a Yankee man-o-war," one of the black gang said. "She's been following the *Argonaut* for the better part of the day. Captain Quill had managed to pull away from her."

"They must have seen or heard the explosions from the *Argonaut,*" another man said. "They probably think we've abandoned Quill's sinking ship."

I glassed the dimly lit figures on her deck.

"Her two deck guns are manned and ready," I said.

Even as I spoke, a puff of smoke erupted from the muzzle of one of the warship's twelve-pounders. Without warning, a live round hurtled toward us, blasting a hole in the sea less than 20 yards off our starboard bow. The explosion sent green water across our scuppers and deck. No doubt about it, they thought we were Quill's crewmen. And, to make matters worse, some of us were more or less dressed in Confederate uniforms. McKenna leapt to his feet, ready to jump overboard, when I grabbed him by the collar and pulled him down.

"Wait," I said, "You'd never make it to shore. We'll cover for you with the Yanks."

McKenna nodded and said, "Much obliged."

"Lower the sail," I shouted. "Hove to. And lay down your weapons. Be quick about it."

I quickly ran up a white flag. Doc did the same on the other boat. Then we braced ourselves for what was to come. I struggled to maintain a hard façade in front of the men, but inside I felt as empty as a spent shell. I had nothing left to give.

The warship lowered a gig. Five men clambered down her monkey lines and into the boat then pushed off and started rowing toward us. When they came alongside, a three-man boarding party climbed aboard brandishing cutlasses and pistols. Their commanding officer, a self-important boson, was a big oaf of a man with a walrus mustache, a pock-ridden face and coal black hair tied in a pigtail. A rum gut strained against his belt. He held a storm lantern in one hand, a pistol in the other.

"On behalf of Commander John Taggert of the USS *Davenport,*" he said, "I hereby seize these blockade runners as property of the federal government."

"You'll do no such thing," I said. There was enough flint in my voice to spark a fire.

Instantly, the Yanks fell back in a half circle as if avoiding a rapier thrust. They crouched, their swords leveled at our bellies, their pistols cocked. Any second could be our last.

"What did you say?" the boson growled.

"These aren't blockade runners," I said. "They're fishing boats crewed by men loyal to the Union. The blockade runner you've been chasing is yonder. We blew a hole in her hull, set her on fire. Her master, Damien Quill, is dead."

"Quill is dead?" the incredulous boson asked.

"I saw it with my own eyes," Jesse answered. "Foster over there hit Quill on the head with a shovel."

Foster nodded.

The boson eyed my ill-fitting Confederate uniform and said, "And just who are you?"

"Ed Canfield. I'm not a soldier. I'm a gladesman from Cedar Keys just like the rest of my crew."

"Canfield?" The boson pivoted to look at the other members of his boarding party then back at me. "The Ed Canfield who ran the *Argonaut* aground?"

"She ran herself aground pursuing us."

The boson thrust his lantern at me, and a blade of light cut across my face.

"The Ed Canfield who was supposed to lead us to Damien Quill's camp?"

"Yes. We were captured by Quill. Some of us were impressed into his black gang but we managed to overpower his crew and escape on these fishing boats."

"Canfield, you must be crazy," the boson said. "Commander Hill ordered you to lead us to the rebel camp."

"It seems as though I did, boson." I jerked a thumb toward the burning hulk of the *Argonaut.* "I not only led you to it, I also saved you the trouble of hanging Quill from the highest yardarm."

"So you did," he laughed, breaking the tension.

The rest of the boarding party and gladesmen breathed a sigh of relief and Jesse pounded me on the back. I was so exhausted the blow nearly knocked me off my feet.

We spent the next few hours on the USS *Davenport,* getting our wounded tended to while the Yanks tried to round up the rebel survivors on the beach. Later, we ate with the ship's master and shared with him what we knew about the rebel operation. He was elated to hear about the death of Captain Quill and promised to put in a good word for us when he made his official report. Afterwards, we returned to our boats where I got the first good night's rest since the attack on Cedar Keys.

~

The next morning, Jesse, McKenna and I joined the detail that went ashore to bury the dead. McKenna and I found Fletcher floating face up on the edge of the surf, his body stiff and bloated. We carried him ashore and went through his pockets until I found a letter he had received from someone. Water had smeared the ink, but I could make out the name of a woman and an address in Athens, Georgia. Fletcher had been married. My eyes teared up. The man had done all I had asked of him and more. And now he was dead.

Just like Private Abner Winslow.

It pains me to think about it even now.

I stuck the letter in my pocket and we carried Fletcher up the beach and onto higher ground. The work detail was digging a mass grave for the other casualties but I wanted Fletcher to have his own grave. We buried him in the shade of a tree and said a prayer. As I prayed, sea gulls hovered so high overhead that they appeared like ashes rising above a funeral pyre.

We never found Hoagg's body; the tide must have carried it off. McKenna said Hoagg wasn't married and there was some comfort in knowing that.

The *Argonaut* was a burned out hulk; her hull bore a gaping hole that allowed cargo to spill out into the sea like the guts of a sea dragon. The crew salvaged what it could then abandoned her carcass to the elements. Strangely, Quill's body could not be found.

The Yanks left marines ashore to ambush and capture the cracker cow hunters while we set out on the voyage to Key West. The man-o-war pulled away from us, traveling at twice our speed. We headed into the gulf where the color of the water ran from emerald green to dark blue.

That first day the air was crisp and clear and the wind out of the southeast lifted the seas in gentle swells. Scattered cumulus clouds indicated good weather ahead. It was smooth sailing. About mid-afternoon, I checked on Broady. He was laying on a tarp, doubled over with stomach cramps, his complexion yellow, blood oozing from his nose and mouth onto his beard.

"What can I do for you?" I asked.

"You can stop rocking the boat."

"Seriously," I said. I crouched beside him and felt his feverish forehead. "This is no time for jokes. What can I get you? Anything?"

"Yeah," he winced. "A pencil and paper."

I tore a page out of the back of the logbook and gave the sheet and pencil to him. He wrote a brief message to his wife Catherine, folded it twice and asked me to give it to her "in case something happens." I promised him I would; then sat beside him, making small talk, until he lapsed into unconsciousness. I closed the lids of his eyes, dipped a sponge into a water bucket, and wiped my friend's face, while thinking back on all the good times we'd had together.

Fifty-percent. Doc said fifty-percent recover after the coma.

Later, I used another sheet of paper to write a letter to Fletcher's widow trying to explain how it was that her husband had died in a pitched battle against other rebels led by a British naval officer. It made no sense and yet that is what had happened. When I finished, I walked over to Jesse who was staring dejectedly in the general direction of Cedar Keys.

"Seen enough of fighting?" I asked.

He wrung his hands as if they were covered in blood. "More than my fair share."

Seeing him do that reminded me of how I had felt after going to war. I couldn't help wonder if my son would be tormented by what had just happened—much as I had been. At least he hadn't killed one of our own men. He didn't have that to live down.

"It gets better with time," I said.

He glanced at me sideways and said, "You're sure about that?"

I chuckled and changed the subject. "Have you given any thought as to what you'll do next?"

"Too soon to say," he answered.

"Well, you'd make a helluva a gladesman," I said.

He just smiled, pointed to his red shirt and said, "I thought I already was one."

"After we get our share of the salvage money," I said, "we should both have enough for a fresh start somewhere."

"I'm not sure where to turn," Jesse said. "Charleston no longer has a place for me and Cedar Keys holds nothing but bad memories. What about you?"

I nodded. "First off, I have to find a buyer for what's left of the gum patch. Then I might try to make a go of it in Key West."

"A Yankee port?" he asked with a wry smile.

"Union or Confederate," I said, "it doesn't make a heap of difference."

"You've always marched to a different drummer," he said. "What will you do to make a living?"

"Hard to say. Key West is a bustling port. There are lots of opportunities there for the both of us. What do you say?"

"I'll think about it. What about you and Maureen Foster?"

"If she'll have me," I said, "I'll ask her pa for her hand in marriage."

"Hell, if her old man doesn't say yes, I'll throw him back where I found him."

We both laughed and kept talking for a good half hour. The more we talked the woozier I felt. At first, I thought it was seasickness because my stomach felt queasy; but then, I felt chilled to the bone and, at the same time, I began to sweat like a horse. My head began to pound. I started to slur my words.

"You feeling all right?" Jesse asked.

"A little under the weather," I muttered.

"A little?" He looked at me again and said, "Don't move. I'm getting Doc."

Doc's boat came alongside and he clambered aboard the smack. When he knelt by my side, I saw a look of concern clearly visible on his face. I forced myself to smile, tried to make a joke.

"Lie down with dogs; get up with fleas," I said.

Doc and Jesse did not laugh. I wasn't feeling too jovial myself. He took my pulse, felt my forehead and neck glands and said, "Stick out your tongue."

Then he spoke the words I dreaded:

"I'm sorry but it looks like yellow fever."

Yellow fever! The very words that had been a death sentence for my mother.

"No way," I said. "That can't be." After all I had gone through, all I had battled, to get this far, it didn't seem fair. I was about to become another casualty, but this time the enemy was my own body and the onslaught was unstoppable.

"I just gave Broady the last of the medicine," Doc said. "The best I can do for now is give you some laudanum and make you comfortable until we get to Key West."

They had me sit down, removed my sweat-soaked shirt and applied a cold compress to my forehead. My teeth began to chatter and I felt myself melting into a pool of rank sweat. I began to retch. I couldn't keep the laudanum down. My fever spiked and I slumped over and started to drift in and out of consciousness. I hallucinated. In my mind, I saw myself slogging through a lake of pitch and tar, trying to reach the other side, while soldiers on both sides of the conflict fired at me.

They tell me that I babbled incoherently for the better part of the voyage. I don't recall anything except the approach to the Key West harbor. I'm told they carried me off the boat, laid me in a wagon and brought me—along with Broady and his brother-in-law—to a home that Doc rented. Then they ran up the yellow jack and began tending to us day and night.

The first round of fever subsided in a few days and I dragged myself out of bed and asked Doc if he had heard any word about Maureen. Doc insisted that I stay in bed and said that he and Jesse would let me know as soon as they heard anything.

Two more days passed without any word of her. The second round of fever set in and I lapsed back into unconsciousness. Time and again, I would struggle to clear my head only to slip back into a state of semi-consciousness. In that troubled state, I saw the seamen on the *Argonaut* getting caught up in the explosion that burned some of them alive. I saw myself being dragged before a firing squad with Captain Quill giving the order to fire.

On the following day, I stirred, opened my eyes and tried to focus on the blurry figures hovering over me. They slowly came into focus: Jesse and Doc.

"He's coming around," Jesse said with a tentative smile on his face.

I tried to speak but my tongue was too swollen, my lips too cracked. "Water," I managed to mumble.

Doc lifted my head off the pillow with one hand and brought a dipper of water to my lips with the other. I swallowed the water greedily.

"Not so fast," Doc said.

My thirst quenched, I searched their faces and asked, "How long have I been here?"

"A little over a week," Doc said. "You've slept most of the time."

I nodded. "I feel older than Methuselah's grandfather."

They laughed a little too hard at my joke. "You look as old as him, too," Jesse said.

I ran the palm of my hand across my chin and felt that my stubble had become whiskers.

"Damn," I said to Doc in mock dismay, "I must be starting to look like you."

"If that's the case," Doc joked, "you're sicker than I thought."

The three of us laughed softly.

"I'll be right back," Doc said.

I sat up expecting to get a better look at myself in the mirror on the nearby wall. That's when I noticed it was covered in black. Someone had just died in this house.

"How is Broady?" I asked Jesse.

He bit the inside of his cheek. "He's gone; so is his brother-in-law. The fever carried them off."

We both searched for words to express what we felt. I had known Adam Broady for seven years. We drank together, fished together and worked side by side in the gum patch. I could always count on him. He was a brick by the cartload. He had a quick sense of humor, too; he knew how to cheer me up. I knew his wife, Catherine, and his kids, too. They called me "uncle" Ed.

My thoughts swirled all about me like a whirlpool that dragged me down into a place I didn't want to go. I was about to give in to a sense of guilt bordering on despair, when Doc reentered the room with a broad smile on his face. He took one look at me and at Jesse, then at the mirror and sized up the situation.

"I believe," he said, "I have just the tonic for what ails you."

He stepped aside to allow Maureen to enter the room holding a bowl of chicken soup. My spirits lifted instantly and I sat up.

"We've all been praying for you, Ed," she said. "Land sakes but you did give us a fright."

Her beauty took my breath away. My heart leapt within my chest. I lay there, speechless, looking up at the very image of a southern belle, her auburn hair parted in the middle and braided into a bun at the nape of her graceful neck. Her eyes gleamed like the flame of a prayer candle. Her black mourning dress clung to her, hinting at the firmness of her figure.

She handed me the bowl of soup then leaned over and kissed me on my forehead, soft as a butterfly's caress. I reached out with one hand for her but she pulled away with a mischievous twinkle in her eyes. Only the fragrance of her rosewater lingered behind.

"See—what did I tell you?" Doc said. "He's feeling better already."

"Yeah," Jesse added, "he'll soon be up and about and causing me no end of trouble."

Maureen gave an exasperated shrug. “I declare, to hear you talk, you wouldn’t think you two loved one another as much as you do.”

She was right. Jesse and I had a strange way of showing it at times, but we had come a long way since that first day on the wharf at Cedar Keys.

~

CHAPTER THIRTEEN

Thanks to Maureen's nursing skills I was up and about in two days, just strong enough to attend a Catholic funeral service for Broady and his brother-in-law at Saint Mary's Star of the Sea, on the southwest side of Duval Street, between Eaton and Fleming Streets. The bodies of the two men had been kept on ice until their relatives could reach Key West.

The Catholic priest, who conducted the service, delivered an emotional eulogy in which he compared Adam's willingness to take up arms to Christ's willingness to take up His cross. He said every Christian had a duty to die to self and, in that sense, to become a martyr. Too many, the priest said, fall short of glory because, unlike Adam, they are unwilling to pay the price.

The priest had it all wrong. Yes, Adam's courage had cost him his life; but, no, he hadn't been following Christ; he had been following me.

Out of the corner of my eye, I saw Catherine Broady wipe tears from her swollen eyes and struggle to remain strong for the children who sat on both sides of her. For their sake, I wished I could have taken Adam's place. I wished I had been the one to die. I asked myself, "Why me? Why had I survived? What was I supposed to do now?" I got no answer.

I looked away and saw Brother Storter taking it all in, smiling to himself, nodding as if he had stumbled upon a new text for his funeral services. I felt heart sick.

After the service, we processed a short way to Passover Lane and through the main gate of the Key West cemetery. We made our way down the white, crushed shell and limestone path where the history of the island was carved in stone, each victim of a shipwreck, pestilence, fever, accident or old age memorialized in row after row of ash-gray, weather-pitted grave markers. In the nearly treeless expanse, the stone angels, saints and crucifixes cast stark, hard-edged shadows. Weed-choked, scrollwork on rust-encrusted iron fences surrounded the larger plots, some with their gates open and askew as if a mourner had just fled in grief.

The funeral party gathered at the graveside beneath an army tent that had been set up to shield us from the sun's intense rays. In the tent's shadow, knots of women, dressed in black, hid their faces beneath lace mantillas and hankies as they clustered together for emotional support. At the corners of the tent, groups of stoic men stood with hands behind their backs, looking at the tips of their boots, talking out of the sides of their mouths.

Jesse, Pemble and Perry were there. So were Nordland, McKenna and the men from the black gang. Seeing McKenna reminded me of Fletcher and Hoagg and of the last time I had seen them alive. I turned my head away only to see a clutch of Negro men and women standing outside the tent, unprotected from the sun. It brought to mind my mother's funeral and the shameful way the white folks had treated Nat and his wife, Sue. All this fighting and killing and nothing seemed to have changed. It made no sense.

I stood with Maureen, off to the side and outside the sheltering tent, avoiding eye contact. I didn't want to talk to any one. I couldn't shake the feeling that Broady might have survived the fever if he had left the camp with Brother Storter, instead of staying to fight alongside me. I tried to tell myself that we had no choice. That the Yanks would never have gone along with a prisoner exchange. It was up to us to free the men in the black gang. But, a voice inside me kept whispering that I had thrown caution to the wind. That I was drawn to danger, even reveled in it—that deep down inside I liked the fighting. Hadn't I recruited Broady and the other men in much the same way that Brother Storter had recruited the young boys he sent off to war? With those conflicting thoughts warring inside me, I steered clear of Broady's widow and three children, the oldest being a boy only twelve years of age.

After the graveside service, Maureen asked, "What's wrong? What's going through your mind?"

"I was just thinking about Catherine Broady and her boys. Who is going to fend for them now that Adam's gone?"

"I know someone who could help," she said in a voice as soft as the morning mist.

"Who?"

"You're going to get your share of the prize money from the wreck, right? Why not give it to them?"

I chuckled at the thought and kissed her on the forehead.

"That's a great idea," I said. "Let's go for a walk."

She gave me her hand and I squeezed it gently, just enough to feel her warmth mingle with mine. I could smell her rose water enveloping me. I could feel the clouds lifting, the sun breaking through the miasma that had settled all around me.

Lost in conversation, we had scarcely covered two blocks when we heard the sound of a horse strutting up behind us, chomping at the bit, pawing the ground with its hooves. Turning, I looked up at P. J. Cornelius astride a big, black steed. He raised his riding crop to the brim of his straw hat and bowed at the waist to Maureen. She curtseyed.

"Good day, Ma'am. Good day Mister Canfield. I see y'all are up and about."

The sun was at his back and I had to shade my eyes, squint up at him. "Yes, sir, the first day."

"I understand you are a very enterprising fellow."

"And a very brave one, too," Maureen said.

"So it would seem," he chortled. "A man like you could go far in my organization, Canfield. Stop by my office later this week. We have some unfinished business to discuss, if you follow my meaning."

Cornelius flicked the reins, kneed the flanks of the horse and pranced off, throwing up clods of dirt.

"Who was that man?" Maureen asked.

"He's Doc's brother-in-law and one of the wealthiest men on the island. He supplied the medicine I brought to the camp."

"What sort of business do you have with him?" Maureen asked.

"I'm not sure. I think he expects me to become a spy."

"Heaven forbid."

"Exactly my sentiments."

We walked down to the beach where I picked up a flat stone and skimmed it across the surface of the water. A startled sea gull took to the air and wheeled about on unseen thermals, drawing other birds into its orbit. The image brought to mind what old seamen said about the gulls being the souls of people lost at sea. I wondered how many men had followed me to their death. More than I cared to count. I asked myself why I had survived.

Why me of all people?

I let out a long sigh and turned to face Maureen. "There is something I have to say about what happened the other day and I'm not sure you're going to like hearing it."

She gave me a puzzled look and said, "Ed, this is Maureen you're talking to. Remember? I was there in the refugee camp. I'm the one who threw the beehive into the tent. So don't talk to me about a lady's delicate sensibilities."

"I know," I said. "You're the strongest woman I have ever met. But there is something you need to know about me."

"What then?"

"There's a part of me that wanted to die in that firefight on the beach. I expected to die. I thought I owed as much to my men."

She knit her brow and said, "How much of Doc's laudanum did you take this morning?"

"This isn't the laudanum talking," I said. "It's me, the firebrand who led those men to their death on that beach."

"You were a hero the other day," she said. "Those men volunteered. They'd follow you to hell and back."

"And hell is where I took them."

"Don't be talking like this," she protested.

"You have to know," I said. "You have to know everything." My voice cracked but I continued. "As an 18-year old, I volunteered to fight the Mexicans. I believed what the bigwigs said about Manifest Destiny and about our nation's right to drive the greasers across the Rio Grande. I believed God was on our side. I was eager to do my duty."

"Yes," she said, "and my father says you went above and beyond the call of duty."

"I was no hero," I said. "I was a fool. The drums of war played mischief with my mind; led me to do things that no right-thinking, God-fearing man would countenance. War taught me what it's like to kill or be killed. I learned there is a part of me that revels in the fury and violence of war and that the smell of gunpowder, like laudanum, can be intoxicating. I was just a kid. A kid. Still wet behind the years. What did I know?"

Then I paused, not certain how she would take what I was about to say. She wiped a loose strand of hair off her forehead and I could see the blood had drained from her face. But I could not stop now.

"The army taught me what it means to be a comrade in arms, ready to lay down your life for the men who serve beside you. Men you love like a brother. But I also learned how easy it is to lose your head in the heat of battle and accidentally bayonet one of your own men; then watch him bleed out in front of you."

I told her about Abner Winslow.

"When I close my eyes at night," I said, "I see Abner lying there, staring up at me in disbelief."

The effort of dredging up all these memories was too much for me. I slumped down on the edge of a pier. She sat down beside me and put her arm around my shoulder.

"I am so sorry, Ed," she said, her voice whisper thin. "But you're not to blame. You didn't mean to—"

She couldn't bring herself to say what I had done, but I could. "I killed him."

"Mercy sakes, it was an accident. It happened almost twenty years ago."

"I still have night sweats and nightmares about it," I said. "Abner bled out that day. I'm still bleeding inside. The wound never heals. Doc Reynolds calls it soldier's heart."

Tears welled up in her eyes. "Is there a cure?"

"How do you cure a memory?"

"Maybe," she said, "you can rid yourself of them by writing down what you remember."

"Writing them down? You mean focus on what I did?"

"Afterwards you could burn the pages."

"I'm not so sure about that. All I do know is I'm sick and tired of all the killing. I swore to myself that I'd never do it again. And, yet, I did. Somehow, I have to find a way to balance the scales. Come Judgment Day, I have to show that I've saved as many lives as I've taken. From here on out, I have to do something more with my life than run a backwater gum patch."

"I declare." There was an awkward pause before she added, "Just how do you propose to save lives? Do you mean doctoring?"

"No, I've seen what Doc does and it's not for me."

"What then?"

"I'm not sure. All I know is a day of reckoning is coming."

"Well," she said, "my father likes to say you can't plow a field by turning it over in your head. You have to roll up your sleeves and go to work. Maybe you need to take the first job you find that will help other people live a better life."

I nodded and said I'd look in the newspaper; see if something caught my eye. We changed the subject, continued walking and started talking about our future together. Nothing more was said about the nightmares.

~

Soon, Jesse and I got our shares of the prize money for what we had helped salvage from the USS *Argonaut.* He met a girl and decided to stay in Key West after all. Next thing I knew he was calling himself by his rightful name, Canfield.

I used most of my money to repair the *Dead Reckoning* and pay Gus Neally for the repairs to his smack. I gave the rest to Catherine Broady along with the note that Adam had written just before slipping into a coma. Then I got word that the pencil company, Eberhard Faber, was interested in buying my acreage in Cedar Keys. To celebrate the good news, I invited Maureen to dinner. I told her she could pick any place she wanted to eat and she chose a popular tavern just off White Street, a place called The Dockside. It was a blustery day with heavy seas and I was glad to be ashore.

Once we were seated, I brought up a subject that needed to be discussed: her father and his opinion of me.

"How is your father doing?"

"Working on that black gang has taken a toll," she said. "But he just got the insurance money from Lloyd's of London and that has been a tonic."

"That's good to hear. What's he going to do with all that money?"

Her face brightened. "He's going to open a new salt works right here in Key West."

"That should help take his mind off what happened."

"Yes," she said. "But he says he's no longer strong enough to do it on his own. He wants me to help him."

"Help him run the business?"

She placed a table napkin on her lap, smoothed it out and looked up at me. "Yes."

"So he's had a change of heart."

"A change of heart?"

"It sounds like you're no longer thought of as his little girl."

She grinned impishly from ear to ear and said, "I must be the apple of his eye."

"And I bet that feels good."

She paused briefly as if reflecting on the past. "Yes, it does," she said.

"Any chance he might change the way he thinks about me, too?"

She pulled her chair closer to the table, leaned in and said earnestly, "Ed, my father is a veteran like you. In his heart of hearts, he knows that Caleb would have enlisted anyway. Caleb was just following in our father's footsteps. Dad is already bragging about Caleb, telling anyone who will listen that his son was the hero of Cedar Keys. He's even commissioned a portrait of Caleb in his uniform to hang next to the one of my mother that's being shipped down from Cedar Keys."

"So you think your father will come around?"

"Just leave him to me," she said. Her eyes twinkled mischievously.

We reached across the table to one another and I inhaled deeply of the scent of her rose water. The waiter brought our order and, for the next half hour, we sat there enjoying a fine dinner while discussing our future together.

Then, just as the dessert arrived, I thought I heard a faint cry from the street:

"Wreck Ashore!"

The waiter froze with the dessert tray in hand. The tavern fell graveyard still. Every diner strained to make sure he or she had heard correctly. The distant voice drew closer, gained in intensity. Racing footsteps pounded furiously up the street. A breathless man wrenched open the tavern door.

"Wreck ashore! The *Osprey* has run aground!"

The *Osprey* was one of Cornelius' schooners. The tavern erupted in bedlam. Men shoved back their chairs, knocked over tables, elbowed one another and dashed for the front door, each one hoping to be the first to the wreck in order to claim a larger share of the prize money. Yelling and cursing, they jammed themselves through the doorway in a mad tangle of flapping arms and legs.

Instinctively, I jumped up, too. But, as I shoved back my chair, Maureen grabbed me by the sleeve.

"Wait. Don't go." Her eyes pleaded with me. The color drained from her face. "You're not well enough," she said.

My pulse started pounding. The room started spinning. The floor began to pitch and roll like the deck of a ship at sea. I reached out for rigging that wasn't there, thrashed at the air like a drowning man and felt the deck rise up and hammer me in the head. Everything went black.

Later, when I came to, lying spread eagle on the floor, Maureen was wiping my brow with a cold compress. The tavern was empty.

"It's just two blocks to Doc's house," she said. "Think you can make it?"

Embarrassed, I nodded, got to my feet slowly and said, "I'll be fine."

She helped me take the first few steps and we pushed through the batwing doors and turned the corner heading down the deserted street toward the house where Doc had been treating me. When we got there, the front door stood wide open; lamps remained lit; yet the house was empty. Doc had evidently heeded the call of "Wreck Ashore."

I lay down on my bed, too weary to remove my boots.

"Let me help," Maureen said.

She sat on the edge of the mattress and removed my boots then turned to me and said, "Are you going to be all right by yourself? Or should I stay?"

She looked down at me expectantly, her big blue eyes filled with concern. She placed a bed sheet over me and I felt the comforting touch of her fingers.

She leaned over and kissed me on the forehead. A stray curl passed across my cheek and I reached out and stroked her hair.

"Blow out the lantern," I said huskily.

She stiffened and whispered, "Doc could be back any minute."

"There's a full moon," I said. "They'll have enough light to work through the night."

She bent over again and blew out the lamp. I groaned and everything went black.

~

When I came to the next morning, I could hear Maureen in the kitchen and smell fresh coffee brewing. I eased out of bed, climbed into my clothes and shuffled to the kitchen doorway.

"Morning sunshine," she said with a warm, affectionate smile. "See you're feeling better."

"Morning," I yawned and scratched my beard.

"Made you some coffee and porridge," she said.

"Thanks. Where is Doc?"

"He isn't back yet. There must have been some casualties in last night's wreck."

I pulled a chair up to the kitchen table and sat down. She put the bowl of porridge and coffee in front of me then sat down across from me, her chin cradled in her hand.

"You didn't talk in your sleep last night," she said.

I picked up the spoon. "Uh, last night," I said, "we didn't—"

"No," she said with a prim grin and a nod toward the next room where I saw Doc's sofa with a rumpled bed sheet lying over the cushions.

I nodded and said. "I think I may be up to walking down to the quay after breakfast. I want to find out about the wreck."

"I'll clean up here while you're gone," she said.

I ate quickly, gave her a peck on the cheek and headed for the quay. On the way, I passed one of my old hang-outs, a dive called the Seaside Saloon. To my surprise, it was boarded up. I entered Mallory Square, where I heard the shouts of a newspaper boy crying about last night's shipwreck:

"Schooner sinks. Two people dead. P. J. Cornelius arrested."

Cornelius arrested?

I reached into my pocket for money to pay the boy and felt something else. I pulled it out and realized it was the letter I had written to Fletcher's wife just before I came down with the fever. A pang of grief and guilt shot through me and I couldn't move.

"You want a paper or not, mister?" the boy asked.

I nodded, fished in my other pocket for the money to pay him.

Then I read the sorry details about the wreck. Two people had died when Cornelius' *Osprey* ran aground. More lives would have been lost were it not for an alert lighthouse keeper.

The newspaper devoted a mere five lines to each of the victims. The rest of the story listed in detail all the valuable cargo that had been recovered from the *Osprey*. The reporter seemed to gloat over the vast quantities of wine, silverware, silk, plumage, linens, cotton, lumber, furniture and other household goods that had been thrown up on the island's shores and into the waiting arms of the salvagers.

In a sidebar, the paper reported that Cornelius had been arrested and charged with conspiring with the ship's master to deliberately wreck his ship for the insurance money. According to the article, Cornelius' schooner could not compete on the open seas with the faster steamships. Rather than take a loss by converting his schooner to a barge, Cornelius had decided to "sell" his problem to Lloyd's of London. His plan went wrong when the wreck claimed the lives of two seamen. One of the survivors told about the plot and the *Osprey's* guilty captain quickly turned against Cornelius to save his own hide. Cornelius swore he was innocent; but a reporter had interviewed Peter Kearns at the ships chandlery and Kearns confirmed that Cornelius had been losing business to steamers. He had wondered how his boss could maintain his lavish lifestyle. In another article, Doc Raymond said he had suspected all along that Cornelius had deliberately sunk the schooner on which he had been the ship's surgeon. So that must have been what Doc was holding over his brother-in-law's head.

Sickened by the news, I turned the page and spotted a help wanted ad that read:

Assistant Lighthouse Keeper Wanted. Must be strong, healthy person of impeccable character and pro-Union sympathies willing to work long nights in fair and foul weather. Contact Charles Howe, Collector of Customs.

The ad reminded me of the alert lighthouse keeper who had just saved lives on Cornelius' wrecked schooner. I glanced over my shoulder at the Key West lighthouse. I thought about Jack Pemble and of all the lives he had boasted about saving as a lighthouse keeper in Cedar Keys.

If only half of Pemble's stories were true . . .

I opened and re-read my letter to Fletcher's wife and the newspaper article with its five brief lines about each of the two victims of the *Osprey*—both of them were married men with children. They deserved more than a passing mention amid all the wreckage thrown up on the reef.

I remembered how I had felt as a boy when the local newspaper carried a mere one-line mention of my mother's passing; followed by a list of all our worldly goods—going under the auctioneer's gavel because my father was in jail. I could still hear the hammer blows of that gavel breaking my heart into a million pieces. Like the drums of war, the memory of that hammering set my pulse to pounding. I gritted my teeth, tore the help wanted ad from the newspaper and headed for the office of Charles Howe, the man who had placed the ad.

As I made my way there, I heard the melancholy voice of Abner Winslow in the back of my head.

"Are you crazy?" he said. "Working on a lighthouse is dangerous. Those beacons stand right on the water's edge. They're buffeted by hurricane winds and high seas."

I ignored the warning.

"The hurricane of '46 destroyed the Key West lighthouse."

I kept walking.

"It killed 14 people who were in the tower."

I lengthened my stride.

"Rebel gunships are attacking the lighthouses."

I reached Duval Street.

"They're out to destroy them."

I crossed the street.

"You're pressing your luck. You'll get yourself killed."

I reached for the front door of the building.

"Don't do this. Don't throw caution to the wind."

I grabbed the latch, opened the door wide, and stepped inside. Then I closed the door behind me, shutting Abner out of my life.

The next day Maureen gave me a gift: the pen that I hold in my hand as I write these recollections.

"And the sea gave up the dead that were in it; and death and Hades gave up the dead that were in them: and they were judged every man according to their works."

(Revelations 20:13)

BOOK CLUB GUIDE

The following questions are best reviewed after you have had a chance to read and enjoy the book; otherwise, the questions might spoil the plotline for you.

1. Why do you think the book is called "The Reckoning"?

2. What do you think is the major conflict in the book?

3. The story opens with Ed Canfield meeting his 16-year old son, Jesse, for the first time. How does their meeting set the tone for their relationship? How do both men change in the course of the story?

4. Do you think that Ed succeeds in making a "gladesman" out of Jesse?

5. Jesse is easily swayed by the war mongering oratory of preachers, politicians and journalists. He wants to join the rebel army with his friends. Do you think today's youth are as easily swayed by authority figures?

6. When Ed sees Maureen Foster for the first time, he is immediately drawn to her. What about Maureen attracts him? How is her character developed through Ed's eyes? Why do you think she is attracted to him?

7. How does the war impact the relationship of Ed and Maureen?

8. When Jesse refers to blacks as "niggers," his father corrects him and says that his turpentine still isn't part of the "slavocracy." How are Ed's views about slavery revealed throughout the story; and, in particular, in his comments about Brother Storter's sermons, and in the letter that Ed writes to Maureen?

9. When Ed learns that his ex-wife is barely getting by as a seamstress, how does he react and what does that reveal about his character?

10. As an ex-sharpshooter, Ed struggles with nightmares about what he did in the line of duty during the Mexican-American War. He suffers from what doctors in that era called "soldier's heart," and, which we now know as post-traumatic stress disorder. Do you know anyone who has suffered from PTSD (in war or otherwise)?

11. Did any of your ancestors fight in the Civil War? What became of them? Do you have any family heirlooms, diaries or journals from that era? Have you ever researched your family history online?

12. Once the Confederacy starts drafting soldiers—instead of relying on volunteers—Ed calls it "a rich man's war, poor man's fight." Why did he say that and why did Maureen become upset when he said it?

13. After Jesse learns that Ed was court-martialed for brawling, Jesse says that his father is still punishing himself by living alone in the backwoods. Do you think that is true? Has Ed grown since leaving the army? Does he grow during the story?

14. Do you think Ed is jealous of Caleb Foster and the way that Jesse looks up to him? Do you think Ed is justified in secretly paying Caleb to enlist in Jesse's place?

15. When Cedar Keys is attacked, Ed and Jesse, are forced to set aside their differences and join forces in order to survive. How do you feel about the way in which they grow together throughout the story?

16. Why does Ed decide to sail for Key West, a northern stronghold during the war?

17. Why does Ed suddenly stop drinking? Do you think of that as a turning point in the book?

18. When Ed reaches Key West, he meets soldiers who used to serve with him. The soldiers tell Ed that he is crazy. Do you think that is true? The fort's commander says Ed is not only fearless but also reckless? Do you agree?

19. Toward the end of the book, Ed shares his darkest secret with Maureen. Do you agree with the way in which Maureen reacts to what Ed tells her? Or, do you think that, once she knows about Ed's violent temper, Maureen should leave him for her own safety?

20. Ed tells Maureen that he fears a day of reckoning is coming when he must account for all the blood he has shed. Do you think he is right?

Questions for Discussion

1. Did this novel change the way you think about the opposing sides in the Civil War?

2. Did the novel cause you to reflect on the legacy of war, the long-lasting trauma of post- traumatic stress disorder and how it affects today's soldiers?

3. Which character in the book appealed most to you?

4. What scene or scenes did you find most surprising?

5. What scene or scenes did you find most moving or troubling?

Made in the USA
Charleston, SC
02 November 2012